GREAT LIVES
Sports

Sports
GREAT LIVES

George Sullivan

Charles Scribner's Sons · New York

Charles Scribner's Sons Books for Young Readers
Macmillan Publishing Company, 866 Third Avenue, New York, NY 10022
Collier Macmillan Canada, Inc.

Printed in the United States of America
First Edition   10 9 8 7 6 5 4 3 2 1

Cover illustration copyright © 1988 by Stephen Marchesi. All rights reserved.

Library of Congress Cataloging-in-Publication Data
Sullivan, George, 1927–   Great lives: Sports.
    Includes bibliographies and index.
    1. Athletes—Biography. I. Title.
GV697.A1S816 1988   796'.092'2 [B]   88–15673
ISBN 0-684-18510-5

Contents

Contents

(by sport)

Acknowledgments

Many people helped me in preparing this book. Special thanks are due John Devaney, who supplied countless bits and pieces of information; Jim Benagh, whose research contributed importantly to the chapters on Wayne Gretzky, Jesse Owens, and Ty Cobb; and Lou Sabin and Howard Liss, who, along with others, helped enormously in choosing the individuals profiled.

Foreword

"Great" is a terribly overused word in sports. Listen to almost any telecast of a sports event. It's sure to be filled with descriptions of "great" players executing "great" plays. There are no ordinary players in the Super Bowl or World Series, and nothing just plain average ever happens—at least not on television.

And how many books and magazine articles have been written about "great" teams and "great" games and their "great" heroes? Attempting to choose the "great" lives, the select list of athletes to be included in this book, was therefore no easy matter. Many hundreds of athletes had to be considered.

Certain criteria were established at the beginning. We wanted about a dozen different sports to be represented, with some emphasis on those that are most popular. That's why the book features more baseball players than gymnasts, more football stars than skiers.

Some individuals were chosen because they were the very best in their respective sports over an extended period of time: Babe Ruth in baseball, for example, and Pelé in soccer.

Another consideration was impact. Some athletes changed the way a particular game is played or influenced it to such an extent that they forced the rulesmakers to change it. Basketball's Wilt Chamberlain is a case in point. So is hockey's Bobby Orr.

Billie Jean King is another example of a person who had enormous impact.

She not only changed women's professional tennis but the status of women in sports in general.

Profiles of some athletes are based on personal recollections. My father took me to my first major league baseball game in the early 1940s, and I have been involved in sports in one way or another ever since. I've watched Jackie Robinson at Ebbets Field, Wilt Chamberlain at Madison Square Garden, Martina Navratilova at the National Tennis Center, and Johnny Unitas in the Super Bowl. I never saw Babe Ruth, Red Grange, Jim Thorpe, and some others featured in this book. In such cases, I have relied on their own writings and on articles and books written by authors whom I respect.

Some readers are not going to agree with the list of athletes chosen—maybe *most* readers. I'm not entirely happy with it myself. I feel bad that Walter Payton and Joe DiMaggio weren't included. I wish we had had room for Kareem Abdul-Jabbar and Arnold Palmer. To their fans, I can only say that I'm sorry and that I probably feel worse than they do.

GREAT LIVES

Sports

Muhammad Ali

The Greatest
1942–

He was the only man to win the world heavyweight championship three times. He earned more than $60 million in prize money during his career.

But Muhammad Ali was more than a boxing superstar. He was a clown, a poet, a religious zealot, an antiwar activist, and a symbol for blacks in every part of the world. From 1960, the year in which he won a gold medal in the Olympic Games, until he settled into retirement more than twenty years later, Muhammad Ali was, to use his words, "the greatest."

Ali was the third in a line of black heavyweight champions of the twentieth century to have an important social impact upon the nation. The first was Jack Johnson, who won the heavyweight title in 1908. Johnson ultimately lost his title to Jess Willard in 1915. He died in 1948 in an automobile accident at the age of 68.

The next important heavyweight champion was Joe Louis, who captured the title in 1937 and reigned as heavyweight champion until 1949. He was black America's first hero. After Muhammad Ali had become heavyweight champion, he told of the time Joe Louis had come to Ali's hometown and happened to lean against a telephone pole on the street where Ali (who was known as Cassius Clay then) and his family lived.

"My momma never forgot," Ali said. "She still can't pass that telephone pole without telling Joe Louis leaned on it."

Louis did a great deal to advance the cause of race relations in the United

States. In January 1942, only a few weeks after Americans had been drawn into World War II by the Japanese attack on Pearl Harbor, Louis enlisted in the Army. He thus became the Good American, a symbol of national togetherness.

The Reverend Jesse Jackson delivered the eulogy at Louis's memorial service in 1981. "We are honoring a giant who saved us in a time of trouble," said Jackson. "He lifted us up when we were down. He made our enemies leave us alone."

Muhammad Ali went beyond Joe Louis. Louis, at least in the early stages of his career, had been what white America wanted him to be. But that was not Ali's way, not for a second. In February 1964, after he had won the heavyweight crown for the first time, he said, "I know where I'm going and I know the truth, and I don't have to be what you want me to be. I'm free to be who I want."

That was Muhammad Ali. He was always himself, just who he wanted to be.

Muhammad Ali was born Cassius Marcellus Clay on January 17, 1942, in Louisville, Kentucky. His father was a sign painter. His mother did housework for other families.

The Clays trace their family name back to the time of slavery. Cassius's great-great-great-grandfather had been one of the slaves of a noted Kentuckian, Cassius Marcellus Clay, the American ambassador to Russia in the 1860s. The slave took the name of his master, and it was passed down from generation to generation.

Young Cassius's interest in boxing began when he was fourteen. One rainy day his brand-new red bicycle was stolen from a Louisville street corner. Cassius reported the loss to Joe Martin, a Louisville policeman, who also gave boxing lessons in a community gymnasium operated by the city's recreation department. Martin never got Clay's bike back, but he did persuade him to take up boxing.

Cassius weighed about 90 pounds at the time. He was an aggressive fighter who wore down his opponents by the sheer number and fury of his blows.

Some of the bouts staged by Martin were featured on a local television program called *Tomorrow's Champions*. Within a few months, Cassius was a regular on the show. "He was just ordinary," Officer Martin once recalled, "and I doubt whether any scout would have thought much of him in the first year. But he was easily the hardest worker of any kid I ever taught."

Clay would rise at five A.M. to run in the park. After breakfast, instead of taking the bus to school, he would run alongside the bus during its twenty-eight-block journey. He often dozed through his classes until lunch, when he would run again.

In the evening at Martin's gym, Cassius skipped rope for hours to strengthen his legs. He flailed away at the heavy punching bag to put power into his punches. He beat out a rapid rat-tat-tat on the speed bag and sparred with his image in a full-length mirror to improve his timing.

Just as important to Clay's will to work was his confidence. "He believed he was the best fighter in the gym," Martin said. "He believed he was going to be the champion."

Martin had only one complaint about his prize pupil. "He always talked too much," Martin said. "He was always mouthin' off."

From the age of twelve through eighteen, Cassius devoted himself to becoming the best amateur boxer in the world. In those six years, Cassius took part in more than one hundred amateur bouts, winning all but a small handful of them. In 1959 and 1960, he captured both the national Golden Gloves and AAU (Amateur Athletic Union) light-heavyweight championships.

Next, Clay won a spot on the American Olympic boxing team. The Olympics were held in Rome in 1960, and Cassius hit the city like a tornado. He seemed to be everywhere, waving, shaking hands, posing for photos, and being interviewed. Weighing in at a sleek 178 pounds and fighting in the light-heavyweight division, Clay disposed of three opponents without great difficulty and won the gold medal.

Louisville gave him a hero's welcome on his return, with parades and dinners in his honor.

Despite the fact that he was the toast of Louisville, Clay was often made to feel the sting of racial discrimination. Louisville was a segregated city in 1960, and Clay was refused service in downtown restaurants. "I don't care what he's won," said one luncheonette owner, "he's a nigger, and he can't eat here." Clay was hurt and outraged by such treatment.

Clay's ambition now was to become a boxing professional, and he turned to the serious business of finding a manager. He and his parents eventually signed a contract with the Louisville Sponsoring Group, a syndicate of eleven white businessmen, most of them Louisville millionaires. The agreement gave Clay a $10,000 bonus, a salary of $4,000 for the first two years and $6,000 for the next four. There was to be a fifty-fifty split on everything Clay earned.

Angelo Dundee, a skilled and experienced trainer, was hired to work with Clay. "I smoothed Cassius out and put some snap in his punches," Dundee once said. "I got him down off of his

Muhammad Ali (then Cassius Clay) won a gold medal for boxing in the light-heavyweight division at the 1960 Olympics before embarking on his professional career. *Courtesy of the United States Olympic Committee.*

dancing toes so that he could hit with power."

On October 29, 1960, Clay won his first professional fight, a six-round decision over a veteran but out-of-shape boxer named Tunney Hunsaker.

Clay was taller now, standing 6-foot-3. His greatest asset was his fighting speed. He had always been faster than his rivals, but now he was bigger than most of them as well. This made for a devastating combination.

Clay defeated one opponent after another. By the end of his second year as a professional, he had scored sixteen straight victories. His ring earnings totaled more than $100,000. He bought his parents a new home in a Louisville suburb and bought himself a black Cadillac limousine.

However, Cassius was attracting much more attention with his mouth than with his fists. He constantly touted his own greatness by reciting rhymes of his own creation. He began naming the round in which he would down his opponent, saying:

They all must fall
In the round I call.

Newspapers called him "Mighty Mouth" or "the Louisville Lip" or "Cassius the Brashest."

Clay's self-advertising helped to fill boxing arenas and earned him bouts with top-ranked opponents. In November 1962, he faced Archie Moore, a former light-heavyweight champion, who was at least twice as old as Cassius. Before the bout, Clay said:

When you come to the fight,
Don't block the aisle,
Don't block the door,
You will go home after round four.

And that is exactly what happened. Clay knocked out Moore just before the fourth round was half over.

Early the next year, Cassius fought at New York's Madison Square Garden for the first time. He filled the arena to capacity, drawing more than 18,000 customers. They saw him win a close decision over Doug Jones. And when Clay went to London for a bout with British Empire heavyweight champion Henry Cooper, 55,000 Englishmen packed Wembley Stadium. It was an easy win for Clay.

All the while, Clay was campaigning to fight the world heavyweight champion, Sonny Liston, a brutish figure with a devastating punch. Liston had not been defeated in nine years, but that didn't matter to Cassius. "I want the big, ugly bear," he kept telling everyone.

In February 1964, Clay got his wish. Not many people thought he had much of a chance against the powerful Liston.

But Clay surprised the experts by taking control of matters at the opening bell, dancing away from his rival's ferocious left hook, then leaping in at every opportunity to deliver barrages of blows to Liston's head.

When the bell clanged to begin the seventh round, Liston remained on his stool, his shoulders hunched, staring at the canvas. His left arm hung uselessly at his side. He had torn muscles in the left shoulder in swinging wildly at the elusive Clay.

The referee took Clay's hand and raised it in triumph. At twenty-two, Cassius had become the world heavyweight champion.

Before leaving the ring, he ranted at the press: "Eat your words! I am the greatest! I . . . am . . . the . . . greatest!"

In the months that followed, Cassius shocked the world again and again. He turned his back on the Christian religion by joining the nation of Islam. That meant giving up his name and acquiring a new one, Muhammad Ali.

"Cassius Clay had no knowledge of his own self," Ali once said. "He thought Clay was his name but found out it was a slave name."

"Ali means 'the most high,'" Ali once explained. Muhammad, he said, means "worthy of the highest praise."

Said Ali: "Cassius Clay had Caucasian images of God on his wall. Muhammad Ali was taught there should be no image of God. No color. That's a big difference."

Many people resented Ali's decision to become a Muslim. Some of those who had supported him in the past now rejected him. When he fought, they wanted him to lose. But Ali kept winning. In a rematch with Sonny Liston, he retained his title by knocking out Liston in the first round. He also beat former heavyweight champion Floyd Patterson.

In 1966, when young men were being drafted and sent to Vietnam to fight, Ali was drafted, too. He was due to be inducted into the Army on April 28, 1967. He refused to take the required step forward during the induction process, however, saying that his religion forbade him to bear arms.

Many Americans immediately branded him a slacker and draft dodger. He was charged by the government with draft evasion and faced a prison sentence. Boxing officials stripped him of his title. For three and a half years, Ali did not box, and his critics were urging his imprisonment or deportation.

At the same time Ali was being branded as a traitor by one segment of society, he was looked upon as a hero by others. Many blacks hailed Ali as a symbol of black manhood, an individual who was unafraid to stand up for his beliefs. He was asked to be the Grand Marshal of the Watts parade in Los Angeles. College students throughout the country applauded Ali for his antiwar stand.

During the years he was not permitted to box, Ali made speeches at college campuses and Muslim meetings. He became one of the most popular speakers on the college lecture circuit, sometimes making four or five appearances a week.

In 1967, Ali married Belinda Boyd, a seventeen-year-old whose Muslim name was Khalilah. His first marriage, which had taken place in 1964, had ended in divorce.

The only fighting Ali did during that time was in the courts. He was eventually convicted of draft evasion and drew a harsh sentence: five years in jail and a $10,000 fine. Ali's lawyers were able to keep him out of jail by appealing his case to higher courts. Eventually, it would go before the Supreme Court.

Ali was also involved in a lawsuit meant to restore his right to fight again. In this he was victorious, the judge ruling he could return to the ring. Ali was pleased with the decision, but he wanted something more than just the right to fight. He wanted his title back. Joe Frazier, nicknamed "Smokin' Joe," was the heavyweight champion. A ferocious slugger, he had beaten every good heavyweight, knocking out most of them. He was undefeated as a professional. Ali fought Frazier on March 8, 1971, at New York City's Madison Square Garden.

No fight in history had ever stirred so much interest; it was called "The Fight of the Century." The purse for each man was to be two and a half million dollars, win, lose, or draw.

Ali wrote a poem for the occasion:

Joe's gonna come out smoking,
And I ain't gonna be joking,
I'll be pecking and poking,
Pouring water on his smoking.
This might shock and amaze ya,
But I'm gonna retire Joe Frazier!

It was a brutal fight. Frazier smashed Ali's body with rights and lefts. Ali stood his ground and attempted to outslug his rival, but he could not. Frazier knocked Ali down in the fifteenth round. Although Ali got up, the decision was unanimous in favor of Frazier. Smokin' Joe was still the champ.

Ali took the defeat in stride. "The world goes on," he said at a press conference after the fight. "You got children to feed and bills to pay, got other things to worry about."

Later that year, one of his biggest worries was lifted from Ali's shoulders when the Supreme Court cleared him of the charge of draft evasion and declared that he should never have been drafted in the first place.

Ali let out a whoop when he heard the news. But he did not celebrate. "I've said a long prayer to Allah," he declared. "That's my celebrating."

Ali continued to fight after he lost to Joe Frazier. He took part in fourteen bouts in the next three years, earning some $5 million. He lost once, to a young fighter named Ken Norton, but he beat Norton in a rematch.

Ali wanted to fight Joe Frazier a second time—and he did. But the heavyweight title was not at stake. Frazier had lost his title to George Foreman. Ali won the rematch with Frazier.

After defeating Frazier, Ali was ready to fight George Foreman for the championship. He got his chance on March 30, 1974, in Kinshasa, the capital of the African nation of Zaire. "A rumble in the jungle," Ali called it.

Sixty thousand people jammed the stadium at Kinshasa. Millions watched on closed-circuit television.

Foreman, who was favored to win, was twenty-five years old, seven years younger than Ali. He had never been knocked off his feet during a bout. Ali took Foreman's best blows on his arms and shoulders. At the same time, he punched back. When Foreman began to tire, Ali stepped up the pressure. He knocked Foreman out in the eighth round with a murderous right cross.

Now that Ali was champion again, every heavyweight wanted to fight him.

One was Joe Frazier. Ali fought Frazier a third time in Manila, in the Philippine Islands, in September 1975. The bout was advertised as "The Thrilla in Manila." Ali defeated his old rival in a brutal slugging match.

"I just want to sit one day and be an ordinary citizen," Ali told sportswriter Dave Anderson of the *New York Times*, "go to the hardware store, cut the grass. Don't be in no more papers, don't talk to nobody, no more lectures. Just rest."

But Ali did not become an ordinary citizen. He felt a need to continue fighting.

On February 15, 1978, a few weeks after his thirty-sixth birthday, Ali lost his title to Leon Spinks, whose greatest asset was his age; Spinks was twelve years younger than Ali. It was one of the most stunning upsets in boxing history. Later in the year Ali defeated Spinks, thus regaining his title a third time.

The next year, 1979, Ali gave up his championship and announced his retirement. But he did not stay retired very long. In 1980, he returned to the ring to fight Larry Holmes for the World Boxing Council version of the heavyweight championship. Holmes gave Ali a sound beating. Then Ali quit for good.

In the years that followed, Ali's health worried his fans as well as his friends and family. Often his speech was slurred, and he moved slowly and unsteadily. Some people gave knowing nods and said that Ali was "punch drunk." The repeated blows to the head that he had received had damaged Ali's brain, they said. Ali was in his early forties now. His face was rounder, his body thicker around the middle.

Early in 1984, Ali underwent a much publicized series of medical tests at Columbia Presbyterian Medical Center in New York City. It was revealed that Ali had been taking medicine to treat the symptoms of Parkinson's syndrome, a nerve disease. Speaking of Ali, Dr. Stanley Fahn, one of his physicians, said: "We expect him to respond very well to medication and lead a normal life."

After the medical tests, Ali spoke to newsmen. "I've taken about 175,000 hard punches and I think that should affect somebody some. But that doesn't make me have brain damage. I feel fine. I'm older and fatter, but we all change."

Early in 1985, Ali was on hand in Las Vegas for a championship fight between middleweight champion Marvin Hagler and junior middleweight champion Thomas Hearns. He was introduced from the ring before the bout, and loud cheers and applause rang out when Ali's name was announced. His fans began to chant: "Ali . . . Ali . . .

Ali." But as Ali climbed through the ropes, a hush fell over the crowd. His movements were slow and faltering, like those of a very old person.

Many of the fans remembered Ali from his days of glory. He would bound into the ring and dance around while waiting for the bell to sound. People who saw him now could hardly believe their eyes.

Afterward, with some sadness in his face, Ali tried to respond to those who were saying that they felt sorry for him. "I have a beautiful wife," he said. "I have two beautiful daughters I'm living with. I have eight kids in all—seven girls and one boy. All are healthy.

"I have more fans and loved ones than any one person in the world. I've been invited to the countries of the world. I have so many people who love me—and I love them.

"I'm happy and doing real good. I'm happier now than when I was boxing. Don't feel sorry for me."

But everyone did.

Additional Reading

Ali, Muhammad. *The Greatest: My Own Story*. New York: Random House, 1975.

Edwards, Audry, and Gary Wohl. *Muhammad Ali: The People's Champ*. Boston: Little, Brown & Co., 1977.

Lipsyte, Robert M. *Free to Be Muhammad Ali*. New York: Harper & Row, 1978.

Roger Bannister

Four Minutes to Fame
1929–

For a couple of thousand years or thereabouts, nobody ran the mile distance in four minutes or less, or even came close to doing it. The reason? No one was capable of doing so. It was believed that the four-minute mile was beyond the reach of any runner.

Then in 1922, Paavo Nurmi of Finland, the "Flying Finn," as he was called, lowered the world record to 4:10.4 (4 minutes, 10.4 seconds). That started athletes dreaming of running the mile in four minutes.

It remained merely a dream, however. During the 1940s, a rivalry between two Swedish runners, Gunder Haegg and Arne Andersson, served to reduce the record by several seconds. When Haegg ran a 4:01.4 mile in 1945, the record ended up his.

But then no one could do better. Any one of a number of milers seemed capable of bettering four minutes, yet years passed and no one did. Breaking the four-minute "barrier" became the biggest challenge in sports. It loomed not only as a physical obstacle but also as a challenge to the human spirit, something like climbing Mount Everest or flying solo across the Atlantic Ocean.

The mile itself is special. It is, after all, a standard unit of distance in English-speaking countries.

It was a distance important to athletes long before anyone dreamed of the magic four minutes. It offers the perfect test of speed, stamina, and strategic planning.

The mile is the right distance for the spectator, too. It is not like a short sprint, where you can blink your eyes and you've missed it. It is not like a race over a long distance, which can be boring. A mile is frequently a thriller from start to finish.

Each mile race has all the ingredients of a well-constructed story, with a beginning, middle, and end. When the gun goes off, runners jockey for position. Once each has assumed a certain role, the race takes on a suspenseful air. Who is going to be the first to challenge the leader? When will he make his move? Will he be successful? And what about the leader himself? Can he maintain the pace?

Lap by lap, the suspense builds. The lead may change hands several times. Then at the finish, there is always the possibility of something unexpected happening. The race's outcome is seldom clear until the final instant.

In December 1952, John Landy, an Australian runner, triggered tremendous interest in the mile by covering the distance in 4:02.1. It was the fastest mile in the world in seven years, since Gunder Haegg had posted the record of 4:01.4 in 1945.

As if to prove what he had done was no fluke, Landy followed his achievement with another mile in 4:02.6. He made no secret of the fact that the four-minute mile was his goal. Every time he stepped out onto a track,

the eyes of the world focused upon him.

A young British medical student at Oxford University was watching Landy more intently than anyone else. His name was Roger Bannister. The tall and ruddy-faced Bannister was deeply involved in a program of scientific study and rigorous training designed to enable him to be the first to run the mile in less than four minutes. The fact that he was badly beaten in the 1952 Olympic Games did not discourage Bannister or cause him to change his training methods. It made him try harder.

Finally, at Oxford University on a cold, dreary, and windswept afternoon in the spring of 1954, it came time for Bannister to put his scientific theories to the test. He went to the starting line with three of the fastest milers in England. That afternoon, in a few minutes of supreme effort, Roger Bannister did what most runners before him had thought impossible to do.

Roger Gilbert Bannister was born at Harrow on the Hill, England, on March 23, 1929. When World War II broke out in 1939, the family moved to the city of Bath.

There Roger ran his first race as an eleven-year-old. The event was his school's junior cross-country race, which was held each year. The race covered a distance of three miles. The whole school turned out, Bannister once said, "except . . . the fat boys, who were excused." Bannister finished eighteenth, completely exhausted.

For the race the following year, Bannister trained hard, running two and a half miles twice a week as fast as he could. Much to the surprise of his friends, Roger won the race. He won it the next year, too, and again the year after that.

Four races (and three victories) in four years amounted to all the serious running Roger did until he entered Exeter College of Oxford University in October 1946. He planned to study medicine.

Roger had been told that at Oxford, "a man without a sport is like a ship without a sail." Roger decided that running would be his sport.

In his first mile race, Roger's time was 4:53. The winner was a full second faster. The race marked the first time that Roger had ever worn spiked track shoes, and they caused him to bound up and down as he ran. "Stop bouncing," he was told, "and you'll knock twenty minutes off your time."

Roger was far from being a dedicated runner at this time. He trained only once a week, then usually raced on Saturday. But his failure to train hard didn't seem to hurt him. Late in the

winter of 1947, the first time he represented Oxford on the track as a miler, Roger won in the quite respectable time of 4:30.8.

That race was a turning point in his career. In it, he had been able to tap a hidden source of energy he always suspected he possessed. That energy reserve enabled him to win by twenty yards. He realized he had discovered what he called his "gift of running."

Bannister improved steadily in the months that followed. The Olympic Games were to be held at London's Wembley Stadium in the summer of 1948. Bannister learned that there was a chance he might be chosen as a member of Britain's track and field team, but he withdrew his name from consideration. He felt he was not yet ready for advanced competition. He figured his chance would come in the 1952 Olympics, to be held in Helsinki, Finland.

Bannister was named captain of a joint Oxford-Cambridge team. In that role, he made his first trip to the United States in June 1949. In a race at Princeton University, Bannister won in a time of 4:11.1, the second fastest mile run in the United States that year. The next year, 1950, Roger cut his time to 4:09.9.

Bannister was using a training system that had been developed by mile record-holder Gunder Haegg. Called *fartlek,* meaning speed-play, it involved running entirely over grass, alternating light jogging with bursts of fast running. The idea was to increase speed as well as build stamina.

By this time, Roger had completed college and had entered St. Mary's Hospital Medical School in London. There he became interested in the medical problems related to running. In laboratory experiments, he ran on a moving belt, calculating to the last decimal point how much oxygen he would need to run the fastest mile in history.

Roger visited the United States again in the spring of 1951 to participate in the Benjamin Franklin Mile at the Penn Relays in Philadelphia. His time of 4:08.3 set a record for the event. The previous mark had been established by Glenn Cunningham seventeen years earlier. His feat earned him reams of publicity back home. He now ranked as one of Britain's foremost sports heroes.

During the winter of 1951–52, Bannister trained hard for the Olympic 1,500-meter race. (There is no mile race in Olympic competition. The 1,500-meter race is the mile's nearest equivalent. The distance of 1,500 meters is about 120 yards less than a mile.) It was a training program of his own design. He did most of his running on a grassy field near his home, and he never ran for more than half an hour at a time. He refused to enter any races, not wanting to use up his energy.

His training program was intended to prepare Bannister to race in one heat, or preliminary race, enjoy a day of rest, and then compete in the final. Not long before the Olympics opened, Bannister was stunned to learn the program had been changed by the addition of a semifinal race. Now he would have to compete in a heat, the semifinal, and then the final: three races in three days.

Bannister knew his training program had not prepared him for so grueling a schedule. He felt he had lost any chance of winning.

His fears proved right. Bannister finished a disappointing fourth in the 1,500-meter run. (José Barthel of Luxembourg was the winner.)

His defeat at the 1952 Olympics made Bannister try even harder. Some days he would run as many as ten quarter miles, each in about 63 seconds, with an interval of only two or three minutes between them. The drill would leave him exhausted for days. Other times, he ran long distances. He ran in sunshine, rain, and fog.

Out of his training and experiments, Roger developed a simple strategy for running the mile. It was based upon the fact that a runner's need for oxygen increases sharply as his speed increases.

To keep his oxygen needs at the lowest possible level, Bannister knew he would have to run the entire race at the lowest possible average speed. That meant four quarter miles—four laps—each of sixty seconds.

Bannister made his first attempt to run a mile made up of four one-minute quarters at Oxford during May 1953. A friend, Chris Chataway, agreed to set the pace in the early stages of the race, running as fast as he could. He would be Bannister's "rabbit."

In the race, Bannister ran the first two quarters a bit too slowly, but still ended up with a total time of 4:03.6, a new British record. Roger had no doubt he was using the right strategy.

Meanwhile, in Australia, John Landy was making an all-out effort to be the first to break four minutes. His training program involved running long distances every day. He also lifted weights. In December 1953, Landy ran a mile in 4:02 on a grass track, his best time ever.

But Landy could not improve upon that time. By April 1954, he had run six more times, but failed to do any better than 4:02. "It's a brick wall," he said after one of his failures.

Beginning in December 1953 and continuing through the early months of 1954, Bannister trained with greater intensity than he ever had before.

He decided he would make his attempt on the record on May 6, 1954, in a race that matched teams representing Oxford University and the British Amateur Athletic Association. Bannister was to run for the A.A.A. As the date approached, Bannister stopped training hard. He wanted to be at a freshness peak on the day he made his try.

Strong winds gusted as Bannister and the other runners lined up for the start. Bannister was to be paced, first by Chris Brasher, then Chris Chataway. About 1,200 spectators, mostly students, were on hand.

The gun went off. Bannister ran almost effortlessly and breezed through the first quarter in 57.5 seconds. He continued to run smoothly, rhythmically, hardly giving any conscious thought to what he was doing. His time for the half mile was a blistering 1:58. Bannister knew he had a good chance.

At the three-quarters mark, Bannister was still moving easily. His time for three quarters was 3:00.5. Now he could hear the roar of the crowd. He knew he had to run the last lap in 59 seconds.

Here's how he described the last 300 yards:

"My mind took over. . . . It raced well ahead of my body and drew my body . . . forward. I felt the moment

Roger Bannister overtakes John Landy in the one-mile race at the 1954 British Commonwealth Games. Both men finished in less than four minutes, prompting observers to call this race "the mile of the century." *Courtesy of AP/Wide World Photos.*

of a lifetime had come. The world seemed to stand still.

"With 50 yards left, my body had long since exhausted all of its energy but it went on running just the same. The last few seconds seemed never-ending. I leaped at the tape like a man taking a last spring to save himself from the chasm. . . . It was only then that real pain overtook me."

At the end, Bannister collapsed, almost unconscious. His arms and legs throbbed with pain.

Then he heard the announcement: "Result of the one mile . . . time, 3 minutes . . ." The rest of the announcement was lost in cheers. But Bannister knew that he had done what no other runner had ever done before.

Bannister's official time was 3:59.4. The psychological block was no more. Just seven weeks later at Turku, Finland, Bannister's record was broken by Landy, who was clocked at 3:58.

Bannister and Landy faced one another in a mile race at Empire Stadium in Vancouver, British Columbia, Canada, on June 21, 1954. The matchup was a feature of the British Commonwealth Games.

The race has been called one of the most dramatic events in the history of sport. Four others were entered besides Bannister and Landy.

At the gun, Landy got off to a fast start. Bannister ran third, then second. Landy continued to lead as they sped through one lap, then another, then a third. As they came into the stretch, Landy looked back over his shoulder. Bannister was not there. Then Landy realized that Bannister had spurted into the lead and was gaining. Bannister won by five yards. His time was 3:58.8 against his rival's 3:59.6.

Bannister was awarded his medical degree in July 1954. The following month, running at Bern, Switzerland, Bannister won the 1,500-meter race in the European Games. That was his last victory in international track competition. He announced he was giving up running because of the pressures of his duties as a physician.

In breaking the four-minute barrier, Bannister opened the floodgates. Great Britain's Derek Ibbotson broke the mile record, to be followed by Herb Elliot of Australia, Peter Snell of New Zealand, France's Michel Jazy, and Jim Ryun of the United States, who lowered the record twice.

Ryun, from Wichita, Kansas, first broke into the headlines in 1965 by running a mile in 3:58.3. What made the feat even more remarkable was that Ryun was a high schooler at the time.

The collegiate record Ryun later established was surpassed by Filberto Bayo of Tanzania and John Walker of New Zealand. Walker was the first to break the 3:50 mile, clocking 3:49.4 in 1975.

That record stood for five years. Then along came a pair of English runners named Sebastian Coe and Steve Ovett. During one eleven-day stretch in 1981, Coe and Ovett traded the mile record three times.

Steve Cram of Britain took more than a second off Coe's record when he ran a 3:46.31 mile in 1985. Those who saw Cram run said he was capable of doing even better.

As for Bannister, in the years following his heroic feat, he became a respected neurologist in England. He was knighted by Queen Elizabeth in 1975. The same year, he was in a serious car accident, in which an ankle was crushed. After that, he did no more running, although he did not have difficulty walking. His serious exercise was limited to bicycling.

Bannister was asked whether being unable to run made him feel deprived. He said no, adding, "I regard life since 1975 as a bonus. I was very lucky not to have been killed." In 1985, Bannister was appointed Master of Oxford's Pembroke College.

Bannister was once asked where he thought the mile record was headed. What was the limit? He said that by the year 2000 the record could be 3:30.

But there is no barrier there. Bannister himself saw to that.

Additional Reading

Bannister, Roger. *The Four-Minute Mile.* New York: Dodd, Mead & Co., 1955.

Larry Bird

Simply the Best
1956–

THE TIME: June 6, 1984.

THE PLACE: The Forum in Los Angeles.

THE EVENT: Game 4 of the 1983–84 National Basketball Association's championship playoffs: the Boston Celtics vs. the Los Angeles Lakers.

It was East Coast vs. West Coast; tradition vs. movieland glamor.

It was the Celtics' rebounding vs. the Lakers' running game.

It was forward Larry Bird of the Celtics vs. Earvin (Magic) Johnson of the Lakers, two of the greatest players in the history of the pro game.

Game 1 of the series went to the Lakers. They simply outblitzed the Celtics, jumping off to a 24–9 lead, then holding on to win.

The Lakers handed Game 2 to the

Celtics on a silver platter. With 15 seconds remaining, Los Angeles had the ball and a 113–111 lead. All the Lakers had to do was let the clock run out. But James Worthy, who had played brilliant basketball throughout the game, tried to force a cross-court pass. The ball was picked off by Boston's Gerald Henderson, who made the game-tying layup with 11 seconds left. The Celtics went on to win in overtime and tie matters.

The Lakers came out firing in Game 3, determined to make amends for their collapse. Magic Johnson, in a peak performance, had 14 points, 21 assists and 11 rebounds. The Celtics were overwhelmed.

Now ahead two games to one in the series, Los Angeles looked to be the better team. If it had not been for that critical moment in Game 2, the Lakers could have been leading in games, 3–0, and the Celtics would have been in an almost hopeless situation.

After Game 3, Larry Bird was upset. He criticized his own performance. He lashed out at his teammates. "I know the heart and soul of this team," he declared in the dressing room after the game. "And today the heart just wasn't there. It was embarrassing. I just can't believe a team like this would let them come out and push us around like they did."

To a newspaper reporter, he said: "They crushed us. We played like a bunch of sissies."

Bird changed that in Game 4. The referee tossed up the ball for the opening tap. The Celtics' Robert Parish got a piece of the ball, but it squirted off several hands and bounded toward a corner. Magic Johnson and James Worthy had position on the ball and darted over to pick it up. The other Lakers sped downcourt. The Celtics backpedaled to get into position.

Remember, it was just the beginning of things. Fans were getting settled in their seats. Players were taking deep breaths in expectation of the game's first scoring thrust.

·Suddenly the calm was broken. Larry Bird was rushing for the ball. When he got close enough, he flung his body into the air, stretching full-length. His big hands clutched the ball just as Magic bent to pick it up. The two men went sprawling, and James Worthy came over and joined in.

A whistle blared. Jump ball.

The jump ball that Bird had forced had no direct influence on the game's outcome, but it sent a message to the Laker players and their fans. In the previous game, Bird had done all the things he was supposed to do—pass, shoot, rebound. That hadn't been enough. Now he was going to do more. It was time to get tough. That was his message.

Other Celtic players got the Bird spirit. In the second period, Boston's Kevin McHale applied a neck tackle on Kurt Rambis of the Lakers. McHale said afterward that he was merely trying to stop an easy basket. The Lakers called it dirty play.

No matter how one describes the act, it was the Celtics' style of play for the rest of the series. It carried them to an overtime victory in Game 4, which tied the series at two games apiece.

In Game 5, back in Boston, the Celtics continued to assert themselves. Bird bombed the Lakers for 34 points, shooting 15 of 20 from the floor. The Celtics won, 121–103.

After the Lakers had knotted the series at 3–3, the teams returned to Boston for the finale. No Boston team had ever lost the seventh game of a championship series. The record remained intact, the Celtics winning, 111–102. It was Boston's fifteenth National Basketball Association (NBA) championship.

Bird was named the most valuable player of the series. He had averaged 27.4 points and 14 rebounds per game.

But the stat sheets gave no hint of Bird's real contribution. All players try hard. Larry Bird tries harder.

Other players score more points than Larry Bird. (Kareem Abdul-Jabbar is one example.) Other players have bigger totals in assists (Magic Johnson), rebounds (Moses Malone of the Washington Bullets), and steals (Michael Jordan of the Chicago Bulls). But Larry Bird is one player who does *all* of these things.

Bird is an incredible passer. He will race down one side of the court and knife through the middle, with players swirling all around him. He will grab a pass; then, suddenly, the ball is gone. Without looking, Bird has flipped it over his shoulder to a man cutting underneath the basket.

Or he will dribble down one side of the court, stop, then go up for a jump shot, but at the peak of his jump, he spots an open teammate, and the ball goes to him.

Former Celtic star Bob Cousy, who is looked upon by many as the best ball handler in basketball history, once said of Bird: "He is the best passer I have ever seen."

When it comes to shooting and scoring, Bird, who averaged 23.6 points per game in his first six years with the Celtics, is in a class with the game's best. He is accurate from any reasonable range. From the three-point distance of 23 feet, 9 inches, Bird makes nearly half of his shots.

"I guess the key thing is that I always know what's happening on the court," Bird once said. "I know exactly what I can and cannot do. I know when and how I can score on a particular defender."

Bird's contributions have not gone unnoticed. In 1978, he was named College Player of the Year, having guided Indiana State University to thirty-three consecutive victories. In 1979–80 he was Rookie of the Year in the NBA; he led the Celtics in scoring, rebounds, and steals. In 1983–84, he was chosen the NBA's Most Valuable Player. It marked only the second time in twenty years that a non-center had been chosen for the honor. (The other was Julius Erving of the Philadelphia 76ers, the league's MVP in 1980–81.)

No one ever questioned whether Larry Bird was *the* forward of the 1980s. He may be the best forward ever.

Playing for Indiana State University, Larry Bird attracted national attention when he was named 1978 College Player of the Year. *Courtesy of Indiana State University Department of Athletics.*

Larry Bird was born on December 7, 1956, in French Lick, a small town in southern Indiana. "A hick from French Lick," is how he has jokingly described himself. He was the fourth boy in a family of five boys and one girl.

After his parents were divorced, his mother, Georgia Bird, raised the children with the help of her parents. A tall and quiet woman, Mrs. Bird went to work as a cook in local restaurants in order to provide for the family. She sometimes worked sixteen hours a day.

Her sons, particularly Mark and Mike, loved basketball. They would go to the courts every day. Larry credits Mark, who is three years older than he, for getting him interested in developing his shooting.

By the time Larry had reached fourth grade, a basketball was almost always his companion. He was active in the "biddy basketball" league sponsored by his school in fourth, fifth, and sixth grades.

Sometimes the teams would perform during halftime of the varsity games. For a shy and skinny youngster like Larry, it was a big thrill.

At Springs Valley High School, Bird, a 6-foot-1 beanpole, was a promising pitcher on the baseball team as well as a guard in basketball. In basketball, he chose to wear Number 33 on his jersey because it had been his brother Mark's number. (He continued to wear Number 33 in college and as a professional.)

Larry was determined to become one of the best players Springs Valley ever had, but in his sophomore season his goal was sidetracked when he broke his left ankle. Even with his foot in a cast, he continued to practice his shooting.

Toward the end of the season, when tournament time arrived, Larry begged the coach for a chance to play. The coach gave him a try, even though he had not played in a varsity contest. Larry made two foul throws that won the game.

By his senior year, Larry was four inches taller and much stronger from lifting weights. "I never saw a kid who played basketball so much," Gerry Holland, Larry's high school coach, once said. "He didn't have a car or much money, so he spent his time on basketball." Larry and his friends would practice in the gym until the school closed, then find a playground court where they could keep practicing until dark. Says Bird: "I played when I was cold and my body was aching and was so tired . . . and I don't know why, I just kept playing and playing." In games Bird's unselfish team spirit was such that, as his coach once recalled, we "had trouble getting him to shoot enough." Bird preferred to pass off. In spite of this "trouble," Bird averaged 30.6 points and 20 rebounds during his senior year.

During the spring of 1974, college scouts by the dozens traveled to French Lick to see Larry in action. A year before, Larry had no plans to attend college. Of course, he didn't know that he was going to grow to be 6-foot-7 as a college senior. Nor did he know that Holland would be describing him as "the best player I ever coached."

About two hundred colleges wanted Larry and offered him athletic scholarships. Larry had trouble making up his mind. A country boy, his roots deep in the Indiana soil, he did not want to travel far from home. A Florida college asked him to visit and sent him a round-trip airline ticket. Larry went to the airport but at the last minute decided not to board the airplane and went back home.

Bobby Knight, coach of Indiana University and one of the most respected college coaches in the nation, came to French Lick to see Larry in action. Knight was very impressed with what he saw. But Larry was not thrilled by the idea of attending Indiana University. It was too big, he felt. He preferred Indiana State University in Terre Haute, a much smaller school.

The townspeople in French Lick who were interested in pushing Larry's career wanted him to pick Indiana University. Its basketball program was better, they said. Larry listened to his friends. He chose Indiana University.

In the fall of 1974, seventeen-year-old Larry Bird went off to the sprawling Bloomington campus of Indiana University and its 31,500 students. Almost from the moment he arrived, Larry felt he had made a mistake. There were masses of students, none of whom he knew. He had to walk miles to classes. The lecture halls were so huge that it was hard to hear what was being said.

Larry felt swallowed up. He missed his pals in French Lick. He began to feel depressed, but it was not Larry's nature to talk to anyone about it. One day, only a few weeks after he had arrived, Larry packed his bag and left.

It was not very pleasant for him back in French Lick. Some of the townspeople felt Larry had let them down. He had been given a chance to play top-flight college basketball, and he had blown it.

Larry then decided to attend little Northwood Institute in West Baden, Indiana. Jack Johnson, the basketball coach there, once described Larry as being "very unsettled." After two months, Larry quit again. He took a job driving a garbage truck and painted park benches for the city sanitation department. When he had spare time, he turned to basketball, playing in an amateur league.

Things got worse. Larry's father committed suicide. Then Larry married, fathered a child, and separated from his wife.

Larry might still be driving a truck or painting park benches had it not been for Bob King and Bill Hodges, the coach and assistant coach at Indiana State University. Hodges went to French Lick to make another attempt to recruit Larry. The two met at Larry's grandmother's house. Larry told Hodges he had been playing amateur basketball. One of his teammates, Larry said, could have been a great college player.

Hodges saw his chance. "Yeah," he said, "someday they'll be saying that about you."

Hodges had struck a nerve. Larry didn't want to be known as a quitter for the rest of his life. He decided to return to college, accepting Hodges' offer of a scholarship.

Bird had to sit out the 1975–76 basketball season. As a transfer student, he was not eligible to compete. He practiced against the varsity, concentrating on improving his defensive skills. He watched from the sidelines as the Sycamores struggled, winning only 13 of 25 games.

The following season, with Larry in the lineup, it was much different. He led the team to a 25–3 record, averaging 32.8 points per game.

Sportswriters struggled to describe Bird. They called him "Super Bird," "Big Bird," "Blond Bomber," and "the Sycamore Sensation."

"Bird operates in one gear—wide open at all times," wrote Jim Kimball of the *Fort Wayne* [Indiana] *Journal-Gazette.*

"Bird has a bigger variety of shots than Heinz has pickles," said Max Stultz of the *Indianapolis Star.*

The next season, 1977–78, Bird was even better. Indiana State sprang into the top ten of the college rankings, and Larry was a first team All-American.

Although Larry was eligible for the pro basketball draft in 1978, he decided to remain in college for another year. He had two reasons for doing so: He wanted to get his degree, and he wanted one more chance at leading the Sycamores to the NCAA (National Collegiate Athletic Association) title.

He told coach Bob King that he would be returning to campus with the understanding that he would not have to talk to reporters. He didn't like answering prying questions posed by people he didn't know. Some of the reporters started calling him "the silent Sycamore."

Bird achieved his first goal: getting his college degree. He just missed the second. The Sycamores were the surprise number-one college team in the nation in 1978–79, winning 33 consecutive games.

In the final NCAA championship game, the team was pitted against Michigan State. The game was billed as a duel between the season's two towering superstars, Bird and Earvin (Magic) Johnson. The two would face one another countless times in the years to come. In this matchup, it was Magic who prevailed. He was the game's high scorer and its most valuable player, as Michigan State won, 75–64.

Bird had had an exceptional season. He had averaged 14.8 rebounds per game, the highest average in the NCAA. He had scored 28.6 points per game. Only one player in the nation had had a higher scoring average. Bird was awarded Player of the Year trophies by both the Associated Press and United Press International.

On June 8, 1979, Bird signed a five-year contract with the Boston Celtics. The contract, which was to pay him $3,250,000, or $650,000 a year, made him the highest-paid rookie in the history of professional sports.

A reporter asked Bird what he intended to do with all that money. "My mother comes first," he said. "I want to do everything I can to help her out. Where I come from, we didn't have much. So I want to give her a little security."

Bird found a home with the Celtics, a club that stressed team play. He liked it that nobody seemed point-hungry. He liked it that the team ran hard on offense but also played tough defense.

Bird had a superb rookie season. In the year before Larry's arrival, the Celtics had won only 29 games of the 82 they had played. Bird, as a rookie, led the team to a 61–21 record. He was the team leader in rebounding, scoring, and minutes played. He helped get the Celtics back into playoff competition (although they lost to the Philadelphia 76ers in the Eastern Conference finals).

Bird was named to the All-Star first team and won Rookie of the Year honors, edging out Magic Johnson, who had become a star performer for the Los Angeles Lakers. Bird was also third in the balloting for the NBA's Most Valuable Player.

The Celtics improved themselves for the 1980–81 season. They obtained Robert Parish, a 7-foot center, from the Golden State Warriors. They also added 6-foot-10 Kevin McHale for backup strength. Both proved to be defensive standouts.

Bird, who started in all 82 games that season, firmly established himself as Boston's Big Gun. He was the driving force as the Celtics captured the Atlantic Division championship, swept the Chicago Bulls, 4–0, in the Eastern Conference semifinals, then faced the tough

Philadelphia 76ers for the Conference title.

Bird was awesome throughout the series. In the seventh game, with the score tied and time running out, he rebounded the ball, dribbled almost the length of the court, then tossed up a 15-foot jumper that clinched the game and the Eastern Conference championship for the Celtics.

There were more heroics for Bird against the Houston Rockets in the championship finals. In the sixth and what was to prove to be final game, Bird turned a nip-and-tuck contest into a Boston victory with a six-point scoring spree in the final period. All of the points came within 32 seconds.

"They came close," Bird told reporters in the joyous Boston dressing room. "But I knew we would win. The coach kept calling my play, and I knew I could make it.

"Everybody was worrying . . . but I wasn't."

In 1981–82, Bird averaged more assists per game than any other of the league's forwards for the second consecutive season. He also led the Celtics in steals for the second time.

Boston's 63–19 record put them in first place in the league standings, but they were eliminated by the Philadelphia 76ers in the playoffs. The next season, 1982–83, the Milwaukee Bucks

ousted the Celtics from playoff competition. In 1983–84, the Celtics could not be denied. Led by Bird, named the playoff MVP, they defeated the Lakers to win their fifteenth NBA title.

Not since the days of Bill Russell of the Celtics and Philadelphia's Wilt Chamberlain have basketball fans been treated to a rivalry as intense as that between Bird and Magic Johnson. Bird has called Johnson one of the three top players in pro basketball. "He's a perfect player," Bird said, "maybe the best."

"We both do the same type of things," Bird once told *Sports Illustrated*, "but we're not the same type player. When you think of the impact we have on the game, with me it's usually scoring, but with him it's always his passing. He gets his hands more on the ball than I do, so he has more control of the situation."

In 1984–85, it was Johnson's turn to celebrate once more. The Lakers, with Kareem Abdul-Jabbar leading the way, downed the Celtics, four games to two, in the championship finals.

It was a season that Larry would like to forget. For much of it, he was plagued with damaged fingers and bone chips in his right elbow. "He's been playing hurt, very hurt," said Boston coach K. C. Jones during the playoffs. "But you'll never get him to admit it."

Larry Bird led the Boston Celtics against their perennial rivals, the Los Angeles Lakers. *Courtesy of Naismith Memorial Basketball Hall of Fame.*

There was back pain, too. Bird sought out a physical therapist through an exercise program and began to overcome the pain. By the time of the All-Star Game in 1986–87, he was beginning to look like the real Larry Bird.

Bird went on to lead the Celtics to the team's sixteenth NBA title that season. They downed the Houston Rockets in the finals, 4 games to 2. Bird, who earlier had been named the league's regular season Most Valuable Player, was also voted the MVP of the finals.

Bird has made no secret of what he wants to do once his professional career has ended. He plans to return to French Lick and coach junior high school basketball. "That's where the real coaching is done," he has said, "in the younger grades."

French Lick will always be his home. It's where he feels comfortable. "People there want nothing from me and I want nothing from them," he has said. "They treat me as just another guy, and that's how, more than anything, I want to be treated."

Additional Reading

Bird, Larry, with John Bischoff. *Bird on Basketball*. Reading, Massachusetts: Addison-Wesley Publishing Co., 1985.

Corn, Frederick Lynn. *Basketball's Magnificent Bird*, New York: Random House, 1982.

Jim Brown

Pro Football Powerhouse
1936–

"You never hit him head on," a defensive back once said of Jim Brown. "What I used to do was let him go by and grab him from behind and hang on, hollering for help. If help didn't come quick, he'd drag you ten yards without breaking stride."

Jim Brown, who played nine seasons for the Cleveland Browns beginning in 1957, was the very model of what a pro football running back is supposed to be. Strong and muscular, he stood 6-foot-2, weighed 230 pounds, and had a 32-inch waist.

He ran with crushing power yet he also had speed enough to outleg most defensive backs. He had a gliding style of running; high knee action was not for him. "You have to stay close to the ground," he once said. "Most good runners I've seen run that way.

"You have to keep your feet close to the ground so you can maneuver. If you lift your feet up high and take too long a stride, you get in a position so you can't move."

His gliding style made Brown a punishing runner. He'd drive so hard that it almost always took more than one tackler to bring him down. "When he comes through that line," linebacker Sam Huff once said, "brother, you forget about yourself and dive in there and try and stop him. You have to hit him from the knees down, or you don't have a prayer. Anything from the hips up, he'll either drag you with him or run right over you. Believe me, he's run over me more than once."

But there was also Brown's speed to reckon with. A dozen or more times during the season, he would pop through the line or streak to the outside, and then turn on the speed, racing all the way to the end zone.

Brown never won any prizes for his blocking. He had no enthusiasm for it. But this failure was hardly noticed. On those rare occasions when he didn't carry the ball, he was often used as a decoy. No defense could ignore him. Whenever he circled out of the back-field, one and sometimes two players went with him. What he accomplished as a potential pass receiver was just as effective as if he had blocked.

Brown's enormous power and sprinter's speed were not what made him a superstar, however. His pride was. One season near the end of his career, the Browns, unbeaten in four games, traveled to New York to play the Giants, champions of the Eastern Conference. Jim was a marked man that afternoon. "Get Brown!" was the New York game plan. Whenever he was going down or in a pileup, the Giant players went for Jim's face, which became a mass of welts and bruises.

Still, Jim managed to have an excellent day, scoring twice. In the Cleveland dressing room afterward, reporters gathered around him and asked him about the dirty play. All he would say was, "It was my most satisfying day—under the circumstances." But he would not explain what he meant by "under the circumstances."

That was typical conduct for Jim Brown. Never complain; never explain. He seldom showed any emotion. Whether one man tackled him or a mob, he'd get up slowly to conserve his energy for the next play. He could be dog-tired or in terrible pain, but you couldn't tell it by looking at his face. In a career that lasted nine seasons, Brown never missed a game.

When he quit abruptly after the 1965 season, Brown was hailed as pro football's greatest running back. Many of the records he set lasted until the mid-1980s, and some are still on the books. Even today, among NFL coaches, their fondest hope is to find a running back they can call "another Jim Brown."

Jim Brown was born James Nathaniel Brown on February 17, 1936, on St. Simons Island, a good-sized chunk of land off the coast of Georgia, just north of the Georgia-Florida border. When he was two years old, his parents separated and his mother moved to Manhasset, Long Island, New York. For a time, Jim stayed behind with a grandmother in Georgia, but when he was seven, he joined his mother, who was working as a housekeeper.

He was involved in sports early, first at Manhasset Valley Elementary School and the Manhasset Police Boys' Club, and later at Plandome Road Junior High School and Manhasset High School.

In high school Jim earned a reputation as one of the best schoolboy athletes in the history of New York State. He starred on the basketball team, once scoring 55 points in a game, a Long Island scholastic record. He was a first baseman on the baseball team and a standout lacrosse player (a game in which opposing teams attempt to send a small ball into each other's goal using a stick at the end of which is a netted pocket for catching, carrying, and throwing the ball). He also excelled in football, averaging 14.9 yards per carry.

By the time he was ready to graduate from high school, Jim could count forty-two offers of college athletic scholarships. He also had been approached by the New York Yankees and Boston (now Atlanta) Braves.

A Manhasset lawyer named Ken Mulloy, who had become his close friend, wanted Jim to go to Syracuse, the school from which he had graduated. Although Mulloy was successful in getting Jim interested in Syracuse, he failed to get Syracuse interested in Jim. University officials would not approve an athletic scholarship for him. That didn't stop Mulloy. He rounded up a group of local citizens who were proud of Jim and eager to see him succeed, and he got them to contribute to a fund to pay for Jim's college tuition and living expenses.

Jim did not know of these arrangements at the time, but later he was to acknowledge what Mulloy had done, saying, "Ken Mulloy exerted the greatest influence on my life. He helped me when I needed it the most." When, in 1971, Brown was named to pro football's Hall of Fame, he chose Ken Mulloy to introduce him at the enshrinement ceremonies.

Jim was an athletic sensation at Syracuse, winning ten varsity letters—three each in football and lacrosse, and two each in baseball and track. He won All-America honors in lacrosse. A fierce competitor, he would hold the ball and net tight to his chest as he barreled down the field under a full head of steam. He once fired the ball so hard it tore through the goal. "Our goalie spent the rest of the day keeping out of his way," one player said.

Jim was also an All-America selection in football. In the final game of his senior season, he scored an incredible 43 points as Syracuse walloped Colgate, 67–6. Immediately afterward, Syracuse was invited to the Cotton Bowl. There Jim was at his dazzling best, rushing for 132 yards and scoring 21 points. Syracuse nevertheless lost to Texas Christian University, 28–27.

Jim was drafted by the Cleveland Browns in the first round of the National Football League's college draft. Paul Brown, then the head coach of the Browns, named him the team's starting fullback when the season opened.

Jim Brown, running back for the Cleveland Browns, developed a gliding style that made him one of the swiftest players on any football field. *Courtesy of the Cleveland Browns.*

Jim's biggest day during his rookie season came on November 24, 1957. The Browns, leading the Eastern Conference by one game, met the Los Angeles Rams in Cleveland before a throng of more than 65,000. Jim put the Browns in front with a touchdown run early in the game. Not long after, he took the ball on a draw play and was belted so hard his helmet flew off, but managed to keep his balance and race 69 yards for another touchdown.

In the third quarter, Jim fumbled, giving the Rams a chance to score. They did, and by so doing took a 28–17 lead.

Embarrassed by the fumble, Jim raged back. In less than four minutes, he scored two more touchdowns. The Browns eventually won 45–21.

It was called the greatest exhibition of running in the pro game. Jim had carried the ball 31 times for 237 yards, a pro record. (Several other running backs were later to surpass the figure.)

Cleveland lost the 1957 championship game to the Detroit Lions. In 1958, they tied the New York Giants for the Eastern Conference title, and Brown set a league rushing record with a total of 1,527 yards. (The record was later topped by Brown himself and several other runners. The present record of 2,105 yards was established by Eric Dickerson in 1984.) Brown also led the league in scoring, with 108 points on 18 touchdowns. But his outstanding season was offset by Cleveland's loss to the New York Giants in the championship game.

In his first five years with the Browns, Jim gained 6,463 yards on 1,269 carries. Many people thought that Paul Brown was overworking his star performer. Brown had a ready answer for his critics. "When you've got a big gun," the coach said, "you shoot it."

The criticism did not die down. "No man, not even a powerhouse like Jimmy, should carry the ball so much," said one of his teammates. "The more he smashes into those big linemen, the more chance he has of getting hurt and ending his career.

"Sure, let him carry a lot, but at least give him a rest once in a while. He's not a horse; he's only a human being."

In a game against the Giants, Jim got banged on the head while carrying the ball in the first quarter. He was in a daze for the rest of the game. He couldn't even remember the score. He sat out the second quarter, but Paul Brown had him back on the field for the third and fourth quarters. The Browns lost, 48–7.

Afterward, one of the Giants said, "It was a crime to send Jimmy back in after he got hurt. There was no point in it. We had the game wrapped up, and the guy was in a daze. He could have gotten hurt pretty badly."

Paul Brown had an answer for that, too. "I'm not in the habit of asking Giant players what to do in a game," said the Cleveland coach. "But I do ask the team doctor."

Jim felt that Brown was wrong in putting him in that game. He seethed—but didn't say anything.

The relationship between the two men kept going downhill. Jim thought the coach was making a mistake by calling all the plays from the bench, not giving the quarterback the freedom to direct the team on the field. He didn't like the way the coach treated the players, making all the rules and decisions himself. More and more he himself felt like a robot. Whenever the coach pressed the button, Jim was supposed to gain five yards.

Things came to a head in 1962. The Browns finished with a 7–6–1 record, their worst in years. Jim, playing much of the season with an injured wrist, gained 996 yards. But he lost the rushing title to Green Bay's Jim Taylor. It marked the first season in his career that Jim had not led the league.

Several of the Cleveland players, Jim included, went to see team owner, Art Modell. They told him they no longer wanted to play football for Paul Brown. If the Browns had been winning cham-

pionships, Modell might have defended the coach. But the Browns hadn't won anything since 1957. So Modell fired Paul Brown and replaced him with Blanton Collier, one of the team's assistant coaches.

Collier was warm and friendly, and Jim and the other players liked him. They also admired some of the tactical changes he made. One was option blocking. Under Paul Brown, a lineman blocked in a specific direction on every play. But option blocking gave each lineman a choice. He simply pushed his opponent in the direction the opponent wanted to go. Then it was up to Jim, or whoever else happened to be carrying the ball, to read the blocking and react accordingly. When the lineman took the defender to the left, for example, the ball carrier simply cut to the right.

Jim called it "instinctive football." He proved perfect for it, carving out one brilliant performance after another. It was his greatest season. He averaged 133 yards per game and gained a record 1,863 yards for the season. He thus became the first player in pro history to gain more than a mile in one season.

One game that year must be mentioned. It took place against the Giants, the Eastern Conference title holders, at New York's Yankee Stadium.

The Giants scored first, but the

Browns came back. With Jim ripping off big gains, Cleveland moved the ball 78 yards to the Giant 1-yard line. Then they handed the ball to Jim one more time, and he fought his way across the goal line for the tying touchdown.

Each team scored one more touchdown in the first half, but the Giants also got a field goal. New York held a 17–14 edge as the third period began.

Jim took charge. Three minutes after the kickoff, he circled wide, grabbed a screen pass, and hurried 72 yards for a touchdown. A few minutes after that, he took a handoff at the Giant 32-yard line, veered to his left, then reversed his field. With his legs churning smoothly, his head up, and warding off tacklers with his forearm, he sped for yet another touchdown. The Browns had all the points they needed for a victory.

Despite Jim's heroics that season, the Browns finished second to the Giants in the conference standings. The next year, 1964, the Browns did win the title, whipping the Baltimore Colts, 27–0, in the championship game. "We finally won the big one," Jim said. He called the victory the "high point" of his career.

The Browns repeated as champions of the Eastern Conference in 1965 and Jim had another exceptional season.

But in the championship playoff, the Browns fell to the Green Bay Packers.

A week later in the Pro Bowl in Los Angeles, Jim was at his explosive best, scoring three touchdowns. No one knew it at the time, but it was Jim's final appearance in pro football.

Jim had already launched a motion picture career. In 1965, he played a minor role in a film titled *Rio Conchos.* "He's the first Negro actor to come along that the average man in Watts or Harlem can identify with," said actor Lee Marvin, later to be one of Jim's co-stars. "He looks like an average guy; he talks like one, not like Sidney Poitier, who goes around all day talking Shakespeare."

Offers of bigger parts followed. In the summer of 1966, as his teammates gathered for the beginning of training camp, Jim was in England filming *The Dirty Dozen*, a movie in which he had a starring role.

Art Modell, the owner of the Browns, was not pleased. He began fining Jim $100 a day for each day of training camp he missed. Jim reacted as many people expected he would. He called a press conference and announced he was retiring.

"It was the right time to retire," he was to say later. "You have to go out on top."

He was thirty years old at the time

he quit. He surely would have had many more standout seasons in pro football.

As it was, he was the Number 1 running back of all time when he retired. In his nine-year career, he gained a total of 12,312 yards. At the time, the next runner on the list was more than 4,000 yards behind Jim. (Walter Payton of the Chicago Bears broke the record in 1984.) Here are some of the other ball-carrying records held by Brown at the time he called it quits:

Most seasons leading league, rushing—6

Most attempts, career—2,359

Most attempts, season—305

Most yards gained, season—1,863

Most games, 100 or more yards gained—58

Highest average gain, career—5.2 yards

Most touchdowns, lifetime—106

Brown's achievements went beyond what he had done as a ball carrier. He set a standard of excellence for his teammates. In the dressing room after the 1964 championship playoff, which the Browns won, coach Blanton Collier went over to Jim's locker. "Jim," he said, putting out his hand, "I want to thank you for your leadership."

In the years following his retirement, Brown made more than twenty movies and dozens of television dramas. Usually he was cast as a tough guy.

That was his image off the screen as well. In 1965, Brown was accused of beating and molesting two teen-age girls. One later dropped the charges. The other filed a paternity suit and lost.

In 1968, Brown was arrested and charged with intent to commit murder when his girlfriend was found semiconscious beneath his apartment balcony. Again, charges were dropped. However, Brown was fined $300 for resisting arrest.

In 1978 he was fined $500 and jailed for one day after being convicted of beating up a golf partner. Their fight was triggered over the placement of a golf ball.

In 1985 Brown was arrested at his home in the Los Angeles area on suspicion of rape. The charges were later dismissed.

Brown always kept an eye on pro football. It pained him to see his records get broken one by one, particularly since he felt that running backs of the 1970s and 1980s had it easier than he did. Standards *were* different. Brown played in a twelve-game season from 1957 through 1960, and a fourteen-game season from 1961 through 1965. The NFL embarked on a sixteen-game season in 1978.

"Gaining 1,000 yards in a fourteen-game season is like walking backwards," he once remarked. "Gaining 1,000 yards in a sixteen-game season isn't even worth talking about."

He called pro football of the 1980s a fake. "I can't accept quarterbacks sliding and running backs running out of bounds," he told *Sports Illustrated* in 1983. "Ever since the merger [of the National Football League and American Football League] in 1966 and the creation of the Super Bowl, the owners have been more concerned with ratings than the level of the game. Coaches put up with players waving into TV cameras, giving high fives, and spiking the ball. That's what sells."

To go with his remarks, Jim posed for a photograph that was used on the magazine's cover. He was wearing a Los Angeles Raiders' jersey and his old number, 32. He had a Raiders' helmet tucked under one arm.

The uniform was more than a random choice. The Raiders have a reputation as pro football's tough guys. That was Jim Brown, all right.

Additional Reading

Isaacs, Stan. *Jim Brown: The Golden Year, 1964.* Englewood Cliffs, N.J.: Prentice Hall, Inc., 1970.

Toback, James. *Jim.* Garden City, N.J.: Doubleday & Co., 1971.

Wilt Chamberlain

Basketball's Big Man
1936–

Kareem Abdul-Jabbar of the Los Angeles Lakers. Moses Malone of the Philadelphia 76ers. Ralph Sampson of the Houston Rockets. Every successful basketball team has had its high-scoring big man. No pro team can win consistently without one.

A seven-footer who can move, score, and block shots can transform a doormat club into a playoff contender. Talented big men are now scouted in high schools and even junior highs. Scouts also range through European and African countries, looking for boys who are abnormally tall and can put a basketball through a hoop—or look as if they can be schooled to do so.

That wasn't always true. For years, very tall players were not looked upon kindly. The few seven-footers who attempted to play pro basketball were found to be slow and awkward. They were called freaks or goons.

Wilt Chamberlain helped to change the tall player's image. Wilt, who stood a shade over 7-foot-1 and weighed 250 pounds, was one of the fastest runners in pro basketball. He had a high-jumper's leg spring and unusually good balance for someone so large. While he didn't move with grace or beauty, he knew how to get around without falling over his feet.

Fans marveled at Chamberlain's achievements. During the 1960–61 season, Elgin Baylor of the Los Angeles Lakers scored 71 points against the New York Knicks at Madison Square Garden. That was the National Basketball Association's one-game record. During that season and the one that followed, Wilt Chamberlain had outbursts of 73,

78, and 100 points. In fact, of the sixty highest scoring performances in National Basketball Association (NBA) history, more than two-thirds of them are Wilt Chamberlain's.

Wilt led the NBA in scoring a record seven times. He averaged 30.1 points during his career. By comparison, Kareem Abdul-Jabbar, pro basketball's outstanding player of the 1980s, averaged around 27 points per game.

Wilt was not merely a scorer. His proudest statistical achievement came in the 1967–68 season, when he led the league in assists and rebounds as well as field goals. He ended his career with more rebounds per game than Bill Russell—22.8 vs. 22.4. Russell is the standard against which all rebounders are measured.

Chamberlain was not a clever ball handler, and he was perhaps one of the worst foul shooters of all time. His average was consistently below .600. High schoolers do better than that. Yet he dominated virtually every game in which he played. "He gets the points, he gets the ball, and he can go all night," is how Bob Cousy of the Boston Celtics once described him. "What else can you say?"

Wilt Chamberlain was born in Philadelphia on August 21, 1936. His father was a maintenance worker. Both of his parents were of normal height.

Wilt and his five brothers and three sisters were brought up in an eight-room, two-story home in the Haddington section of West Philadelphia. Neighbors of the Chamberlains remember Wilt climbing to the roof of his front porch and leaping across the yawning gap to the porch roof of the house next door. Then he'd leap to the house next to that, and so on, down the entire block.

Porch-jumping was a hazardous activity—for other youngsters. But not for Wilt. His legs were so long and so limber, he could soar from one roof to the next without putting his life in jeopardy.

There were other sports besides porch-jumping. At the George Brooks Elementary School, where teachers remember him as being "well-liked and well-behaved," Wilt played dodge ball at recess. After school and on weekends, the sport was wall-ball, a type of handball played off the side of a house.

Wilt was taller than his boyhood friends, and his height earned him a nickname. He was always bumping his head in doorways or wherever there were low ceilings. One day when he was playing in an empty house, he struck his eye on a piece of pipe. The eye puffed up.

His friends kidded him about it. They told him he should learn to "dip under" whenever he came to a hazardous object. They started calling him "Dipper"—and the name stuck.

While Wilt was tall, he was not so tall that people stared. Not yet. Friends and neighbors thought he was probably going to sprout to about the same height as his brother Wilbert, who was 6-foot-6.

During his elementary school years, Wilt showed little interest in basketball. In fact, he considered it something of a sissy sport.

In the years when Wilt was growing up, black youngsters did not play basketball in the numbers they do today. The sport, at least in the professional ranks, was a white man's sport. Flip through the pages of the *Official NBA Guide* and glance at the photos of the championship teams through the years. Black faces don't begin appearing until the mid-1950s. It was during those years that the sport was touched by the great social changes that were taking place.

In Wilt's neighborhood, there was evidence of what was happening. A couple of neighborhood churches laid down basketball courts, and the Philadelphia Department of Recreation built Haddington Center at 57th Street and Haverford Avenue in West Philadelphia. Just a few minutes from Wilt's home, Haddington Center became a focal part of his life. It was there that he learned the fundamentals of basketball. He played on a team that represented Haddington Center in citywide competition. He also played on a church team and a YMCA team.

As he got older, Wilt's height became something of a problem for him. In school, he had to crouch down to get through his classroom doorway. To write on the blackboard, he had to bend his knees. Wilt's father raised the chandeliers and other light fixtures because Wilt kept hitting them with his head. Getting clothes that fit was another problem. He outgrew shirts and trousers almost by the time his mother got them home from the store.

Everywhere he went, people stared at him. Wilt was beginning to feel like a freak. But on the basketball court it was different. There he was accepted. Indeed, his height made him a hero. He was cheered for what his height enabled him to do. Little wonder that basketball became his greatest interest in life.

James "Blinky" Brown coached Wilt at Haddington Center. "At first he was a little too timid for the game," Brown once recalled. "And he took a lot of punishment because of it. If you chucked an elbow in his ribs, he wouldn't elbow you back. What he'd do would be to block your shot. That was his way of retaliating."

Wilt was one month past his sixteenth birthday when he entered Philadelphia's West Overbrook High School. He was a sixteen-year-old the likes of which few people had ever seen. He stood 6-foot-11. To speak to him, you had to tilt your head back, like looking up a tall building. Wilt's growth had slowed some, but he wondered if it was ever going to stop.

He had a big upper body with spindly arms and pipestem legs. A reporter for the *Philadelphia Bulletin* called him "Wilt the Stilt." Wilt didn't like that name. "It sounds like some kind of an ugly bird," he said. He preferred being called "Dipper" or even "Dip."

By the time he had reached high school, Wilt had lost his early awkwardness. He could move fast and with great dexterity.

His best shot was his jumper. Because of the height at which he delivered it, the ball traveled on almost a straight line. He usually banked it in off the backboard.

He had no problem dunking the ball. After all, when he stood flat-footed under the basket, he was able to reach up and come within an inch or two of the rim. In pregame warmups, Wilt liked to impress the opposition by going up with a ball in each hand, and then, while in midair, stuff first one ball and then the other.

Overbrook was virtually unbeatable with Wilt in the lineup. His coach usually kept him in the game for only the first half. Otherwise, the opposition would be humiliated by the score. Of course, in close games Wilt played every minute.

Wilt shattered every high school scoring record in his years at Overbrook. Once he scored 73 points in a game; twice he scored 90 points. Overbrook lost only three games in the three years Wilt played. His talents began earning him nationwide attention. *Sport* magazine profiled him in an article titled "The High School Kid Who Could Play Pro Ball Now."

But Wilt had decided he wanted to go to college before trying professional basketball. Which college? So many were hounding him he had difficulty making up his mind. In his last two years at high school, he could not answer the doorbell or pick up a telephone without being confronted by someone who represented one college or another. "They gave me no rest," Wilt said.

In the spring of 1955, Wilt decided he would attend the University of Kansas. There he became a popular student. He roomed with track star Charley Tidwell. A special 7-foot-6 bed was built for him.

He had apparently stopped growing,

finally topping out at 7-foot-1. However, he refused to allow himself to be measured.

Playing for the freshman team, Wilt made his basketball debut at Kansas in a game against the varsity team. More than 14,000 crammed their way into the University of Kansas fieldhouse to watch the contest. Wilt put on a splendid show, scoring 42 points as the freshman whipped the varsity. That had never happened before.

Wilt was so fearsome he forced rulemakers to change the game. He had devised an out-of-bounds play in which a teammate would lob the ball over the top of the backboard. Wilt would grab it and stuff it in. A rule was passed prohibiting anyone from throwing the ball in-bounds from directly underneath the basket.

In his first varsity game at Kansas, Wilt scored 52 points and gathered in 31 rebounds. His team romped to an easy victory over Northwestern. Kansas was instantly hailed as the nation's Number 1 basketball power.

As the season continued, Wilt led Kansas to one win after another, averaging about 30 points a game. He did this despite the fact there were always two or three enemy players guarding him.

In the NCAA tournament, Kansas faced North Carolina for the national championship. North Carolina's strategy was to keep Kansas from getting the ball to Wilt. And the strategy worked. At the end of regulation play, the score was tied, 46–46. Wilt had scored one half of his team's points. It took three overtime periods to settle matters finally, with North Carolina edging ahead, 54–53, in the final seconds.

The following season Kansas struggled to an 18–5 record. It was a disappointing year for Wilt. Teams would freeze the ball for long periods of time, preventing Kansas from getting possession. And when Kansas did get the ball, players would drop off to guard him, often battering him with elbows and knees.

No one was very much surprised when Wilt quit college at the end of his junior year. But he wasn't planning on becoming a pro player, at least not in the ordinary sense. He signed with the Harlem Globetrotters. He would spend a year as a basketball clown.

He explained the reasons for his decision in an article in *Look* magazine. "The game I was forced to play at K.U. wasn't basketball. It was hurting my chances of ever developing into a successful professional player.

"The barnstorming tour will also give me a chance to make some money. My father, 57, still has to work as a handyman for $60 a week. My mother, 56, still has to hire out as a domestic. I want to fix it up so they can stop working and enjoy life more."

In 1959, following his year with the Globetrotters, Wilt signed with the NBA's Philadelphia Warriors. (The present Philadelphia team, the 76ers, did not begin play until 1963.)

"He's great, that's all," said Red Auerbach, coach (and later president) of the Boston Celtics. "He'll take over this league. The first time he meets Russell, we could fill Yankee Stadium."

Auerbach was right. Boston Garden was jammed to the rafters the first time the two players opposed each other. Russell, in his fourth year as a pro, was already being hailed as the finest defensive player in the history of the game. Wilt was a couple of inches taller than Russell, stronger, and had a two-inch reach advantage. He had been averaging 39 points per game. It was the rookie star against the master of defense.

The duel was pretty much of a standoff. Russell finished with 22 points and 35 rebounds. Wilt, who took 19 more shots than Russell, had 30 points and 28 rebounds. Boston won, 115–106.

Russell won the game's opening tap and then blocked Wilt's first shot, a fallaway jumper. Never before—not in high school, nor in all those games at Haddington Center nor in college—had that ever happened before. It was a shocker.

"He's the best rookie I've ever seen," Russell said after the game. "The guy's no freak. By the end of the season, he could be the greatest player of all time. . . . There's no stopping him."

While there were nights that Wilt did seem unstoppable, with Wilt's team it was a different matter. The Warriors were stopped with some degree of frequency. The team finished a distant second to the Celtics in the Eastern Division standings, then lost to them in the playoffs, four games to two.

Wilt went on one scoring rampage after another during the 1961–62 season. He scored 50 or more points in 46 of his team's 80 games and finished the season with an incredible average of 50.4 points per game. In the years since, no player has come within hailing distance of that record. San Francisco's Rick Barry averaged 35.6 points per game during the 1966–67 season. Nobody has gotten any closer than that.

In Los Angeles on December 8, 1961, Wilt set a league record by scoring 78 points in a triple overtime game. That night, Frank McGuire, the coach of the Warriors, had warned, "Someday soon Chamberlain is going to score a hundred. He'll do it even if five men are guarding him."

When Wilt Chamberlain (number 13) joined the University of Kansas basketball team, its national ranking soared to first place. *Courtesy of the University of Kansas.*

On March 2, 1962, the Warriors traveled to Hershey, Pennsylvania, to meet the New York Knicks on a neutral court. Only a few games remained in the regular season. The Knicks were in last place and going nowhere. The Warriors had second place nailed down and were waiting for the playoffs.

When Wilt came out onto the court, he was warmly cheered by the crowd. A month or so before, Wilt had recorded a rock 'n' roll piece called "By the River." As he began his warmups, someone played the record on the public address system. Wilt enjoyed hearing it. As he loosened up, he was singing to himself and laughing.

Once the game began, Wilt began scoring at a frantic pace. He hit on every kind of shot he tried, including nine foul shots in a row.

The first quarter ended with Philadelphia ahead, 42–26. Wilt's contribution had been 7 of 14 shots from the field and the 9 free throws—23 points. Although it was early, a game-scoring record was on everyone's mind.

Wilt was being guarded by husky, 6-foot-10 Darrall Imhoff that night. But Imhoff couldn't cope with the big man. Wilt's favorite weapon was his lovely fallaway jumper. He also bulled his way past Imhoff to stuff rebounds with his awesome dunk, slipped in a few delicate underhand shots, and even raced down the floor with his teammates to either shoot or follow up off fast breaks.

Imhoff shook his head in frustration. "He was so strong," the Knick center was to say afterward, "that he was picking us up and stuffing us through the hoop with the ball. We collapsed three men around him and it didn't do any good. And I don't think I've ever seen him get down the floor so fast. I couldn't keep up with him."

The Knicks fought valiantly. Behind 16 points at the end of the first quarter, they battled back to close the gap some, drawing to within 11 points at halftime, 79–68. Wilt scored 18 more points (7 field goals, 4 free throws) during the second period. That gave him a total of 41 points.

In the Philadelphia dressing room at halftime, no one spoke of the record, but Wilt's teammates were well aware that if he continued to score as he had, the record was sure to fall. The crowd realized it, too, and when Wilt returned to the floor to begin the third quarter, his every move was cheered.

Wilt kept pouring in points. He hit 10 of 16 shots from the floor and 8 of 8 free throws during the third quarter, giving him 69 points for the game. Wilt was now just four points shy of his own record for a regulation game. Oh, yes, the Warriors led, 125–106.

Once the fourth quarter began, the Warriors attempted to get the ball to Wilt whenever possible. He curled in a soft underhand shot. He banked in a jumper. With slightly more than ten minutes remaining in the quarter, he slammed in a rebound. Now Wilt had 75 points, a record for a regulation game.

Hundreds of fans left their seats to ring the court. *"Give it to Wilt. Give it to Wilt,"* they chanted whenever the Warriors got possession.

Imhoff fouled out, making it even harder for the Knicks to shut Wilt down. With 7 minutes, 51 seconds remaining, Wilt took a pass from Guy Rodgers and eased in a one-hander from near the foul line for his 79th point. The crowd cheered and cheered. No one had ever scored more points in a professional game.

Wilt's point total spurted into the high 80s. But the crowd wanted more. Whenever any member of the Warriors besides Wilt attempted a shot, he was booed. A little more than 5 minutes remained. Al Attles passed up an easy basket to toss the ball to Wilt. The giant center sprang high above the hoop, then slammed the ball through. Now Wilt had 89 points.

The Knicks tried mobbing Wilt with three or four defenders and constantly fouled him. But this strategy didn't work either, because Wilt continued to hit from the foul line. Three free-throw shots and a long jumper boosted Wilt's total to 94 points. The fans at courtside and those remaining in the stands roared their approval after every point.

Rodgers dribbled the ball over the midcourt line, managed to elude a defender, then fired the ball to Wilt. He lost control of it momentarily, then got it in his grasp again, and fired another jump shot for his 96th point.

The Knicks tried to freeze the ball. But someone knocked it loose. Larese picked it up and dribbled into the forecourt. He spotted Chamberlain, who had stationed himself near the basket. Larese lofted a high pass to Wilt, who reached over the heads of a couple of Knicks to grab it. *Whoosh!* He slammed it through. The crowd raised the roof with its cheers. Wilt's Warrior teammates were standing and shouting. Wilt had 98 points with 1 minute 19 seconds to go.

When the Knicks tried to pass the ball in-bounds, Wilt darted up to intercept it. He turned and fired a one-hander. The ball hit the rim and bounced away. The crowd groaned.

New York got possession and brought the ball down court. A Knick shot missed. The Warriors got the rebound. Wilt took a pass from Ruklick, tossed up a one-hander that missed, then grabbed the rebound and missed again. The clock kept running. About one minute remained.

Luckenbill outfought the Knicks for

the ball and passed to Ruklick. As Chamberlain moved toward the basket, every eye followed him. Ruklick flipped a high pass above the rim. In one sweeping motion, Chamberlain rose up, got both hands on the ball and jammed it down through the hoop. He had scored his 100th point.

Although there were still 46 seconds to play, hundreds of fans swarmed onto the court. They mobbed Wilt, clapping him on the back and grabbing his hand to shake it. Even the Knick players came off the bench to congratulate him. It took several minutes before security guards could clear the floor.

When the final buzzer sounded, the Warriors were ahead, 169–147. Wilt had scored 31 points in the final quarter.

He finished with 36 field goals in 63 attempts. He hit an amazing 28 of his 32 free throws. He also contributed 25 rebounds.

In the dressing room Wilt was surrounded by grinning teammates. "Honestly," he kept repeating, "I never thought I could do it. Never in my life. It's really something. Like nothing that ever happened to me before. I sure feel different. Triple figures. Wow!"

What Chamberlain accomplished that night in Hershey ranks as one of the outstanding achievements in the history of American professional sports. No one has ever hit five home runs in

a baseball game or scored six touchdowns in football. Should either of these ever be achieved, it would compare to Wilt's 100-point outburst.

"Chamberlain is the greatest basketball player alive, no doubt about that," Bill Russell said in the early 1960s. "He has set the standards so high, his point totals are so enormous that they've lost their impact."

Russell spoke of the competition between himself and Wilt. "There can never really be a rivalry, when in my best year I averaged 18 points and in one of his worst years he averaged 37," he said. "The highest total I've ever had for a single game is 37, and when Wilt is 'held' to 37 they say he's had a bad night."

While Wilt was frequently the scoring champion, the Boston Celtics usually wound up with the league title. Beginning with the 1958–59 season, Boston captured eight straight NBA championships, and nine in ten years. Wilt had some difficult seasons. Sometimes moody and unapproachable, he created friction with his teammates and coaches. The Warrior franchise was switched from Philadelphia to San Francisco just before the 1962–63 season. Then, partway through during the season that followed, Wilt was traded back to Philadelphia, to the 76ers.

Some observers say that Wilt played

Wilt Chamberlain, playing for the Los Angeles Lakers, invariably dominated every game. *Courtesy of Naismith Memorial Basketball Hall of Fame.*

the best basketball of his career during the season of 1966–67. He passed off more. He worked harder than ever to block shots. He played aggressively at both ends of the court.

The 76ers won the Eastern Division over Boston by eight games, then crushed Boston in the playoffs, four games to one. In the last game of the playoff series, Wilt beat Russell in points, 29–4, in assists, 13–7, and in rebounds, 36–21. The 76ers demolished the Celtics, 140–116. They then went on to beat San Francisco, four games to two, for the title. Wilt was a winner at last.

A year later Wilt was traded to the Los Angeles Lakers. There, in 1971–72, he teamed with Jerry West and Elgin Baylor to win a second NBA championship. The following season, Wilt's last in the NBA, the Lakers lost to the Knicks in the playoff finals.

At the time of his retirement, Wilt reigned as the greatest offensive player in the history of the game. In 1984, Kareem Abdul-Jabbar surpassed Wilt's career total of 31,410 points. Wilt was asked how he felt on seeing the record broken. He shrugged, pointing out that it was only one of ninety or so records he still held, some of which meant more to him than total points.

Additional Reading

Chamberlain, Wilt. *Wilt*. New York: Macmillan & Co., 1973.

Ty Cobb

Baseball's Fierce Immortal
1886–1961

Ty Cobb was perhaps baseball's greatest all-around player. Even though he played his last year of major league baseball before most people alive today were born, he is still remembered for his fire and genius at the plate and on the basepaths.

Cobb dominated the American League for more than a decade—from 1907, his rookie season with the Detroit Tigers, until after World War I. Then along came Babe Ruth, who hit all those home runs. The emphasis in baseball shifted from base hits and base-running to the long ball. Even so, Cobb continued as one of the game's top-flight players for another decade, until 1928.

Cobb won the American League batting title in his first full year in the American League and kept on winning it for the next eight seasons. He finished second once, and then won it three more times in a row.

His lifetime batting average for twenty-four seasons was .367. He hit over .400 three times. His record of 4,191 career hits lasted for more than half a century, eventually falling to Pete Rose in 1985.

Cobb's 892 stolen bases remained a record until fairly recent times. Of those 892 steals, 35 were swipes of home. That's a record that has endured to this day.

Cobb led the American League in RBIs (runs batted in) four times, in runs scored five times and in slugging average eight times. He even led the major leagues in home runs one year.

Cobb's greatest year was 1911, when

he batted .420 on 248 hits, including 47 doubles and 24 triples. He scored 147 runs, had 144 RBIs, and 82 stolen bases.

Baseball strategy at the time Ty Cobb entered the game was much different than it is today. Pitchers dominated. Home runs were rare. (In 1909, when Cobb led the American League in home runs, he had only nine of them.) The idea was to get a base hit, steal, or get sent to second by a bunt or a hit-and-run play.

The batter stood close to the plate, choked up several inches on a heavy, thick-handled bat, and tried to slap the ball between infielders or maybe poke it over their heads. Wee Willie Keeler, the game's best hitter at the turn of the century, once revealed the secret of his success. Said Keeler: "I hit 'em where they ain't." That's what every batter tried to do.

Cobb took his position at the plate in a slight crouch, his feet ten or twelve inches apart, his knees slightly bent. He gripped the bat with his hands two or three inches apart, holding it well away from his body. He slashed line drives, punched the ball through the infield, bunted, or sought to work the pitcher for a base on balls.

Besides being skilled at the plate, a good ballplayer of the early 1900s had to be able to steal a base when called upon to do so or take an extra base on a hit to the outfield. Stolen bases occurred more frequently than they do today. It wasn't that runners were faster. Catchers of that time took their positions a foot or two farther back of the plate than they do nowadays. That meant they had to throw a longer distance, particularly to second base.

Cobb was a terror on the basepaths. He would go from first to third on a bunt, or from second to home on an infield out. He wouldn't do it every time, but he did it enough to give opposing infielders the jitters. There was no runner like Cobb until Jackie Robinson made his debut with the Brooklyn Dodgers in 1946.

Cobb seemed to enjoy getting hung up between bases. He felt that his quickness and ability to react in the blink of an eye would force his rivals into making mistakes.

Despite his deserved reputation as a daredevil, Cobb did not slide head first. Early in his career, he had gone into second head first, and the catcher's throw beat him. As the second baseman tagged Cobb out, he pressed his knee down onto the back of Cobb's neck, grinding his face into the dirt. His teammates kidded Cobb about the slide, saying it was "bush." Cobb seldom went into a base head first after that.

Cobb developed a style of driving

for the base and staying on his feet until the last moment. He'd then drop into a sudden slide, slashing to either the left or right. He'd hook the base with a toe or grab it with one hand as he went sailing by.

"Infielders didn't know what the hell he'd do next, and neither did he until the last split second," Rube Bressler, a rival of Cobb's for many years, told Lawrence Ritter for his book *The Glory of Their Times.* "You couldn't figure Cobb. It was impossible."

In the decades following Cobb's death in 1961, baseball went through another period of important change. The barriers against blacks were removed, and scores of players with great speed, quickness, and agility entered the major leagues. They triggered a new era in base-stealing.

One by one, Cobb's stealing records began to fall. In 1962, the year following Cobb's death, Maury Wills surpassed Cobb's single-season base-stealing mark, ending with 104 steals for the season. Five times in his career, Wills stole at least 50 bases.

In 1974, Lou Brock eclipsed Wills' record, stealing 118 bases. Brock later wiped out Cobb's record for career steals, accumulating 938 of them by the time he retired in 1979.

Three years later, Rickey Henderson reached 130 steals in a season. It seemed possible that Henderson, under the right circumstances, could average a steal a game.

During the early 1980s, Pete Rose mounted an assault on Cobb's record for career base hits. Rose, who played for and managed the Cincinnati Reds in 1985, was often said to play baseball the way Cobb had. Both were durable, hard-driving players. But there were few other similarities. Cobb was a better hitter than Rose, and a much faster and more daring base runner. Rose had little power at the plate and was notably slow-footed. In his later years, Rose was no better than average as a fielder.

Cobb, at the time of his retirement, held forty-three records for batting, base stealing, and longevity. But the record book scarcely tells the story of Ty Cobb. He was always a fierce competitor. He had "that terrific fire, that unbelievable drive," said Rube Bressler. "I never saw anybody like him. It was *his* base. It was *his* game. *Everything* was his."

Tyrus Cobb was born on December 10, 1886, in The Narrows, the name given to several farms at the northern edge of Banks County, Georgia. His father was a schoolteacher. Another son was born to the Cobbs in 1888, and, in 1892, a daughter.

When Tyrus Cobb was still very

Ty Cobb was famous for his distinctive, sudden slides into base. *Courtesy of the National Baseball Library, Cooperstown, N.Y.*

young, the family moved to Royston, Georgia, a farm community of less than six hundred people. Mr. Cobb not only taught school there, but farmed, ran a weekly newspaper, and eventually became Royston's mayor.

Tyrus was stubborn and quick-tempered as a boy. He once beat up a schoolmate for misspelling a word in a spelling bee, a lapse that had allowed the girls' team to beat the boys' team.

One of his classmates once recalled that there was something very different about young Tyrus. "He just seemed to think quicker and run faster," the classmate said. "He was always driving and pushing, even in grade school."

His father had high hopes for Tyrus. It was planned that he would go to college. His father thought that Tyrus might become a lawyer or a doctor.

But Tyrus was not always serious

about his studies. Things outside of school distracted him.

Baseball was one of the distractions. Like many American communities during the early part of the century, Royston had its own baseball team. The Royston Reds, as they were called, played teams representing nearby towns every Saturday afternoon all summer long. Players weren't paid; they played for the fun of it.

There was also a team for young boys in Royston that was known as the Rompers. Tyrus played for the Rompers until he was fourteen.

One Saturday, when the Reds suddenly found themselves without a shortstop for a game, they called upon Tyrus to fill in. He played well in the field and cracked three hits. He was soon playing with the Reds on a full-time basis.

One afternoon that summer, Tyrus, playing center field, made a diving catch of a fly ball to snuff out a rally and save the game for the Reds. So thrilled were the fans, they showered the field with coins. Tyrus picked up between ten and eleven dollars. It was the first money he ever received for playing baseball.

The game became the most important thing in young Tyrus's life. During the summer vacation, he played whenever he could, that is, when he was not made to do household chores or work in the fields on the family farm. By the time he was sixteen, Tyrus stood 5-foot-10 and weighed about 150 pounds. He became a star for the Royston team, playing either the infield or outfield, drilling line drives, and running the bases recklessly but with success.

When he was seventeen, Tyrus, without telling his father, wrote letters to teams in the South Atlantic League asking for tryouts. The Augusta [Georgia] Tourists answered, inviting Tyrus to spring training, as long as he agreed to pay his own expenses. The club said he would be paid $50 a month if he made the team. Tyrus dreaded telling his father that he planned to turn his back on college to seek a career as a baseball professional, but he somehow managed to get his father to agree to let him give baseball a try. "Get it out of your system," his father said.

Tyrus was in the starting lineup in center field for the Augusta Tourists on opening day, but only because the regular center fielder was not available. When the missing player returned, Tyrus was dropped from the team.

Stunned and hurt, Tyrus didn't know which way to turn. Then he learned that a semipro team in Anniston, Alabama, needed an outfielder. Ty Cobb went to Anniston and won a place on the team.

Before the season ended in Anniston,

Tyrus received a telegram from the Augusta Tourists asking him to rejoin the team, and he did. He also played for Augusta the next year, 1905.

Within a short time, Ty, the nickname given him by his teammates, was one of the outstanding players in the South Atlantic League. Scouts from major league teams began turning up at Augusta games regularly to watch him. Ty heard a rumor that the Detroit Tigers were interested in signing him. He was told it was only a matter of days. Ty could hardly contain his excitement.

At that point, one of the most tragic events in Ty's life occurred. On August 9, 1905, he received a telegram from Royston telling him that his father had been killed in a shooting accident. And then, on returning home, he learned that his mother, having mistaken her husband as an intruder, had done the shooting.

The accident scarred young Ty for life. "I made the major leagues the same month my father was killed," he was to say in later years. "He never got to see me play. But I knew he was watching me. I had to play superbly for him. I overcame every obstacle for him."

Just three days after he returned to the Augusta team, Ty was told he had been sold to the Tigers. He was to report to the team by the end of the month.

Cobb did not become a star right away. As a hitter, he was no better than average. Left-handed pitchers were a big problem for him. His play in the outfield was uneven. One day he'd make a sensational catch, but the next he'd drop a ball. On the bases, he was wild and unpredictable.

Yet he showed flashes of his enormous talent. The *Sporting News* described him as being "a bit too fast for the good of his team. He is not content to catch flys that go to his territory, but he wants to get those that go to left and right as well."

Cobb's greatest difficulties in his early years were not with rival players but with his teammates. He had trouble fitting in. In those days, rookie players were often the victims of ridicule and humiliating tricks. They might find their shoes nailed to the clubhouse floor. Their favorite bats would be sawed in half. On the bench, the veteran players would ignore the rookies.

Most rookie players merely shrugged and ignored their plight. Soon the hazing ended. But Cobb could ignore no slight. He fought back, storming, cursing his tormentors. He had a fight with pitcher Ed Siever, whom he knocked down and kicked. He had two fights with the team's catcher, Charlie Schmidt, who broke Cobb's nose in one of them. He feuded with Marty McIntyre, the team's left fielder. Things got so bad that the manager found that he could not play them side-by-side in the outfield. McIntyre had to be shifted from center field to right field, as far away as possible from Cobb in left.

Little by little, tempers cooled. But Cobb never got over being distrustful of many of his teammates.

Despite these problems, Ty improved steadily as a player. He figured out how to hit left-handers by adjusting his stance from the middle to the back of the batter's box. This gave him an added fraction of an inch to gauge the left-handed curve as it broke. Then, by closing his stance and shortening his swing, he found he could slice the ball into left field.

Playing the outfield, he realized that he had to charge ground balls instead of waiting for them to reach him. He studied rival batters by the hour and learned how to play each one. He was constantly shifting his position in the outfield, drifting in, backing up. When the ball fell, Cobb was often standing right under it. He thereby made almost every fly ball look easy.

On the basepaths, he learned to watch the infielder's eyes as the man prepared to take the throw from the outfield. Then Cobb would try to twist his own body accordingly, often getting in the path of the thrown ball and blocking it with his back or shoulders.

In 1905, the year that Cobb joined the Tigers, he played in 41 games and batted .240. But the next year he boosted his average to .320. And in 1907, he hit .350 and led the league, the first of his nine consecutive batting championships.

For three straight years beginning in 1907, the Tigers won the American League pennant. But they never could win a World Series.

The 1909 Detroit team was the last pennant winner on which Cobb played. Over the next nineteen years, his teams came close to the league title only once. Yet in those years Cobb would outperform every other player at bat and on the basepaths. He never stopped being a hothead, however, squabbling and battling from the moment he stepped out onto the field.

Cobb was easy to recognize, even from the most distant seats. He always turned up the collar of his jumper and rolled down his sleeves to cover his wrists. Sometimes he only had to step out of the dugout to start the stands buzzing.

Not only did Cobb fight with rival players and occasionally with teammates, he also had several highly publicized brawls off the field. One of the most noted occurred in 1921, when Cobb went into the stands in New York to attack a fan who had been abusive

Neither the opposing infielders nor the fans could guess what Ty Cobb might do. His speed, daring, and quick reflexes dazzled everyone. *Courtesy of the National Baseball Library, Coopers-town, N.Y.*

toward him. He punched and kicked the man and had to be dragged away. Cobb was handed a suspension, which triggered a one-day strike by his Tiger teammates. Cobb also had disputes with waitresses, cashiers, clubhouse attendants, and police officers.

In 1921, at the age of thirty-four, Cobb, while continuing to play, began managing the Tigers. He continued in the role for six seasons, moving the team from seventh place to second, before it fell back again. After he was dismissed as manager and released by the Tigers, he played his last two seasons with the Philadelphia Athletics.

Cobb broke the record for hits on September 20, 1923, exceeding the previous mark of 3,430, held by Honus Wagner. It is interesting to compare the way in which the fans and press responded as Pete Rose closed in on Cobb's record, and the way they reacted when Cobb eclipsed Wagner.

In September 1985, the final stages of Rose's quest were covered by approximately three hundred photographers and newspaper and television reporters. There were so many journalists following Pete around that it was impossible for him to grant individual interviews. Instead, he held press conferences before and after games. When he eventually broke the record, it was front-page news in newspapers from coast to coast.

By contrast, when Cobb broke Wagner's record, statistics were not worshiped as they are now, and hardly anyone noticed. The Tigers played the Red Sox in Boston that day. The *Boston Globe* reported that Cobb had delivered four "safe hits," but failed to point out that one of them lifted him past Wagner.

Of the several papers that covered the game in depth, only the *Detroit Times* made mention of what Cobb had achieved, noting that on the all-time hit record he was now two ahead of Wagner. "Doubtless," said the *Times*, "Ty will make many more hits before he quits the game, and in all probability will quit with a record that may never be equaled."

Even after Pete Rose had topped Cobb's record for base hits, scarcely anybody believed that Rose was a better hitter than Cobb. Rose required approximately 2,300 more at bats than Cobb to break the record. Rose played in about 400 more games.

"There is no doubt that he [Cobb] was the best hitter who ever lived," Rose himself said. "Look at his lifetime average of .367. And he led the league in hitting for nine straight years, missed it once, and then led it again for three more years."

In retirement, Cobb seldom had a good word to say about baseball. He hated fence-swingers. Brute power ruined the game, he said. He was convinced the game's most glorious years paralleled his own career.

Cobb proved to be just as shrewd as a businessman as he was in analyzing rival pitchers. He became a millionaire several times over through investments in such companies as General Motors and Coca-Cola.

Old age did not put a damper on Cobb's fiery nature. Even in his seventies, he was seldom at peace. He was married twice and divorced twice. His five children had little to do with him.

Yet he sometimes showed another side. He established the Cobb Educational Foundation to provide money for Georgia youngsters who could not afford to go to college. He built a hospital in Royston, Georgia, in honor of his mother and father. He sometimes sent money to needy old-time ballplayers or their widows.

In his last days, dying of cancer, he often drank too much. He lived in a fifteen-room mansion in Atherton, California, but he had no lights, heat, or hot water because of a squabble over a $16 electric bill.

Death came to Ty Cobb on July 17, 1961. "He was one of the greatest players who ever lived," said Davy Jones, a former teammate. "And yet he had so few friends. I always felt sorry for him."

Additional Reading

Alexander, Charles. *Ty Cobb*. New York: Oxford University Press, 1984.

McCallum, John D. *Ty Cobb*. New York: Praeger Publishers, 1975.

Nadia Comaneci

Young and Perfect
1961–

During the early weeks of July in 1976, the world's best gymnasts began gathering in Montreal, Canada, for the Olympic Games. The strongest women's teams were from the Soviet Union and other Eastern European countries—East Germany, Romania, Hungary, and Czechoslovakia.

The Russian women, Olympic champions every year since 1952, were favored to win again. Their deeply talented team included tiny Olga Korbut, who had won two gold medals at the Olympic Games in 1972. With her yarn-tied pigtails, pixie smile, and friendly hand waves, Olga had charmed audiences throughout the world. She was the first to demonstrate that gymnastics could be fun. Because of Olga, many thousands of American girls had taken up gymnastics.

Yet Olga was not looked upon as the best of the Soviet gymnasts. Her teammate, Ludmilla Turishcheva, was. A veteran performer of twenty-four, Turishcheva was making her third appearance in the Olympics. She had won the all-around title at the 1972 Games.

Nelli Kim was another of the Soviet stars. Like Ludmilla Turishcheva and Olga Korbut, Nelli Kim was expected to pick up a gold medal or two at Montreal.

Gymnasts for the United States, Holland, West Germany, Italy, and Japan were also arriving in Montreal. The American team was led by strong and determined Kathy Howard of Oklahoma City, Oklahoma. Kathy, eighteen years old, was the American national champion.

But when the competition was over,

there was only one star, a fourteen-year-old mechanic's daughter from Onesti, a factory town in the mountains of Romania. Her name was Nadia Comaneci (pronounced NAD-ya CO-ma-neech).

Lean and trim, Nadia weighed 86 pounds and stood less than five feet. She had straight dark eyebrows and soulful eyes. She wore her brown hair in a ponytail and bangs.

Nadia had strength and stamina, agility and courage. She made gymnastics look like child's play. She became queen of the sport and, thanks to television, a worldwide celebrity. And she did it without saying any more than twenty words or so. She did it with her daring exploits alone.

The young girl who was to become the world's best gymnast was born on November 12, 1961, in Onesti, a town of about 40,000 some sixty miles west of the Russian border. Romania has a Communist government, and in 1956 the town was renamed Gheorge Gheorghiu-Dej after an official of the Romanian Communist party. But the local residents still call it Onesti.

Nadia was six years old when she first met Bela Karolyi, a big bear of a man who was to become coach of Romania's Olympic gymnastics team. The meeting changed Nadia's life.

Karolyi and his wife, Marta, often scouted kindergartens searching for young girls who might be talented enough to become members of Romania's national gymnastics team. One day the Karolyis visited Nadia's school. It was recess time, and the children were playing.

Two girls were running and jumping about, pretending to be gymnasts. Suddenly the bell rang, and the girls ran back into the school before Karolyi or his wife could speak to them. Karolyi made up his mind he would never leave the school until he found the two girls. He went from classroom to classroom. In each he would ask the question, "Who likes gymnastics?"

A few girls would raise their hands in each room. But in one, two girls sprang to their feet and shouted, "We do! We do!" One of the girls was Nadia.

Shortly after, Karolyi visited Nadia's parents and asked them whether they would allow her to undergo training in gymnastics. She would join other young girls who were already being schooled by the Karolyis.

Sports and physical education are an important part of life in Romania, East Germany, and other nations of Eastern Europe. The best athletes are trained in special schools. They and their families lead lives of privilege. Mr. and Mrs. Comaneci were happy to give their permission.

Before she was accepted by the Karolyis, Nadia first had to pass a test. It was divided into three parts. Nadia had to sprint 15 meters (about 50 feet), jump as far as she could, and then walk back and forth on a balance beam.

The beam is a piece of gymnastics apparatus that is 16 feet long, only 4 inches wide and 4 feet above the floor. It is something like a tightrope without a net. Gymnasts use the beam to perform steps, turns, leaps, and other acrobatic moves.

If a girl happened to be timid on the beam and was afraid of falling off, Karolyi would not take her as a pupil. But Nadia treated the beam as if it were her private stage, moving with poise and confidence. "She knew no fear," said Karolyi.

Karolyi found Nadia to be the ideal pupil. She had a delicate figure, with small hips and long legs. But her physique wasn't as important as her enthusiasm, her fire.

She was usually the first to arrive at the gym for daily workouts and the first to begin warming up. She would do the same exercise over and over without getting bored or showing signs of tiredness. "It is important for a child to love gymnastics as Nadia does," Karolyi said.

Karolyi also found Nadia to be very serious and emotionally stable. "I don't remember ever seeing her cry," he said.

The uneven parallel bars were Nadia's favorite piece of equipment. They are called "uneven" because they are placed at different levels. (The lower bar is, at the most, 4 feet, 11 inches from the floor; the upper bar is 7½ feet from the floor.) With her hands gripping the bars, the gymnast performs swinging, spinning, and vaulting movements in a carefully developed routine.

"I can put in many more moves," Nadia once said of the bars. "They're more challenging."

While the bars were Nadia's favorite piece of equipment, Karolyi came to realize that she performed her best on the beam and the vault. Vaulting begins with a headlong sprint down a 75-foot strip of mat toward a stationary leather horse (a padded piece of equipment about 5 feet long and a foot wide that stands 3½ feet above the floor).

Just before she reaches the horse, the gymnast pounds down on a small springboard that shoots her into the air. She lands with both hands on the horse, then thrusts herself into the air to perform twists, turns, and somersaults. Nadia was to become a powerful performer on the horse, startling observers with her maneuvers.

Besides the training she was receiving in gymnastics, Nadia was schooled in ballet. This helped her to become more graceful and precise in the way she moved. These qualities are important on the beam and also in floor exercise.

In floor exercise, performed on a thick mat that measures 40 feet on each side, the gymnast has one and a half minutes to perform a routine consisting of three tumbling moves connected by leaps, turns, pirouettes, and other dance movements. Floor exercise is the only gymnastics event performed to music.

As soon as Nadia had developed a "feel" for each piece of equipment, Karolyi began to enter her in local gymnastic meets. As each gymnast performed on each piece of apparatus, judges watched carefully. Each performance was graded in hundredths on a scale from one to ten. Typical scores were 8.75, 9.35, or 9.65. A score of 9.85 or 9.90 was considered excellent.

In 1969, when Nadia was eight, Karolyi entered her in the Romanian National Junior Gymnastics Championships. She was the youngest of all the competitors. She finished in thirteenth place. It was not a bad showing for so young a girl, but Karolyi did not tell Nadia that. He gave her a little sealskin doll that he had bought on a trip to Canada. "This is for you," he said, "to remind you never to finish thirteenth again."

The next year Nadia carried the doll to the National Junior Championships—and won. After that, whenever she was going to compete, she never failed to take the doll with her for good luck.

In 1971, Nadia became a member of Romania's national gymnastics team. It was a proud moment for her when she put on the white uniform with its narrow red, yellow, and blue sleeve stripes for the first time.

Nadia's best friend, Teodora Ungureanu, was also a member of the team. She was smaller than Nadia but very quick and strong. Teodora was to become one of the world's best gymnasts.

That year, Nadia won the Romania all-around gymnastics title for her age group. She repeated her victory the following year.

Also in 1971, Nadia went to Bulgaria for the Friendship Cup Meet, the annual competition among gymnasts representing Communist countries of Europe and Asia. There she emerged as a champion again, winning gold medals for her performances on the bars and beam.

In 1972, on her eleventh birthday, she captured the National Junior Championships a third time. In the Friendship Cup competition the following year, she defeated some of the best gymnasts in the world in winning three gold medals.

By this time, Nadia's life followed a strict routine. She and her schoolmates attended classes every day except Sunday from eight o'clock until noon. After class, Nadia had lunch and then a nap. Her nap was followed by three or four hours of strenuous gymnastics training. In the evening, Nadia did her homework.

Doll collecting was Nadia's favorite hobby. Whenever she traveled to a foreign country to compete, she purchased a doll as a souvenir. By the time she was fourteen, there were more than two hundred dolls stacked on shelves in her bedroom.

Whenever an important gymnastics meet was scheduled, Nadia and her teammates received special training at a government-operated camp in the Romanian capital of Bucharest. The girls remained at the camp for several weeks. There, gymnastics drills began each morning at eight o'clock. After lunch and a nap, Nadia and her teammates returned to the gym for more workouts.

Not only were the finest gymnastics instructors in the country there, the camp also offered a choreographer who helped Nadia create ballet movements for her floor exercise routine. A music master gave her advice on what music to choose. If she injured herself, she could see a doctor who was a specialist in sports medicine. She also had a masseur to massage her tired muscles.

While the girls' diets were carefully controlled, they were allowed tiny snacks of chocolate twice a day. Nadia and her teammates slept in a big dormitory. Everyone was awakened at seven-thirty A.M. It was lights out at ten-thirty P.M.

In January 1975, Nadia became eligible to compete as a senior. Four months later, in her first such competition, the European Championships at Skien, Norway, Nadia won gold medals in the vault, bars, beam, and in all-around competition. She took the silver medal in floor exercise.

She presented many new and daring exercises in her performances. On the beam, for example, she performed a back aerial somersault. Most gymnasts have difficulty executing a *front* aerial somersault on the beam. "She's unbelievable," said one judge. "She's doing things I never thought possible," said another.

Nadia and her teammates competed in the United States and Canada for the first time during March 1976. They participated in pre-Olympic meets in Tucson, Arizona; Albuquerque, New Mexico; San Francisco, California; Denver, Colorado; and Toronto, Ontario.

Late in the month, Nadia appeared at New York City's Madison Square Garden for the American Cup competition. Here she would face the best American gymnasts.

For the vault, Karolyi suggested that Nadia perform the difficult Tsukahara vault. This involved taking off in a layout position—that is, with her body stretched out straight. After snapping off the horse, she would execute a full twist before going into a back somersault and landing. No woman had ever performed the Tsukahara vault in competition before.

Nadia performed the vault with magical ease, finishing with her feet firmly planted, her arms upraised. The huge crowd cheered loudly.

Every pair of eyes turned to the scoreboard to see how many points Nadia had earned. There was a brief pause and then the number 10 flashed on the board. The crowd screamed. A 10 meant that Nadia had executed the vault perfectly. Hers was the first perfect 10 ever scored in gymnastics competition in the United States.

It happened that the famous Japanese gymnast Mitsuo Tsukahara was also competing in the meet. It was he who had developed and given his name to the vault that Nadia had performed. When Tsukahara himself performed the vault, he earned a score of 9.30.

Nadia thrilled the crowd with another 10, this time with her floor exercise routine. Her perfect score helped Nadia win the American Cup championship. When she was presented with a big trophy, she accepted it wearing a serious expression. "Smile! Smile!" the photographers shouted. Nadia did smile, but only for an instant.

Reporters crowded about her. One of them asked Nadia how many gold medals she expected to win at the Olympic Games at Montreal, which were to be held in just a few months.

"Five," she said firmly.

The reporter grinned. Five was the total number of events that Nadia would be permitted to enter in Montreal.

When Nadia returned to Romania, she began training for the Olympics. It was hard work. Karolyi added new flips and twists to her bars routine and put new and difficult aerials into her beam performance. He urged her to go higher on her vaults and added a double back twisting somersault to her floor exercise routine.

When Nadia arrived in Montreal for the Games, what impressed her the most was the huge number of Canadian soldiers and police who had been assigned to the Olympic Village, where the athletes lived. During the previous Olympics, held in Munich, Germany, in 1972, Arab terrorists had invaded the dormitory where members of the Israeli team stayed and killed two of them. Canadian authorities were determined that nothing like that would happen in Montreal.

Nadia Comaneci's extraordinary performance on the uneven parallel bars at the 1976 Olympics earned an unprecedented perfect score. *Courtesy of AP/Wide World Photos.*

At the stirring ceremonies opening the Games, the athletes of ninety-four nations marched proudly into the enormous stadium filled to capacity with more than 70,000 spectators. Eighty doves, each meant to symbolize one year since the beginning of the modern Olympics, were released. They circled the stadium and soared high into the afternoon sky.

Gymnastics competition was held in the Montreal Forum, the home of the city's professional hockey team, the Montreal Canadiens. Day after day, sellout crowds filled the arena. Millions upon millions watched on television.

Competition on the uneven parallel bars was scheduled first. Nadia was very serious-minded as she prepared herself. She did stretching exercises to keep her muscles loose and blew on her hands to dry them. She never once looked at her rivals.

Olga Korbut went first. She whipped and whirled about, earning a score of 9.90. It seemed unbeatable.

Nadia was next. She chalked the bars and then her hands so there would be no friction. Then she stood motionless and faced the bars, staring straight ahead.

Suddenly Nadia exploded toward the low bar, whipped to the high bar, and then began dazzling the crowd with handstands, fast hip circles, and grasps and regrasps. She ended with a breathtaking twisting midair somersault, landing on her feet, her hands reaching for the rafters.

The audience sat in stunned silence for a moment, then stood and cheered. Then came the announcement that Nadia had earned a perfect 10 with her performance. It was the first perfect score in the history of the Olympics. Another burst of cheers and applause poured from the stands.

Beam competition took place the next day. When it was Nadia's turn, she leaped to the beam, posed for a split second with one leg in an L position, then dropped back into a handstand. A flurry of skipping steps was followed by a series of back flips, an aerial somersault, cartwheels, a split leap, and another handstand.

Her performance hushed the crowd. Jim McKay, the American television broadcaster, watched in disbelief. He described Nadia as "swimming in an ocean of air."

Nadia ended the routine with a double twisting somersault that brought her to a standing position on the mat. The huge crowd went wild. "She's so good," said one spectator, "you get a chill." Nadia was awarded another 10.

In floor exercise the next day, Nadia performed her routine as the piano played, "Yes Sir, That's My Baby," an American jazz tune of the 1920s. As she neared the end of her routine, she smiled and brushed a hand across her lips, as if she were throwing a kiss to the audience.

Never did any performer dominate the Olympics as Nadia did. She scored seven 10s in all, four of them on the uneven parallel bars. She won a gold medal for her beam performance, a gold for the bars, and a gold for all-around. She led Romania to a silver medal in the team competition behind the Russians. She captured a bronze medal in floor exercise and just missed another bronze with a fourth-place finish in the vault.

When Nadia mounted the winner's platform to accept her gold medal for the all-around, she was her usual serious self. But when her name was announced and thunderous cheers came from the stands, she thrust her hands over her head and grinned. Then Nelli Kim, who finished second in the all-around, shook her hand. And Ludmilla Turishcheva, who had placed third, drew Nadia close and kissed her lightly on the cheek.

In a press conference held in Montreal, Nadia told reporters that her victories came as no surprise to her. "I was sure I would win," she declared. "I knew that if I worked hard I would win."

A few days later, when Nadia arrived back home, thousands of happy, smiling Romanians stormed the gates of the Otopeni Airport in Bucharest to welcome her, carrying flowers, small Romanian flags, and posters that bore her picture. Nadia appeared sad. When asked why, she explained she was a little upset because one of her dolls lost its head on the plane.

Late in 1976, at an official welcome held at the Palace of Sports and Culture in Bucharest, Nadia received a gold medal making her a Hero of Socialist Labor. It was the highest honor the country could confer. Nadia was the youngest woman ever to receive the honor.

Nadia continued to compete in the years that followed, but she didn't always win. There were reports from Ro-

mania that she was in a slump and was overweight. In October 1978, she lost the world title to Russia's Elena Mukhina.

But early in 1979, Nadia captured the European championship and in June that year took the World Cup in Tokyo.

Nadia occupied the world stage again in 1980 at the Olympic Games in Moscow. American athletes did not participate in the games that year. Soviet troops had invaded Afghanistan late in 1979, and President Jimmy Carter ordered an American boycott of the 1980 Olympics to protest the Soviet invasion. More than fifty other nations joined the United States in refusing to participate at Moscow.

Despite the boycott, Nadia faced a strong field of competitors in Moscow. This was a different Nadia. She now stood 5-foot-3. She weighed 99 pounds. She had filled out and shaped and shortened her brown hair. She wore red lipstick, mascara, and competed with a gold chain about her neck.

Again she performed with brilliance, winning a gold medal for her beam performance and sharing a gold with the Soviet Union's Nelli Kim in floor exercise. Nadia also captured two silver medals. A rare fall during her routine on the bars kept Nadia from successfully defending her all-around title.

While she was one of the outstanding athletes at the 1980 Games, she was not the princess of the games as she had been four years earlier at Montreal. Yet no one doubted that in the world of gymnastics she was still the reigning queen.

In 1981, the Nadia Comaneci story took an odd twist. Bela Karolyi, Nadia's coach, and his wife traveled to New York with the Romanian team for the American Cup competition. During the trip, the Karolyis came to a decision: They would not return to Romania. They would defect and adopt the United States as their country.

The Karolyis settled in Houston, Texas. There they ran a gymnastics school for young girls.

Their most promising student was sixteen-year-old Mary Lou Retton of Fairmont, West Virginia. At the 1984 Olympic Games in Los Angeles, the dynamic Mary Lou Retton stole the show. When she won a gold medal in the all-around competition, it marked the first time an American woman had ever won an individual medal of any kind in Olympic gymnastics competition.

Nadia was in Los Angeles for the Games, not as a competitor but as a coach of the Romanian team. She lived in the Olympic Village with the athletes and was introduced each night to receive an ovation from the crowd.

In her role as a coach, Nadia couldn't help but be pleased by the showing of the Romanian women. They won gold medals in floor exercise, the beam, and vault. They also captured the team gold medal. The United States team took the silver medal. (The Soviet Union, proclaiming that the safety of their athletes would be jeopardized by a lack of security in Los Angeles, boycotted the Games. To many observers it seemed that the Soviets were simply retaliating for President Carter's boycott of the Moscow Olympics four years earlier.)

When the Romanian team returned home, Nadia continued to serve as a coach. Just as her past has been dedicated to gymnastics, so too will her future. Not only does she plan to stay with the national team as a coach, she wants to be a recruiter. "Visiting the kindergartens to find suitable little girls, the way Karolyi found me, that's what I like," she says.

Additional Reading

Grumeza, Ion. *Nadia*. New York: K. S. Giniger Co., 1977.

Babe Didrikson

World's Greatest Female Athlete
1914–1956

Martina Navratilova. Chris Evert. Mary Decker Slaney. Nancy Lopez. During the 1980s, many female athletes were household names.

It wasn't always so.

Before the general prosperity and increased leisure time that came upon the heels of World War II and widened opportunities for women, very few tried professional sports. The civil rights movement and the women's movement of the 1960s also helped to propel women into sports. Before these important events, only a small handful of women managed to make sports history. One was Babe Didrikson.

In the summer of 1932, when she was eighteen, the wiry little Texan put on a track and field performance that has never been matched. "Super Girl"

is what newspapers of the day started calling her.

At the time, Babe competed for the Golden Cyclones in Dallas, Texas. Her coach, studying the records of American women athletes, realized that Babe stood a good chance of winning several events in the national AAU (Amateur Athletic Union) Women's Track and Field Championships to be held that summer on the campus of the University of Illinois in Evanston. Indeed, Babe could be an entire "team." The coach entered her in eight events.

On the day of the meet, team after team was introduced. With each introduction, a group of fifteen or twenty women would sprint out into the center of the huge arena. When the Golden Cyclones of Dallas were introduced, out came the lone figure of Babe Didrikson, lean and muscular, waving her arms and grinning as the crowd cheered.

Babe spent the next three hours hurrying from one event to the next. Officials sometimes delayed race starts to wait for her. She got extra minutes to rest between events. The special treatment angered her rivals. Babe didn't help matters by parading around the infield, announcing to the other athletes, "I'm going to win every event I enter."

She came close to doing just that. When the afternoon was over, Babe Didrikson had won the National AAU Women's Track and Field title single-handedly. Of the eight events she entered, she won five, tied for first place in the sixth, and placed second on the seventh. She failed to place in the eighth. Her individual total of 30 points was almost twice that achieved by the twenty-two members of the second-place team. They scored 16 points.

Babe Didrikson launched her phenomenal athletic career that afternoon. She was to be the dominant figure in women's sports for the next quarter of a century.

Babe's performance in the AAU championships at the University of Illinois was a warmup for the 1932 Olympic Games in Los Angeles. There Babe easily qualified for five events. She was,

however, permitted to compete in only three of them. She won two of the three. She failed to win the third—the high jump—because officials objected to her jumping style.

In baseball, she once struck seven homers in seven at-bats in the Texas Twilight League. That feat earned young Mildred Didrikson her nickname. Babe Ruth, the home-run hero of the New York Yankees, was then an idol in the world of sports.

During her lifetime, Babe Didrikson won championships in running, javelin throwing, swimming, diving, high jumping, hurdling, baseball, boxing, rifle shooting, horseback riding, and billiards.

"I never played football," she wrote in her autobiography, *This Life I've Led*. But in the same book she tells how she and her older sister, Lillie, once played football on a street near their home in Beaumont, Texas, with boys who had been warned by their mothers not to tackle girls.

To most people, Babe was known for her prowess at golf, a sport she did not discover until she took it up professionally in the late 1930s. During the mid-1940s, she set a record by winning seventeen major tournaments in a row. She won the National Women's Open three times. In 1947, she became the first American woman to capture the

At the 1932 Olympics, Babe Didrikson won two gold medals and set two world records, including those for the 80-meter hurdles. She might have won a third gold medal had the Olympic judges approved of her controversial jumping style. *Courtesy of the United States Olympic Committee.*

British Women's Amateur Golf Tournament.

Babe Didrikson was the only woman to be voted the Associated Press's "Woman Athlete of the Year" six times—in 1932 for track, and in 1945, 1946, 1947, 1950, and 1954 for golf. It was really no surprise when, in 1950, the Associated Press named her "Woman Athlete of the Half Century." In the year 2000, when voting for "Woman Athlete of the Century" takes place, the Babe is very likely to be the winner again.

The Babe was born Mildred Ella Didrikson at Port Arthur, Texas, on June 26, 1914. She was the second youngest of seven children of Ole and Hanna Didrikson, who had come to the United States from Norway. The family moved to Beaumont when Babe was three.

Her father was a carpenter and cabinetmaker. As Babe said in her autobiography, ". . . with seven kids to support, he generally didn't have any dimes or quarters to hand out for picture shows. . . ." To keep his children entertained, Mr. Didrikson built a backyard gymnasium for them, complete with chinning bars and weight-lifting equipment. There the Didrikson kids worked out together.

Babe learned to play basketball in elementary school, Beaumont's Magnolia School, which had a big gym and four outdoor courts. The Beaumont junior high and high school girls' basketball teams would come to Magnolia to practice.

Babe learned the basics of the sport from the older girls. She would often challenge them to free-throw shooting contests in which she would usually outscore her older rivals, tossing up the ball one-handed. Most of the other girls could barely manage shooting with two hands.

At South End Junior High and later at Beaumont High School, Babe was a member of the girls' basketball team. In high school, she also competed in volleyball, tennis, baseball, and swimming.

Sports became her only interest. She did only enough work in school to stay on the teams.

Most high school girls of the time wore stockings, high heels, and lipstick, and curled their hair. Their chief interests were good grades and dates with boys. Babe was different. She liked boyish clothes. She wore her short brown hair straight, with bangs. She never dated. When she talked with boys, it was always about sports.

The other girls ignored Babe or called her names, such as "Tomboy" or "Toughie." This made Babe try even harder, and frequently she would brag about herself. "I can beat Raymond all to little bits and pieces at kicking," she said to the high school football coach about the player who kicked extra points. When the coach gave her a try-out, Babe proved she knew what she was talking about. She kicked farther and straighter than Raymond.

Babe never got to play on the high school football team, but she did win a spot on the boys' basketball team. A forward, she was talented enough to win All-City and All-State honors.

Babe's fame reached Dallas and the ears of Colonel Melvin J. McCombs, director of the women's athletic program at the Employers Casualty Insurance Company. The firm sponsored a women's basketball team called the Golden Cyclones. The colonel was always looking for talented point-getters for the squad. He went to Houston, where Babe's team happened to be playing, to scout her. The 5-foot-7 Babe put on a dazzling show, scoring almost at will against much taller girls. Afterward, Colonel McCombs invited Babe to come to Dallas to play for the Golden Cyclones.

In those days, there were very few opportunities for girls to play basketball beyond high school. There were no women's college basketball scholar-ships. There were no pro leagues for women.

Babe was eager to accept the colonel's offer. She was able to convince her parents to let her drop out of school and go to Dallas. She did, however, promise to return in June to take her final examinations and graduate with her class.

The Employers Casualty Company paid Babe to be a secretary, but her real job was to play basketball. She announced she planned to be a forward on the team. And not just an ordinary forward. "*Star* forward" is what she said.

And she was a star from the beginning, becoming the Golden Cyclone's leading scorer. She steered the team to second place in the National AAU Basketball Tournament in her rookie year. The Golden Cyclones came in first the following season.

One spring day in 1930, Colonel McCombs took Babe to a track meet at Southern Methodist University in Dallas. Babe had never seen track and field competition before. She watched the sprints and hurdles, the long jump and javelin throw. It all looked like great fun to her.

Not long after, Colonel McCombs organized a Golden Cyclone women's track team. Babe, performing in a wide variety of events, soon became the star of that team, too.

Babe excelled at throwing and jumping events. The baseball-throw was an AAU event in those days. Babe once threw a baseball a record 296 feet. Some major league outfielders cannot throw a ball that far.

During the 1930 and 1931 track seasons, Babe personally won ninety-two medals. She set Texas records, all-South records, and American records. Her spectacular one-woman performance at the 1932 AAU track and field championships pointed her toward even greater days.

Although the United States was in the midst of the Great Depression, the 1932 Olympic Games in Los Angeles were held in lavish style. A magnificent new stadium—the Los Angeles Coliseum—had been built for the occasion. Record throngs were to turn out for the festivities.

From the moment she arrived in Los Angeles, Babe was a sensation. Newspaper reporters flocked about her when the train carrying Babe and her teammates pulled into the station.

"Yep, I'm going to win the high jump and set a world record," she predicted. "I don't know who my opponents are and, anyways, it wouldn't make any difference."

Time after time, Babe proclaimed that she had come to California to "beat everyone in sight." Her teammates grew tired of Babe's bragging and strutting. But the newspaper reporters encouraged her to make outrageous statements. She was "hot copy."

Babe backed up her words with glittering performances, even though some of her methods were unusual. Her javelin-throwing technique, for example, resembled a catcher pegging the ball to second base to nab a stealer; the javelin never got higher than 10 feet from the ground. But on Babe's first throw, the javelin flew 143 feet, $3^{11}/_{16}$ inches, beating the world record by some 11 feet. No one beat Babe's first throw.

After winning the gold medal for the javelin, Babe had a day off to rest before the next event, the 80-meter hurdles. Babe came flying from behind to snatch a gold medal at the finish line. Her time of 11.7 seconds was another world record.

Babe looked forward to winning a third gold medal in the high jump. When the bar was raised to 5 feet, $5^1/_4$ inches, only two hurdlers were left, Babe and teammate Jean Shiley. Babe sailed up and over the bar. So did Jean. They were tied for first place.

The judges raised the bar to 5 feet, $6^1/_2$ inches. Both women missed at that height to remain tied.

Babe and Jean were expecting the judges to lower the bar and ask each woman to try again, but after a long huddle near the jumping pit, the judges announced that Babe was being disqualified. She had "dived," they said, in going over the bar, and that was illegal. (In those days, the high-jumper's feet had to go over the bar first. That rule is no longer in effect.) The gold medal went to Jean Shiley. Babe protested. But it did no good. She was awarded the silver medal for second place and had to be content with that.

When the Games were over, Babe returned to Dallas to be honored with a big parade. Bands played and spectators lined the streets. Babe waved from a car filled with red roses. In her hometown of Beaumont, the high school band was called from summer vacation to help welcome her.

In the fall of 1932, Babe returned to her job at Employers Casualty. She felt she should be earning much more money than she was being paid as a secretary, but there were very few opportunities for women in sports in the 1930s. Today, for example, an Olympic gold medalist can earn hundreds of thousands of dollars by endorsing athletic equipment and other products. There were no such contracts in Babe's day. There was no professional league for women who played basketball. There were no professional golf or tennis tours for women.

Babe turned to show business. For the next two years she toured the country, exhibiting her many skills. At a theater in Chicago, for instance, she sprinted at top speed on a treadmill and demonstrated her talent as a golfer by driving plastic balls out to the seats. To end the act, she played popular songs on the harmonica, an instrument she had learned to play as a child.

Other times, she entertained by speeding around a baseball diamond and sliding head first across home plate. She did trick shooting on the basketball court and played exhibition basketball on a team made up of men and women. She pitched against major league baseball teams, including the Red Sox, Dodgers, and Phillies. At one time, she considered an offer to sprint against a race horse.

People bought tickets to see her because she was a celebrity. Babe loved the crowds and the attention.

But when she returned to Dallas in the fall of 1934, once again to work for Employers Casualty, Babe realized she was not completely happy. She wanted to compete again.

The sport she chose was golf. Colonel McCombs gave her a membership in the Dallas Country Club, and Babe began spending her leisure hours there sharpening her skills. She found golf a difficult sport to master. While she could smack the ball a long distance, her drives lacked accuracy.

The more the game frustrated her, the harder she worked. She sometimes showed up at the golf driving range at five A.M. She would hit as many as 1,500 balls in a day. Her hands would blister and bleed. She plastered them with tape so she could keep on hitting.

She practiced putting at home on the living room carpet. Babe would sometimes spend fifteen or sixteen hours a day practicing.

In April 1935, Babe entered and won the Texas Women's Amateur Golf Tournament in Houston. "I was on top of the world," she wrote afterward. "It had taken me longer than I had originally figured to get going in golf, but I was rolling at last."

To win the approval of the country club patrons who were now her fans, Babe began wearing dresses. She let her hair grow and began curling it. But she refused to wear stockings. Nothing could make her do that.

She often laughed and joked with spectators. "Look close, boys," she would say as she got set to swing, "'cause you're watching the best."

To her caddie, far out on the fairway, chasing her booming shots from the tee, she would shout, "Move back, boy. This ain't no kid hittin'."

Babe's aggressive style of play helped to change women's attitudes toward the game of golf. Before the Babe, women played with grace but seldom power.

It was rare, indeed, for a woman to score in the low 70s.

Babe helped turn women into attacking hitters. And since Babe shot scores in the low 70s, and even posted rounds in the 60s, other women came to believe that they could do the same. Babe broke down the barriers.

In January 1938, Babe entered the Los Angeles Open, a well-known men's tournament. One of her partners in an early round was a husky, dark-haired professional wrestler named George Zaharias. It was practically love at first sight for Babe and George. Before the year's end, they were married.

For the next seventeen years, George was Babe's devoted husband, manager, and golf coach. He got to be a familiar figure following Babe around the course.

During the summer of 1946, Babe won five golf tournaments in a row. She wanted to take a long vacation. But George urged her to keep playing. "You've got something going here," he told her. "You could build your win streak into a record that will never be forgotten."

George convinced Babe to go to Florida for the winter tour. There she continued to win.

With her tournament streak at fifteen straight, Babe entered the British Women's Amateur Tournament in Scotland. It was number sixteen in

Babe Didrikson, shown with fellow golf champion Richard Arlen, helped to establish the Ladies Professional Golf Association. *Courtesy of the World Professional Golf Association Hall of Fame.*

a streak of seventeen wins without a loss. No other golfer—man or woman—has ever approached that record.

Babe left her mark upon golf in other ways. She helped to establish the Ladies Professional Golf Association, the LPGA. The LPGA tournaments offer women professionals millions of dollars in prize money annually.

Misfortune caught up with Babe at the height of her golf career. She suddenly found herself in the hospital, a victim of cancer.

After an operation in 1953, Babe came back to win the National Women's Open and the Tam O'Shanter All-America Tournament. Soon, however, she was back in the hospital fighting for her life. She died in 1956 at the age of 42. She left a legacy that women sports stars of the 1980s and beyond may never equal.

Additional Reading

Knudson, R. R. *Babe Didrikson, Athlete of the Century.* New York: Viking Penguin, Inc., 1985.

Johnson, William O., and N. P. Williamson. *Whatta-gal! The Babe Didrikson Story.* Boston: Little Brown & Co., 1977.

Zaharias, Mildred Didrikson. *This Life I've Led: My Autobiography.* New York: A. S. Barnes, 1955.

Julius Erving

The Fabulous Doctor
1950–

The Philadelphia 76ers, playing on their home court, trail the San Antonio Spurs by 11 points. There are nine minutes remaining in the game.

Forward Julius Erving comes in for the 76ers. He gets the ball and moves toward the San Antonio basket. Mark Olberding, preparing to defend against a drive, steps back and dares Julius to shoot. He does—arching in a 17-foot jump shot.

The next time the 76ers come down the floor, Julius gets the ball near the right sideline. Olberding covers him like a coat of paint. Erving dribbles and steps around Olberding, then springs into the air. Two Spurs go up with him. Erving slips the ball to Henry Bibby, who then passes to Doug Collins. Collins pops in a 12-foot jump shot.

After an outburst of shooting by the Spurs, the 76ers get the ball to Erving again. This time he dribbles toward the basket, then abruptly stops and pushes off his left foot into the air. Two defenders, their hands raised, leap as high as Julius. He flicks the ball up underhanded. It hangs on the rim. Center Darryl Dawkins pushes it in.

Time after time, Erving gets the ball. Sometimes he drives, dribbling like a guard, around or between his legs, twisting his body in a dozen different directions. Other times, taking a running start, he leaps from the foul line and floats in to slam-dunk the ball. Still other times, he pulls up for bank shots or drops the ball to open teammates.

With 39 seconds left, the 76ers forge into the lead. Erving blocks a shot and Philadelphia runs out the clock to win.

That was a typical performance for

Julius Erving, the Doctor, during his years of glory. He was capable of taking command of a game for long stretches, dominating it by force of his personality and artistry. Always an electric figure on the court, he made jaws drop and hearts pound.

People did not think of Erving as a scorer. Yet he ranks as the third highest point-getter in the history of NBA–ABA (National Basketball Association–American Basketball Association). Only Wilt Chamberlain and Kareem Abdul-Jabbar outscored the Doctor. He averaged nearly 20 points a game.

Julius Erving is also important for the changes he made in pro basketball. He showed there was a different way to play the game.

One thing he did was take what had always been thought of as a smaller man's game—ball handling, passing, and such—and bring it to the front court.

Second, he took what had been traditionally the big man's game—rebounding and shot blocking—and demonstrated that he could handle that, too, even though he was "only" 6-foot-6.

In other words, Doctor J. blended two different styles of play that had always been considered separate and distinct. He had the size and strength of a big man but played with the grace and fluid motion of the guard. It was

as if the chief talents of Bill Russell, the great defensive star and shot blocker, and those of Bob Cousy, a playmaker without equal, had been combined in the same player.

That's not all. The most important contribution made by Doctor J. had to do with style, with showmanship. "My overall goal," Julius once told *Esquire* magazine, "is to give people the feeling that they are being entertained by an artist—and to win."

What Julius offered, as he once described it, was "the playground game . . . refined." *Esquire* explained what Julius did in these terms: "He once and for all, no turning back, blackified pro basketball."

Julius Erving was born in Hempstead, Long Island, New York, on February 22, 1950. He was the second child born to Julius and Callie Erving. He had an older sister, Alexis. When Julius was three, a brother, Marvin, was born.

Not long after Marvin's birth, Julius's parents separated, and Mrs. Erving was left alone to support her three young children.

The family lived in a low-income housing project. Callie Erving did housework in other people's homes to support herself and the children.

Julius was a serious child, perhaps because of his father's absence and out of an appreciation of his mother's struggle. His sister, Alexis, once said of him: "Julius was an old man when he was a boy."

Julius was introduced to basketball when he was very young. The courts at the Hempstead project where he lived were usually occupied by older boys, but Julius and his friends would take over whenever they got the opportunity.

When he was ten, Julius started playing basketball for a team that represented the Salvation Army Youth Center of Hempstead. They played other teams from different parts of Long Island. It was an important experience for Julius. "I came to see that basketball represented an avenue of getting out and seeing things," he once said. "And the more I saw, the more I wanted to see."

When Julius was fourteen, his mother remarried. The family moved to Roosevelt, Long Island, a largely black, lower-middle-class community, a few miles from Hempstead. Practically the first thing that Julius did after the family arrived was to get on his bike and go searching for a basketball court. He found two asphalt courts at Roosevelt Park, about a mile from his new home. There Julius would develop the skills that were to make him a superstar.

Basketball as played at Roosevelt Park was the version of the game that is common to big-city ghetto playgrounds. It was black basketball.

The object of black basketball is not merely to play well and win, but to do so with style and flair. Playground basketball features the behind-the-back dribble and the between-the-legs pass.

And, of course, there's the dunk, the shot made by leaping up high into the air and stuffing the ball down through the basket with one or both hands. Julius was to become to the dunk what Shakespeare is to the English language, raising it to its greatest heights.

Black basketball is also very much a game of self-expression. As David Wolf, in his book, *Foul!*, says, "For many young men in the slums, the schoolyard is the only place they feel true pride in what they do, where they can move free of inhibitions, and where they can, by being spectacular, rise for the moment above the drabness and anonymity of their lives." In other words, a slam-dunk or a reverse layup can make a boy, at least for a moment, feel special.

Julius himself has spoken about the psychology of the playground game. "[It] makes you want to beat a guy in a way that makes him pay twice," he once said. "You want to outscore him and you also want to freak him out with a big move or big block."

Every moment Julius was not in

school or running errands or helping out at home, he was practicing at Roosevelt Park. If he wasn't involved in a game with other boys, he would be playing one-on-one with a friend or shooting baskets by himself.

Julius was not particularly tall. But he had big hands, which enabled him to control the ball well, and he could jump. He was very proud of his jumping ability. However, he had not been born with it. He had to work hard to become a good jumper.

One day when he was in sixth grade, and while his family was still living in Hempstead, Julius actually dunked the ball for the first time, even though he was not yet six feet tall. Dunking is a skill usually associated with very tall players, but Julius was able to dunk because of his exceptional jumping ability. By comparison, Kareem-Abdul Jabbar, the legendary pro center, was not able to dunk the ball until he was an eighth-grader. By that time, Kareem stood 6-foot-8.

Julius was in seventh grade when he palmed the ball for the first time—that is, he was able to control it in one hand the way an ordinary person might control a grapefruit.

Today, there is a sign at the playground at Roosevelt Park that says: THIS IS WHERE JULIUS ERVING LEARNED THE GAME OF BASKETBALL.

When Julius started attending Roosevelt High School, he still had not reached 6 feet; he weighed about 140 pounds. He could not always practice when he wanted to because all three of the Erving children were expected to help out by working. Julius, throughout his high school years, had jobs running errands, washing cars, or washing dishes.

Julius played on the freshman team in his first year in high school. The next year he played on the junior varsity. He was undoubtedly good enough to play on the varsity team, but his coach believed in letting the older boys, the juniors and seniors, do most of the playing. Besides, basketball was serious business at Roosevelt High. There were plenty of talented players. Julius watched and learned.

During this period, he concentrated more on playing "team" basketball. Except for dunking, which he loved to do, he did not try to distinguish himself with an assortment of "playground" moves.

By the time he was a senior, Julius was averaging 25 points and 17 rebounds per game. He was named to the All-Long Island High School Team by *Newsday*, Long Island's largest daily newspaper. While Julius was not particularly tall and not very well-known nationally, colleges throughout the country had become aware of his talents. He received more than one hundred scholarship offers.

Julius chose a school that was reasonably close to home. His sister was about to get married. His brother, Marvin, was very sick with a rare skin disease. Julius didn't want to be too far from his mother. He chose the University of Massachusetts.

When he went out for the basketball team, the coach checked his size. Julius was 6-foot-3½; he weighed 165 pounds. Over the next two and a half years, Julius would grow another 2½ inches.

During the spring of his freshman year, Julius received an emergency call from his mother. His brother was dying. By the time Julius arrived home, Marvin was dead. Julius cried all day. Today he does not like to talk about his brother's death, but in the years after he reached stardom, when he was often asked how it felt to be so talented, so well known, and so well paid, Julius would grow serious-faced and answer, "What I really want most, I can never get back."

Julius was a sensation during his freshman year at the University of Massachusetts. Students stood in line for hours to buy tickets for the freshman games. He set records for scoring and rebounding, and he led the team to its first undefeated season ever.

As a sophomore, Julius averaged 26 points a game and was the second leading rebounder in the nation. The team was invited to play in the National Invitation Tournament in New York City's Madison Square Garden. Never before had a University of Massachusetts basketball team been invited to a post-season tournament. They were invited back the following year, too. In both years, however, the team failed to reach the finals.

The summer after Julius's sophomore year, the National Collegiate Athletic Association (NCAA) sent a team of college All-Stars on an exhibition tour of Europe and the Soviet Union. Julius won a spot on the team, then went on to be voted the tour's Most Valuable Player.

"That was a turning point in his career," Jack Leaman, Julius's college coach once said. "He realized that he was as great as any college player in the country."

Julius had wanted to be a doctor. That was how he came to be given his nickname. In elementary school, when the students got up in class to say what they wanted to be when they grew up, Julius said, "A doctor." His classmates started calling him "Doctor."

Later, when he started playing basketball for the University of Massachusetts, Julius saw the nickname become public property. At the home games, the public address announcer sometimes called Julius "The Claw" because of his large hands. Julius didn't like that name. One day he said to the announcer, "Look, if you're going to call me by a nickname, use the one I already have. It's 'The Doctor.'" From then on, that's what he was called. When he arrived in pro basketball, the players refined it to "Doctor J."

As a junior, Julius had another outstanding college year. He averaged 27 points and 19 rebounds per game. Again he was the Number 2 rebounding forward among the nation's college players. "People only saw the scoring and rebounding," his coach once pointed out, "but he was a great passer and a standout on defense."

Pro scouts had been watching Julius. In the spring of his junior year, he received an offer to play basketball for the Virginia Squires. It was an offer that had to be carefully weighed. The Squires were not members of the old, established National Basketball Association (NBA). They represented an upstart league, the American Basketball Association (ABA).

The ABA had been organized four years before, in 1967. It competed fiercely with the NBA. In the past, pro teams had followed a policy that did not permit them to sign college players until they were seniors and ready to graduate. That rule was no longer being observed. With two leagues and twice as many teams to staff, there weren't enough college seniors to go around. Now the pros were signing juniors, too.

Julius figured if the ABA wanted him, he'd prefer to play for a New York team, so he told his agent to give the New York Nets a call and offer his services. But the Nets weren't interested in Julius.

One day in April 1971, Julius and his agent met with the owner of the Virginia Squires. They quickly came to an agreement. Julius called home to make sure what he was doing had his mom's approval. Then he signed a four-year contract calling for a salary of $500,000.

Julius made his first appearance for the Squires in a preseason exhibition game against the Kentucky Colonels. He quickly established himself as the most exciting player on the floor—leaping, whirling, and spinning. And dunking. Three times that night, Julius dunked the ball over Artis Gilmore, Kentucky's 7-foot-2 center. Gilmore was thoroughly bewildered by young Julius.

In the months that followed, the Doctor elevated his dunk to an art form. His specialty was the leaping dunk from the foul line. He personalized each one,

"Doctor J" brought artistry and showmanship to professional basketball. *Courtesy of Naismith Memorial Basketball Hall of Fame.*

jamming some in with his famous "tomahawk" slam, in stuffing others with his back to the basket. Three or four times during a game, Julius would bring the fans to their feet, and even opposing players would shake their heads in disbelief.

Julius had not been permitted to dunk in college. The rulemakers had issued a ban on the shot in 1967. "The no-dunking rule came in my senior year in high school," Julius once recalled, "so I hadn't been allowed to slam for four years. At first, I couldn't get enough of it."

With his dunks and other spectacular moves, Julius was soon being compared to some of basketball's all-time greats, to Elgin Baylor, a 6-foot-5 forward who was known for his twisting layups and unbelievable jumpers. Baylor is one of the NBA's career scoring leaders. And, with his fine defensive play, Julius also reminded people of center Bill Russell, an exceptional shot-blocker and rebounder.

Eventually, of course, Julius was recognized for what he was—an "original." No one ever played the game quite the way the Doctor did.

Julius might not have become an instant sensation had he played in the NBA, where most teams played a calm and serious grind-it-out type of basketball. The Boston Celtics were, at the time, the only NBA team to feature the fast break.

But the ABA, in an effort to get itself established with the fans and sell tickets, encouraged a wide-open style of play built around the dunk. It was playground basketball, black basketball. And that was Julius's game.

The Virginia fans loved Julius. Attendance at Squires games hit record levels. But Julius was not happy with the Squires. Much of the money he was to receive was in "deferred payments." He would not receive much of his salary until after his contract had expired. Although he was a star, Julius was almost broke.

When the Atlanta Hawks of the NBA offered him a contract that would end his financial worries, Julius signed it. He played only three exhibition games before a federal court judge ordered him back to Virginia.

After a second season with the team (in which he led the league in scoring with an average of 31.9 points per game), the Squires traded Julius to the New York Nets. The Nets played their home games at Long Island's Nassau Coliseum, not far from where Julius had grown up.

Julius had some of his greatest days with the Nets. Twice he led the team to the ABA championship. Three times he won the league scoring title, and three times he was named the ABA's Most Valuable Player.

After the 1975–76 season, Julius's career took a sharp turn. The NBA ended its war with the ABA and absorbed three of its teams, including the Nets. More than a few observers say that the real reason the NBA made peace with the ABA was to get Julius. The older league simply could not go on allowing a crowd-pleaser like the Doctor to operate outside its domain.

As the 1976–77 season drew near, Julius looked forward to the challenge of competing against NBA teams, but Julius and the Nets could not agree on contract terms. The Nets then sold Julius to the Philadelphia 76ers for $3.6 million. Julius was able to reach an agreement with Philadelphia. The club promised to pay him $3.5 million over the next six years.

Julius quickly found it was much different playing for the Sixers than for the Nets, where he had been top dog. Now Julius had to share the limelight with forward George McGinnis and other stars. No longer was he able to be the creative daredevil he had once been. He showed only glimpses of the real Doctor.

The team was not successful. Some people said they played "out-of-control" basketball.

Before the next season began, the Sixers decided to shape the team around Julius's ability as a leader. Those who did not fit—such as George McGinnis and guard Lloyd Free—were traded.

Julius did everything he had to do to get the Sixers to win. When necessary, he was a playmaker. Or he could be a defensive ball hawk. And always he was the whirling, dunking scorer.

The Sixers reached the championship finals in 1980 and again in 1982 but were eliminated both times. In 1983, it seemed as if the team might finally fulfill its promise. The Sixers swept the New York Knicks, four games to none, in the Eastern Conference semifinals, then breezed past the Milwaukee Bucks, four games to one, to capture the Conference finals.

That put them in the championship series against the defending champion Los Angeles Lakers. In one game after another, Julius contributed slams and steals and blocked shots at what always seemed to be just the right moments. The 76ers won the first three games.

Late in the fourth game, played in Los Angeles, Erving took charge, scoring 7 points within the space of 98 seconds. The spree helped to clinch a 115–108 win for Philadelphia, giving the team its first NBA title in sixteen years.

When the team returned to Philadelphia, the city went crazy. An estimated 1.7 million watched the Sixers parade down Broad Street to Veterans Stadium, where a crowd of 55,000 waited to greet them. The championship helped to wipe out a mountain of frustration for Julius. Many of the Lakers admitted during the finals that if they were unable to repeat as champions, there was some comfort in the fact that the good Doctor was finally going to get a championship ring.

Following the 1986–87 season, Erving retired. He concerned himself with promotional activities and public service and charitable appearances. He watched over his financial investments. He and his wife, Turquoise, watched the four children grow up.

In his final years with the Sixers, the Doctor was less dominant and acrobatic than he once had been. Only rarely did he take control of a game. That surely influenced his decision to call it quits. He had been the foremost member of every team on which he played. He did not wish to play any supporting role.

Additional Reading

Bell, Marty. *The Legend of Dr. J.* New York: New American Library, 1975.

Haskins, James. *Doctor J: A Biography of Julius Erving.* Garden City, New York: Doubleday & Co., 1975.

Peggy Fleming

Ballerina on Ice
1948–

A slender brunette, only 5-foot-3, 109 pounds, Peggy Fleming was the nation's sweetheart, a graceful and daring blue-eyed young woman who spun, leaped, and glided her way into the hearts of Americans as the Olympic gold medalist in figure skating. "Flawless" and "superb" were words often used to describe her.

Dick Button, America's Olympic gold medalist in 1948 and 1952, once called Peggy a "delicate lady on ice." But she was more. She presented a unique combination of strength, grace, and poise. As such, she helped to trigger the "new ice age" of the 1980s, when skaters' routines would feature breathtaking jumps and the art of dance.

This kind of skating requires the athletic ability of a track star and the grace and elegance of a ballerina. That was Peggy Fleming.

Peggy Gale Fleming was born on July 27, 1948, in San Jose, California, to Albert and Doris Fleming. She had an older sister, Janice. Later, two other girls were born to the Flemings, Maxine and Cathryn.

When Peggy was nine, the family moved to Cleveland. It was there Peggy discovered skating. She found it fun; she found it easy. "She took to it right away," her sister Maxine once said. "She started skating as though she been at it a long time."

Not long after Peggy started skating, the family moved back to California, settling in Pasadena. At her father's urging, Peggy began thinking seriously about skating and competing in local events. After less than a year on skates, she won her first title.

Early in 1961, the world of skating was dealt a heavy blow. A huge airliner crashed near the airport in Brussels, Belgium, killing seventy-three persons, including eighteen members of the United States figure-skating team. "My coach, Billy Kipp, was on the plane, but I didn't know any of the skaters," Peggy once said. "I hadn't been skating very long when it happened. It all seemed so awful that I could hardly believe it."

As Peggy became more skilled and experienced, she moved up quickly in the age ranks, finishing third or better in each of the several divisions. In 1962, she captured second place in the National Novice Championship, and the following year she won the Pacific Coast Senior Ladies Championship.

In January 1964, at the age of fifteen, and in the very same arena where she had first laced on skates, Peggy won her first women's national senior title. She was the youngest woman ever to win the championship. A reporter for the *New York Times* said that she skated with the "flow and ease of maturity."

The 1964 Winter Olympic Games, to be held in Innsbruck, Austria, were at hand. The American team was still very weak as a result of the tragic plane

crash in Belgium three years before.

Peggy, because of her victory in the nationals, was assured a berth on the American Olympic team. She placed sixth in women's singles competition, a remarkable achievement for a fifteen-year-old.

In 1965, Peggy's career took an important turn. In March that year, she finished third in the world figure-skating championships held at the Broadmoor World Arena in Colorado Springs, Colorado. Peggy's father felt she would have done better if she had been accustomed to the high altitude of Colorado Springs. (The city is perched in the Rocky Mountains at an altitude of 5,980 feet.) Because of the thin air, Peggy got tired quickly. Mr. Fleming also realized that the following year the world championships were going to be held at Davos, Switzerland, which, in terms of altitude, was similar to Colorado Springs.

Peggy's father thought it would be a good idea for the family to move to Colorado Springs so that his daughter could train at Broadmoor and get accustomed to living a mile above sea level. There was another important factor. At Broadmoor, Peggy would be coached by Carlo Fassi, the former European men's skating champion. The energetic Fassi would be able to give Peggy the kind of advanced schooling she would not be able to get elsewhere.

So it was that the Fleming family moved to Colorado Springs. Mr. Fleming found a job as a pressman with a newspaper in Colorado Springs. He often worked overtime to help pay for Peggy's training. Mrs. Fleming made all of Peggy's costumes on her home sewing machine.

Each of Peggy's sisters was encouraged to pursue her own career. Janice, the oldest, decided to become a nurse. Maxine, three years younger than Peggy, developed a special interest in fashion while in college. Cathy, six years younger than Peggy, loved to skate, but not in competition—"just for fun," she said.

Perhaps because the Flemings moved so often, the girls found it easy to make friends. Their house in Colorado Springs became a gathering place for neighborhood youngsters. The girls loved sewing their own clothes. They also had an art studio in the garage. "Home is where the fun is," Peggy once said.

Skating, of course, dominated Peggy's time. She was up at dawn to begin practice at six A.M. School didn't begin until eleven A.M. Peggy attended Cheyenne Mountain High, located about a mile from the Broadmoor Arena. It was a school that numbered among its students several other skaters with promis-

ing careers. Class schedules were adjusted to fit their needs.

After school, Peggy went back to the arena, and there she practiced from five P.M. until eight P.M.

Carlo Fassi was now Peggy's instructor. He quickly recognized that she had the special grace and elegance of a ballerina. He believed that these qualities should be developed more and recommended that Peggy work with a choreographer, a person who specializes in composing and arranging ballets and other dances.

Fassi, in fact, started Peggy working with not one choreographer, but two of them—Bob Paul, a Canadian skater well known for his creativity, and Bob Turk, a choreographer for the Ice Capades. Today, the importance of choreography is recognized throughout the skating world. Choreographers work alongside coaches at major skating schools. But in the mid-1960s, it was considered unusual.

During this period, Peggy was also aided by Dick Button. He nagged her about her poor eating habits. If a restaurant didn't have her favorite dish—macaroni and cheese—Peggy would walk away without eating. Button said that when she did eat, she ate too much starch and too little protein.

When Peggy went to Davos, Switzerland, for the world championships in

February 1966, she was in top form. Carlo Fassi went with her. The competition was held outdoors in bitter cold. Fassi had a trainer rub Peggy's legs with liniment each time she went out on the ice so the muscles would be warm. Then, after each turn, Fassi would have the liniment rubbed off with alcohol so her legs wouldn't overheat.

Skating competition is divided into two parts—compulsory figures and free skating. In the compulsories, each contestant must skate a series of figures (called school figures), which are designs or patterns that are etched upon the ice. They include tight circles, three-turns, loops, and brackets.

Each performer is required to skate each of six figures three times. The skater is judged on her precision in making the figures, on her smoothness and body position.

Free skating—or freestyle—is completely different. In free skating, the competitor performs a carefully worked out program of jumps, spins, spirals, and other "free" movements performed to music. Each performance is graded on the basis of style, grace, and rhythm, as well as the proper execution of each movement.

In her compulsories at Davos, Peggy was never better. She traced and retraced her figures with such precision that she piled up 1,233 points, leaving Canada's Petra Burka, the defending champion, far behind.

In her free-skating performance, Peggy, wearing a tight-fitting dark rose costume, leaped and pirouetted to the strains of Verdi and Tchaikovsky. Not only did Peggy display her usual remarkable skill but newfound stamina, too.

As she skated off the ice, Peggy rushed for her mother and coach Fassi, who hugged her. "It was perfect, Peggy," Fassi said, "just perfect!" His face wore a wide smile.

One of the judges confirmed Fassi's opinion, awarding Peggy a 6, the mark of perfection in skating. It was the only 6 handed out during the women's competition. When the other judges reported their scores, it was clear that Peggy had won the world championship.

With her victory, Peggy became the first American woman to win a world title since Carol Heiss in 1960. At last, the United States had a skater for the Olympic Games in 1968.

Before returning home, Peggy and several other skaters took part in a European tour sponsored by the International Skating Union. France, England, Austria, Russia, and Germany were among the countries they visited. It was hard work, but it was fun, too. Peggy could relax at last, even stay out late.

France's Alain Calmat, who had won the men's world figure skating title the year before, was Peggy's guide around Paris. She had first met him in Colorado Springs when he had visited there to compete. It was a happy time for Peggy.

In the Soviet Union, the group performed in Moscow. When their tour of Russia was over, the skaters assembled at the busy Moscow International Airport for a flight that was to take them to Germany. As they waited, a man walked up to Peggy's mother and began talking to her. As Peggy watched, her mother put her hand to her face. Peggy hurried over to her mother and learned that her father had suffered a fatal heart attack. Peggy and her mother took the next flight home.

The close-knit Fleming family had to adjust to their great loss. Peggy had graduated from high school, and now she plunged into her studies at Colorado College in Colorado Springs, while continuing her rigorous practice schedule.

Peggy won the United States women's championship for a third time in 1966. In March the following year, she traveled to Vienna, Austria, to defend her world title. There were twenty-two competitors from twelve countries on hand. A victory, Peggy realized, would be another big step toward a career as a professional, a goal she had set for

herself not long after her father's death.

At the end of the first three days of competition, Peggy held a big lead and looked unbeatable. Several rinkside observers marveled that she was about the only skater who had no bruises. Most were covered with black-and-blue patches from falling down during practice sessions, but Peggy had such a keen sense of balance and skated with such grace and ease that she rarely fell.

During the free skating, Peggy glided over the ice to her music. Spectators noticed that she skated softly and rhythmically one moment, then would display a more rugged approach the next. Suddenly the unthinkable happened. Peggy fell. She was trying to finish a double axel, a jump with one and a half turns, and ended up on the seat of her pants, sliding toward the wall. Spectators gasped when she went down.

While the audience sat in stunned silence, Peggy got to her feet and charged off again. She performed a fast sequence of spins, splits, and loops. Then it was time for another double axel. Peggy was perfect. The audience stood and cheered.

There was a tense moment as the judges prepared to announce their scores. Had Peggy's fall cost her the championship? Amazingly, it had not. Her 2,273.4 points, 94 more points than those accumulated by runner-up Gabriele Seyfert, earned Peggy the world title for the second year in a row.

The next year, 1968, would bring the Olympic Games. The skating competition was to be held in the Stade de Glace at Grenoble, France.

In the year leading up to the Olympics, Peggy worked even harder on her ballet approach to skating. Norman Cornick, a dance instructor at Colorado College, tutored her for several hours each week in both modern and jazz dancing. Cornick felt that most of the top skaters never seemed to be good dancers, but Peggy, he said, had "a feeling for music."

At Grenoble Peggy built an almost overwhelming lead in the compulsory figures, earning a margin of 77.2 points over her closest rival, Gabriele Seyfert of East Germany.

For the free skating competition, Peggy's mother had made her a special beaded and sequined costume in fluffy chartreuse chiffon. Chartreuse is not only a color (green with a yellowish tinge), it is also the name of a strong, sweet, green-and-yellow alcoholic liquor made by monks living near the city of Grenoble. Mrs. Fleming felt that color would have special appeal for the people of Grenoble. She had picked up the material for the costume in New York on her way to the Olympics.

There were 32 skaters entered in the competition, and 21 of them performed before Peggy. She followed Czechoslovakia's Hana Maskova, who pleased the audience with a routine full of high, floating leaps and spins.

When Peggy stepped out onto the ice, she almost met with disaster. She caught the rhinestones on her sleeve against her beige tights. She skated out with the uneasy feeling that she might have ripped something. More than once during her routine, Peggy faltered briefly. Carlo Fassi could not bear to look. He covered his eyes and groaned.

But Peggy overcame her lapses to put on a dazzling performance. One of her routines included the spectacular double axel spread-eagle. It involved leaping in the air from a backward-leaning spread-eagle position—that is, with the arms and legs outstretched—spinning two and a half times in midair, and landing back in the same position. No other woman in international competition had mastered the routine.

Peggy was not happy with her performance. When she came off the ice, she broke into tears.

But as the judges soon confirmed, Peggy had won easily. Her total score of 1,970.5 points was 88.2 points better than that of the second place finisher, Gabriele Seyfert. Hana Maskova took third place, 141.7 points behind Peggy.

Peggy Fleming's mastery of spectacular leaps helped her capture a gold medal for figure skating at the 1968 Olympics. *Courtesy of the United States Olympic Committee.*

Peggy was teary-eyed as they played "The Star-Spangled Banner" and she received her gold medal. Just three weeks later, she retained her title in the world championships, held in Geneva, Switzerland. Her score of 2,179 points surpassed her Olympic total. It marked the third time that Peggy had captured the world crown. Peggy was the national champion five times.

When she returned to the United States following her triumph in Geneva, Peggy was welcomed home by President Lyndon Johnson at the White House. Shortly afterward, she signed contracts to appear in television specials and in ice show spectaculars, such as the Ice Follies. Her first television special was called "Here's Peggy Fleming." One television critic called it "very special."

Another of her TV programs was titled "Peggy Fleming Visits the Soviet Union." The first American television show filmed entirely in Russia, it was shown both in the United States and Soviet Union the same evening.

Peggy married Dr. Greg Jenkins, a

After Peggy Fleming turned professional, she continued to demonstrate the agility of a champion skater and the grace and musicality of a ballerina. *Courtesy of Peggy Fleming.*

dermatologist, in 1970. She and Gregory had met five years before, when Peggy, who was living in Colorado Springs at the time, had coached his fraternity hockey team at Colorado College. A son, Andrew, was born to the couple in 1976.

During the 1980s, Peggy continued to spend a good amount of time on the ice. She made guest appearances with the Ice Capades, on more TV specials, and on the Pro Skate circuit, which presents top-flight professional skaters to audiences at arenas throughout the country.

Peggy was also busy as the representative of several nationally known companies. One of these distributed her own line of clothing. Designing clothes was something she said she enjoyed almost as much as skating.

Peggy admitted that she no longer executed the daring and tricky double axels and flying camels that were part of her presentation at the 1968 Olympics. She said she simply didn't have time to practice such maneuvers. But those who saw her, either in person or on television, continued to applaud her ice artistry, the special grace and softness she brought to every performance.

Additional Reading

Van Steenwyk, Elizabeth. *Peggy Fleming, Cameo of a Champion*. New York: McGraw-Hill Book Co., 1978.

Red Grange

Football Giant
1903–

The 1920s were called the Golden Age of Sport. World War I had just ended, and Americans were ready for some entertainment. Big sports stars were covered lavishly by the press. Motion pictures, which had just learned how to talk, presented accounts of important sports events through weekly newsreels. Radio covered sports, too.

Baseball had Babe Ruth and Ty Cobb. Tennis had Bill Tilden; boxing, Jack Dempsey. In football, it was a college player, Red Grange.

A halfback at the University of Illinois, Grange was both fast and elusive. In the twenty games he played at Illinois, Grange scored 31 touchdowns, many of them on spectacular long runs. Sportswriter Grantland Rice nicknamed Grange "the Galloping Ghost."

Grange's last appearance as a college player was against Ohio State. The game drew 85,200 spectators, the biggest crowd ever to see a sports event in the United States up to that time.

They had gathered, Grantland Rice wrote, "To hear for the last time the thudding hoofbeats of the Redhead's march. . . ." Rice said it was "like a tremendous circus, multiplied ten or twenty times. And every tongue was spinning just one name—Grange."

After the game, won by Illinois, Grange did a shocking thing. He signed a contract to become a professional, joining the Chicago Bears.

Pro football was a scruffy, ragtag business in those days, about as popular and well organized as picnic softball is today. It was college football that at-

99

tracted crowds and got important space on the sports pages.

The league was a hodgepodge of some twenty teams spotted through the East and Northeast and Midwest. New York, Cleveland, Chicago, and Detroit were represented, but so were such towns as Canton, Ohio, Rock Island, Illinois, and Pottsville, Pennsylvania.

The schedule was a haphazard affair. Rival teams arranged games whenever it suited them. On a good day, they would draw four or five hundred fans. Players were paid $50 to $75 a game.

Grange's decision to play pro football was debated far and wide. Some people believed that Grange, who was guaranteed the unheard-of salary of $3,000 a game, was smart to cash in on his name. Others couldn't understand his decision. They felt he was betraying the college game by accepting money from a pro team. Being paid to play football was looked upon by many as being somehow unholy or indecent.

In those days, there was no rule that prohibited a pro team from using a player in the same season he had played college football. So George Halas, owner of the Bears, decided to put Grange into action right away. "There are millions of people who haven't had a chance to see Grange play this year and want to," Halas said. "We'll give them a chance."

The Galloping Ghost played his first professional football game on Thanksgiving Day 1925 at Chicago's Wrigley Field. The Chicago Cardinals furnished the opposition. Grange didn't do much galloping that day. Paddy Driscoll, the star kicker for the Cardinals, refused to boot the ball anywhere near Grange. "Kicking the ball to Grange is like grooving one to Babe Ruth," Driscoll said. Grange got his hands on the ball only three times, and his longest run was 7 yards.

Yet the game was a tremendous success, the first sellout in pro history. It drew 36,000 people, and so many of them charged out onto the field at the final gun that the Redhead needed a police escort to get to the dressing room.

Grange and the Bears then barnstormed through the Midwest and Northeast, playing ten games in seventeen days, seven of them in one nine-day period. (Teams today, during the regular season, play sixteen games in sixteen weeks.) Wherever they played, it was a big event. In St. Louis, Boston, Pittsburgh, New York, Philadelphia, and Washington, huge crowds turned out.

The incredible tour changed people's minds about pro football. It helped to launch the game toward its decades of success. It was probably the greatest single influence until the sport was discovered by television during the 1950s. In other words, Red Grange put pro football on the map.

The son of a lumberjack, Harold Grange was born in Forksville, Pennsylvania, on June 13, 1903. When he was five, his mother died. His father moved Harold and his brother to Wheaton, Illinois. Two sisters were left behind in Forksville for an aunt to raise. In Wheaton, Red's father became chief of police.

Red spent his boyhood in Wheaton, except for one year at the age of fifteen, when he lived on an uncle's farm. It was a tough life. Red would get up at dawn, do farm chores, then bicycle two miles to school. After school, he'd bicycle back to the farm, where he would work until dusk.

The hard work and exercise hardened Red's muscles. When he returned to Wheaton, he was so strong that he won a dollar bet from the town iceman by hoisting a seventy-five-pound block of ice onto his shoulders. So impressed was the iceman that he gave Red a job delivering ice. In later years, Red would be nicknamed the "Wheaton Iceman."

At Wheaton High School, football was not Red's favorite game. He liked baseball and track more. He ran the 100- and 220-yard sprints, the low and high hurdles, and the broad jump (called the long jump today) and high jump. He was a four-time sprint champion.

He also had an outstanding high school football record, scoring 75 touchdowns and kicking 82 extra points. Since colleges of the 1920s did not offer athletic scholarships, Red might easily have skipped college if it had not been for his father. "He was set on my going," Red once said. "He wouldn't hear of anything else." A neighbor convinced Red he should go to the University of Illinois. He earned money for tuition by working summers on the ice truck.

In his first varsity game, Grange broke loose for touchdown runs of 35, 65, and 12 yards. "Grange showed remarkable speed, dodging, hip shift and change of pace," one reporter wrote, "and when he was caught by several tacklers, the man simply put on steam and drove and whirled ahead, leaving a wake of would-be tacklers strewn in his path."

Illinois enjoyed an undefeated season and Red was hailed as the man most responsible for it. As the season of 1924 approached, opponents of Illinois knew what they were going to have to do if they expected to win: "Stop Grange!" Coaches spent the summer plotting special strategy to bar Grange's long runs.

Coach Fielding H. ("Hurry Up") Yost of the University of Michigan was one of the plotters. In 1923, Michigan, like Illinois, had gone undefeated. Their meeting on October 18, 1924, would probably decide which one of the two teams would be the national champion. "Mr. Grange," said Yost before the big game, "will be a carefully watched young man every time he takes the ball. There will be just about eleven clean, hard Michigan tacklers headed for him at the same time. I know he is a great runner, but great runners usually have the hardest time gaining ground when met by special preparation."

Bob Zuppke, the Illinois coach, had some strategy of his own. He made certain that Red saw every newspaper story in which Yost boasted how Michigan was going to put a damper on Red's running. The more fired up Red got, Zuppke knew, the tougher it was going to be for Yost and his Michigan team.

Zuppke also developed special strategy for the game. During practice sessions, he had Red run an unusual sideline-to-sideline play. Taking the snap from center, Red would start around right end, race toward the right sideline, then abruptly cut diagonally across the field to the left sideline. He would move downfield for a few yards, then speed back to the other side of the field again.

In the opening game of the season, Zuppke never used the play. Whenever Red got the ball, he would swing around the end, shoot over to the sideline, and stay there as he raced downfield. Although Illinois won the game, Grange did not have a good day. The Nebraska defenders had little trouble tackling him or knocking him out of bounds.

The next week, when Illinois played Butler, it was more of the same. Red ran down the sidelines whenever he carried the ball, and again he was stopped easily.

Scouts for the University of Michigan observed both games. When they handed in their reports to Yost and he read them, he felt certain that Grange was not going to be a problem. "All we have to do," Yost told his team, "is charge straight for the sideline and knock him out of bounds."

On the day that Illinois and Michigan were to renew their bitter rivalry, more than 67,000 people jammed the Illinois stadium. Michigan kicked off. The ball floated in Red's arms at the 5-yard line. He cut to the right sideline. Michigan tacklers, following Yost's instructions, swarmed toward him.

But Red surprised them. He cut sharply to his left and across the entire field, then ran down the left sideline for about 20 yards. When the Michigan tacklers drew a bead on him, Red scam-

Red Grange ran from one sideline to the other toward victory in the historic 1924 game between the University of Illinois and the University of Michigan. An astonished sportswriter dubbed him "the Galloping Ghost." *Courtesy of the Athletic Association of the University of Illinois at Urbana-Champaign.*

pered back to the right sideline and then into the end zone. Illinois led, 6–0.

On the Michigan bench, Yost decided it was just a fluke. He wanted Grange to get the ball again as quickly as possible. He was sure his tacklers would flatten him and demoralize Illinois. With the choice of kicking off or receiving, Michigan kicked off.

Again the ball went to Grange. This time he was brought down on the Illinois 20-yard line. Illinois had to punt. But not long after, Illinois got the ball back on its own 30.

On second down, the snap went to Grange. He sprinted around left end, then headed for the left sideline. Hemmed in by Michigan tacklers, he reversed his field, sprinting for the right side of the field. Only one of the Michigan tacklers stayed with Red. As he closed in, Red faked with his hip and then veered to his left again. As the tackler grasped handfuls of empty air, Red sprinted for another touchdown.

A few minutes later, Red had the ball again. At the Illinois 44, he started down the right sideline, cut back to the left, broke free, and hurried for the end zone. Soon after that, he took off from the Illinois 45-yard line, ran the crisscross pattern again, and scored his fourth touchdown.

Four touchdowns. And the game was only twelve minutes old.

There was more. In the third quarter, Red ran 12 yards for another touchdown. In the fourth quarter, he passed 18 yards for still another. Illinois won, 39–14. Red had touchdown runs of 95, 67, 56, 45, and 12 yards. He had gained 402 yards in 21 carries. He completed six passes for 78 yards. That was the day he earned his nickname "the Galloping Ghost."

Grange went on from the Michigan game to gain a total of 1,164 yards rushing and 534 yards passing for the season. He had a career record of 4,280 yards gained—3,637 on the ground, 643 in the air—and 31 touchdowns.

Bob Zuppke, his coach at Illinois, told Red to ". . . stay away from professionalism." But Red couldn't understand Zuppke's attitude toward the pro game. "You coach for money," he said to Zuppke. "Why isn't it okay to play for money?"

Grange performed in his final college game for Illinois on a Saturday, signed his contract with the Bears the following Monday, practiced with the team on Tuesday and Wednesday, and made his first appearance as a Bear on Thursday, Thanksgiving Day.

Three days after his debut, Grange and the Bears were in action again at Wrigley Field against the Columbus (Ohio) Tigers. It was another successful day, with more than 28,000 fans paying their way into the park. On Wednesday the following week, the team sold out the park in St. Louis. In Philadelphia, 35,000 people were on hand despite a cold drizzle.

With one night's rest, the show moved to New York, where the Bears were to play the Giants. The crowd began gathering during the morning hours, and every seat in the old Polo Grounds was sold by noon. Thousands crashed through the gates when they weren't able to buy tickets.

No one knows for sure how many people saw that game. At the very least, the number was 65,000. Whatever the figure, it was the biggest crowd ever to see a pro football game.

Grange thrilled the huge crowd by intercepting a New York pass during the fourth quarter and streaking thirty yards for a touchdown. It didn't matter that the touchdown contributed to the home team's defeat. These people had come to see Red Grange. He sent them home happy.

After New York, it was Washington, Boston, Pittsburgh, Detroit, and then back to Chicago. The following week, the Bears played in Washington, D.C., and Boston, where they faced the Providence Steamrollers on what was the coldest day of the year in Massachusetts. By this time, the murderous

Fans of collegiate football were shocked when Red Grange signed with the Chicago Bears in 1925. *Courtesy of the Chicago Bears.*

schedule had taken its toll on Grange. His black-and-blue body ached in a hundred places. On the field he moved listlessly, and fans were beginning to boo him.

During a game in Pittsburgh, Grange tore a muscle in his left knee. He was not able to play in Detroit the next day. Thousands of dollars had to be refunded to ticket holders.

After a final game in Chicago, Grange and the team rested, but not for long.

Halas had scheduled a second tour. This included Jacksonville, Tampa, and Miami in Florida. After a stopover in New Orleans, they moved on to the Pacific Coast. In Los Angeles, the Bears defeated a team called the Tigers before 75,000 fans.

When Grange's train arrived in San Francisco, he was met by the mayor and other city officials. There was a parade up Market Street and a reception at City Hall. Later in the day, Grange visited a hospital for crippled children, where he handed out miniature footballs.

By the time the Bears arrived in Seattle, the final city on the tour, on January 31, they had played nineteen games in seventeen cities in sixty-six days.

Grange, besides receiving a fee for each game in which he appeared, also earned a percentage of the gate receipts. A Chicago newspaper published a box score of his earnings, figuring that he made an average of $300 an hour, 24 hours a day, over the first eleven days of the exhibition schedule. In total, the tour is said to have netted Grange and his manager, C. C. Pyle, about half a million dollars.

When the tour was over, Grange returned to Wheaton to rest his battered body. In the fall of 1926, he was ready to try pro football again. He and his manager asked George Halas, the owner of the Bears, to give them a share of the team. When Halas refused, the two men tried to get a National Football League franchise in New York. They were refused again. So Grange and Pyle started their own league, with Red playing for the league's New York team, the Yankees.

While the Yankees drew big crowds, none of the other teams in the league did. At the end of the 1926 season, the league folded. Permission was then granted to Grange and Pyle to operate their New York team in the NFL, even though the league had another team there, the Giants.

In the third game of the season of 1927, Grange took the Yankees to Chicago to play the Bears at Wrigley Field. More than 30,000 fans were on hand, the biggest hometown crowd since Grange had broken in two years before.

Late in the game, Red bolted into the line. When he tried to twist into the open, his cleats caught in the ground. At the same moment, George Trafton, the Bears' big center, slammed into him. With one leg fixed to the ground, Red was jerked backward. A badly twisted knee was the result.

Red was on crutches for a month and out of football for the rest of the season and all of 1928. Without him, the New York Yankees folded.

"The accident took most of my running ability away from me," Grange once said. "I was just another football player after that."

But he was wrong. While he could no longer shift direction as quickly and cleverly as he had done before, Grange was still very fast. And he could still block and tackle and catch passes and play tough defense.

In 1929, George Halas invited Red to return to Chicago as a member of the Bears, and he accepted. He remained with the Bears for six more years. During those years, he was known almost as much for his defensive skills as for his ability as a runner. (In those prespecialization days, everyone played both offense and defense.) Grange won All-Pro honors in 1932.

Grange played in his last game on January 27, 1935. It was an exhibition contest against the Giants. Red took a handoff at the Bear 20-yard line and broke into the open—to the 30, then the 40. He was nearing midfield when he felt himself being grabbed from behind. The next thing he knew he was flat on his face.

Red had been chased and caught by a 230-pound lineman. He was 32 years old. His knee had been bothering him. Being outrun by a beefy lineman was the last straw. Red knew it was time to retire.

During the 1940s, Grange was named president of the proposed United States Football League (no relation to the USFL of the 1980s). He resigned before the league became a reality. He then turned to sports broadcasting. He did the Bears games on radio and television for fourteen years.

Through the years, Grange was often singled out for his accomplishments in football. In 1963, when the National Football League established the Pro Football Hall of Fame in Canton, Ohio, and a panel of writers and editors began selecting members, Grange was one of the very first players chosen. And in 1969, in honor of college football's one-hundredth anniversary, the Football Writers Association of America selected an all-time All-America team; Grange was the only player who was a unanimous choice.

During the 1970s and into the 1980s, Grange and his wife lived in the retirement community of Indian Lake Estates in central Florida. He once told a visitor that he spent most of his time cutting the grass and fishing—"doing nothing."

When asked about his achievements, he always shrugged off what he had done. "I played football the only way I knew how," Grange once told John Underwood of *Sports Illustrated*. "If you have the football and eleven guys are after you, if you're smart you'll run. It was no big deal."

Wayne Gretzky

The Great One
1961–

As an athlete, he was always doing things ahead of everyone else. At the age of six, he was competing against ten-year-olds. At sixteen, he was dominating twenty-year-olds.

At seventeen, he was the youngest athlete in North America playing a major professional sport. At twenty-one, he smashed the National Hockey League's single season scoring records. That's Wayne Gretzky of the Edmonton Oilers.* "I've always done things early," he admits.

In his first eight years in the National Hockey League (NHL), Gretzky won about all the hardware it was possible to win. He captured the Hart Trophy as the league's Most Valuable Player eight consecutive years. He won seven straight Art Ross trophies for leading the league in scoring.

He won the Conn Smythe trophy as the playoff MVP in 1985. He won the Lady Byng trophy, awarded for gentlemanly conduct, in 1980.

Gretzky, at the age of twenty-five, held or shared 38 NHL records in regular season, all-star, and playoff competition. That's 27 more records than his idol, Gordie Howe, "Mr. Hockey," whose career spanned almost three decades.

In 1981–82, Gretzky startled the world of hockey with 92 goals and 120 assists for 212 points. (Each goal and each assist is worth one point.) Mike Bossy, the NHL's second leading scorer that season, trailed Gretzky by 65 points.

Statisticians at the Elias Sports Bureau compared Gretzky's achievements to performances in other sports. The

Great One's 92 goals were equivalent to hitting 56 home runs or batting .393 in a baseball season; or gaining 2,304 yards rushing or tossing 43 touchdown passes in football.

What Gretzky did reminded sports historians of the 1961–62 season in the National Basketball Association, when Wilt Chamberlain led the league in scoring with a 50.4 average. Walt Bellamy, the league's Number 2 scorer that season, had a 31.6 average.

But Chamberlain's feat could be explained, at least in part, by the fact that he was a shade over 7 feet tall and exceptionally strong. Gretzky is a hair under 6 feet; he weighs about 170 pounds. He looks as if a solid hit could wipe him out. But Gretzky rarely takes a solid hit. "He goes with every check," said Ron Low, a one-time teammate of Gretzky's. "He doesn't try to withstand it or stop it. Hitting Gretzky is like hitting a pillow."

Gretzky is fast on the ice but not super fast. Several of his teammates could probably outdo him in a straight sprint. Nor does he have a graceful skating style. He bends over awkwardly when he skates.

But Gretzky is fast enough to get the job done. The Edmonton offense is based on an intricate weaving style. The ability to skate extremely fast in a straight line is not a necessity.

"Gretzky is great coming down the middle of the ice because he has great lateral speed," said Ron Low. "He has eight million moves to either side, so the defensemen have to back off, give him room." Wayne then just glides to either side, and his speedy wingers fly past him.

Gretzky's shot, while fast, is not the fastest in the league. But he is very accurate with it. His coach at the Oilers, Glen Sather, once described a goal that Gretzky scored against the Rangers. "The puck was right in front of their defenseman, who went down to block the shot, and their goalie went down behind him. Wayne was in front, with an opening of about six inches in the goal. The puck went straight up for that spot. I don't think anybody else could do that."

Gretzky is always among the leaders in the scoring percentage. "It's his release more than anything," said Ron Low. "He can open up the blade of his stick and make the puck drop, or close it and make it dive, and he never gives any inkling of what he intends to do."

Another of Gretzky's "secrets" is that he expanded the shooter's target area by zeroing in on the top corners of the net. During the 1970s, as shooting speed increased, goalies' protection failed to keep pace. Masks were primitive in those days. As a result, players were told to "keep the puck down" in practice sessions. It was natural for them to do the same thing in games.

But Gretzky doesn't necessarily keep the puck down. A shot from his stick is as likely to be around the top of the net as the bottom. This gives him another foot of target area with which to work.

Wayne's style always stresses brains over brawn—he is like Bobby Orr or Gordie Howe in that respect. He doesn't waste any energy. Countless times he goes to a spot on the ice, and then the puck goes there. Scores of observers hail Wayne for this ability to anticipate, to always seem to know where the puck is going.

Reporters often ask Gretzky how long he thinks he might continue to play. "If I play until I'm thirty," he once said, "that would be fourteen years. That would be long enough."

A fourteen-year career would surely enable Wayne to break records that it took Gordie Howe twenty-six seasons to set. "He [Howe] is a long way away," Gretzky said in 1985. "If I finished second to him—he's the greatest player ever—I'd be happy. Perhaps I'll be fortunate to pass him."

Barring a serious injury, Gretsky *will* pass Howe. Everyone agrees with that. And being fortunate will have very little to do with it.

The young man who one day would be hailed as the greatest offensive hockey player the game has ever known was born in Brantford, Ontario, Canada, on January 26, 1961. He was the first of four children, all boys, born to Walter and Phyllis Gretzky. Mr. Gretzky, a telephone company technician, had once played junior hockey, but he had been too small to be successful as a professional.

Wayne's father never forgot his own dreams of becoming a hockey star, and he put his own son on skates not very long after he had learned how to walk. There are films of Wayne skating with a tiny hockey stick when he was two.

Mr. Gretzky built a rink in the backyard. He never flooded the rink with a hose; that might have made the surface too uneven. Instead, he carefully sprayed coat after coat with a lawn sprinkler. One year, the sprinkler broke, and Mr. Gretzky asked his wife to buy another one. When she got home with it, she told her husband she would never do that again. The clerk in the hardware store thought she was crazy buying a lawn sprinkler in February.

Mr. Gretzky taught Wayne special drills. He arranged tin cans on the ice, and Wayne would skate patterns around them. He placed hockey sticks on the ice, and Wayne would hop over them while his father sent him passes.

There were also target-shooting drills. Mr. Gretzky tipped a picnic table on its edge and slid it in front of the net, so it blocked out all but the outer edges. Wayne would then shoot at the net corners.

Mr. Gretzky and Wayne practiced for hours every winter afternoon. They would have supper and then return to the rink, practicing under lights that Mr. Gretzky had strung.

When Wayne was five, Mr. Gretzky tried to find a youth team that his son could join. But the rules required players to be six years old, so the Gretzkys went home and practiced together some more.

During the summers, Wayne played other sports. He was a star sprinter, which helped him build up his legs for hockey. He also played lacrosse, a game in which opposing players attempt to move a small ball into each other's netted goal. Each player is equipped with a long-handled stick at the end of which is a rawhide-strung pocket. The ball is picked up, caught and thrown by means of the pocket. "I learned how to roll a body check in lacrosse, and how to spin away when a guy cross-checks you," Wayne has said. "It's carried to hockey. I've been hit but I've never been decked."

Wayne was seven years old and had been playing organized hockey for only a year when he began being noticed. He scored 27 goals in a youth league. At the age of eight, competing against much older boys, he scored 104 goals for the seasons. Newspaper reporters were now interviewing him.

In January 1972, Wayne turned eleven, but he did not look it. He stood 4-foot-4; he weighed 70 pounds. Yet he was a goal-scoring demon, getting goals in bunches, often 6 or 7 in a game. He scored 378 goals in 68 games that season.

His stardom put Wayne under great pressure. Newspapers throughout Canada were writing articles about him. He was constantly being interviewed by television reporters. He was also invited to speak at banquets. At one banquet, Gordie Howe was another speaker. Wayne had always idolized Howe. When Wayne didn't know what to say, Howe helped him out. Later the two were photographed together. It was an unforgettable experience for Wayne.

Despite the pressure on Wayne, Mr. Gretzky realized that his son needed tougher competition. When Wayne was fourteen, his father arranged for him to move up the Bantam league ladder to Junior B hockey. But to play with a Junior B team, Wayne had to move to Toronto, about 70 miles northeast of Brantford. "There was so much pressure around Brantford," Wayne said, "that I wanted to move to a bigger city, so I could lead a normal life."

Wayne had never been away from home before. It was not easy at first, even though he moved in with family friends of the Gretzkys. It was not easy on the ice, either. Wayne was fourteen, and most of the Junior B players were fifteen, sixteen, and seventeen—and some were even older. But by the second year of his Junior B experience, Wayne was playing a starring role again.

Junior A hockey, the highest level for an amateur player age twenty or younger, was the next step up. Wayne joined the Junior A Sault Sainte Marie Greyhounds in the spring of 1977, several weeks after his sixteenth birthday. He moved some 150 miles to the west to Sault Sainte Marie and lived with friends.

Again, Wayne had no problem scoring goals. The fans loved him and attendance doubled at Greyhound games. It was at Sault Sainte Marie that Wayne acquired his nickname, "The Great Gretzky." It was derived from the famous book *The Great Gatsby*, by F. Scott Fitzgerald. Sportswriters and television broadcasters began using the name, and it stuck.

Something else happened at Sault Sainte Marie that was to leave its mark on Wayne's career. He was assigned uniform Number 99 to wear. That is not a common jersey number in any sport, but some of the greatest players in the history of the National Hockey League had worn Number 9, among them Gordie Howe, Bobby Hull, and Maurice "Rocket" Richard. Wayne was given two Number 9s, not merely one.

A handful of athletes have made their uniform numbers famous. After the players are no longer active, their clubs retire their numbers. This is what happened in the case of Bill Russell (Number 6 of the Boston Celtics), Willie Mays (Number 24, the New York Giants) and Red Grange (Number 77, the University of Illinois). Gretzky wore Number 99 with the Sault Sainte Marie Greyhounds and has continued to do so throughout his career. Someday it surely will join him in retirement.

Canada's Junior A program is traditionally a stepping stone to professional hockey. Wayne followed in that tradition. After the 1977–78 season, in which he was clearly a star, Wayne decided to turn professional. He was seventeen at the time.

There were two major leagues in hockey in 1978. One was the National Hockey League (the NHL), which had been in operation since 1917. There was also the upstart World Hockey Association (the WHA), organized in 1972.

Before the opening of the 1978–79 season, Wayne signed a contract with the Indianapolis Racers of WHA. He scored three goals and had three assists in eight games with the Indianapolis team. Then, in November 1978, the Racers, under financial pressure, sold Wayne's contract to the Edmonton Oilers, another WHA club.

The Oilers were on much firmer financial footing than the Racers. The Oilers were, in fact, given a good chance of getting into the National Hockey League after the expected merger of the WHA and NHL.

The Oilers were thrilled with their new young star. On January 26, 1979, Wayne's eighteenth birthday, the club tore up his old contract and gave him a new one. It was worth more than $5 million to Wayne, and it made him an employee of the Oilers until 1999.

"We feel we are going to be in the National Hockey League," Peter Pocklington, the owner of the Oilers, said at the time. "We need a superstar, and Wayne is going to be the one."

In Wayne, the WHA now had the youngest player in major league hockey. The league also happened to have the oldest player—51-year-old Gordie Howe, who played for the New England Whalers. That year they played together on the WHA's All-Star team. Wayne was nervous before the game. After all, how often does a young athlete get to play on a team with his idol?

Howe noticed that Wayne seemed jittery. In the dressing room just before the players were called out onto the ice, Howe went over to Wayne and said, "Gee, Wayne, I'm nervous."

Wayne grinned—and relaxed. "An amazing man" is how Wayne describes Howe today.

With 46 goals and 64 assists, Wayne finished his WHA season as the league's third best scorer. After the season end, the WHA and NHL merged, and the Oilers became an NHL team.

Some people questioned how Gretzky would fare competing against NHL teams night after night. The truth is that he had few problems. Just as in his amateur days and his season in the WHA, goals and assists seemed to come easy to him. On February 15, 1980, Gretzky tied a thirty-three-year-old record by getting 7 assists in a game, against the Washington Capitals. On April 2 that year, he became the youngest player in league history to score 50 goals in a season.

Wayne finished his first NHL season with 51 goals and 86 assists, giving him a total of 137 points. That tied him for the leadership in total points with Marcel Dionne of the Los Angeles Kings. But in the case of a tie, the league rules give the title to the player with the most goals, and Dionne had 53.

The decision did not please Wayne. "I have younger brothers," he remarked. "They and their friends have

Wayne Gretzky of the Edmonton Oilers has broken records, won trophies—and may have transformed the style of professional hockey. *Courtesy of Bob Mummery.*

all been brought up to believe that an assist is just as important as a goal. Kids are going to have second thoughts about that now."

Wayne, however, did win the Hart Trophy as the league's most valuable player for the season. He was also awarded the Lady Byng Trophy as "the league's most gentlemanly player." No player so young had ever won two such important hockey honors.

From his first days in the NHL, Wayne had his critics. Some people said that he would have had difficulty earning a spot on an NHL team back in the 1950s or 1960s. It was a different game then, more defense-minded, more violent. Small players were at a disadvantage.

Gretzky feels that a player of his size would have been seriously injured then. "Today's game is a lot quicker, the puck is moving more, the training is better. The emphasis now is not on toughness and fighting, but on the ability to skate and move the puck effectively."

Other observers criticized Gretzky for doing little defensively, for being strictly a "one-way player." *The Hockey News* conducted a poll among NHL coaches, scouts, and managers during the 1981–82 season, asking each one which player he would prefer to have in his lineup *to win one game*, Gretzky or Bryan Trottier, center for the New

York Islanders. Trottier won because of his ability and willingness to bodycheck.

Gretzky's lack of interest in defensive hockey never hurt his popularity. He was the Number 1 attraction in the NHL. No team outdrew the Oilers on the road. *Sports Illustrated* once said of Gretzky, ". . . no one has appealed to the general public like Gretzky since Bobby Hull appeared on the cover of *Time* in 1968." (Gretzky appeared on a *Time* cover in 1985, although he had to share it with Larry Bird.)

The ability to pack arenas pays very well. Gretzky earned about $1 million a year in salary. He was said to earn another million each year from endorsements and investments.

Although Wayne, even in his early years with the Oilers, could boast a bigger income than almost any other athlete, held dozens of records, and was showered with personal honors, what he really wanted to do was win the Stanley Cup. The NHL's championship trophy, the Stanley Cup is awarded to the team that wins the four-out-of-seven-game playoff series at the end of the season.

Winning the Cup remained merely a dream for four years. In 1980, the Oilers were beaten in the preliminary playoff round. In 1981, they lost in the quarterfinals; in 1982, they were eliminated in the semifinals. In 1983, they managed to hold on until the finals, only to lose to the New York Islanders.

In 1984, Wayne and his Oiler team-mates vowed it would be different. Once more they faced the Islanders, winners of four straight championships, in the playoff finals.

They shocked the Islanders in Game 1, shutting them out, 1–0, on Grant Fuhr's goaltending. After the Islanders rebounded to win the second game, the series moved to Edmonton for Games 3, 4, and 5.

The Oilers blasted the Islanders, 7–2, in Game 4. Gretzky, however, had not yet scored against the New York team. He ended his drought in the first period of Game 5 with a breakaway on which he faked out Islander goalie Billy Smith and slid in a backhander. "Without question, it's the most relieved I've ever been," said a grinning Gretzky afterward. Wayne also scored the last goal of the game, as the Oilers won by 7–2 again.

One more victory and the Stanley Cup would belong to the Oilers.

Gretzky opened the game with a pair of goals in the first period. The Oilers added two more in the second period, then went on to win, 5–2.

At the end of the game, scores of fans streamed onto the ice to surround the Oiler players. Gretzky and his team-mates seemed not to notice the swarm.

They skated around the rink with Wayne in the middle, holding the Cup over his head.

In the 1985 playoff finals, the Oilers overwhelmed the Philadelphia Flyers, four games, to win the Cup a second time. Gretzky captured the Conn Smthye Trophy as the most valuable player of the playoffs.

After the Oilers had won their second straight Stanley Cup, some people said the team was on its way toward becoming the NHL's latest "dynasty." Winning championships in long sequences happens often in pro hockey. The Islanders won four straight titles from 1980 to 1983. Before that, it was the Montreal Canadiens, winners of four championships in a row from 1976 to 1979. The Philadelphia Flyers were champions in 1974 and 1975.

One reason that championship teams tend to repeat as champions in hockey is because there is so little player movement from one team to another. NHL teams mostly stay together, changing only two or three players a season.

As for the Oilers, their future was deemed bright because their star players were so young. Gretzky, Paul Coffey, Jari Kurri, and Mark Messier were in their mid-twenties when they won their first Stanley Cup. "They're young but they're veterans," said John Muckler, co-coach of the Oilers.

Many people believe that the Oilers

opened up a new era in hockey with the Stanley Cup victories. They demonstrated that an imaginative and high-scoring offense can overwhelm a traditional bump-and-grind defense. "We proved that an offensive team can win the Stanley Cup," Gretzky said. "We showed that you can win by skating and by being physical and without having to fight all the time."

Ken Dryden, the former goalie for the Montreal Canadiens and later a hockey analyst, is one of those who thinks that Gretzky may have a lasting impact on the way hockey is played. "His legacy will be a sense of movement, of speed, of just breaking into openings wherever they happen, whenever they happen," Dryden once told *Sport* magazine. "He'll leave behind a terrific sense of this combination game, that any individual star, no matter how great, is fairly easy to stop but is much harder to stop if he works with others to their advantage and his advantage."

It may well be that Gretzky, by putting a much greater emphasis on fast and creative skating and team play, has triggered a new age in hockey. If that is true, to say that he is the best scorer in the history of the game is not saying nearly enough.

Additional Reading

Benagh, Jim. *Picture Story of Wayne Gretzky.* New York: Julian Messner, 1982.

Fischler, Stan. *The Great Gretzky.* New York: William Morrow & Co., 1982.

Gretzky, Walter. *Gretzky: From the Backyard Rink to the Stanley Cup.* Toronto: McClelland & Stewart, 1984.

---

*In August 1988 Gretzky joined the Los Angeles Kings.

Gordie Howe

Hockey's Ageless Wonder
1928–

It is November 1963. The Detroit Red Wings are playing the Montreal Canadiens at the Olympic Stadium in Detroit. More than 15,000 fans have jammed their way into the arena. Some 3,000 have had to be turned away.

Late in the second period, Marcel Pronovost slips a pass to Detroit's Gordie Howe. When Howe gets the puck on his stick, he instantly passes to Billy McNeill at center. McNeill speeds over the Detroit blue line and toward the Montreal net. Defenseman Bill Gadsby is on his left, Howe is on his right. McNeill drops the puck to Howe, who is 30 feet from the goal.

The moment he feels the puck on his stick, Howe flicks his powerful wrists. The puck flies toward the net.

Goalie Charley Hodge moves out of the net slightly to cut down the angle. He leaves a 6-inch space between his left pad and the goal post. Normally, a 6-inch opening can be covered by a goalie, but this time the puck is rocketing so fast it knifes through the opening before Hodge can move.

As soon as the puck bulges the cord, Howe's stick flies up. He leaps as he circles the net and then falls to his knees. His teammates pour over the boards to clap him on the head and back.

With the goal, Gordie Howe surpassed Maurice "Rocket" Richard's National Hockey League record of 544 career goals. It was a record that had long been considered impossible to break.

After, it was considered impossible for anyone to score 600 career goals. Howe did.

Then it was considered impossible to score 700 of them. Howe did that, too.

Howe ended his career with 801 goals and 1,850 points (goals plus assists) in regular season play. He also established National Hockey League (NHL) records for total assists, single-season point-scoring championships, and Most Valuable Player awards. No wonder Howe's nickname was "Mr. Hockey."

Gordie Howe joined the Detroit Red Wings in 1946 when he was eighteen years old. Big and strong, he was 6-feet tall and weighed 190 pounds. He had sloping shoulders and a thick neck. In October that year, Howe scored his first NHL goal. "It was a crazy kind of goal," he once said. "I just pushed it in. I thought I was going to go on to big things, but I got only six more goals the rest of the season."

It took Howe three seasons to attain stardom, but once he achieved it, he never gave it up.

The evidence of Howe's greatness is readily apparent. Skating with the Detroit Red Wings, with whom he spent most of his career, Howe won the Hart Trophy as the league's Most Valuable Player in 1952, 1953, 1957, 1958, 1960, and 1963.

Howe, the only player of his day able to shoot and stick-handle from both the right and left side, led the NHL in scoring in 1951, 1952, 1953, 1954, 1957, and 1963. "His shot was uncanny," said goalie Glenn Hall, a member of hockey's Hall of Fame, "because it would come at the net in so many different ways."

About the time of Howe's twenty-fifth anniversary with the Red Wings, the NHL coaches named him the league's "smartest player, the best passer, best playmaker and best puck carrier."

If the coaches had thought of other categories, Howe undoubtedly would have been named the master of them, too. He was the best there was at feinting goalies out of position and getting defensemen to commit themselves.

Not only did Howe outperform all of those who challenged him, he also outlasted them. He holds the records for games played and seasons played.

Or look at it like this: When Bobby Orr, the great defenseman for the Boston Bruins, was born in 1948, Howe was already a star. (He was an idol of Orr's, in fact.) When Orr retired in 1979, Howe was still playing major league hockey. Howe played against Dit Clapper, whose career began in 1927, and he also played against Wayne

Gretzky, who will probably still be driving goalies crazy in the year 2000.

In the final stages of his career, Howe was sometimes kidded by players who were younger than the youngest of his hockey-playing sons. Once, as he lined up for a faceoff against Philadelphia, Bill Barber of the Flyers turned to Gordie and said, "Hi, Mr. Howe. I haven't seen you since I was a kid at your hockey camp."

Gordie Howe was born on March 31, 1928, in Floral, a town on the outskirts of Saskatoon, Saskatchewan, in the heart of Canada's prairie country. He was the fourth oldest in a family of nine children. After an unsuccessful try at farming, his father moved the family into Saskatoon, where he got a job in a garage. It was there that young Gordie learned to skate and play hockey.

Like many other families of the 1930s, the Howes were hit by the Great Depression. Gordie's first pair of skates was secondhand.

"As a kid," he once told hockey writer Stan Fischler, "the only equipment I had was skates and a stick. I took magazines and mail order catalogs, stuck 'em in my socks, and had shin pads. I held them in place with rubber bands made from inner tubes. We played with tennis balls instead of pucks."

In Saskatoon, where the winter temperatures sometimes plummeted to 50 degrees below zero, every school and playground had a skating rink. The Howes also had a rink in their backyard. Mrs. Howe spread newspapers on the kitchen floor so that when the children came in for lunch they could keep their skates on and not damage the linoleum.

"I guess I always knew he'd become a hockey player," his mother once said. "He used to practice at night under the light from the streetlamp."

Gordie quit school to take a job with a construction company that was building sidewalks. Lifting 85-pound bags of cement built up his arms, shoulders and chest, but construction work was never anything more than a way of filling the summers between hockey seasons.

By the time he was fifteen, Gordie was being sought by scouts from several NHL hockey teams. A scout from the New York Rangers visited the Howe family in Saskatoon in 1943. He invited Gordie to Winnipeg, where the Rangers were holding tryouts. Gordie stuffed a shirt, a pair of socks, and a set of underwear into a bag with his skates and took the overnight sleeper train to the camp.

But Gordie's stay in Winnipeg was very brief. He felt out of place among the pro veterans. He had no idea how to adjust the pads and other equipment the Rangers issued him. "I just dropped

A goalkeeper could only let his jaw drop in amazement when Gordie Howe scored one of the 801 goals achieved in regular season play. *Courtesy of Foremost Photographic Services.*

the gear on the floor in front of me," he once recalled, "and watched the others. I found out pretty early that the best way to learn was to keep my mouth shut and my eyes open."

Living in the big city, Gordie became homesick. Not long after his roommate left, Gordie, too, departed.

The next year, a scout from the De-troit Red Wings came knocking at the Howe family's front door. He asked Gordie to come to a Detroit camp at Windsor, Ontario. Older and more confident now, Howe so impressed everyone he was signed to a contract by the Red Wings. He was then assigned to the Wings' junior farm team at Galt, Ontario, but because, at sixteen, he was too young to play professionally, he merely practiced and played exhibitions for a year.

The next season, Gordie was promoted to Omaha, and in 1946 he joined the Red Wings. During his first three years with the team, Gordie scored 7, 16, and 12 goals. He began to emerge as a star during the Stanley Cup playoffs in 1949, when he scored 8 goals and had 3 assists, giving him 11 points. No other player equaled that output in Cup competition that year.

The following season, 1949–50, Howe was one of the league's scoring leaders. Stationed at right wing, he scored 35 goals and had 33 assists for 68 points. That may seem somewhat modest when compared to point totals of the 1980s, but during the 1940s and 1950s there was much more of an emphasis on defense in pro hockey.

Howe's career was derailed in the 1950 Stanley Cup playoffs. In the opening round, the Red Wings faced their bitter rivals, the Toronto Maple Leafs. Ted Kennedy, the Leafs' captain and center, was bringing the puck into the Wings' zone, when Howe, skating at top speed, swerved diagonally across the ice in an effort to intercept him. Suddenly, Kennedy pulled up and, according to the Red Wings, fouled Howe with his stick. Howe went flying head first into the wooden sideboards, then crumpled to the ice with a fractured skull. (Players did not wear helmets in those days.)

At the hospital, doctors worked to save Howe's life, drilling a hole in his skull to relieve pressure on the brain. Howe's parents were sent for from distant Saskatchewan. Howe's survival was at stake. Even if he lived, few people believed he would ever play hockey again.

Howe was not only back on his skates for the next hockey season, but he astounded everyone by becoming the league's scoring leader once more. He then went on to lead the league in scoring for each of the next three years.

Howe was successful because he could do more things better than anyone else. He could skate, shoot, score, and set up goals. He not only took his regular turn on the ice, but killed penalties and worked the power play. He played defense and probably would have played goal if they had let him. In the early stages of his career, he averaged forty minutes a game on the ice. Most forwards were ready to call it quits after twenty-five minutes.

Besides being a peerless performer, Howe had a reputation as a fighter. Indeed, Muzz Patrick, former general manager of the New York Rangers, once called Howe "the meanest and toughest man in the league."

Gordie Howe (number 9) could locate just the right angle from which to score a goal. *Courtesy of Foremost Photographic Services.*

Howe was not a brawler, not a player who got involved in gang wars. The Howe style was more subtle. Vic Stasiuk, a one-time coach of the Philadelphia Eagles, described it in these terms: "There would be a play where somebody spears Howe or trips him, and the referee doesn't call it. Well, everything might be real cool for a few minutes and then, all of a sudden, you notice the guy that speared Howe or tripped him is lying on the ice as stiff as a frozen mackerel. You can bet that Gordie slipped him a forearm."

Stasiuk said that Howe did not even like having opponents get close to him on the ice. Three feet was about his limit. The Philadelphia coach said that Howe built himself a "working area"; he "skated around inside an invisible glass tube." Anyone who penetrated the "tube" had to pay the consequences.

Howe's engagements with the enemy took their toll. During his first year in the NHL, he lost all of his front teeth. He had operations on both knees. He suffered a dislocated shoulder, torn rib cartilage, and a broken wrist. His nose was broken several times. He had over three hundred stitches on his face alone. And the accident that almost cost him his life in 1950 left him with a damaged optic nerve that caused a never-ceasing blink.

The seasons slipped by, but neither old injuries nor advancing years seemed to have an effect on Howe. In practice sessions, he still popped in goals with ease, faked out defensemen as if they were standing still, and checked with his usual authority.

Brian McIntyre, who later was to become the public relations director for the National Basketball Association, once recalled an encounter with Howe that took place in 1966, when the Detroit star was thirty-eight. "I was a pretty fair high school player," said McIntyre, "and my lifetime ambition was to play professionally."

In his senior high school year, McIntyre enrolled in a Red Wings' instructional camp. "The first thing they asked us to do was to skate as fast as we could," he said. "There I was, going flat-out,

and I looked up to see Gordie lapping me—skating backward. That was the instant I knew I would have to find another profession."

Did Howe slow down toward the end of his career? This is how he answered that question: "I don't have as many real good games. I used to go night after night, killing penalties, playing in the power play, going the whole route. If I'm feeling good, it means nothing to me to do all the things I used to do, but I don't feel that good that often anymore."

Gordie had married Colleen Joffa in 1953. They have four children—Marty, Mark, Cathleen, and Murray.

Howe often said that one of his fondest wishes was to skate on the same line with his eldest sons, Mark and Marty. Howe got his wish on February 17, 1971. The Detroit Red Wings played the Junior A Red Wings in an exhibition game, the proceeds going to charity.

Gordie's two boys played for the Junior A team at the time, and that night he skated alongside them. "It was a game I'll never forget," Gordie said afterward. Howe and his sons were to skate together many times in the years that followed.

Howe, joking, always said: "I'll probably never retire—they'll have to fire me."

Well, Howe wasn't actually fired, but they came close. In 1971, his twenty-fifth as a player, the Red Wings forced Howe into retirement, handing him a virtually meaningless front-office job.

Howe couldn't stand the inactivity. After two years, he startled the hockey world when he signed a contract with the Houston Aeros of the World Hockey Association (WHA). It wasn't only the forty-five-year-old Howe that the Aeros were taking on, but also his sons: Marty, twenty years old at the time, and Mark, nineteen. The three-player package earned the Howes about $2.5 million over a four-year period.

So began one of the most amazing comebacks in the history of sports. Slower, but still capable of exceptional hockey, Howe led the Aeros to the WHA championship in 1972. With that out of the way, Gordie was chosen to play for Team Canada against the Soviet Union's All-Star team. Howe returned to Houston and the Aeros to win the WHA's Most Valuable Player award in 1974 and guide the team to another championship in 1975.

Howe and his sons played with the Aeros until 1977, then signed with the Hartford Whalers, another WHA team. When Hartford joined the National Hockey League in 1979, huge crowds turned out to see the team. Fans wanted to find out whether the fifty-year-old Howe could skate with such young stars as Bryan Trottier, Marcel Dionne, and Wayne Gretzky.

Gordie proved he could. In the team's first year in the NHL, the Whalers were the only former WHA club to earn a playoff berth. "We can thank Gordie for that," said Howard Baldwin, president of the Whalers.

A year later, Howe retired at the age of fifty-one. He spent most of his time promoting the Hartford Whalers. He was also involved in oil exploration, real estate, banking, publishing, movie and TV production, hockey schools and camps, and as a sales and public relations representative for a number of firms.

His income from his many interests far exceeded what he had earned as a player. Obviously, Howe scored as well in the business world as he had in the National Hockey League.

Additional Reading

O'Reilly, Don. *Mr. Hockey: The World of Gordie Howe*. Chicago: Regnery, 1975.

Walter Johnson

Baseball's Greatest Arm
1887–1946

"I just throw as hard as I can when I think I've got to throw as hard as I can." That was the pitching philosophy of Walter Johnson, who quite possibly threw a baseball faster than any pitcher in baseball history. There were no electronic devices to measure a pitcher's speed in those days, but Johnson's blazing fastball enabled him to set pitching records that have never been matched.

How fast was Johnson? Fast enough to make batters blink in amazement. Roy Chapman of the Cleveland Indians once dropped his bat on home plate and walked away after taking two Johnson fastballs for called strikes. "That's only strike two," said plate umpire Billy Evans.

"You can have the next one," Chapman shouted back. "It won't do me any good."

Another time, Detroit first baseman Lu Blue, tossing away his bat after striking out on a Johnson fastball, was heard to ask, "How can you hit 'em when you can't see 'em?" That phrase summed up how many batters felt about Johnson and his speed.

Johnson never used his lightning fastball to intimidate a batter. The brushback pitch was not a part of his repertoire. A kind and gentle man, he always feared he might injure someone with his great speed.

During the 1980s, television and the press kept baseball fans posted on the steady advances of Steve Carlton, Gaylord Perry, Tom Seaver, and Phil Niekro toward victory number 300. They all eventually reached it.

It seems almost unbelievable that any pitcher could win more than 400 games, but Walter Johnson did. In a major league career that spanned twenty-one seasons, all of them spent with the usually pathetic Washington Senators, Johnson recorded 416 victories. Only Cy Young, with 511 wins, had more.

It would take an entire page to list all of Johnson's pitching records. These are the most important ones: He pitched the most American League games—802; he led the league in strikeouts the most years—12; he pitched the most complete games—531; he struck out the most batters—3,508.

Johnson pitched the most innings—5,925; he pitched the most shutouts—113; he pitched the most consecutive shutout innings—56; he recorded the lowest earned run average for 300 more innings in one season—1.09.

What's extraordinary about Johnson's record is that he was able to win so many games with such a poor ball club. In his twenty-one years with the Washington Senators, the team was frequently in last place or close to it. But year in, year out, Johnson was a big winner.

Walter Perry Johnson was born on a farm near Humboldt, Kansas, on November 6, 1887. He was the second of six children.

When Walter was fourteen, his family moved to Fullerton, California.

There Johnson was introduced to baseball, becoming a catcher on his high school team. Halfway through his first game, the manager noticed that Walter was firing the ball back harder than the pitcher was throwing it in, so he sent Walter to the mound.

It was not a happy debut. Walter got beat, 21–0. The reason for the defeat had nothing to do with Walter's lack of skill or experience. The Fullerton catcher wasn't able to corral his steaming fastballs. Batter after batter who struck out reached first base because the catcher was unable to hang on to third-strike pitches. Once the team acquired a catcher who could get a glove on Walter's fastball, he became a winner.

After Johnson finished high school, he spent part of his time working in the oilfields around Fullerton and another part pitching in a semipro league. In the spring of 1906, a friend persuaded Walter to join Tacoma (Washington) in the Northwest League, but he was quickly released for being "far too green."

Walter made his way to Weiser, Idaho, where he pitched for a semipro team for the last two months of the season. His contract provided him with $75 to dig postholes for the Weiser Telephone Company as well as pitch.

The next spring, Walter was back in Weiser. Now his brilliance began to show. By midseason, he had won 13 games and lost but 2. During one masterful stretch, he pitched 86 consecutive scoreless innings.

Johnson's talents might have gone unnoticed for years, except that a fan of the Washington Senators, doing government work for the U.S. Geological Survey, happened to visit Weiser and saw him pitch. The fan began bombarding Washington manager Joe Cantillon with letters about the young right-hander with the blazing fastball. "He has blinding speed," wrote the fan, "and although a bit green will make good in short order."

Cantillon was accustomed to receiving such letters and seldom paid any attention to them. But this fan kept writing, and each letter was more enthusiastic than the next. Cantillon finally relented and agreed to send a scout to Weiser to take a look at Johnson.

The scout arrived in time to watch Walter pitch 12 scoreless innings, ultimately losing, 1–0, on infield errors. The scout was so impressed he offered to take Johnson back to Washington with him. But Johnson was wary. He had no intention of taking the long train ride back to Washington without some guarantee. He made the scout agree to provide him with a return-trip train ticket. Thus, for an investment of about

$250, the Washington Senators acquired Walter Johnson. It has been judged the biggest bargain in baseball history.

The sandy-haired Johnson, 6-foot-1, 195 pounds, nineteen years old, joined the Senators in August 1907. He pitched with a long, loose sidearm motion, showing not the slightest strain as his arm whipped through.

In his first game, Johnson faced the Detroit Tigers, who boasted Ty Cobb, then in the early stages of his magnificent career. When Johnson took his windup and let the ball go, Cobb barely saw it. "The ball just hissed with danger," Cobb said. Not only was Johnson the fastest pitcher that Cobb had ever seen, but he had pinpoint control, a rare quality for a rookie.

Cobb managed to outwit Johnson in his first at-bat by laying down a bunt that the gangly Johnson was unable to field. Johnson left the game for a pinch-hitter in the ninth inning, with the Senators trailing, 3–1. The team eventually lost, 3–2, but as Cobb was to state in his autobiography, he and his teammates "knew we'd met the most powerful arm ever turned loose in a ballpark."

Cobb, incidentally, figured out how to cope with Johnson and his tremendous speed. He realized that Johnson was kindly and even-tempered, and thus he could take advantage of him by crowding the plate. Johnson would not drive Cobb back, as other pitchers did, for fear he would hit, kill, or maim him with his deadly fastball. As a result, Cobb hit Johnson consistently during the twenty-one years that the two played against one another.

Johnson ended his first season in the majors with a 5–9 record. The following year, Johnson performed his famous "ironman" stunt, hurling three consecutives shutouts against the New York Yankees (known as the Highlanders in those days). Starting on Friday, September 4, Johnson blanked the New Yorkers, 3–0, on four hits. The next day he tossed a three-hitter, winning 6–0. There was no game the following day because Sunday baseball was then illegal in New York, but on Monday Johnson whipped the New York team a third time, pitching a two-hitter and winning, 2–0. Sportswriter Grantland Rice, who watched all three games, noted, "He was faster in the third game than he was in the first."

It was Rice who nicknamed Johnson "The Big Train" for the whistling speed of his fastball. In a story before an important series, Rice wrote: "The Big Train comes to town today." The name was applied to Johnson throughout his career.

His teammates, however, often called him Barney, after Barney Old-field, the famous racing-car driver of the time. Johnson earned that nickname because he liked to barrel along the open highways at full throttle, sometimes hitting speeds as high as 40 miles per hour. However, in letters to his friends Johnson always signed himself "Walter."

Johnson won twenty games in a season for the first time in 1910, when he wound up with a 25–17. The Senators finished seventh in the eight-team American League. Since Washington managed to win only 66 games that season, well over one-third of the team's wins were Johnson's.

During the season of 1912, Johnson won sixteen games in a row, a streak that began on July 3 and ended on August 23. It could easily have continued, except for a quirk in the rules. Johnson had come into the game in the eighth inning in relief of Tom Hughes. The score was tied, 2–2; two men were on base. Walter gave up a hit that drove in the runners, and he was charged with the defeat.

A storm of protest followed. He hadn't put the runners on base, his supporters said; thus he should not have been tagged with the loss. Years later, organized baseball established the present rule, which charges the loss to the pitcher who puts the winning runs on base.

Johnson was hailed far and wide for the 32–12 record he compiled in 1912. The next year, to the surprise of even his most fanatical supporters, he went beyond that, posting a 36–7 record. In terms of both number of wins and percentage (.837), he never had a better season. It was also the year in which Johnson put together a record string of 56 consecutive scoreless innings.

Johnson had another reason to remember 1913. It was the year Walter, the quiet bachelor who never drank or joined in clubhouse card games, met Hazel Lee Roberts, the daughter of a United States Congressman from Nevada. They were married in 1914. The couple bought a farm near Bethesda, Maryland, not far from Washington, and had five children. Hazel died suddenly in 1930 at the age of thirty-six, the victim of a lung infection. Her death was the greatest tragedy of Johnson's life.

In the years from 1914 through 1925, Johnson was seldom less than masterful. In eight of those twelve seasons, he won twenty or more games. But seldom were the Senators ever a factor in the pennant race. The saying, "George Washington—first in war, first in peace, and first in the hearts of his countrymen," was adapted to become "Washington—first in war, first in peace, and last in the American League."

Time after time, mistakes by his teammates would cost Johnson victories. But he never lashed out at anyone for lack of support, never even complained. Once, Clyde Milan, a usually dependable outfielder, dropped a fly ball in the eleventh inning that led to Walter's getting beat, 1–0. In the clubhouse afterward, Johnson was told he had every right to be angry at Milan. He answered with a shrug, saying, "Oh, I don't think so. You know, Clyde doesn't do that very often."

Finally, in 1924, Johnson's eighteenth season with the club, the Senators won their first American League pennant. The New York Giants, managed by the fiery John McGraw, were the winners in the National League. Johnson, who boasted a 23–7 record that season, went to the mound in the first game of the World Series, played at Washington's Griffith Stadium. A crowd of 35,760, including President Calvin Coolidge, squeezed into the tiny ballpark.

The Washington fans had little to cheer about as the Giants won in twelve innings, 4–3. Johnson pitched his heart out, striking out twelve. Washington won two of the next three games to knot the series at two games apiece. Manager Bucky Harris then named Johnson to start the fifth game. Again he went down to defeat. The Giants

Walter Johnson of the Washington Senators may have pitched the fastest baseballs ever. Some of the records he set between 1907 and 1927 have never been broken. *Courtesy of the National Baseball Library, Cooperstown, N.Y.*

raked him for thirteen hits to win, 6–2.

Johnson got one more chance. In the ninth inning of the seventh and deciding game, the score tied, 3–3, Harris called on Walter a third time. Griffith Stadium was again the scene. Walter retired the side in the ninth, and with the Senators unable to score in their half of the inning, the game went into extra innings.

Johnson was magnificent. Whenever the Giants threatened, he bore down and slammed the door. He struck out the dangerous Frankie Frisch with a man on base in the eleventh inning. He got the powerful Hack Wilson to fan with a runner on first in the twelfth inning.

With one out in the bottom of the twelfth, Muddy Ruel doubled for the Senators. Johnson, allowed to hit for himself, grounded to short, but the shortstop fumbled the ball, and both runners were safe. Center fielder Earl McNeely lashed a ground ball that became famous as the "pebble hit." It took a weird bounce over Freddy Lindstrom's head. Ruel scampered around third to cross home plate with the winning run.

The Senators were baseball's world champions! The fans cheered wildly. As Johnson, the winning pitcher, came off of the field, President Coolidge was waiting at the dugout to shake his hand. For almost an hour, fans remained in the darkening stadium, cheering and shouting. In downtown Washington there hadn't been such celebration since the day World War I ended.

That game marked the peak of Johnson's career. The following season he won 20 games for the twelfth time and helped steer the Senators to their second consecutive pennant. But the World Series, in which Washington faced the Pittsburgh Pirates, was a disappointment.

Johnson started and won the opening game, 4–1. He shut out Pittsburgh in the fourth game, 4–0. For the second straight year, the series went to seven games, and once more Johnson was called upon with all the chips on the line.

The scene was Forbes Field in Pittsburgh on a cold and gray afternoon. Rain had turned the field into a sea of mud. In the eighth inning, with two out, and the Senators leading, 7–6, Johnson gave up two consecutive doubles. Now the score was tied. An error and another double accounted for two more runs, and shortly after, the Pirates were celebrating a world championship.

The Pittsburgh fans cheered their heroes loudly, but they remembered Walter, too. As he trudged off from the mound, they called out to him: "Tough luck, Walter," and, "Sorry it had to be you." Seldom are such words of sympathy showered on an enemy.

Washington manager Bucky Harris was hotly criticized for starting Johnson in the third game, which stretched him beyond the breaking point. There were plenty of rested pitchers on the Washington bench. Even American League President Ban Johnson entered the controversy, saying that Walter had been used "for sentimental reasons." But Walter himself would not get involved. "It's tough," he said, "but they had the better ball team out there, and they won. And that's all there is to that."

Johnson began his twentieth season in major league baseball by shutting out the Philadelphia Athletics, 1–0. The win marked the fourteenth time he had started on opening day and the ninth time he had won. Johnson pitched before five different United States Presidents.

One reason that Johnson was able to go on and on was because he paced himself so carefully. When he was ahead in the count, 0–2 or 1–2, he liked to experiment with his curveball, which hardly curved at all. And when he had a big lead with which to work, he did not worry if runners reached base. He knew he could always bear down and

get outs when he had to. In his final season of 1927, Walter had a 5–6 record.

After his retirement as a player, Johnson managed for several seasons, in Newark for a year, in Washington from 1929 to 1932, and in Cleveland from 1933 to 1935. He was much more successful as a pitcher than as a manager.

Johnson's name was in the headlines again in 1936. On February 22, Washington's Birthday, that year, he hurled two silver dollars across the Rappahannock River at Fredericksburg, Virginia, duplicating a feat said to have been performed by George Washington as a boy.

That same year, 1936, when the first group of five players was named to the Hall of Fame, Johnson was one of those included, right along with such giants as Babe Ruth and Ty Cobb.

Johnson was active in politics in Montgomery County, Maryland, for many years. He was also a radio announcer for baseball games. But what he liked best was working his land, hunting with his dogs, and raising chickens, ducks and turkeys. He lived the life of a country gentleman until his death in 1946.

Johnson was never conceited or boastful, but once, many years after he had retired, he was invited to Griffith Stadium by baseball writer Shirley Povich to watch the Senators play the

Cleveland Indians. Bob Feller, whose brilliant pitching career was based upon his legendary speed, was on the mound for the Indians. "Rapid Robert" was Feller's nickname.

Johnson took note of Feller's speed. "Mighty fast," he said to Povich. "He smokes the ball, good gracious."

After a few innings, Povich turned to Johnson and said, "Tell me, Walter, does Feller throw the ball as fast as you did?"

Johnson, who was known throughout his lifetime for always telling the truth, thought for a moment, then looked Povich in the eye and said, "No."

Jean-Claude Killy

Fastest Man on the Mountain
1943–

Nobody skied like Jean-Claude Killy. The lean and handsome Frenchman attacked a course, nose-diving down, his legs wide apart, his arms flailing.

"I have always skied on instinct," Killy said. "If people say I look pretty in a race, then I know I'm not winning."

Nobody skied with the success of Jean-Claude Killy, either. In 1965, the first year he became internationally known, Killy won the European championship. In 1966 he captured the world title.

In 1967, Killy startled the world of skiing by winning all of the big races in the Alps of Switzerland, France, and Italy. He also won in the White Mountains of New Hampshire and in the Colorado Rockies. He won twenty-three victories in all, including all three of

the World Cup titles—the slalom, giant slalom, and downhill.

The next year, 1968, was Killy's most golden. He won the World Cup championship again. He won three gold medals in the Winter Olympics.

Killy had won everything there was to win. He was called the greatest ski racer of his era, even the greatest of all time.

Thanks to his many professional profitable business tie-ins and sponsor contracts, Killy became a millionaire. He shared the company of famous men and beautiful women. He owned a large and imposing home that overlooked Lake Geneva in Switzerland.

Then, in the summer of 1972, Killy decided he wanted to race again. He joined the North American professional ski racers tour. Few people believed that Killy could regain his winning form after a four-year absence from the slopes.

But Killy worked hard. On days he was not skiing competitively, he did not rest but went out onto the course to practice. He got stronger and stronger each week and began winning regularly. He ended the season as the pro champion and skiing's biggest money winner. Then he retired for good.

The descendent of an Irishman named Kelly who fought in the army of Napoleon and then settled in France, Jean-Claude Killy was born in Saint-Cloud, a suburb of Paris, on August 30, 1943. His parents were divorced when he was very young. Jean-Claude and a younger brother and sister were raised by their father.

The family moved to Val d'Isère, a ski resort high in the French Alps. It is possible to ski ten months a year in Val d'Isère. Many outstanding skiers have been developed there.

The elder Killy first operated a sporting goods store and then a restaurant. He later owned a hotel in the middle of Val d'Isère. Called La Bergerie, the hotel had seventeen rooms, a French flag draped below its steep slate roof, and a big aquarium in the dining room. It was a very popular resort.

The Killys had not been in Val d'Isère very long when Jean-Claude's father found he was spending all of his spare time wondering where Jean-Claude was. "From the age of three, he would disappear on skis for hours," he once recalled. "I had to demand that the lift operators not let Toutoune [his nickname for Jean-Claude] go up more than two or three times a day."

By the age of six, Jean-Claude was hurtling down the slopes as fast as his father. By the time he reached his teens, there were very few skiers around Val d'Isère who could compete with him. "I skied then almost as fast as I ski now," Jean-Claude once told *Life* magazine after he had become a champion, "only I was always falling."

As a teen-ager, Jean-Claude was constantly absent from school because he was traveling long distances to compete in ski meets. He quit school at age fifteen, a decision that later saddened him. "I wish I could have continued school and skiing, the way Americans do," he once said. "The biggest grief in my life is that I have not had more education. That is why I try to read books often. To fill in, yes?

"But always I remembered that when my teacher asked me what I wanted to be when I grew up, I replied, 'Ski champion.' From the age of fifteen, I have devoted everything to that."

Expertly twisting around the slalom gates, Jean-Claude Killy triumphed in the slalom event of the Hahnenkamm races at Kitzbuehel, Austria, one of the twenty-three championships he won in 1967. *Courtesy of AP/Wide World Photos.*

A boy in France usually wins his first important medal in skiing at age thirteen or fourteen. Jean-Claude won his at nine. Even then, he was skiing slalom only a second behind his instructor. (The slalom is a race against the clock in which each competitor skis down a zigzag course passing between pairs of poles, called gates.)

No one can ski as recklessly as Killy did and not break a few bones. At the age of fourteen, he broke his left knee in a junior slalom. After he recovered from the injury, he won three events in the French junior championships in 1960. He also won a place on the French national junior team.

In 1962, Jean-Claude's career was interrupted again when he broke his leg in a downhill race. Later, during a tour of duty in the army, Killy became seriously ill with jaundice. Even though he was not near his best physical condition, Killy rejoined the French national team in 1964. His performance at the 1964 Olympic Games at Innsbruck, Austria, was a big disappointment. He fell in the downhill and lost one of his skis in the slalom. He was better in the giant slalom, finishing fifth. (A giant slalom is a ski race that contains the elements of both a slalom and a downhill. The giant slalom course has only about half the number of gates of a slalom course, but they are set farther apart.)

There were no world championships during the 1965–66 racing season, but Jean-Claude won just about everything else there was to win. In 1966–67, Killy won all the big races in Austria, France, and Italy. He visited the United States early in 1967 and promptly won three races in the White Mountains of New Hampshire. He went on to Vail, Colorado, to win another three. Killy's downhill victory at Vail clinched the world championship for the French team.

The downhill, skiing's most glamorous and dangerous event, gave the most vivid proof of Killy's superiority. In the years before Killy, if a racer captured only one of the major downhills he was held in high esteem. In 1966–67, Killy captured *seven* of them. That is roughly the same as a baseball player winning the triple crown (for the best batting average, most hits, and most RBIs), taking the base-stealing championship, and maybe picking up a Golden Glove award, too.

Killy had an explanation for his string of successes. "I train harder now during the racing season," he told *Sports Illustrated*. "I think about nothing but ski, eat, and sleep. I used to make jokes, you know, with my good friends, the Americans. But they are trying more seriously. They are not as much fun because they are trying to beat me."

By winning all those downhills in

1966–67, Killy came to be idolized in France the way a rock star or Super Bowl hero might be in this country. At one time, he received as many as five hundred letters a day. He had to learn to protect himself from swarms of fans, mostly females, who often descended upon him after races, ready to tear his clothing into souvenirs.

Naturally, Killy was a heavy favorite to win the three Alpine events—the downhill, slalom, and giant slalom—at the 1968 Winter Olympics. The competition was to be held at Grenoble, France, home ground for Killy and his teammates.

Only once before in Olympic history had any skier won three gold medals. That was in 1956, when Austria's Toni Sailer performed the feat. Although many acknowledged that Killy was the finest skier of the day, most people believed he would need an enormous amount of good luck to be able to do what Sailer had done.

First of all, there were many more good racers in 1968, about three times as many as when Sailer was at the peak of his form.

Second, there had been a change in the rules in the giant slalom competition that required each racer to ski the course twice. One run was all that was required in Sailer's day.

Third, another change required that Killy compete in preliminary races that led up to the slalom finals. Sailer never had to worry about eliminations.

And last, there was the pressure. The whole French nation was expecting Killy to win three gold medals. Even General Charles de Gaulle, the President of France, was a Killy fan and planning to be on hand for the competition.

While Killy was heavily favored among his countrymen, he himself realized that there were several skiers who had a real chance to beat him. Among them were two Austrians, Gerhard Nenning and Karl Schanz. Nenning had already won two downhill races that year while Killy had not won any. Killy also respected America's Billy Kidd.

Day by day, the pressure built. Killy, usually jovial and fun-loving, became tense and irritable. Disaster struck about a half an hour before the downhill race began. Killy skied over a patch of ice and scratched the coating of wax that had been applied to his ski bottoms. The wax had been selected and applied with the greatest care. Now it was ruined, and there was no time to rewax.

"Don't worry," a friend told him. "I've been down the course. You'll win anyway. Just get a good start." But Killy knew he had been dealt a heavy blow.

In downhill, skiers start one after the other at one- to two-minute intervals. The racer with the best time wins. Killy was assigned to start fourteenth. As he got set in the starting gate at the top of the steep, windswept course, he knew exactly what was expected of him. Guy Périllat, a teammate of Killy's, starting first, had posted the best time—1:59.93, a record for the slope. Killy had only to beat Périllat's time to win.

Killy exploded out of the starting gate to nose-dive down the slope. At the hairpin turn, he fought for more speed rather than hold steady as the previous skiers had done. In the series of S turns at the middle of the course, Killy slashed and skated his way through. He leapfrogged over some low jumps. Then he dived through the rest of the course to the finish.

When he crossed the line, Killy threw both of his arms over his head in triumph. He had beaten Périllat by .08 of a second. The gold medal was his.

The giant slalom competition was next. Skiers had to make two runs over the course. Each competitor was timed on each run. The skier with the best combined times would be the winner.

Killy was very confident as he readied himself. Normally, he did better in the giant slalom than any other event, but just before he left the starting gate he broke two buckles on one of his boots. There was no time to get new boots, so he pulled his safety straps tighter on that boot. He made up his mind

not to let the mishap bother him. "I was sure I was going to win anyway," he said later.

Perfect conditions—a hard track, a cloudless sky—prevailed for the first run, and Killy responded with a brilliant effort, finishing 1.2 seconds ahead of his nearest competitor.

It was foggy for the second run, so Killy skied more cautiously, but the poor conditions didn't affect the outcome. For the two runs, Killy finished more than two seconds ahead of his closest challenger. Now Killy had two golds. The big question was whether he could score a historic triple by winning the slalom.

Killy first had to qualify for the finals, however. This did not please him. "It is ridiculous," he said, "that I am obliged to beat British and Lebanese racers in order to make the finals." When he did make the qualifying run, he posted the fastest time of the 102 racers.

The finals loomed as one of the most exciting days in skiing history. Many thousands of spectators were expected. Millions would watch on television.

Unfortunately, the weather did not cooperate. On the day of the race, thick fog blanketed the mountain. One spectator said it was so bad that if you leaned forward a little and adjusted your binoculars, you could see your feet. The racers complained that when they snaked their way down the slope, they could never see more than two gates ahead. But officials refused to reschedule the race. Any postponement, they said, would cause conflicts with other events on the schedule.

Killy had the fastest time on the first run over the fog-shrouded course. He also posted the fastest time on the second run.

But as Killy and his supporters were celebrating his magnificent victory, a Norwegian skier named Hakon Mjoen emerged from the gloom to knife across the finish line. His time was announced as being faster than Killy's, but Mjoen admitted to missing at least two gates in the dense fog and was disqualified. Killy still owned the gold.

Then Karl Schranz arrived. He, too, posted a better time than Killy. Schranz began to celebrate. He told a reporter: "You always expect a victory like mine when you train as hard as I did."

Schranz stopped celebrating when a gatekeeper on the course reported that he had swept past two gates, 18 and 19, the same ones that Mjoen had missed. When Schranz protested that he had not missed any gates, officials called a meeting. It lasted five hours. The officials looked at television tapes of the race and heard testimony from the gatekeeper. They decided to dis-

qualify Schranz. The third gold medal was Killy's to keep.

The gold medals changed Killy's life. He turned his back on the life of a ski racer, on the hard training and the discipline. He signed contracts endorsing magazines, ski resorts, ski clothing and equipment, automobiles, and an airline. He posed for advertisements, attended sales meetings, and went on personal appearance tours. He starred in his own television show and made a movie.

Then in 1972 Killy shocked the ski world by announcing he was giving up the comforts of his retirement to return to the slopes. He was not going to be competing for gold medals. He was going to turn professional and compete for prize money as a member on the American ski racing tour.

In his first four races, Killy won nothing. Only occasionally did he show glimpses of his old dash and skill. But week by week, Killy improved. As the tour entered its final stages, he was winning regularly. He ended up by winning pro skiing's individual championship and also was the tour's leading money winner.

After his triumphs as professional, Killy retired a second time and set up headquarters in Geneva, Switzerland, as an international businessman. He manufactured ski clothes and tested skiing equipment. He married former actress Danièle Gauber. He and his wife have three children.

Killy enjoys being a businessman. He often said that there was nothing in the world that could entice him to compete again. He had, he said, "proved all there was to prove." Nobody could argue with that.

Additional Reading

Killy, Jean-Claude, with Al Greenberg. *Comeback*. New York: Macmillan Publishing Co., 1974.

Billie Jean King

Wonder Woman
1943–

When Billie Jean Moffitt (King is her married name) was a student at Poly Technical High in Long Beach, California, in the late 1950s, she had to make an important decision.

She absolutely loved sports. She played basketball, softball, and tennis. But in those days, girls weren't supposed to be jocks. "The kids at school thought I was crazy," she once recalled. "They laughed at me. I was an outcast."

Billie Jean had to make up her mind. Was she going to continue being a jock and risk being called a weirdo the rest of her life? Or was she going to give up sports and become a nice, quiet little girl, just so everyone would think she was "normal"?

"The heck with being 'normal,'" Billie Jean said to herself. She decided to follow her dream.

She was eleven when she bought her first tennis racket out of earnings from neighborhood odd jobs. That same year, she played her first important match. Her opponent was a much older girl, Marilyn Hester, a junior at the University of Southern California. In women's tennis, a match is made up of three sets of games. The first player to win two sets is the winner of the match. Billie Jean managed to win, 6–3, 6–4, but she was still so inexperienced that she wanted to quit after winning the first set.

Billie Jean first created a stir in 1962 when, as a pudgy eighteen-year-old, she upset Margaret Smith of Australia in the first round of the All-England Tennis Championships at Wimbledon. Smith was regarded as the world's best women's tennis player at the time. Although Billie Jean lost in the quarter-finals of the singles, her stunning victory was a sign of what was to come.

For almost a full decade beginning in 1966, Billie Jean won just about every tennis championship worth winning. She won the U.S. Open women's singles title in 1967, 1971, 1972, and 1974. At Wimbledon, she did even better, winning the women's singles crown in 1966, 1968, 1972, 1973, and 1975.

Counting her singles titles, plus her championships in women's doubles and mixed doubles, Billie Jean captured a total of twenty Wimbledon titles. That's a total no other player, man or woman, can match. She also won the Italian Open in 1970 and the French Open in 1972.

Thanks to her remarkable record, Billie Jean holds a place among the immortals of the game, but she ranks as much more than a tennis champion. She was a pioneer. As a female superstar in a sport traditionally dominated by men, she attacked the established order with all the fire and determination she displayed on the court. Thanks to her vigorous personality and tireless efforts, women today are accepted on a par with men by tournament organizers, the press and television, and the public. It was Billie Jean who, almost single-handedly, led tennis out of the Dark Ages.

It was a long struggle. "Slowly, day by day, things got better," Billie Jean once recalled. "Finally, I woke up one day and no one was laughing at us anymore. No one was putting us down. No one was telling us we were weirdos."

Billie Jean Moffitt was born on November 22, 1943, in Long Beach, California. Her father was a fireman. Her mother took care of the home.

Both of Billie Jean's parents were interested in sports, and so was her younger brother, Randy. His favorite sport was baseball. Randy eventually became a major leaguer, a pitcher for the San Francisco Giants during the 1970s.

As an eleven-year-old, Billie Jean, stocky and nearsighted, played shortstop on girls' softball teams. She was also a star forward on a girls' basketball team. She was so good in softball that whenever the fire department had a picnic, the men invited her to play on one of their softball teams. Billie Jean's mother wasn't altogether happy about her daughter's choice of sports. She was always saying to her, "Why can't you be a lady?"

Billie Jean asked her father to suggest a sport that was more ladylike. Her father named tennis. "What's tennis?" Billie Jean asked. Her father explained it was a game in which people used rackets with strings to hit balls back and forth over a net. It sounded like fun. She decided to give the game a try.

Billie Jean learned to play tennis on the public courts of Long Beach. From the beginning, she was an attacker. Her coach wanted her to stay back at the baseline and hit ground strokes. That wasn't Billie Jean's style. She kept charging the net, asking, "What's that shot where you hit the ball before it bounces?"

"It's called a volley," she was told. The volley would become a favorite weapon of Billie Jean's in the years that followed.

Billie Jean played tennis every day during the summer vacation, and after school and on weekends when she started attending high school. She talked about wanting to be a champion. Her dream was to play at Wimbledon.

During her teen-age years, it seemed as if Billie Jean's dream would never be fulfilled. Her style of rushing to the net to hit the ball on the fly caused her problems. The girls Billie Jean faced played steady, conservative tennis. They stayed back at the baseline, striving to merely keep the ball in play and waiting for Billie Jean to make a mistake.

Usually they didn't have to wait very long. Often Billie Jean hit the ball so hard it landed outside the court, costing her a point each time. Although she played in many junior tournaments in California, she never won any of them.

Her coach told her to be patient. His advice was not to worry about winning but to concentrate on developing a strong, all-around game. Billie Jean did just that.

Her coach's advice paid off. When Billie Jean was fifteen, she won the Southern California junior championship in her age group.

In 1960, when she was sixteen, Billie Jean reached the finals of the national championship tournament for girls eighteen and under, but she lost to seventeen-year-old Karen Hantze.

The next year Billie Jean was invited to play at Wimbledon. There she teamed with Karen Hantze to win the Wimbledon women's doubles championship. The two American teen-agers were the youngest pair ever to win the Wimbledon doubles crown. In 1962, again teamed with Karen Hantze, Billie Jean won the Wimbledon doubles crown a second time.

At Wimbledon in 1963, Billie Jean fought her way into the singles finals before losing to Margaret Smith (later Margaret Smith Court) of Australia. Afterward Margaret gave Billie Jean some advice: "You know, you've got all the shots. But I always wear you out. I know you don't practice. You don't play enough. I know you could win Wimbledon one day. Why don't you give it a go?"

Billie Jean did, indeed, want to "give it a go." But something was holding her back. At Los Angeles State College (now California State College in Los Angeles), where she had been taking courses, she had met another student, Larry King, and they had decided to get married. Billie Jean figured she would give up tennis and settle down and keep house for her husband.

But Larry encouraged her to seek a tennis career. "You have the potential to be the best in the world," he told Billie Jean. "You can't give that up."

Billie Jean and Larry were engaged in the fall of 1964. Soon afterward, Billie Jean left Larry behind and flew to Australia to spend three months training with Mervyn Rose, a world-class player. "I'm leaving to become the Number 1 player in the world," Billie Jean told her family and friends.

Mervyn Rose showed Billie Jean how to get more slice into her serve and put greater topspin on her forehand drives. He helped her to increase her understanding of tennis strategy. During the training period, Billie Jean also sprinted and jogged to improve her stamina.

Billie Jean returned from Australia in 1965 a much smarter and stronger tennis player. Not long after her return, she and Larry King were married.

In the early months of 1965, Billie Jean swept to one victory after another. Her big test came in the U.S. Open that summer. There she faced Margaret Smith in the finals. Billie Jean surged to a 5–3 lead in both sets—but eventually lost. After the match, Margaret told Billie Jean that she was the best player she had ever faced.

"Right then," Billie Jean once recalled, "I knew I had it."

In the years that followed, Billie Jean scored one triumph after another. She won the first of her six Wimbledon singles championships in 1966, overpowering Maria Bueno of Brazil with her blistering serves and strong volleys. The next year, 1967, Billie Jean won the first of four U.S. National Open singles championships. Ann Haydon Jones was her victim in the final.

Her ability to cope with pressure was one reason Billie Jean was able to build such an enviable tournament record. The bigger the match, the better she liked it. "I've always played better under pressure, even as a youngster," she once recalled. "It's just that I seem to get my adrenaline flowing, and my concentration gets better, and everything starts working right."

Despite her many championships and her status as the Number 1 player in the world (a ranking she was to hold seven times), Billie Jean was not content. She felt that female players were victims of discrimination. When Rod Laver or Arthur Ashe, the best male players of the day, won tournaments, they were hailed in headlines. Accounts of Billie Jean's tournament wins were buried in the last paragraphs of the story.

Newspaper reporters didn't take women professionals seriously. They asked Laver and Ashe about their plans for upcoming tournaments. They asked Billie Jean when she was planning to settle down with her husband and have children.

But what bothered Billie Jean more than anything else was the unfair distribution of tournament prize money. Wherever she competed, the men always received more money than the women. The situation reached a low point in May 1970. Billie Jean had just

Billie Jean King's powerful concentration helped propel her to victory in the 1966 Wimbledon women's singles tournament, the first of six times that she was to win that title. *Courtesy of AP/Wide World Photos.*

won the women's singles title in the Italian Open. She stood by as the men's winner was presented with a check for $7,500. Then Billie Jean was handed her check—for $600.

Billie Jean started campaigning for a new series of tournaments for women players. "You women don't have a chance," reporters kept telling her. But Billie Jean kept fighting. "I believed," she once said, "that if women were worth anything, then we could somehow convince people to come and watch us play."

By 1971, the Women's Tennis Circuit was a reality. Big cash prizes were offered by the sponsor, Virginia Slims cigarettes. Billie Jean racked up so many wins in Virginia Slims competition in 1971, she became the first woman athlete to earn more than $100,000 in a year.

Billie Jean also helped to convince her fellow players to form a labor organization to represent them in their dealings with tournament officials and television networks. The organization came to be named the Women's Tennis Association. Billie Jean was elected its first president. She remained active with the organization in the years that followed.

What was perhaps Billie Jean's most significant match didn't take place at Wimbledon or Forest Hills or the National Tennis Center. It didn't involve Margaret Smith, Evonne Goolagong,

Chris Evert, or any of the other top female players.

The match took place at the Houston Astrodome on the night of September 20, 1973. Her opponent was Bobby Riggs, a 55-year-old former Wimbledon champion and one of the cleverest players in tennis history. Their match was one of the most watched events of all time.

It came about as a result of a challenge issued by Riggs. "You say that women provide a brand of tennis equal to men," Riggs told Billie Jean. "Well, prove it. I say that you not only cannot beat a top male pro, you cannot even beat a tired old man like me."

Billie Jean had never said that women players were as good as men. What she had said was that women could attract crowds that were just as big as those men drew. She rejected Riggs' challenge.

Then Riggs challenged Billie Jean's old rival, Margaret Smith, to a match. Margaret agreed—and Bobby beat her.

"Any man can beat any woman," Riggs boasted afterward. "Women always choke."

When Riggs challenged Billie Jean a second time, she accepted. She wanted to avenge Margaret's loss and put Riggs in his place. She also wanted to collect the $100,000 in prize money that was to go to the winner.

Some people said that Billie Jean made a mistake in accepting Riggs' challenge. It was believed that he would set the pace and tempo of the match with his soft serves and feathery·lobs. Said Arthur Ashe: "Bobby will jerk Billie Jean around so much she'll look like a yo-yo."

More than 30,000 people turned out for the match. Fifty million more watched on television. A band played loud and brassy music. Big banners, the kind usually seen only at baseball or football games, were hung about the Astrodome by the fans.

Once the match got underway, it was all Billie Jean. Her strong serves, powerful groundstrokes, and sharp volleys put Riggs on the defensive. She made him keep running from one side of the court to the other. When he tried lobbing the ball high into the air, hoping she'd lose sight of it in the bright lights, Billie Jean smashed it back past him. It was one of the best performances of her life. She won in straight sets, 6–4, 6–3, 6–3.

Billie Jean was delighted with her win. She called it the most important of her career.

Billie Jean continued to play tournament tennis well into the 1980s. Sometimes her opponents were women who were half her age. As recently as 1982, she was ranked in the Top 10 among American women.

During the late 1980s, Billie Jean continued to compete, playing in about five tournaments a year on the 35-and-over circuit. "My racket works fine," she said, "but I have lost power. I can't cream an egg."

Billie Jean's pioneering spirit never ebbed. In 1985, her husband founded Team Tennis, a tennis league that planned to operate teams in eight American cities. Billie Jean was named to head Team Tennis. As such, she was the first woman commissioner of a sports league.

Not long after she took on the job, a writer for *Tennis* magazine asked Billie Jean how she hoped to be remembered. This was her answer: "If I've motivated people to do more, be happier or have higher self-esteem, then that's fine. Maybe I'd like to be remembered as someone who made a difference." There can be no doubt that she will be.

Additional Reading

King, Billie Jean, with Frank Deford. *Billie Jean*. New York: Viking Press, 1982.

Bob Mathias

King of the Decathlon
1930–

Only ten weeks before the Olympic Games in 1948, Virgil Jackson, coach of the Tulare, California, high school track team, said to his star performer: "Bob, what do you know about the decathlon?"

"The decathlon?" said seventeen-year-old Bob Mathias. "What's a decathlon?"

The decathlon, explained Jackson, was the most demanding test of track and field skill and endurance ever devised. It involved competing in ten different events in a period of two days.

The decathlon was to be one of the featured events of the Pasadena Games, to be held in June. Did Bob want to enter, Jackson wanted to know. If he did well in the event, then continued to train and compete, he might even have a chance to qualify for the 1952 Olympics, four years away.

"Why not?" said Mathias. Although he had never entered a decathlon before, and five of the ten events were brand new to him, Mathias won the decathlon competition at the Pasadena Games that summer with an amazing 7,094 points. Bob Mathias was on his way.

No test in sports is as tough as decathlon. Every competitor has to be able to run a fast short race, a fast long race, and do well in an endurance run. He has to have the spring of a high jumper and the strength of a shot-putter. It takes plenty of courage, too.

In other words, the decathlon athlete has to be able to do everything a good athlete should be able to do. It's often said that the Olympic decathlon champion is the greatest all-around athlete in the world. What's incredible about Bob Mathias is that he was able to claim that billing not once but twice.

Excellence in sports was something of a tradition in the family of Robert Bruce Mathias, who was born on November 17, 1930, in Tulare, California. He was the second child in a family of three boys and a girl. Bob's father, a physician and surgeon, had been an All-State football player at the University of Oklahoma.

When Bob was still very young, he and his brother Gene, who was three years older, dug a cave in a hillside near their home. They'd squirm their way into it, build a fire and roast potatoes. When their father learned about the cave, he ordered the boys to seal it up. "It can collapse at any time," he told them. "You'd both be killed."

To replace the cave, Dr. Mathias had an array of gym equipment installed in the Mathias's spacious backyard— swings, chinning bars, and weight-training equipment. He also had a short track for sprinting built. The area soon became a popular meeting place for neighborhood youngsters. "Mornings, afternoons and nights, it seemed there was a track meet going on in our backyard," Mrs. Mathias once said. "On

Sundays the parents would come over to watch their kids compete."

Bob was a big winner in those Sunday get-togethers in the Mathias backyard. The same was true at track meets at grade school. In high jump competition at the age of twelve, Bob once cleared 5 feet, 6 inches, a remarkable height for a grade-schooler.

At Tulare High School, where he became the senior class president, Bob was a sports sensation. As a 6-foot, 190-pound running back on the football team, he averaged 9 yards every time he carried the ball. In basketball, he averaged 18 points a game.

He was even better in track and field. In three years of competition, Bob won 40 first places and broke 21 records. In 1947, he reigned as the state champion in the discus, shot put and high hurdles, and he was the second best performer in the high jump.

Virgil Jackson, Bob's coach, couldn't have been more impressed. It was rare for an athlete to do so well in so many different events. Jackson had an idea. "I think you could compete for the Olympic decathlon championship," he said to Bob. "Of course, we're too late for the 1948 Olympics. But if you start right now, I think you could be ready for the Olympics in 1952."

Bob shrugged and said he'd think about it. It was fall, and there was football to prepare for. And after that, there'd be basketball.

In the spring of 1948, Virgil Jackson and Bob talked again about starting a four-year training program that would prepare Bob for the 1952 Olympics. Of the ten decathlon events, Bob knew little or nothing of five of them. He had never run the 400-meter or 1,500-meter races, except in practice. He had never broad-jumped in competition. (The broad jump is called the long jump today.) He had never pole-vaulted and he had never even seen a javelin.

Every day that spring, from after school until darkness fell, Bob practiced on the dusty Tulare track. He ran sprints to increase his speed. He ran long distances to build his stamina.

Early that summer Jackson entered Mathias, then seventeen, in the annual Pacific Coast games at Pasadena, California. Bob threw the javelin 171 feet and pole-vaulted 11 feet, 6 inches. Both efforts were good for first-place finishes.

Scoring in decathlon competition is on the basis of a complicated point system, with the judges awarding a certain number of points to each athlete in each event, depending on his performance. When the judges added up each athlete's points for all ten events, Mathias was the surprise winner.

Afterward, Bob was bursting with confidence. "Coach," he said to Jackson, "I don't see any point in waiting for 1952. I want to compete *this* summer."

Jackson wasn't quite as confident as his pupil. "The tryouts are only two weeks away," he said. "They're way back east in New Jersey. And you'll be up against the top guys from all over the country. Do you really think you'll have a chance?"

"Yes," Bob said, "I do."

Two weeks later, in Bloomfield, New Jersey, the unknown competitor from Tulare, California, went up against the top decathlon athletes of the country. They included Irving (Moon) Mondschein, the three-time national champion. Mathias outscored Mondschein and everyone else by a healthy margin.

One month later, on a hot July afternoon, Bob was in London, attired in his blue and white uniform, as the United States team marched into Wembley Stadium for opening ceremonies of the Games. A crowd of 82,000 cheered the more than 6,000 athletes. Then a lone runner, carrying a torch, circled the red clay track and lit the Olympic flame, thereby signaling that the Games were officially opened.

The decathlon competition was held on two successive days—five events one day and five the next. Twenty-six athletes from nineteen countries had entered the competition.

Bob Mathias is the only athlete to have twice won the Olympic decathlon. *Courtesy of the United States Olympic Committee.*

The first event was the 100-meter sprint. Bob finished second in 11.2 seconds.

The broad jump was next. Bob's inexperience was obvious, and he finished. eighth. In the shot put, he managed to heave the 16-pound metal sphere only 42 feet, a poor showing.

Bob was far behind the leaders as he readied himself for the high jump. He knew that if he didn't do well in this event he might as well pack his bags and head for home. At 5 feet, 9 inches, a height that he had cleared hundreds of times, Bob brushed against the bar, knocking it into the pit. Then he failed a second time. On his third and final try, Bob exploded over the bar, and when he tumbled into the pit he could tell from the crowd's loud roar that the bar was still in place.

Bob continued clearing the bar until he had been raised to 6 feet, 1 inch, which enabled him to finish in a tie for first place. He then won the 400-meter run. At the end of the first day, with five events completed, Bob was in third place, 51 points behind the leader.

At nine-thirty the next morning Bob was back out on the track, jumping up and down to keep warm. A cold drizzle was falling, making for hazardous footing, but the rules would not permit a postponement. Because of the bad weather, the program soon fell behind schedule. The final events—the pole vault, javelin throw, and 1,500-meter run—had to be conducted as darkness gathered.

In the pole vault, officials lit the runway with flashlights. Bob used a white sneaker to mark his takeoff point. Despite the conditions, he managed to clear 11 feet, 5 inches to take first place.

The javelin competition was even more bizarre. Officials held flashlights to indicate the foul line. When Bob threw, the javelin disappeared into the darkness. Everyone listened for the thud. Then officials with flashlights scurried about to look for the mark created by the spear when it touched down. Bob threw the javelin 31 feet farther than his closest competitor.

By the time of the final event, the 1,500-meter run, Bob held a commanding lead. Even a slow time in the race would give him the championship. When he crossed the finish line, a small, weary band of Americans cheered him. The 8,042 points Bob accumulated in winning broke a fourteen-year-old record.

Back in Bob's hometown of Tulare, the news of his victory set off a celebration. People ran into the streets shouting the good news. Factory whistles blared, auto horns honked, and there was a hastily organized parade in his honor. Two weeks later, when Bob came home, more than 10,000 people lined the streets cheering him. A huge banner over the town's main street read: TULARE, HOME OF BOB MATHIAS, OLYMPIC AND U.S. DECATHLON CHAMPION.

Bob's record as a student at Tulare High did not come close to equaling his athletic performance, and he had failed to pass his college entrance examinations. Thus, after his return from London, from the Olympics, he returned to school, enrolling at Kiskimineta Springs School—Kiski Prep, for short— in Salzburg, Pennsylvania.

At Kiski Prep in the fall of 1949, Bob played football well enough to receive dozens of college scholarship offers. He chose Stanford in Palo Alto, California. There he became an outstanding running back and a member of Stanford's Rose Bowl team on January 1, 1952.

But Bob had his eye on the 1952 Olympic Games, which were to be held in Helsinki, Finland. He wanted to become the first athlete in history to win the Olympic decathlon twice.

Bob took every opportunity to perfect his form. In 1949 and 1950, he won the national decathlon title a second and third time. He captured the championship a fourth time in 1952. No other athlete had ever won the national title four times.

Between Olympics, Bob grew 3 inches and gained 17 pounds. At 6-foot-3, 204 pounds, he scarcely resembled the seventeen-year-old who had stunned the world in 1948.

Despite his increased size and strength, Bob realized that winning the championship again was not going to be an easy matter. He would have to overcome several obstacles. For one thing, the executive committee of the International Amateur Athletic Federation had changed the decathlon scoring system. Mathias's world record of 8,042 points had been reduced to 7,443 points. The new system of scoring gave added importance to the decathlon's running events, in which Europeans excelled.

Another stumbling block was the caliber of the competition. After the 1948 Olympic Games, in which Russian athletes had fared poorly, the Soviet Union had embarked on an all-out effort to establish itself as the Number 1 nation in amateur sports. Russian athletes were going to be a major force in Helsinki.

Perhaps the most difficult obstacle of all was psychological. No one had ever won the decathlon in two Olympics. The thought occurred to Bob that perhaps it was impossible to do so.

On the opening day of the decathlon competition, the Russians beat Bob in the discus. Then Bob pulled a thigh muscle and could do no better than finish sixth in the broad jump.

Bob Mathias set world records at the 1948 Olympics—and broke them in 1952. *Courtesy of the United States Olympic Committee.*

But in the next event, Bob fought off the stabbing pain to sprint 400 meters in 50.2 seconds, the fastest time of his life. Then he leaped off that pulled muscle to win the high jump, clearing the bar at 6 feet, 3 inches.

Mathias entered the second day of competition in real pain, his leg heavily bandaged, but he was far out in front of the competition. He could coast and still win.

But Bob had no thought of doing less than his best. In the javelin, he unleashed his all-time best throw—194 feet. Then he cleared 13 feet in the pole vault.

Only one event remained, the 1,500-meter run. By now Bob had already won the gold medal. His coaches told him to merely jog around the track for easy points, but Bob knew he had a chance to beat the world record he himself had established in 1949. Despite his pain and fatigue, Bob ran away from the field, finishing in 4:50.8, a record time for the decathlon. He thereby shattered his own world record, scoring 7,887 points (under the revised scoring system).

Bob Mathias never entered another decathlon. After his graduation from Stanford, he served for two years in the Marine Corps, then moved on to a career in films. He appeared in four movies, including one devoted to his life story. Mathias then joined the U.S. State Department, until in 1965 a friend asked him whether he would like to run for a seat in the U.S. House of Representatives, representing his home district of Tulare. Politics loomed as even a bigger challenge than the decathlon. Bob decided to give it a try. He won four consecutive congressional terms.

Like a good number of Republicans, Mathias was defeated for reelection in 1974 in the wake of the Watergate scandal. He then became a full-time consultant to the President's Council on Physical Fitness and a part-time fund-raiser for the U.S. Olympic Committee (U.S.O.C.).

The 1976 Olympic Games were a disappointment for the United States. Athletes from the Soviet Union and East Germany dominated the competition. The U.S.O.C. announced a long-range program to improve the performance level of American athletes. A key element would be an official U.S. Olympic Training Center to be established at Colorado Springs, Colorado. The U.S.O.C. wanted Mathias to be the first director of the training center. Would he accept the job?

"After all the Olympics had done for me, I jumped at the chance," he said. "I thought the center could fill an important need. We're so different from the Soviets and the Eastern bloc countries, with their centralized regimes and their ministries of sport.

"We really needed some continuity and direction within our democratic system to help our athletes. I considered it a real challenge."

When Bob arrived at Colorado Springs to begin work, he found nothing but an abandoned Air Force base. "For the next two years," he said, "I was in the construction business—fixing pipes, putting in light bulbs, and redoing the barracks to make them liveable."

Under Mathias's direction, the center became the permanent home of the U.S. national teams in weightlifting and volleyball. Being trained at the center became the goal of every athlete who showed world-class promise. By March 1983, more than 12,000 American athletes had benefited from the center's facilities.

Late in 1983, confident that the center was running smoothly, Mathias moved on, taking a job as the first executive director of the National Fitness Foundation based in Indianapolis. The foundation represents an organized effort to educate schools and businesses about the benefits of exercise.

Mathias continues to be concerned about his own fitness. He weighs himself every day. At age 55, he is only 16 pounds heavier than he was at seventeen. He follows no special diet, but when his weight edges above 220, he starts cutting back. "I gave up peanuts," he once said.

Mathias starts each morning with stretches and situps and works out regularly on a miniature trampoline. He hates jogging. "I had to run too much when I was training, and I found it boring," he said. Instead, he stays trim by playing tennis and racquetball. And he skies all winter.

Throughout his life, Mathias has remained a legend in American sports. He paved the way for other celebrity athletes, notably Rafer Johnson, who captured the decathlon title for the United States in 1960, and Bruce Jenner, the winner in 1976.

But Mathias is the only athlete to have won the decathlon twice. Even today, Mathias himself shakes his head in amazement at the thought of what he did.

Willie Mays

The Amazin' One
1931–

Excitement. Perfection. Those were the words for Willie Mays, the first black teen-ager to break into the major leagues. In a career that began in 1951, when Mays was a rookie center fielder for the New York Giants, and spanned more than two decades, he electrified crowds with his sensational fielding, explosive hitting, and daring base-running.

Anyone who ever saw him play has one memory or another of Mays in a hero's role, a moment in which he hit a clutch home run, made a fantastic catch, or uncorked an incredible throw.

There was the 1964 All-Star Game, for instance. Mays, who had been held hitless, came to bat in the bottom of the ninth, with the National League trailing by one run.

On the mound for the American League was Dick Radatz, at 6-foot-5, 260 pounds, the Monster Man of the Boston Red Sox. He was one of the best, if not *the* best, relief pitchers of the time. He had been called into the game two innings before and had retired six straight men, four on strike-outs.

Radatz fired two quick strikes. The third pitch was in close and Mays leaned back. Willie fouled off the next pitch and the one after that. He was merely trying to protect the plate, waiting for a pitch he could hit.

Willie continued to foul off pitches, eight of them in all, eventually working the count to 3-and-2. Then Radatz missed by a fraction of an inch on the outside. Mays went hurrying down to first base.

A baseball strategist would not be

likely to advise a runner to steal with his team a run behind in the ninth inning with nobody out. But Willie sometimes set his own strategy. "When I see a base out there," he always said, "I just want to get it."

Orlando Cepeda came to the plate. As Radatz got set to pitch, he peered over his shoulder at Willie. He was obviously bothered by him, afraid that he was going to take off for third.

Second baseman Bobby Richardson, noting Radatz's discomfort, edged closer to the base. That was a mistake. Cepeda lifted a fly into short right field toward the foul line. Because he was out of position, Richardson could not get to it. Willie had rounded third base by the time first baseman Joe Pepitone picked up the ball.

Willie faked a move toward home. Pepitone, afraid Willie would beat the ball, hurried his throw. It was far off target. Willie exploded for the plate, sliding in with the tying run.

Later in the inning, Johnny Callison hit the game-winning home run for the National League. But no one had any doubt who was the real hero.

Most people agree that Mays's greatest moment in baseball involved a catch. It occurred off of the bat of Cleveland's Vic Wertz in the opener of the 1954 World Series. The game, played at the old Polo Grounds in New York,

was a 2–2 tie in the eighth inning, with the Indians at bat. Runners were on first and second; nobody was out.

Left-hander Don Liddle whipped in a pitch to Cleveland's broad-backed slugger, Vic Wertz. Wertz smashed a tremendous line drive toward right-center field, way over Mays's head. It looked as if the ball was headed for the bleachers, 460 feet away.

Willie turned his back to home plate and started running. He had his arms stretched out in front of him, the glove out. He kept running and running. Then he glanced over his left shoulder and the ball fell into the glove while he was still on the dead run.

There was more to it than that. Although off-balance, Willie whirled and fired the ball to the distant infield in an effort to keep the base runners from moving up.

Mays had turned a triple or an inside-the-park homer into a long out. The Indians lost the game on that catch, for the Giants put across the winning runs in the tenth inning on a home run off the bat of Dusty Rhodes.

That kind of play was fairly typical for Willie Mays. He played center field with a dazzle that has seldom been approached.

Yet Mays is remembered more for his hitting than for his glove. He smacked 660 home runs during his career, which puts him third on the all-time list behind Hank Aaron (with 755) and Babe Ruth (714). But neither Aaron nor Ruth had the all-around baseball ability of Mays, who also had 338 stolen bases.

Mays batted over .300 ten times, including seven years in a row, and he had eight consecutive seasons with at least 100 RBIs (runs batted in). He had a career batting average of .302. He was the National League's Most Valuable Player in 1954 and again in 1965. He was elected to the Hall of Fame in 1978, the first year he was eligible for the honor.

Throughout his career, Mays was often compared to Mickey Mantle, one of the game's most feared power hitters, a superstar with the New York Yankees at the same time Mays was toiling for the Giants.

Their lives and careers were similar in many ways. They were both born the same year, 1931. They both arrived in the major leagues in the same city in the same year, 1951. They played the same position, center field.

Almost immediately, fans began to ask, which one is the best?

Mantle could hit the ball farther than Mays, and he could do it from either the right or left side of the plate. Mays was strictly a right-hand hitter. And Mantle was one of the fastest men in the game. But Mays had better all-around ability, was a much better fielder. He seemed to make an incredible catch almost every game. And Mays not only hit home runs, he hit consistently. A batting average that sometimes got quite gaudy was proof of that.

The debate went on for years. But in 1957, Mantle injured his shoulder, which made it difficult for him to throw. (By 1965, the pain was so bad he could hardly throw at all.) Then, in 1963, Mantle broke a bone in his left foot and tore cartilage in his knee. Although Mickey continued to play until 1968, he was at a point of retiring in 1965.

But Willie, in the mid-1960s, was getting his second wind. In 1965, he hit a sparkling .317 and won Most Valuable Player honors. He also began hitting home runs at an unprecedented pace— 47 in 1964, 52 in 1965. Early in 1966, Willie hit home run number 512. That homer broke Mel Ott's National League record. At the time Willie retired, only Babe Ruth was ahead of him on the all-time home-run list.

Mantle and Mays were very different in personality. Mantle was moody and often suspicious when not among close friends. He had great pride, great determination.

Willie, in his early years with the Giants, was open and friendly. He played baseball with a great joy, as if swinging a bat and chasing down a long fly ball were the most wonderful things in the world.

After he retired from the game in 1973, Mays was sometimes asked who was the best player he ever saw. "I was," he always answered. He got very few arguments on that.

Willie Mays's roots are in Alabama. He was born in Westfield, a steel-mill town not far from Birmingham, on May 6, 1931. His father was an outfielder for the Birmingham Black Barons of the Negro National League. He was known as "Kitty Cat" because of the fluid grace with which he moved. By the time Willie was three, he and his father often played catch.

Willie's parents were divorced when he was still a small child. He then went to live with an aunt, Sarah Mays, in Fairfield, Alabama.

At the Fairfield Industrial High School, Willie took courses in cleaning and pressing. The high school had no baseball team, but Willie starred in football and basketball. "I was the best athlete the school had," he once said.

He played baseball for local semi-pro teams. When he was sixteen, his father got Willie a tryout with the Black Barons. Willie made such a good impression on Piper Davis, the manager, he was asked to join the team.

Willie was sixteen, a high school sophomore at the time. During the school year he played only on Sundays in the Birmingham area, but during the summer months he crisscrossed the country with the Barons in their creaky bus, playing local black teams. "The older guys watched over me," he once recalled. In the two years he played for the Barons, Willie developed a good batting eye, hitting .310.

At this time, major league baseball was going through a period of enormous change. In 1947 the Brooklyn Dodgers had signed Jackie Robinson, the first black player in modern major league history. Robinson was named the National League's Rookie of the Year in 1948 and helped the Dodgers win the pennant.

Suddenly major league clubs were very interested in black teams and got busy scouting them. Young black players such as Willie realized that there were now career opportunities in the majors.

In the spring of 1950, when Willie was still a member of the Barons, a scout for the New York Giants saw him play. Scouts look for young players who can hit, hit with power, have good speed on the bases, and own a strong and accurate throwing arm. Willie got high marks in every category.

After he graduated from high school,

Willie was offered a $5,000 bonus to sign with the New York team. The Giants also gave the Barons $10,000.

The Giants then assigned Willie to their Class B farm team at Trenton (New Jersey) in the Inter-State League. Willie felt as if he was being demoted. The Black Barons, he knew, were a much better team than Trenton.

Willie was a star at Trenton, batting .353 in 81 games. He was rewarded with a promotion to the Minneapolis (Minnesota) Millers in the American Association, a Triple A league. After 35 games with the Millers in 1951, Willie was hitting a lofty .477.

One May day, Willie had the afternoon off. He went to a double feature. When the first film had ended, the lights went on and a man walked out on the stage.

"Is Willie Mays here?" the man said. "Your manager wants you at the hotel."

Mays ran to the hotel where the team was staying, worried that something had happened to his father or his aunt Sarah.

But the manager was smiling when he greeted him. "Congratulations!" he said. "The Giants want you! You're going to the big leagues." Willie was eighteen days past his twentieth birthday.

Willie began his long career with the Giants with one hit in his first 26 at-bats. He began having doubts whether he could hit big league pitching. But manager Leo Durocher, hailing Willie as "the best rookie I've ever seen," told him not to worry, that he would remain in the lineup no matter what he did or didn't do. Soon after, Willie was in the midst of a hitting streak. At the same time, he was, as one sportswriter put it, covering center field "like a tent."

Willie's hustle and zest for the game ignited the Giants. On August 11 that season, the team stood 13½ games behind the Brooklyn Dodgers (later the Los Angeles Dodgers). The Dodgers began losing; the Giants kept winning.

On the last day of the season, the two teams were tied. The Giants won the playoff. Willie was named the National League's Rookie of the Year.

In the World Series against the New York Yankees, won by the Yankees in six games, Mays had 4 singles in 22 at-bats.

Willie has one memory of that series he will never forget. Before the first game, a photographer approached and said to Mays, "Come on, Willie. We want to take a picture of you and Joe DiMaggio together."

The 36-year-old DiMaggio, one of the greatest players of the day, was in the final season of his glorious career. He had always been Willie's idol. It was a great thrill for Willie to meet DiMaggio

Willie Mays's most famous play was this seemingly effortless catch of a ball hit to deep center

and chat with him. The two men later became close friends.

Willie's baseball career was interrupted in 1952. The Korean War had erupted in 1950. North Korea, aided by Communist China, attacked South Korea, which was supported by the United States and other members of the United Nations. Willie, like many other young men, was drafted into the army. He spent almost two years at Fort Eustris, Virginia, where he was assigned to the athletic department.

The Giants finished second in the standings in 1952 and fifth in 1953. When Willie returned in 1954, he hit .345 to lead the league, smacked 41 home runs, drove in 110 runs, and was named the league's Most Valuable Player. The Giants won the pennant and swept the Cleveland Indians in the World Series, four games to none.

Mays and the Giants moved west to San Francisco in 1958. Willie found making the change difficult. He had been adored by the press in New York.

field in the opening game of the 1954 World Series. *Courtesy of AP/Wide World Photos.*

The fans there had idolized him. It was not like that in San Francisco. Willie heard some boos. But in time, Willie proved to the people of San Francisco that he was as good as everyone in the East had said he was.

As a San Francisco Giant, Willie hit .347 in 1958, the highest average of his career. His 141 RBIs in 1962 and 52 home runs in 1965 were other career highs.

The Giants won the pennant in 1962. Again they faced the Yankees in the World Series, with the Yanks winning in seven games.

Mays always believed the seventh-game victory should have gone to the Giants. The Yankees clung to a 1–0 lead as the Giants came to bat in the bottom of the ninth inning. Two men were out. Matty Alou occupied first base. Mays came to the plate against starter Ralph Terry. He cracked a low line drive toward the right field corner. Right fielder Roger Maris scooped up the ball cleanly and fired it toward the infield, holding

Alou at third base. Willie went into second with a double.

The San Francisco fans were on their feet and screaming for a hit that would win the Series. Willie McCovey was the batter. He promptly belted a line drive that had base hit written all over it, but second baseman Bobby Richardson, playing deep, gloved the ball for the final out.

"That was a base hit that McCovey hit," Mays once told sportswriter John Devaney. "Richardson would never have caught the ball except he was out of position. He was playing on the outfield grass in short-right field. If he had been where a second baseman should have been, the ball would have gone through for a hit. Alou would have scored, I would have scored, and we would have won the Series."

The Giants traded Mays back to New York in 1972. As a Met, Willie helped the team win a pennant in 1973. He was then forty-two years old, in the twenty-second year of his career. In the World Series against the Oakland As, his age showed. Willie hit well enough, but he stumbled and fell under a fly ball and also took a spill on the basepath. After the season he retired as a player, becoming a Met batting coach and goodwill ambassador.

In his last years with the San Francisco Giants and during his years with the New York Mets, Mays had none of his youthful sunniness. He could be rude with autograph seekers and surly with newspaper and television reporters.

His sometimes sour disposition showed when, in 1983, the Giants announced they planned to retire Willie's uniform Number 24. Mays's reaction was that the Giants should have done that years before. "I left the game in 1973," he said, "and they're just now retiring my number. Making it to the Hall of Fame was the thing for me in baseball. I'm not looking for any special favors now."

One thing that embittered Mays was that baseball commissioner Bowie Kuhn had made him give up his coaching and public relations work after he had taken a job as a representative for an Atlantic City gambling casino. Gambling and baseball don't mix, the commissioner said. Mickey Mantle, who also worked for a casino, had been similarly penalized.

But in early 1985, a new baseball commissioner, Peter Ueberroth, reversed Kuhn's ruling, lifting the ban on both Mays and Mantle.

Mays said that he was happy to resume his ties with baseball. The fans surely were glad to have him back. The press, too.

"Never another like him," sportswriter Red Smith once wrote. "Never in this world."

Additional Reading

Mays, Willie, as told to Charles Einstein. *Born to Play Ball*. New York: G. P. Putnam's Sons, 1955.

Mays, Willie, with Howard Liss. *My Secrets of Playing Baseball*. New York: Viking Press, 1967.

Mays, Willie, with Lou Sahadi. *Say Hey: The Autobiography of Willie Mays*. New York: Simon & Schuster, 1988.

Martina Navratilova

Queen of the Courts
1956–

When twenty-four-year-old Martina Navratilova arrived in New York late in the summer of 1981 to compete in the U.S. Open championships, she was more determined than ever to win. Looked upon as the strongest player in women's tennis, Martina had twice captured the All-England championships at Wimbledon, the most respected title in tennis. She had won the French Open and Italian Open and dozens of other tournaments. The U.S. Open was the only major title she had not won. She had never, in fact, even managed to reach the finals.

Martina realized that without the U.S. Open title, she could never claim to be one of the greatest players in tennis history. Champions are supposed to win everything.

There was an added reason why win-

ning the Open was important to her now. Martina, who had been born in Czechoslovakia, had just become an American citizen after six long years of waiting. A victory, she felt, would win her the approval of her new fellow-citizens. That was something Martina wanted very much.

Martina breezed through the tournament's early rounds. In the semifinals, she defeated the popular Chris Evert, who had won the U.S. Open no less than five times. When Martina won the final point to take the game, set, and match, she leaped into the air. Now she was only one step away from the championship. In nine previous tries, she had never before been this close.

Eighteen-year-old Tracy Austin from California was Martina's rival in the final match. Tracy had captured the Open in 1979. A record crowd of 18,892 looked on as Martina crushed Tracy, 6–1, in the first set. She felt certain this was going to be her day. But then Martina began to have problems with her serve. Tracy took the second set. Then Martina's game fell apart completely. The third set and the championship went to Tracy Austin.

Photographers and television cameramen crowded about Martina, who collapsed on a chair and buried her face in a towel. The announcer called out Martina's name as the winner of the runner-up trophy, a small silver ball. Then a marvelous thing happened. The huge crowd stood and started applauding and cheering. The ovation lasted for more than a minute. Martina began crying, but these were tears of appreciation, not sadness. "I knew they were cheering me as Martina," she said in her autobiography. "But they were also cheering me as an American."

When Martina stepped to the microphone, she said, "It took me nine years to get the silver ball. I hope it doesn't take me nine years to get the championship."

The crowd started cheering again. "It was really strange," said Martina. "I never felt anything like it in my life: acceptance, respect, maybe even love." It was one of the most memorable moments of her career.

Two years later, Martina did win the U.S. Open singles championship. She won it again in 1984, 1986 and 1987. She won her eighth Wimbledon singles championship and sixth in a row in 1987. By that time, she was being called the finest women's player in tennis history.

There have been long stretches when Martina was unbeatable. She lost only twice during 1984, a year she captured a record 74 matches in a row. In 1983, she won 16 of 17 tournaments in which she played.

A left-hander, Martina is quick and agile with lightning reflexes. She is known for her cannonball serves and punishing volleys. (When a player at the net hits the ball before it bounces, it's a volley.) Her forehand shots leap off her racket with tricky topspin. Her overheads, as one observer has noted, "make teeth chatter."

There have been periods in her career when Martina has played so well that she has occupied a "zone of her own," as *Sports Illustrated* once put it. In order to beat her, an opponent would have to have a charmed day. Martina has simply been too good for the sport.

Martina Navratilova (pronounced nav-RAH-tee-low-vah) was born on October 18, 1956, in Prague, Czechoslovakia, a mountainous central European country about the size of New York

State. She was not the first tennis player in her family. Her grandmother, Agnes Semanska, had been an outstanding amateur. Her mother, Jana, a big, strong woman, was a good player.

Skiing was the sport that Martina learned first. The family lived at a ski center in the Krkonose Mountains. Martina's mother, a skiing instructor, taught her to ski at the age of two. Martina showed the promise of becoming a great skier. She enjoys the sport to this day.

When Martina was three, her parents were divorced. She seldom saw her father after that. He died when Martina was nine. Years later she learned he had taken his own life.

After the divorce, Martina and her mother moved to the home of her mother's family in Revnice, a suburb of Prague. Her mother joined the local tennis club, and Martina spent so much time at the courts she thought of herself as a "regular court rat."

In 1961 Martina's mother married Mirke Navratil. (In Czechoslovakia, a girl adds the feminine ending "ova" to her father's family name. Martina's real father was Miroslav Subert, so she was Martina Subertova. After her mother's remarriage, she became Navratilova.) Once, in speaking of her stepfather, Martina said: "If he got a dollar for every hour he spent with me, my stepfather would be a millionaire. He loved me so much."

When the weather turned warm and the snow melted, the family spent almost every nice day at the tennis courts. Martina would practice for hours, simply hitting a ball off a wall, using a regulation-sized racket. Sometimes her mother would drag her away from the wall, but as soon as her mother's back was turned Martina would go back to pounding the ball again.

One day her stepfather took Martina out onto the court. The first time she felt the joy of smashing the ball over the net, Martina knew she was in the right place. She remembers that moment to this day. Another time he took her to the Sports Center in Prague to watch a match that featured Rod Laver, the Rocket, one of Australia's great players. Martina stared open-mouthed at Laver, marveling at his power and agility. That's the player I want to be, she thought.

Her stepfather recognized Martina's talent and began coaching her. When she was eight, Martina entered her first tournament, for the twelve-and-under age group. Although officials protested that Martina was too small to compete, she made it to the semifinals before being beaten.

When Martina was nine, her stepfather brought her into Prague to meet

George Parma, one of Czechoslovakia's foremost players, who ran the best coaching program in the city. Martina tried out for the program by hitting balls with Parma. Afterward Parma said to Martina's stepfather, "I think we could do something with her."

Martina began practicing with George Parma every day, even though it meant having to take a train sixteen miles into Prague. She improved steadily, but her life was becoming very hectic. She was always either playing tennis or in school.

In the summer of 1968, when she was eleven, Martina went to the town of Pilsen to play in a junior tournament. While she was there, Czechoslovakia was invaded by Russian armies that crossed the eastern border and rolled across the countryside. Except for riots by some students and workers, the Czechs did not resist. Martina knew her homeland would never be the same.

The invasion cost Martina her coach. George Parma, who had gone to Austria with his wife just before the invasion, did not want to return. He wrote to Martina's father outlining an instruction program she should follow for the rest of the year.

After the Soviet invasion, Czechoslovakia became a "depressed society," Martina has said. No one had any optimism about the future. "I saw my country lose its soul," she said. Even though she was only eleven, Martina began thinking about getting out of Czechoslovakia.

Tennis enabled Martina to visit other countries. In 1969, thanks to her success in junior tournaments at home, she was invited to a tournament in West Germany. She beat one West German player after another and returned home with several medals and a stack of newspaper clippings praising her.

The trip was revealing to her. The people in West Germany were free. They read uncensored newspapers and magazines. They could say what they wanted to say about the government. Not so in Czechoslovakia. Life was becoming hard. People had to wait in long lines to buy food or clothing. Everybody seemed gloomy. There was nothing to laugh about.

By the time Martina was fourteen, she had captured her first national title in the fourteen-and-under age division. Within the next two years, she won three national women's championships and the national junior title to become the nation's top-ranking female player.

In what spare time she had, Martina skied and swam. She also played soccer and ice hockey to strengthen her legs. She had little interest in anything but sports. She was the best student in her class, but she seldom studied. Eventually, Martina dropped out of school.

She now traveled frequently to play in tournaments. She went to West Germany again, then to Hungary and other nations of eastern Europe. She went to the Soviet Union. "Things were worse there than in Czechoslovakia," she noted.

In 1973, Martina was permitted by Czechoslovakian tennis officials to visit the United States for several weeks to compete. Stops on her tour took her to Florida, Massachusetts, Ohio, and New York. Her first impression of America was of the friendliness of the people. They called her by her first name and shared personal thoughts with her right away.

The food in America impressed her, too. She became almost addicted to junk food, particularly pancakes, pizza, ice cream, and Big Macs. In her two-month stay in the United States, Martina gained twenty pounds. She couldn't fit into any of her tennis clothes.

Martina continued to improve as a player. The following year, she fought her way to the finals in the French Open and Italian Open, although eventually losing both. Back in the United States later in the year, she won a Virginia Slims tournament in Orlando, Florida. Her impressive showing on the Virginia Slims tournament circuit helped her to win Rookie of the Year honors from *Tennis* magazine.

Despite her success, Martina was not happy with her game. Although her power and speed enabled her to dominate many opponents, experienced players often simply waited for her to make errors or they hit to her often ineffective backhand. When Martina returned home, she spent almost two months hitting backhands to her stepfather. She also slimmed down.

The hard work paid dividends. In 1975 Martina reached the finals of seven major tournaments, including the French and Italian Opens. With her partner, Chris Evert, she took four doubles titles. She also won another Virginia Slims title. Martina's prize winnings for the year amounted to $200,000. *Tennis* magazine singled her out again, this time naming her Most Improved Player of the Year.

Despite all the good things that were happening, serious problems were developing with officials of the Czechoslovakian Tennis Federation. They objected to Martina's long stays in the United States. They said she was too friendly with Billie Jean King, Chris Evert, and other American players. They said that Martina, who loved American music and food and dressed like an American teen-ager, was acting more and more like an American and less and less like a Czech.

The Czech government wanted "total control" over me, Martina has said. "But the more I won, the less they could control me."

Czech officials toyed with the idea of not allowing Martina to play in the U.S. Open in 1975, but eventually they did grant her permission. During the tournament Martina took a big step. She turned her back on her native Czechoslovakia, asking the American government to let her stay in the United States. U.S. officials granted her request. She was given what is called "permanent resident status." She could live in the United States but she was not a citizen. It was six more years before Martina was granted citizenship.

Martina was not yet nineteen when she made her decision to defect. The year that followed was a lonely one. She was cut off from her family and friends. She knew that if she returned to Prague the Czech government might detain her—that is, take her into custody.

Martina felt rootless and confused. She often spent money in wild sprees but she wasn't really happy. She put on extra weight again.

Her tennis suffered. During her first year in the United States, Martina failed to win a single tournament. In the U.S. Open in 1976, she was beaten in the opening round. Afterward, Martina broke down and wept.

Good friends helped Martina to bounce back. One was Sandra Haynie, a well known professional golfer. Sandra got Martina to practice more. She got her to give up junk foods in favor of healthful foods—fish, fruit and vegetables. For a time Sandra Haynie managed Martina's money and her career. Martina eventually returned to top form.

"No matter where you come from in Europe," Martina once said, "Wimbledon is the tennis championship you honor above all others." It is at Wimbledon, which is just outside London, that the All-England championships are contested. Martina had been hearing about the tournament all of her life. The Czechs who had managed to merely *play* at Wimbledon were greatly honored in her homeland.

At the 1978 Wimbledon championships, Martina was ready to go. She defeated several tough competitors on her way to the finals. There she faced Chris Evert. Known at the time as "America's princess," Chris had been ranked as the best woman tennis player in the world for four consecutive years.

Nervous at first, Martina dropped the first set. Although she trailed in each of the next two sets, she came back to win both, thus becoming the Wimbledon champion and fulfilling her lifelong dream. She was so excited she scarcely felt Chris pat her on the back or heard her words of congratulation.

The year following her first win at Wimbledon, Martina was ranked the world's Number 1 women's tennis player. She continued winning in 1979, capturing Wimbledon a second time. She was ranked Number 1 for the second consecutive year.

Martina's game turned sour in 1980, and she dropped from Number 1 to Number 3. Just as she had been helped by Sandra Haynie at a difficult period earlier in her career, so now two other friends came to her rescue—Nancy Lieberman and Renee Richards.

Nancy, from New York's borough of Queens, was a basketball star. She had won All-America honors at Old Dominion University and then, playing with the Dallas Diamonds of the Women's Professional Basketball League, had become the best player in the sport. (The league folded in 1981.)

Martina and Nancy met in 1981 and became friends right away. Nancy was quick to realize that Martina needed help. She could see that Martina was not in top-notch physical shape. She needed to train harder, to build her strength. Martina, in a bad slump, was ready to try almost anything. She hired Nancy as her trainer.

Nancy pushed Martina harder than she had ever been pushed in her life. She goaded her into running a few miles every day. Together the two women jumped rope and worked with weights. After Nancy taught Martina how to play basketball, the two would spend hours in heated one-on-one competition. And Nancy got Martina to increase her tennis practice sessions to as much as three hours. Previously, forty-five minutes was Martina's limit.

It was difficult for Martina. There was a great deal of pain and more than a few tears. But it worked. Martina shed some pounds she didn't need and added muscles where she had never had them before. She began to feel like a new person.

The same year she began working with Nancy Lieberman, Martina hired Renee Richards as her coach. Renee convinced Martina to work on her serve, getting her to jump into it more, which produced greater power. She taught Martina to add topspin to her backhand, making the ball much tougher to return. She told Martina that she didn't have to accomplish any miracles in order to be a champion. All she really had to do was play steady tennis, forcing her opponents to make mistakes.

Martina also hired a nutritionist, Robert Haas, to advise her about her diet. He got her to stop eating mayonnaise, butter, oils, sodas, and most meats. "Eat to win" was Haas's philosophy. Martina felt lighter yet stronger, thanks to the new diet.

In 1982 Martina was never better, churning out one victory after another. She won 91 of 93 matches. She finished first in 15 of 18 tournaments. In May that year, she again took over the Number 1 spot in the women's tennis rankings.

Illness prevented Martina from doing her best in the U.S. Open in 1982, but she won the event in 1983, defeating Chris Evert. "Mentally, this has to be my biggest win ever," she said after. She won the U.S. Open a second time in 1984. Again, Chris Evert was her victim.

During this period, Martina also captured a Grand Slam. To achieve a Grand Slam in tennis, one must win the four major tournaments—Wimbledon, the U.S. Open, French Open, and Australian Open—in one calendar year. In all of tennis history, only five players have achieved Grand Slams.

During one stretch in 1983 and 1984, Martina won six consecutive Grand Slam events. Maybe that achievement should have been called a Grand-Slam-and-a-half.

During the same period, Martina won 74 consecutive matches, an incredible streak. The previous record, 54 straight, had been held by Chris Evert.

Both of Martina's streaks were halted during the semifinals of the Australian Open in 1984. There, as Martina put it, "History caught up with me."

Helena Sukova was the player who defeated Martina. Sukova, a Czech, was well known to Martina. Her mother, Vera Sukova, was the national women's coach in Czechoslovakia in the years Martina was rising to prominence. Helena, Martina recalled, used to be a ball girl for some of her matches in Czechoslovakia.

In the weeks that followed Martina's loss to Helena Sukova, Martina suffered several other defeats. There was talk that Martina, at twenty-eight, was beginning to slip. Then the real problem surfaced. Martina was having trouble seeing the ball. Once she started wearing eyeglasses, she began winning again.

At Wimbledon in the spring of 1985, Martina faced her old rival, Chris Evert, in the finals. In the months immediately before their meeting, Martina had beaten Chris consistently. But Chris, working with weights, had become stronger and upgraded her game. Martina lost to her in the French Open earlier that year.

As the match got underway, Martina was her aggressive self, attacking the

Martina Navratilova served up defeat to her rival Chris Evert in the final match of this Virginia Slims tournament in 1983, the year in which Navratilova won sixteen of the seventeen tournaments she entered. *Courtesy of AP/Wide World Photos.*

net at every opportunity. Chris won the first set, but Martina took the next two to capture the Wimbledon title once more.

It was Martina's sixth Wimbledon victory and her fourth in a row. In 1987, when she won her eighth Wimbledon Championship, she tied Helen Wills Moody for the most overall Wimbledon singles trophies. Besides her four U.S. Open titles, she also has three Australian Open and two French Open crowns.

Throughout her career, Martina was frequently asked about her goals. She had a standard answer to such questions—"To win a place in tennis history as the best women's player ever." Many people say that is a goal that Martina Navratilova has already achieved.

Jack Nicklaus

The Golden Bear
1940–

He played better than anyone else for twenty years. He won more often. From his first U.S. Amateur win in 1959 to his fourth PGA (Professional Golfers Association) victory in 1980, he dominated the world of golf.

That could only be Jack Nicklaus, called by many the greatest golfer of all time.

Golf is a game that demands great mental discipline. Since the mind controls the body, it is important for the golfer to be able to visualize the perfect swing in his or her mind before playing. This is then reflected in the golfer's shots.

It is in this aspect of the game that Nicklaus was without equal. His mental discipline showed in his cool and deliberate putting stroke. Nick Seitz, editor

of *Golf Digest*, once wrote: "If you had to choose a man to try one putt for all that you own—your house, car, *everything*—you would have to pick Nicklaus."

Whenever Nicklaus thought about his swing or his game in general, he always thought in positive terms. There was no room for negative thoughts.

Pro golfer and later TV announcer Tom Weiskopf once told the story of being on a putting green with Nicklaus as he was lining up a 15-footer. Said Weiskopf: "You've never missed one of those in your life, have you, Jack?"

Nicklaus looked at his friend unsmilingly, then replied: "Not in my mind, I haven't."

Nicklaus's ability to discipline himself mentally, to concentrate, went back to his early days in golf. From the time he took up the game as a ten-year-old, Nicklaus hit every single practice shot as if it counted. There were no unimportant shots, none to be hit carelessly or without thinking.

As a result, Nicklaus was better able to deal with pressure than most other golfers. To him, every shot was serious business. Why should one produce any greater tension than another?

To go with his mental discipline, Nicklaus had marvelous physical gifts. Enormous power, for one. He had massive legs, thighs that were 29 inches around, as big as some golfers' waists. Those legs enabled him to pound every drive 300 yards and more.

Nicklaus always made intelligent use of his power. He never failed to play for position. Explaining his tee shots, he once said, "I try to hit the ball to a specific section of the fairway, not just the fairway in general." By so doing, he would always be in good position for his second shot.

Nicklaus was able to hit his iron shots sky-high, higher than any of his golfing rivals. This meant that they landed softly and stayed put. Seldom would a Nicklaus iron shot go caroming off the green. One writer described his talent in these terms: Jack Nicklaus's iron shots, he wrote, "land as softly as a butterfly with sore feet."

Blond-haired Jack Nicklaus was 6-feet tall and weighed about 180 pounds. He was quite bulky during his early years in competitive golf, and someone suggested "The Golden Bear" as a nickname for him. The name stuck.

Once Nicklaus trimmed his weight and began winning tournaments regularly, it was pointed out that the nickname didn't fit very well. Nicklaus just wasn't bearlike, for often he displayed the killer instinct that all great champions possess. "The Tiger" would have been a better name for him. It suggested how ferocious Nicklaus could be when victory was in sight.

For evidence of Nicklaus's greatness as a golfer, one need look only at his record in the most important tournaments, the so-called "majors." Nicklaus won the U.S. Amateur twice (in 1959 and 1961) and finished second in the U.S. Open before turning professional.

In his years as a pro, Nicklaus won the Masters six times (1963, 1965, 1966, 1972, 1975, and 1986), the U.S. Open four times (1962, 1967, 1972, and 1980), the British Open three times (1966, 1970, and 1978), and the PGA five times (1963, 1971, 1973, 1975, and 1980).

Counting the two amateur titles, that's a total of twenty major championships. Bobby Jones, a golf immortal of the 1930s, won thirteen. No one else came close. Ben Hogan, a golfing great of the 1940s and 1950s, had nine. Arnold Palmer won eight.

Nicklaus also won more than fifty other tournaments. He earned more than three and a half million dollars in prize money, a record.

Nicklaus feels that his record for winning major tournaments will be broken one day. Scarcely anyone agrees.

Jack William Nicklaus was born in Columbus, Ohio, on January 21, 1940. His father, Charles Nicklaus, who owned a chain of drugstores in Columbus, introduced him to golf.

Mr. Nicklaus had suffered an ankle injury in a volleyball game. During his period of recovery, his doctor told him to walk two hours a day to strengthen the ankle. Mr. Nicklaus decided to take up golf. Young Jack went along to keep his father company.

Jack was ten years old when he tried the sport for the first time. He shot 51 for nine holes. He was to show steady improvement for most of the next twenty years.

"By the time Jack was twelve," his father once said, "I couldn't handle him anymore. I remember one day I hit as good a drive as I could hit, maybe 260 yards. I told Jack, 'If you outhit that one, I'll buy you a Cadillac convertible.'"

Jack unleashed a mighty swing. The ball soared high into the air, then came to earth to bound 25 to 30 yards beyond the ball his father had hit. Mr. Nicklaus shook his head in astonishment. "I never outhit him again," Mr. Nicklaus once recalled. (Young Jack didn't let his father forget the promise of a new car. He settled for a Mercury convertible when he graduated from high school.)

Jack Grout, a golf professional who gave lessons in the sport at the Scioto Country Club in Columbus, was one of the first to recognize that Nicklaus could become a champion. He enrolled Jack in his Friday morning instruction class.

Grout encouraged his students to hit the ball as far as they could as a means of stretching their muscles and developing power. When Jack drove the ball, he did not have the smooth swing of other golfers. His stubby fingers choked the club, and he brought his arms back stiffly, his right elbow flying away from his body. But the swing itself, as one writer described it, was "pure thunder," the power pouring into the club head. "Nicklaus hits the ball as squarely and as solidly as a golf ball can be hit," said one observer.

Jack was a good all-around athlete and played other sports besides golf. He was a quarterback in football and did the team's kicking. He played basketball in the winter and baseball in the spring. But golf was his favorite by far. He didn't have to round up a bunch of kids when he wanted to play. He could compete by himself.

"When I got the golf bug, I went overboard," Jack once told *Golf Digest*. "It was nothing for me to go out in the morning in the summertime, hit golf balls for an hour or two, go play 18 holes, come in, have lunch, hit more golf balls until dark." That was a "normal routine" for Jack during his early teen-age years.

The Nicklaus family never took summer vacations. Jack never went to summer camp as a kid. "I played golf," he once said. "That's what I wanted to do."

When he was thirteen, Jack shot a 69 over the 7,095-yard course at Scioto. Even for a top-ranked professional, such a score would have been considered excellent. Some people were already beginning to compare Jack with Bobby Jones, one of golfing's all-time greats. Jones was the first golfer to win the Grand Slam of golf, which meant winning the sport's four major tournaments in one year. Jones had accomplished the feat in 1930 at the age of twenty-eight. (In Jones's day, the Grand Slam consisted of the United States Amateur and United States Open titles, and the British Amateur and British Open championships.)

When, in 1955, Jack competed in his first United States Amateur tourna-ment, Jones was on hand to watch him. All of the attention made Jack jittery, and he played poorly, getting beaten in an early round. It was one of the very few times in his career that Jack faltered because of pressure.

During his four years at Upper Arlington High School in Columbus, Jack continued to work hard to improve his game. In 1956, his junior year in high school, he won his first major tournament—the Ohio Open. He shot a record 64 in the first round.

When it came time for Jack to graduate, he could count a dozen scholarship offers he had received from colleges. His father said, "He was talking about how much this one or that one had offered, how good a deal he could get. I told him to stop thinking about the fun and money and think about getting an education."

Following his father's advice, Jack decided to attend Ohio State University at Columbus. Ohio State had not made Jack a scholarship offer. But he had decided to follow in his father's footsteps and become a pharmacist, and he enrolled in Ohio State's prepharmacy programs. The training he got enabled him to work in his father's stores during vacations. Jack later switched from pharmacy to business administration.

He was also devoting himself to golf. While he did become an outstanding collegiate golfer, Jack failed to make

Jack Nicklaus combined athletic prowess with superb mental discipline, winning tournament after tournament during his remarkable career in professional golf. *Courtesy of the World Professional Golf Association Hall of Fame.*

much of a name for himself on the national scene. In his first National United States Open tournament and in National Junior competition, he did poorly.

A turning point came in 1959, when Jack was chosen to be one of the nine-man team of American amateur golfers to oppose a team of British amateurs in the Walker Cup matches. Held every two years, the Walker Cup is named for George H. Walker, a former president of the United States Golf Association and the organizer of the competition.

The matches were played at Muirfield, Scotland. Jack toured the course like a veteran, winning two of his matches and making a big contribution toward the victory achieved by the American team.

The experience gave Jack's confidence a big boost. He said to himself: "Here I am, playing right alongside these better players. I must be on a par with them." Jack began to demand much more of himself. As a result, he began playing better than he ever had before.

In the months that followed the Walker Cup competition, Jack became one of the best amateur golfers of all time. In September 1959, he captured the National Amateur title. In June 1960, while still an amateur, he finished second to the great Arnold Palmer in the United States Open. Jack's 72-hole score of 282 was the best ever shot by an amateur in National Open history.

The month after his spectacular showing in the Open, Jack married Barbara Jean Bash, whom he had met at Ohio State University. Their first child, a boy, was born the following year.

Jack had been planning to remain an amateur golfer and earn his living in the insurance business, but in November 1961 he changed his mind, announcing he planned to become a golf professional. "I just decided I wanted to play golf," he said at the time. "And I owed it to my family to become a professional."

During his first five months of professional competition, Jack entered seventeen tournaments. While he didn't win any, he never failed to finish in the money.

In June 1962, the world's best professionals and amateurs gathered at the famed Oakmont Country Club near Pittsburgh, Pennsylvania, for the U.S. Open championship. Arnold Palmer, the best-known golfer of the day and the reigning king of the game, was favored to win.

Nicklaus battled Palmer to a tie in four rounds of exceptional golf. Then, in the 18-hole playoff, he defeated Palmer by a score of 71 to 74. Not only had Nicklaus dethroned the king, he had become, at twenty-two, the youngest Open champion in golf history.

Palmer was idolized by millions during his magnificent career. It was he who had brought glamor and excitement to professional golf. He drew bigger crowds when practicing his putting than other golfers attracted on the course. His fans cheered him on during tournaments with cries of "Go get 'em, Arnie!" and "Go, Arnie, go!"

When Nicklaus upset Palmer in the United States Open in 1962, he was unprepared for what followed. Members of "Arnie's Army," as Palmer's fans were called, were so upset that they began to hoot and jeer at Jack. They even booed his good shots. They stood in out-of-bounds areas and held up signs that read: HIT IT HERE, JACK.

Sometimes Arnie's fans were cruel. Jack, who was overweight at the time, heard himself called such names as "Blob-o" and "Whaleman." Not once did Jack lash out at those who taunted him. He endured it all with quiet grace.

Instead, Nicklaus let his shot-making do the talking for him. In 1962, the same year that Nicklaus won his first U.S. Open, Palmer won the British Open. Palmer won the Masters in 1964. Although Palmer continued as a top-flight golfer into the 1970s, he never beat Nicklaus in a major tournament again.

During 1971, the thirty-one-year-old Nicklaus won his second Grand Slam. To capture golf's Grand Slam, one must win the U.S. Open, British Open, Masters, and PGA title in one year. In winning the Grand Slam twice, Nicklaus achieved what no other golfer had ever achieved.

After Arnold Palmer faded, other golfers stepped forward to challenge Nicklaus. Among them were Gary Player, Johnny Miller, Lee Trevino, and Tom Watson. Each would be hot for a time, then drop back into the pack. Nicklaus remained at the top by himself.

Despite his enormous success, Nicklaus never allowed golf to rule his life. He found time for many other interests, most involving his family—his wife, Barbara, and their five children.

Jack's closest friend in North Palm Beach, Florida, where the family lived, was the athletic director at Benjamin High. That's where Jack's kids went to school. Two of the Nicklaus boys were football and basketball stars. Another showed signs of becoming a champion golfer.

When Nicklaus wasn't practicing on the golf course, he was likely to be taking part in some other athletic activity. He enjoyed tennis and bicycling, skiing and basketball, and fishing and hunting. He also did some weightlifting.

Nicklaus watched over a wide range of business interests. Building golf courses was his favorite. "My golf game can only go so long," he once said. "But I'll always be a part of golf because I have the courses."

Nicklaus's victories in the United States Open and Professional Golfers' Association championships in 1980 were his eighteenth and nineteenth major tournament wins. He won a couple of tournaments after that, but no majors.

Year by year, Nicklaus continued in his quest for a twentieth major. Advancing age began to erode his skills. At one tournament, he would drive the ball well but putt poorly. A week later, his putting would be on target but the rest of his game would cause him difficulty.

In 1985, playing in the qualifying round at the United States Open at Oakland Hills in Birmingham, Michigan, Nicklaus missed the cut—that is, he was eliminated from tournament competition because he failed to post a good enough score. It was the first time since 1963 that Jack Nicklaus had missed an Open cut.

Despite the setback, the forty-five-year-old Nicklaus had no thought of retiring. "I've got two choices—try to play well or quit," he said to reporters afterward. Then, grinning, he added, "And I ain't about to quit."

It was a wise decision. In 1986, at the age of forty-six, Nicklaus, with an eagle and two birdies on the closing holes, won the Masters Tournament for a record sixth time. Shooting a stunning 7-under-par 65 on the final round, he beat Greg Norman and Tom Kite by a single stroke.

Walking up the fairways on the last few holes, with cheers resounding on every shot, Nicklaus often had tears in his eyes. "This may be as fine a round of golf as I ever played," he said afterward. "I haven't been this happy in years."

Most golf experts say that Nicklaus's record of twenty victories in major tournament is unbeatable. In that regard, it's similar to Joe DiMaggio's 56-game hitting streak of 1941. And some say the hitting streak mark is likely to be topped before Nicklaus's record of winning twenty majors is broken.

Additional Reading

Nicklaus, Jack, with Ken Bowden. *On and Off the Fairway: A Pictorial Autobiography.* New York: Simon & Schuster, 1978.

Bobby Orr

Lightning on Ice
1948–

How good was Bobby Orr?

"The best, the best ever," said Phil Esposito, the third highest goal scorer in the history of the National Hockey League.

"He was in a class above the superstars," said John Ferguson of the Montreal Canadiens. Ferguson played on five Stanley Cup teams.

"I played in the Orr era," said Don Awrey, a defenseman in the National Hockey League for fifteen seasons. "The other defensemen, like Denis Potvin, Brad Park, Larry Robinson, Serge Savard, and Borje Salming, as great as they were, they couldn't carry his skates."

Bobby Orr stood 5-foot-11, and he weighed about 180. He had blue-gray eyes and thick, light brown hair. He had all the moves, fakes, and tricks that excite the fans. He had a whistling slap shot. He could bring the crowd to its feet with one of his rink-long rushes.

When he was on the ice, the puck was on his stick half the time. Bobby Orr *ran* things.

Orr revolutionized hockey with his magnificent skills. He showed that a defenseman doesn't necessarily have to concentrate on defense, that he can be a scorer, too. Bobby's idea of defense was to poke the puck away from a rival, then skate the length of the rink for either a shot or a pass to a teammate.

Before Bobby joined the National Hockey League (NHL), no defenseman had ever scored more than 20 goals or totaled more than 65 points in one season. (A point is earned for each goal and each assist.) In the season of 1970–71, Orr totaled 139 points. In 1974–75, he scored 46 goals. Orr not only topped the previous marks; he doubled them.

Bobby, who was the NHL's Rookie of the Year in 1967, had assembled an impressive collection of silverware by the time he retired in 1979. He won the Norris Trophy as the league's best defenseman for eight straight years beginning in 1968. Despite being a defenseman, he managed to win the Art Ross Trophy for the league scoring championship in 1970 and 1975.

He won the Hart Trophy as the NHL's most valuable player in 1970, 1971, and 1972, and the Conn Smythe Trophy as the Most Valuable Player in the Stanley Cup playoffs in 1970 and 1972.

Orr established all-time career records for defensemen, including most goals (270), most assists (645), and most points (915).

Denis Potvin of the New York Islanders passed Orr in all three categories during the mid-1980s, but Potvin made it clear that he was no Bobby Orr. "He was the best," Potvin said. "He was the one who came in like Gretzky and changed the game."

Bobby's style of play was called the "Orr effect." It had an enormous impact on the way professional hockey is played. Kids on rinks and frozen ponds all over Canada began imitating Bobby. By the mid-1980s, some of them were playing in the National Hockey League and contributing to the scoring explosion the sport experienced.

Robert Gordon Orr was born on March 20, 1948, in Parry Sound, Ontario, Canada. He was the third of five children. Most boys and girls in Canada learn to skate when they are very young, and Bobby was no exception. By the time he was four years old, he could move across the ice with speed and grace.

Parry Sound offered hockey competition for boys of all ages. The youngest played in the Minor Squirt division. As they got older, they advanced to Squirt, Pee Wee, Bantam, Midget, and Intermediate leagues. Bobby played in them all. A fast skater and slick stick handler, he starred at every level.

From the beginning, Bobby was a defenseman—seeking to take the puck away from opponents, intercepting passes, and blocking shots. Once Bobby got the puck on his stick, he controlled it masterfully. Seldom could anyone knock it away from him.

At the age of eleven, Bobby stood 5-foot-2 and weighed 110 pounds, which was small for a defenseman. Nevertheless, he was playing with fourteen-year-olds on the Parry Sound Bantams.

Bobby's father approached his coach and suggested that he be switched from defenseman to forward. "No," said the coach. "The kid is in his natural position. Anybody can play forward. He's too smart for forward. He belongs on defense."

By the time he was twelve, Bobby's talents had been sniffed out by scouts representing several National Hockey League teams. The Boston Bruins were the first to move toward getting Bobby under contract. In those days, a professional team could gain control of a young player by putting his name on a "protected list." That's what the Bruins did with Bobby.

When he was fourteen, the Boston club signed Bobby to a junior amateur contract and then assigned him to the Oshawa (Ontario) Generals in the Junior A Division of the Ontario Hockey Association. Junior A hockey is a stepping stone to the professional ranks.

Mr. and Mrs. Orr wondered whether this was a good move. "Heck, the boy is only in ninth grade," Mr. Orr told friends. "They want him to go up against players who are four and five years older."

Mrs. Orr believed that Bobby, at fourteen, was too young to leave home. Oshawa, near Toronto, is about 150 miles south of Parry Sound.

But Wren Blair, who had scouted Bobby for the Bruins, assured the Orrs that their son was good enough to play against older boys. If Mrs. Orr didn't want Bobby to leave home, the Orrs could drive him to Oshawa for a game, then drive him back afterward. Sure, it meant driving 300 miles every time Bobby played, but the move was considered vital for his development.

That's how it was done, at least for Bobby's first year at Oshawa. Bobby lived at home and his father drove him back and forth between Oshawa and Parry Sound every time the Generals had a home game.

This arrangement meant that he was not able to practice with the team. Some of the older players grumbled about Orr's being the coach's pet. Their grumbling didn't last long, only until Bobby got a chance to display his skills. He controlled the puck and ran the game whenever he was on the ice. He scored 30 goals in his first season at Oshawa, an exceptional total for a defenseman.

The next season, the Orrs allowed Bobby to live in Oshawa. He boarded with a local family and attended Oshawa High School.

Bobby kept getting better and better. During the 1964–65 season, he scored 34 goals and collected 59 assists, for 93 points. (Each goal and each assist is worth one point.) Never before in the history of the Ontario Hockey Association has anyone scored that many points. The next season, Bobby whipped in 37 goals and had 60 assists for 97 points, breaking his own record. By now, all of Canada was talking about him.

"He not only seems to know what the opposing defense is going to do when he's on the attack," said his coach, Bep Guidolin, "but his judgment of defense is absolutely uncanny. It's almost like he had a magnet on the end of his stick, the way he attracts the puck."

As soon as he reached the age of eighteen and became eligible to play professional hockey, the Bruins called Bobby to Boston to discuss a contract. Bobby shocked the Boston management by bringing an agent, attorney R. Alan Eagleson, with him. No player had ever negotiated with an agent before.

The Bruins offered Bobby a $5,000 bonus for signing and a salary of $8,000. That's about what rookies were paid in those days. Bobby refused the offer, saying that he would not sign unless he was rewarded with an amount that matched his ability. The Bruins ended up paying him $41,000 a year for two years.

Bobby's contract sent shock waves through the hockey world. In comparison to what Bobby was going to receive, just about every other player in professional hockey was underpaid. The con-

tract helped in organizing the National Hockey League Players' Association, the body that now serves as the players' bargaining agent in their negotiations with the owners. S. Alan Eagleson, Bobby's agent, headed the Players' Association.

Although Bobby was only eighteen when he joined the Bruins, quiet and rather shy, he was the team's leader right from the start. As soon as the players got onto the ice, they looked for Orr. "Take it, Bobby! Take it!" became a familiar cry on the rink at the Boston Garden.

One of a defenseman's primary jobs is to get the puck out of his own end and down the ice. Some players perform the task with all the ease of a man destroying a wooden crate with a fire ax. Bobby did it with relative ease and grace. "As soon as Bobby gets the puck on his stick," said Tom Johnson, his coach, "you *know* it's coming out. People take it for granted."

During his first season with the Bruins, Bobby missed nine games with a knee injury. He still managed to score 13 goals and assisted in the scoring of 28 others, for 41 points. He won the Calder Memorial Trophy as the Rookie of the Year.

That same year, Harry Howell of the New York Rangers won the Norris Trophy as the league's best defenseman.

Agile Bobby Orr (center) could elude an opposing team's best defenses. Here Orr skates past Black Hawk goalie Tony Esposito after scoring for the Boston Bruins in the 1970 Stanley Cup playoffs. *Courtesy of AP/Wide World Photos.*

Howell said he was very glad to have won it because nobody else would win it again for as long as Bobby Orr was in the league.

When Bobby joined the Bruins, they were a sad team. The year before, they had finished in last place. Bobby could not lift the team out of the cellar by himself. The next season, after the team had been strengthened by the addition of Phil Esposito and several other players, the Bruins managed a third-place finish and a berth in the championship

playoffs for the Stanley Cup. Boston was stopped in the first round by Montreal.

While Bobby played with greater poise and confidence that season, and captured his first Norris Trophy as the league's best defenseman, he suffered another knee injury. Surgery was required. As a result, Bobby missed most of the second half of the season.

Orr had not been playing major league hockey for very long before his charitable activities had become legendary. He was forever running off to hospitals to visit the ill or injured, or handing out donations to this person or that. A teammate once described him as being "too damn good," implying he was devoting too much of his time and energy to his various charities.

A friend of Bobby's once said: "Every time I turn around in his apartment there are five kids from Cerebral Palsy and a photographer there, and it's time to go to the game, and Bobby's saying, 'No, no, this is more important . . .'"

During the 1969–70 season, when he was relatively injury free, Bobby whacked 33 pucks into the nets and had 87 assists, the most for any player, forward or defenseman, in league history. He finished with 120 points that season. He thus became only the fourth player—and first defenseman—to score more than 100 points.

In the Stanley Cup playoffs that season, the Bruins downed the New York Rangers and then the Chicago Black Hawks. Against the St. Louis Blues in the final round, the Bruins took the first three games.

The fourth game was played in the Boston Garden on a spring afternoon in May. The old arena was filled to capacity with screaming fans. Were the Bruins to win, they would be the world champions.

The Bruins jumped off to a 1–0 lead. Then St. Louis surged ahead, 2–1. A goal off the stick of Phil Esposito tied the contest at 2–2. Then St. Louis took over again, 3–2. But once more Boston managed to tie matters, 3–3.

The clock ran out of time before either team could score again. Boston Garden was a madhouse. As in all playoff games, playing time was extended. The first team to score in overtime would win the game.

At the faceoff beginning play, the puck bounced to Orr. He saw teammate Derek Sanderson in the right corner. He fired the puck to Sanderson, then took off for the St. Louis net in one of his famous give-and-go bursts.

Sanderson saw Bobby blazing for the St. Louis goal. He shuttled a pass in his direction.

Bobby veered between a defenseman and the goaltender. He stopped the puck with the blade of his stick and in the very same motion smacked the black rubber disc into the corner of the net.

Goal! The Bruins had won the Stanley Cup. They were champions of the hockey world.

The Bruins captured the Stanley Cup again in 1972, a win that represented the peak of Bobby's career. The following season, with teammate Phil Esposito sidelined by injuries, Bobby was unable to steer the Bruins past the opening playoff round, and they were upset by the New York Rangers. The

1973–74 season belonged to the Philadelphia Flyers.

Bobby's left knee was a never-ending problem. One operation followed another. He lost count of the number. Eventually the knee drove Bobby out of hockey.

His last years were seldom happy. When he did play, his knee caused him agonizing pain. There was a bitter dispute with the Bruins over his contract. In 1976, he stunned the hockey world by leaving the Bruins and signing a multimillion-dollar contract with the Chicago Black Hawks. At the time, Kevin White, the mayor of Boston, called Orr "the equivalent of a great natural or historical treasure, like Paul Revere's house or Bunker Hill monument."

The years of decline continued. Orr played twenty games in his first season with the Black Hawks and only half that number the next season. He announced his retirement in 1978. He had played twelve seasons, the last three of which he spent mostly on the injured list.

After his retirement, Orr, his wife, Peggy, and their sons, Darren and Brent, settled down in a comfortable home outside of Boston. He became a successful businessman, representing several companies. He often traveled about the country making personal appearances and giving hockey clinics for young players.

Orr became increasingly concerned about youth hockey. What bothered him was that children imitated the roughneck tactics of the pros. Orr said that hockey should be fun for kids, and often it was not. Neither of his sons played hockey. Orr said that didn't matter to him. He wanted them to be active in sports, and they were. Baseball and soccer were the sports they played.

When Orr left hockey, the sport was hurt. Attendance went into a tailspin at more than a few arenas, and the fact that the NHL lost its network television contract about the same time that Bobby's knee betrayed him is regarded as more than just a coincidence.

During the 1980s there were a half-dozen richly talented defensemen playing for NHL teams, but it was universally agreed there was no one who could replace Bobby Orr.

Additional Reading

Devaney, John. *The Bobby Orr Story.* New York: Random House, 1973.

Orr, Bobby, with Dick Grace. *Orr on Ice.* Englewood Cliffs, N.J.: Prentice Hall, Inc., 1970.

Orr, Bobby, with Mark Mulvoy. *Bobby Orr: My Game.* Boston: Little Brown & Co., 1974.

Jesse Owens

Track Athlete of the Century
1913–1980

The year was 1936. The nations of Europe were on the brink of World War II. Adolf Hitler, the Nazi dictator, was nearing the peak of his power as the most feared man in the world. His presence loomed large over the 1936 Olympic Games, which were to be held in Berlin.

Hitler had mobilized the nation's manpower and spent more than $50 million with the idea of using the Games to prove that German athletes were the supermen of the world, the prime examples of his "master race" theory. Battalions of workers had toiled day and night for almost two years to build a new olympic stadium, considered the finest facility of its type in the world.

But from the beginning, things did not go as Hitler had planned. At the opening ceremonies of the Games, the Americans did not dip their flag in a salute to the German leader. Hitler showed no emotion at the snub, keeping his face frozen in a tight smile.

Hitler was to suffer much greater discomfort in the days that followed. The source of his anguish was a 5-foot-11, 165-pound, 22-year-old track and field star from the University of Ohio named Jesse Owens. A world record holder in sprinting, hurdling and jumping, Owens, who was black, made a joke of Hitler's racial theories with one dazzling performance after another.

Born James Cleveland Owens in Oakville, Alabama, on September 12, 1913, Jesse was the seventh of eleven children. His father, the son of a slave, was a sharecropper, working a white farmer's land in return for food and a place to live. Sometimes he worked for as many as eighteen hours a day. It was better than slavery, but not much better.

Jesse was often sickly as a child. He suffered from pneumonia almost every winter. Because of his frequent illnesses, Jesse did not have to go to work in the fields as a child as his brothers and sisters did.

When Jesse was still very young, his father, tired of overwork and abuse, decided to move the family to Cleveland, Ohio. There Jesse attended public schools. When he was in the fifth grade, he was asked to try out for the track team. Jesse explained that he had jobs after school and could not practice with the team, so the coach arranged for him to work out every morning before school began. The coach would meet him at a sidewalk near the school. When Jesse broke his first record six months later, his coach called him the "sidewalk champion."

Later, at East Technical High School in Cleveland, Jesse set several national track records.

After graduation, Jesse wanted to attend Ohio State University in Columbus, Ohio. There were no athletic scholarships to Ohio State in those days. To pay his tuition and living expenses, Jesse held three different jobs, working six days a week. He ran an elevator, worked in the school library, and waited on tables.

During his sophomore year at Ohio State, Jesse catapulted into the headlines with the greatest one-day performance in the history of track and field. The date was May 25, 1935. The event was a Big Ten track meet at the University of Michigan at Ann Arbor. Owens, who was suffering from a bad back, had to convince his coach that he was in good enough condition to compete that day. The coach agreed to let Owens enter the 100-yard dash, the first event on the program. If Jesse didn't do well in that event, it was agreed that he would withdraw from the rest of the races.

Despite the pain, Jesse, at precisely three fifteen that afternoon, sped through the 100 yards in 9.4 seconds, winning the race by five yards and equaling the world record that had been established five years earlier.

At three twenty-five, Owens competed in the broad jump (known as the long jump today). Since his back was still bothering him, Owens made up his mind to leap as far as he possibly could on his first jump, so he then could sit back and watch his rivals try to beat him.

At the time the world record for the broad jump was 26 feet, 2½ inches. Owens casually measured off that distance and placed a handkerchief in the sand pit to mark it. Then he jumped—and soared six inches beyond the handkerchief.

At three forty-five, Owens won the 220-yard dash in 20.3 seconds, breaking the world mark and establishing a record that was not to be equaled for fourteen years.

At four o'clock, Owens climaxed his incredible one-man performance by sailing over the 220-yard low hurdles in 22.6 seconds to shatter another world record.

In the history of track and field, only a handful of athletes—less than half a dozen—have set or equaled two world records in one day. Owens, within the space of one hour, had broken three world records and tied a fourth. An eyewitness said: "It was one of those rare moments in sports when you can't believe what you're seeing."

Owens won lasting fame that day at Ann Arbor. What happened at the 1936 Olympic Games would make his name a household word.

No one had any doubts that Hitler planned to use the Games for propaganda purposes. Not long before the Games were to open, German's Max Schmeling had scored a startling knockout victory over American heavyweight boxing champion Joe Louis, the greatest black hero of the day. It was Louis's first defeat.

Hitler offered his congratulations to Schmeling and sent flowers to the boxer's wife. On the eve of the Olympics, he paraded Schmeling in the Olympic Village as a symbol of his doctrine of racial superiority.

More than a million German citizens lined the streets of Berlin on August 1, 1936, to watch and cheer as Hitler was driven in triumph to the Olympic Stadium for the opening ceremonies. At a little before four o'clock that afternoon, sixty trumpeters on the stadium tower sounded a fanfare that was answered by booming salutes from distant cannon. At a signal, 3,000 white doves were released. As they circled the stadium like a white cloud, a tall, blond sprinter circled the arena to light the Olympic flame. A newspaper described it as "a day of triumph [for Hitler], exceeding perhaps any that have gone before."

Once competition began, it was apparent the Games were not going to follow Hitler's script. On the first day, under gray skies that threatened rain, Owens breezed to victory on a 100-meter heat. (A heat is a preliminary race in which competitors attempt to qualify for entry into the final race.) He later captured the 100-meter quarterfinal and semifinal races.

The next day, the finalists in the 100-meter sprint took their marks. Starting blocks were not legal in those days, so each contestant dug starting holes in the crushed cinder track. Hitler was in his private box, confident that the German sprinter, the bull-necked Erich Borchmeyer, would outduel Owens.

Jesse exploded out of his holes and blazed to victory in 10.3 seconds, equaling his world and Olympic record. Hitler scowled as Owens was awarded the gold medal.

The following day, the qualifying rounds were held in the broad jump. Each competitor had to jump at least 23 feet, 5 inches to be eligible for the finals. That distance was a cinch for Owens and the other leading contestants.

Before competing, Owens, as was his custom, paced down the runway while still wearing his sweats, and continued through the pit. He was merely testing conditions. He was thus shocked to see an official waving the red foul flag. Owens had been charged with an illegal try.

Visibly upset, Jesse stripped off his sweats for his first real effort at qualifying. He sped down the runway and bounded into the air. Although he seemed to have hit the takeoff board cleanly, the red flag signaled another foul. Now Jesse had only one more chance in which to qualify.

Lutz Long, a German jumper, went over and talked to Jesse, suggesting that the American move his starting point to several inches behind the takeoff board to avoid fouling out. Jesse did exactly as Long advised, and easily qualified.

After a break for lunch, it was time for the broad-jump finals. In the early stages, Lutz Long matched Jesse jump for jump. Every eye was focused on the two men as they got set for their final attempts. Hitler followed the action through binoculars.

The two athletes were still tied when Jesse lined up for his last jump. He pounded down the runway like a speeding bullet, hit the takeoff board with inches to spare, then soared to an Olympic record of 26 feet, 5 5/16 inches.

The crowd went wild. As for Hitler, it was reported his mouth became a tight slit and his face reddened with rage.

The 200-meter heats were held the same day as the broad-jump finals, and Owens had to keep shuttling back and forth between the two events. Seeking to conserve his strength, he was content merely to qualify for the event. But in the 200-meter finals the next day, Jesse went all out, streaking to the tape in 20.7 seconds. It was another world record and another gold medal. Never before had any runner bettered 21 seconds in the 200-meter run.

Jesse Owens (second from right) won not only four gold medals at the 1936 Olympics in Berlin but a victory over Nazi racism. *Courtesy of the United States Olympic Committee.*

Shortly before Owens was to receive his third gold medal, there was a flurry of activity in the official box. Hitler gathered his close officials and left the stadium.

On the final day of the track and field competition, Owens added a fourth gold medal and helped in setting another record as the lead runner in the American four-man 400-meter relay team. By that time, "America's black auxiliaries," as the German press called the black athletes, had won six of America's twelve golds.

Jesse returned to the United States a hero. New York City held a big parade in his honor. He was glorified in the press and showered with honors at every turn. But no one came forward with an offer for a job. And a job was what Jesse wanted. He was married now, the father of two children. He wondered how he was going to support his family.

The problem was that there was no market for black athletes in the 1930s. Jesse was forced to drop out of college. The best job he could get was as a playground instructor for the city of Cleveland. It paid $30 a week.

Later, a promoter offered Jesse a chance to earn good money by touring the country and running exhibition races against race horses. Jesse hated that worse than working at the playground, but the money he was paid enabled him to provide for his family and return to college.

Despite the honors that had been heaped upon him, Owens was often the victim of racial segregation. As he once noted, "I came back to my native country and I couldn't ride in the front of the bus. I had to go in the back door. I couldn't live where I wanted.

"I wasn't invited to shake hands with Hitler—but I wasn't invited to the White House to shake hands with the President, either."

In 1951, Owens returned to Germany for a visit. Adolf Hitler's war machine had been destroyed in World War II. Hitler himself was dead. Jesse was invited to appear at the Olympic Stadium where he had scored his magnificent track and field victories fifteen years before. Seventy-five thousand people cheered him, when, dressed in his old track outfit, he made a ceremonial run around the stadium track.

This time there was no arrogant dictator to turn his back on him. The mayor of Berlin sat in the official box. When Owens jogged over to him, the mayor rose, held out both hands, and said, "Fifteen years ago, Hitler would not shake your hand. Here, I give you both of mine." And he threw his arms around Jesse and hugged him.

The hero of the Berlin Olympics eventually received the thanks of his own country. In 1976, President Gerald Ford awarded Owens the Medal of Freedom, the highest civilian honor a president can bestow in peacetime.

By that time, Owens was a successful public relations executive. He died in 1980, a victim of lung cancer.

More than half a century has passed since Owens's triumphs at the Berlin Olympics and his incredible record-breaking day at the Big Ten track meet at Ann Arbor, Michigan, in 1935. The records that Owens established on those two occasions have been bettered, but his record for setting records has stood the test of time. It is not likely any athlete will ever equal it.

Additional Reading

Owens, Jesse with Paul G. Neimark. *Blackthink, My Life as Black Man and White Man.* New York: William Morrow & Co., 1970.

Pelé

Soccer's Greatest Player
1940—

Imagine a soccer player who, while sprinting down the field, could flick the ball from one foot to the other, controlling it as if it were at the end of an invisible string.

Imagine a player who, when trapped by a rival, could cuff a pass to an open spot for a teammate to gather in; a player who could kick the ball rod-straight with either foot or, when he had to, curve it to either the right or left. Imagine a player who could always head the ball with precision.

Imagine a player who was a master strategist, who seemed to know where all the other players on the field were positioned, teammates and opponents alike, and who was able to sense what each was going to do next. Cool and unhurried, even when under attack, he could use this knowledge to plan and

execute quick and effective scoring thrusts in the blink of an eye.

Such a player was no myth. He was real. He was Pelé, the greatest soccer player in the history of the game.

From Brazil, Pelé (pronounced pay-LAY) electrified fans with his daring dribbling and pinpoint passing and shooting. He held every scoring record in his native country. In international competition, Pelé averaged about one goal per game. That is something like a major league baseball player hitting a home run in every game of the World Series.

Pelé, an inside left forward, began playing with Santos of Brazil in 1956. He helped steer the team to five South American and three World Cup championships.

Wearing the uniform of the Brazilian

national team, Pelé led Brazil to its first World Cup victory in 1958. (The World Cup is symbolic of the world championship of soccer. The Cup is held permanently by any national team that wins it three times.) Brazil won the Cup a second time in 1962, and again Pelé played a major role. Incredibly, Pelé was still great in 1970 when Brazil won the Cup a third time.

In those three championship seasons, Pelé played in every qualifying game, every training game, and in every World Cup match. In all of soccer history, Pelé is the only three-time Cup champion.

Pelé was not only the greatest of idols in Brazil but an international hero. He played soccer in sixty-five countries. "He has done more goodwill than all the ambassadors of the world put together," Brazil's ambassador to the United States once said.

Charles de Gaulle, the President of France, paid Pelé one of that nation's highest honors, making him a Knight of the Order of Merit.

In the early 1970s, the war between Biafra and Nigeria was stopped for two days because a soccer match featuring Pelé was scheduled and both sides wanted to see him play.

When Pelé visited Pope Paul VI, the Pope said to him, "Don't be nervous, my son. I am more nervous than you because I have been wanting to meet Pelé personally for a long time."

Pelé retired in 1974, then "unretired" a year later, signing a three-year contract with the New York Cosmos of the North American Soccer League. He retired a second time after leading the Cosmos to the league championship in 1977.

Worldwide fame and more money than he could ever spend wisely did not change Pelé. He always seemed to be wearing a smile. He would pose for snapshots and talk to strangers almost as if they were doing him a favor. He would sign autographs until his arm ached.

From the beginning of his career to the very end, every time he went out onto the field, it was as if he were taking part in a great adventure. Every goal was a thrill, an event to be marked by leaping high and thrusting a fist into the air. Pelé loved the game more than anything else in the world.

The man who was to be known as Pelé was born in the small Brazilian town of Três Corações (which is Portuguese for Three Hearts) on October 23, 1940. The oldest of three children, he was baptized Edson Arantes de Nascimento. Often asked about his nickname, Pelé said he did not know how or when he received it.

As an adult, Pelé once went to see the house where he was born. It was part of a shabby row of dwellings of reclaimed brick, with walls of cracked plaster and peeling paint. "Everyone I knew lived in a house like that," Pelé said.

Pelé's father was a professional soccer player. In keeping with a custom in Brazilian soccer, he was known in the sport by a nickname—Dondinho. In Dondinho's only chance to play soccer with an important club, he injured his knee severely. He continued to play the game despite the fact that the knee was often swollen and painful. It was the only way he knew how to earn money.

When Pelé was four years old, the family moved to the town of Bauru, where Dondinho had been promised a job playing soccer. He was also told that work as a civil service clerk had been arranged for him. But the promises were never kept. The family soon grew to know the meaning of poverty.

Pelé learned what it was to wear hand-me-down clothes that did not fit and never to have shoes. On cold nights, the entire family huddled about the woodburning stove in the tiny kitchen, trying not to sleep on one another.

But the poverty was much more of a problem for his parents than for Pelé himself. "I was always happy in Bauru," he declared in his autobiography. It happened that there were many children about the same age as Pelé living in the neighborhood. "We played from dawn to dusk," Pelé once said, "and the game we played was soccer."

Pelé and his friends couldn't afford a soccer ball, so they did what the other kids did. They would take the largest men's sock they could find, stuff it with rags and crumpled-up newspapers, roll it into a ball shape, and then lash string around it. That was their soccer ball.

Pelé entered school in Bauru, but he was not a good student. He often skipped classes. His grades were low. It took him six years to complete four grades. Then he dropped out.

He got a job in a shoe factory, stitching boots. He also helped a Japanese friend in his dry-cleaning store and the family in their fruit and vegetable market.

But soccer was the most important thing in his life. His father helped Pelé to develop his skills. Dondinho would take his young son to an abandoned field near their home and watch as he dribbled the ball and kicked it. Dondinho would often play goalkeeper, stationing himself before an imaginary net where old goalposts had once stood. Pelé seldom managed to get the ball past his father. "Dondinho always seemed to know instinctively where to go to block," Pelé once said.

When Pelé was nine, he and his friends organized a neighborhood soccer team. They managed to outfit themselves with shirts and shorts but were unable to raise enough money to buy shoes. They named the team "The Shoeless Ones." In going into neighboring communities in search of opponents, they found that just about every other team had the same lack of footwear and the same nickname.

At the age of eleven, Pelé came under the guidance of Waldemar de Brito, coach of the Bauru city team. The coach had watched the small, rail-thin Pelé dart about the field with the ball at his feet, outmaneuvering older and more experienced players. He put Pelé on the Bauru junior team.

Pelé learned quickly. Within three years, he was a star. Led by Pelé, the Bauru team won the junior championship three years in a row.

The coach saw a bright future for Pelé. After getting his parents' permission, de Brito arranged a tryout for Pelé with Santos, an important professional team.

In trying out, Pelé had to test his skills against Santos's veteran players. He was nervous at first, but once the game began he loosened and played as well as he ever had. He felt satisfied with his performance.

Afterward, the Santos coach spoke to him: "I liked the way you played today. The only thing is, you're very small. We'll just have to wait until you're bigger and a little older, and then we'll see. What do you weigh?"

"I weigh almost 130 pounds," Pelé answered in a weak voice.

"Well," said the coach, "you can play with the juvenile team and get practice and experience with them."

Having to play with the juniors was a disappointment for Pelé, but he went along with the coach's decision.

He did not have to wait very long for his status to change. The Vasco da Gama team in Rio de Janeiro desperately needed players for a tournament. Santos lent them four, including Pelé. His sparkling play with Vasco da Gama earned Pelé a promotion to Santos's first team. Pelé was on the way.

In 1957, his first full year with Santos, Pelé scored 17 goals, a league high. A year later, his reputation was such that he was one of twenty-two players chosen to represent Brazil in World Cup competition.

Pelé's exceptional play was a vital factor as Brazil rolled over one opponent after another in the 1958 Cup matches. In a scoreless game against Wales, Pelé banked an overhead shot off an opposing player, then booted the rebounding ball into the net for the winning goal. Pelé scored twice in the final against Sweden. Brazil won, 5–2.

The whole nation was delirious. Schools were closed; a public holiday was declared. Church bells rang. Flags waved. Firecrackers exploded. In Rio de Janeiro, a million people lined the motorcade route from the airport to the presidential palace, where the players received medals.

The triumphal season, the stunning victory in World Cup and the wild celebrating—all of these happened before Pelé had reached his eighteenth birthday.

In the years that followed, Pelé's name was in the headlines often as he led the Santos team to even greater international fame. He did so despite the fact that he was always closely marked—that is, guarded—by the opposition. Often he was marked too closely. "I've been kicked from pillar to post . . ." he once wrote in a soccer yearbook. "At first I was shocked, and then I became angry. Sometimes I hit back and, because my name was Pelé, news of such incidents made every newspaper in Brazil."

Once, in a game against Argentina, Pelé was grabbed, tripped, and stepped upon. He fought back by breaking his opponent's nose with a head butt.

In the 1962 World Cup play, Pelé was sidelined because of a pulled muscle. He could only cheer from the sidelines as Brazil downed Czechoslovakia, 3–1, in the final.

Pelé and the Santos team visited the United States in 1966 for a match against Milan International at Yankee Stadium in New York. The game, played on Labor Day, drew more than 41,000 spectators. Pelé scored once and passed with his usual brilliance, as Santos won, 4–1.

After seeing him in action, Pete Axthelm, writing in *Sports Illustrated*, observed: "On every play, he seems to be two steps ahead of the players around him. . . . He shoots harder and more accurately than anyone in the game. When he rumbles through the offensive zone toward the goal, Pelé captures the imagination in a way only the most dramatic of athletes can."

In 1970, Brazil faced Italy in the World Cup final. Both teams scored a goal in the first half. Brazil's was the result of a header by Pelé.

In the second half, Pelé passed for two goals and headed in a third, making the final score: Brazil, 4; Italy, 1.

Not long after, Pelé announced that he would no longer participate with the Brazilian national team. He did continue to play for Santos, however, until 1974. He closed out his eighteen-year

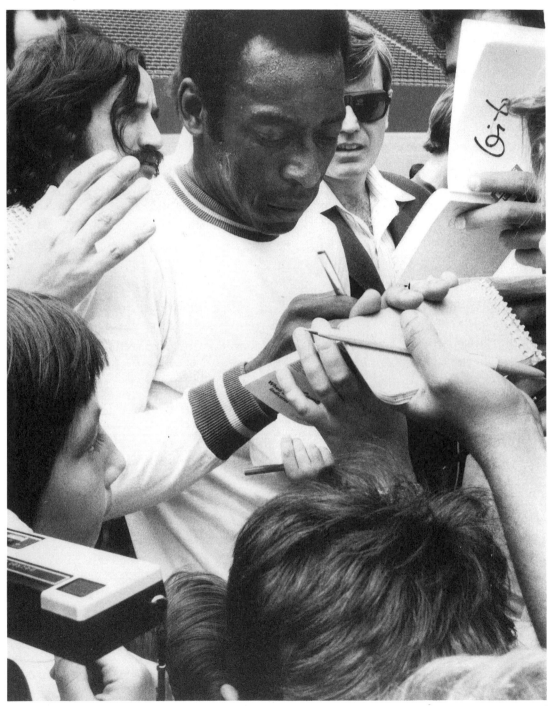

Brazilian star Pelé almost single-handedly created a soccer craze in America when he played in the North American Soccer League for three seasons. *Photo by the author.*

career with the team on October 2, 1974.

But the very next year, Pelé took the world of soccer by surprise with the announcement that he was returning to competition, not in Brazil or some other soccer-mad country but with the New York Cosmos of the North American Soccer League.

Professional soccer was of little importance in the United States, being overshadowed by baseball, football, basketball, tennis, golf, and several other sports. It was beginning to develop some momentum, but the pro teams that did exist were losing money. The sport's future was doubtful at best.

Why would Pelé, the king of the sport, want to get involved in American soccer? It was almost like the Most Valuable Player in the World Series announcing that he was quitting his team to play baseball in Mexico or Argentina.

Clive Toye, president of the Cosmos, had been pursuing Pelé for three years. Toye and league officials realized what American soccer needed was a superstar, an individual who could win the hearts of the nation's youth and also capture the fancy of television and the press.

Toye had many meetings with Pelé. During one, he offered him a six-year contract, which called for Pelé to play three years and then serve three years as a public relations representative. Pelé was to be paid approximately $5 million.

It wasn't merely the money that convinced Pelé that he should give up retirement and his Brazilian homeland to play soccer in a nation where only a relatively few cared about the sport. Clive Toye told Pelé, "You can go down in history as the man who truly brought soccer to the United States, the one country in which it has not caught on." For a humble man who started his career kicking around a sockful of rags, that idea had great appeal.

In June 1975, Pelé made his first appearance at an American soccer game, arriving by helicopter at the shabby stadium at Randall's Island in the East River of New York City, where the Cosmos played their home games at the time. The fans mobbed him. They continued to mob him for the next three years, trying to get a look at him, trying to touch him.

In his first game in a Cosmos uniform, Pelé assisted in the scoring of one goal with a splendid pass, and scored another himself with a perfect header. Throughout the contest, which ended in a tie, Pelé dazzled the crowd with his masterful ball control and brilliant passing. "American soccer has arrived," one television broadcaster declared.

Although the Cosmos played their home games in a rundown stadium,

Pelé did not complain. Even though more than a few of his teammates lacked skill and experience, Pelé said nothing. The fact that the players on the team represented more than half a dozen different nationalities and spoke several languages, chiefly English, did not seem to bother him.

In seeking to get Americans interested in soccer, Pelé did more than merely play in Cosmos games. He went to the White House and posed for pictures with President Gerald Ford, showing him how to head the ball. He was a guest on the Johnny Carson show. Pelé was featured in magazines and newspapers that scarcely even noticed soccer before.

He contributed in other ways. Because Pelé had become a member of the Cosmos, other internationally known stars signed with other American teams. Two of the best-known—Italy's Giorgio Chinaglia and West Germany's Franz Beckenbauer—joined the Cosmos.

In 1976, with interest in the sport picking up and attendance at games beginning to build, the Cosmos were in the thick of playoff competition until they were eliminated by Tampa Bay. The following year, with the Cosmos playing in sparkling new Giants Stadium in East Rutherford, New Jersey, attendance soared. People who had never dreamed of going to a soccer match before came out to watch Pelé and his Cosmos teammates.

On August 14, 1977, for a playoff game against the Fort Lauderdale Strikers at Giants Stadium, a standing-room-only crowd of 77,691 turned out, a league record. They cheered loudly throughout the afternoon as the Cosmos whipped the Strikers, 8–3.

Average attendance at Cosmos games reached 40,000 that season. Other clubs around the league also experienced record throngs. Newspapers and television increased their soccer coverage. Franchises doubled in value, then doubled again. No one had expected so much so soon.

The Cosmos were just as successful on the field as they were at the box office. They swept through the playoffs, then met the Seattle Sounders in the Soccer Bowl. The thirty-seven-year-old Pelé played every minute of the game at top speed, and when it had ended and the Cosmos had won, the crowd surged out of the stands to pick him up and carry him about on their shoulders. Pelé laughed and threw kisses.

That was Pelé's final game in official competition. His farewell was staged in October 1, 1977, when the Cosmos played Santos, the team that Pelé had led to several championships in his native Brazil, in an exhibition match. Pelé was to play for the Cosmos in the first half and for Santos in the second half.

The day was gray and wet. Although it rained steadily before the game began, some 75,646 people were on hand. Among them were former Secretary of State Henry Kissinger, boxing champion Muhammad Ali, rock star Mick Jagger, and actor Robert Redford. There were also 761 journalists from twenty-five countries.

Before the game, Pelé spoke briefly to the huge crowd. In his broken English, he said: "I want to take this opportunity to ask you in this moment—when the world looks to me—to take more attention to the young ones, to the kids all over the world. We need them too much. And I want to ask you—because I think love is the most important thing in the world that we can take in life—people, say with me three times: LOVE, LOVE, LOVE!"

After each time he said, "LOVE," the crowd repeated it.

Then Pelé bowed his head and wept.

Once the game began, Pelé provided one last memorable moment. The Cosmos were trailing, 1–0, when, late in the first half, Pelé was assigned to take a free kick at a point some 30 yards from the goal. He charged the ball and drove it low and hard, a bullet that stayed on target all the way to the left corner of the Santos goal. The goalie flung himself at the shot, but it was beyond his fingertips.

It was Pelé's 1,281st goal, in his 1,363rd game, and it tied the match, 1–1. The Cosmos eventually won, 2–1.

It had been thought that Pelé would leave the field with two or three minutes remaining, but he played the entire game. When it ended, he removed his Santos jersey with the familiar Number 10 and gave it to the team's coach. Then, as the crowd shouted "Pelé! Pelé!" he ran a victory lap around the field.

On the basis of all that was happening, Phil Woosnam, commissioner of the North American Soccer League, predicted that within ten years soccer would be Number 1 in the United States. "More people will watch and play soccer here than any other sport," the commissioner said.

Of course, anyone who is the least bit familiar with sports in America knows that this never happened. Indeed, quite the opposite took place. Soccer went through one of the swiftest declines in the history of professional sports.

Some people said that there were simply too many other sports with which soccer had to compete. In most foreign nations, soccer has center stage to itself. There are no other professional sports of any importance.

Other observers pointed out that the United States was not, by tradition, a soccer-playing nation. "Games are not grafted onto societies like clothing styles," said Larry Merchant in the *New York Times*. Still others blamed television, which never got very interested in soccer. The absence of Pelé was surely a factor, too.

The Cosmos, victims of front office squabbling and dwindling attendance, were kicked out of the North American Soccer League in 1985. Not long after, the league itself folded.

Pelé, once he stopped playing soccer, entered a new world. He continued to work for Warner Communications, the corporation that owned the Cosmos franchise. He lent his name to coffee, credit cards, soft drinks, and athletic equipment.

He made a movie titled *Victory*, which was released in 1981. Set during World War II, the movie portrayed a group of prisoners and concentration camp victims who are recruited to play Germany's best in a soccer match. At the same time, a plot is afoot for the prisoners to tunnel their way to freedom.

"As for Pelé, no one asks him to act," said one reviewer. "He is required to be what he has always been, a magical figure."

A magical figure—that is a good description of Pelé. He was attractive and glamorous, a wizard, an enchanter. Soccer—indeed, American sports—has never seen quite his equal.

Additional Reading

Pelé and Robert L. Fish. *Pelé, My Life and the Beautiful Game*. New York: Warner Books, 1977.

Jackie Robinson

The Man Who Changed Baseball
1919–1972

It was the spring of 1947. World War II had ended about eighteen months before. American servicemen were returning home to their families. American industry was changing over from wartime to peacetime production. Harry S Truman occupied the White House.

On April 15 that year, twenty-eight-year-old Jackie Robinson appeared in the lineup of the Brooklyn Dodgers (now the Los Angeles Dodgers) for the first time. Robinson was the first black player in the major leagues in sixty years. Up until Robinson, baseball had been all white. Black players had to play on all-black teams in what were called "Negro leagues."

Blacks had played professional baseball as early as 1872, but their participation ended in 1887 when Adrian (Cap) Anson of the Chicago White Stockings, the most prominent player of the day, got his team to boycott an exhibition against Newark in the International League because the starting pitcher was black. Blacks were banned from baseball until the arrival of Jackie Robinson.

There were no protests, no marches on behalf of black athletes during that period. Newspapers never said a word about the situation. Black athletes, with only a handful of exceptions, were simply ignored. Most Americans were not yet aware of their own racism.

There were many other American institutions that were just as segregated as baseball in the 1940s. Most black children went to all-black schools. In some parts of the country, blacks could not vote, use public parks or swimming pools, or occupy the front seats of public buses.

It took the civil rights movement of the 1950s and 1960s to end segregation. But Jackie Robinson played an important role. "[My life] produced understanding among whites," Robinson once said. "And it gave black people the idea that if I could do it, they could do it, too, that blackness wasn't subservient to anything."

The son of a sharecropper and the grandson of a slave, Jackie Robinson was born in Cairo, Georgia, on January 31, 1919. Six months after Jackie's birth, his father deserted the family.

When Jackie was about fifteen months old, he, his sister and three brothers were taken to Pasadena, California, by their mother. There Mrs. Robinson worked as a housekeeper. She eventually saved enough money to enable the family to move out of their crowded apartment into a small house on Pepper Street in Pasadena.

The Robinson children were all taught to look after one another. This arrangement worked well until Jackie's sister, Willa Mae, reached kindergarten age. Who would now watch over Jackie, the youngest member of the family?

Mrs. Robinson decided the best solution to the problem was to have Jackie go along to school with Willa Mae. But

school officials would not approve the plan. "If I stay home and take care of Jackie," Mrs. Robinson argued, "I'll have to go on welfare. It'll be cheaper for Pasadena to allow him to go along with Willa Mae."

It was a convincing argument. School officials gave in. Each day Jackie went off to school with Willa Mae. He played in the sandbox while she went to class.

When Jackie was older and still in elementary school, he did odd jobs in his neighborhood, using the income to help the family. He delivered newspapers, watered shrubs and gardens, and collected junk, which he sold. He also sold hot dogs at the Rose Bowl. The famous stadium, site of the annual Rose Bowl game, was about a mile from the Robinson home.

As a student at John Muir Technical High School, Jackie won letters in track, football, baseball, and basketball. He had great pride; he hated to lose.

A catcher on Muir Tech's baseball team, Jackie was chosen to perform on the Pomona All-Star team in 1937. One of his teammates was Ted Williams, who, like Jackie, would go on to a legendary baseball career.

After he graduated from high school, Jackie attended Pasadena Junior College. There he continued to excel in sports, earning several offers of college scholarships. He decided to attend UCLA (University of California/Los Angeles). "My mother wanted me to be a doctor or a lawyer," Robinson once recalled, "but I never wanted to be anything but an athlete."

One of Jackie's brothers, Mack, had been a star athlete while at Muir Technical High School and later at Pasadena Junior College. A sprinter, Mack went to the Olympic Games in Munich in 1936. He finished second to Jesse Owens in the 200-meter dash.

As for Jackie, he was an athlete without equal at UCLA, becoming the school's first four-letter athlete—that is, he won athletic letters in each of four different sports.

In basketball Jackie, a forward, twice led the Pacific Coast Conference in scoring. In his first college baseball game, he stole five bases. In track, he captured the NCAA (National Collegiate Athletic Association) broad-jumping title. (The sport is called long-jumping today.) He was a star running back on the football team, averaging 12 yards per carry.

While at UCLA, Robinson met Rachel Isum, a nursing student. They later married. "Rachel became the most helpful and encouraging and important person I ever met in my life," Jackie once said. "When I was bitter or discouraged, she was always there with the help I needed."

In the spring of 1941, Jackie dropped out of UCLA. His mother needed someone to help support her. One older brother had died. Another was married. The burden fell upon Jackie, who took a job as an assistant athletic director for the National Youth Administration.

But the job paid poorly. Jackie left the NYA to join the Los Angeles Bulldogs, a semipro football team.

Early in December, the Bulldogs played in Hawaii. Afterward, the players boarded the passenger ship *Lurline* for the return voyage to California. They had been aboard only a short time when they heard an announcement from the captain: "The Japanese have just attacked Pearl Harbor. We are heading back to California with all deliberate speed."

The United States had been plunged into World War II. Jackie, like millions of others, was drafted into the army. At about the same time he was celebrating his twenty-third birthday, Jackie was being commissioned as a second lieutenant in the army.

This achievement did not come without a struggle, however. When Jackie first applied for schooling as an officer, he was told blacks were not eligible for such training. Jackie protested. Eventually, he forced the army to relent, opening the way for himself and several other blacks.

After he had won his commission and was serving at Fort Hood, Texas, Jackie was involved in another racial incident.

He refused to leave his seat beside a white woman and move to the back of a bus. Charges were brought against him and Jackie faced a court-martial, but a judge dismissed the charges.

In December 1944, Jackie was given an honorable discharge. His army service had often been marked by struggles against oppression and injustice. They signaled what the future was to bring.

During World War II, major league baseball continued to be played. Most able-bodied men were in the armed services, however, so teams operated with a patchwork assortment of over-the-hill players and others who had been rejected as unfit for military service. One team, the St. Louis Browns, employed a one-armed outfielder.

After World War II ended in September 1945, baseball executives moved forward with team-building efforts. The owners of the Brooklyn Dodgers had hired sixty-two-year-old Branch Rickey as general manager and given him the responsibility for the team's future.

Everyone agreed the Dodger owners had made an excellent choice. A former lawyer and Methodist lay preacher, Rickey, in twenty-six years as head of the St. Louis Cardinals, had guided the team to six National League pennants and four world championships. He was considered a genius in the development of young talent. "Rickey could look in-side a guy's muscles and see what was going on," one reporter said. "He could spot things in a man's play, a man's run, a man's throw, that nobody else could."

Rickey realized that black players represented an enormous untapped source of baseball talent. He announced to the owners of the Dodgers that he was going to have his scouts search "for a Negro player or two." The owners gave Rickey the go-ahead.

Rickey's scouts eventually singled out Jackie Robinson as the best candidate. After he had been discharged from the army, Robinson had signed a contract to play for the Kansas City Monarchs of the Negro American Baseball League. He batted .340 and was a sensation in the field. While with the Monarchs, Robinson's every move was watched and evaluated by the Dodgers.

Rickey also asked friends to check on Robinson's character. They reported that at high school and college Robinson had been a high-spirited young man, with guts, brains, and self-respect. He had been known as a Negro who "talked back" to white players and officials. For that reason he had not always been popular.

In August 1945, Rickey and Robinson met for the first time. Rickey began by announcing that he wanted Jackie to play for the Brooklyn organization. "We have scouted you for weeks,"

Rickey declared. "What you have done is a matter of record. But this is much more than just playing baseball. The main question is, do you have the guts to make it. Have you the courage?"

"What do you want?" Robinson asked. "A player who is afraid to fight back, a coward?"

"I want," Rickey answered, letting the words come slowly, "a ballplayer with guts enough *not* to fight back."

Then Rickey explained that there was virtually no one on their side, no other club owner, no umpires, and perhaps only a few newspapermen. An "impossible position," Rickey called it.

"But we can win," he said, "if we can convince everyone that you are not only a great ballplayer but also a great gentleman."

Rickey acted out typical game situations that Robinson might face and taunted him to test him. "You will hear much worse and go through much more pressure before you are through," Rickey said.

The meeting ended with Robinson signing a contract with the Montreal Royals, a minor league team operated by the Dodgers, for the season of 1946. He received a $3,500 bonus for signing and a salary of $600 a month.

Once installed in the Montreal lineup, Jackie was under tremendous pressure from the beginning. Some of the tension was triggered by the admir-

ing Montreal fans who turned out in record numbers to see him play and mobbed him at almost every opportunity. The tension also developed from the open hatred Jackie experienced, the screaming curses from racist players. There were even threats on his life.

Jackie finished the season with a league-leading batting average of .349, and he stole 40 bases. Montreal won the International League championship.

After Jackie's outstanding season with Montreal, few doubted that he would be promoted to the Brooklyn team for the 1947 season. The Royals and the Dodgers trained together the next spring. Then, just before the season opened, Rickey announced that Jackie would be joining the Dodgers.

Most of the Brooklyn players took the announcement in stride, but a small handful objected and said they would not play on a team with a black man. Rickey told them that they were free to quit baseball if they wanted, but the "Robinson experiment would continue." No one quit.

Wearing the blue Number 42 on the back of his white Brooklyn uniform, Robinson, stationed at first base, made his debut with the Dodgers on April 15, 1947, the season's opening day. The attendance was announced at 26,623. Jackie went hitless in three at-bats. Brooklyn defeated Boston, 5–3.

It was not easy for Robinson that season. He took terrible abuse from the players and fans. The season was only two weeks old when the first of several bitter incidents occurred. The Dodgers were playing the Philadelphia Phillies, a team that had several racist players. "Hey, you black nigger," one of them yelled the first time Robinson came to bat, "why don't you go back to where you came from?"

"Yeah," said another, "pretty soon you'll want to eat and sleep with white ballplayers."

As the taunting continued, Jackie almost lost his temper. He started to drop his bat and go over and punch someone, but he remembered what Branch Rickey had told him. He pretended he didn't hear the insults.

Off the field, there were problems, too. Some restaurants where the team ate would not serve blacks. Some hotels where the team stayed refused to accept them. Robinson had to room with other blacks.

At the beginning, Robinson took the abuse in silence. He put all of his efforts into succeeding on the field and at bat. In the dugout or dressing room, he was a quiet figure. He seldom spoke unless spoken to.

That soon changed. A turning point came in a game against the St. Louis Cardinals. Enos Slaughter, a St. Louis outfielder, raced down the first-base line and, when he reached the bag, stepped on Robinson's foot with his spikes, inflicting a painful injury. The Dodgers were enraged. Pitcher Ralph Branca said, "The next time that guy comes up, I'll stick one in his ear for you."

Robinson told Branca to forget what had happened. "Just pitch," he said. "We want to win the game."

But the incident helped to show that Robinson had been accepted as a teammate. He once said that he knew from that point on that he would have little trouble.

Everywhere Robinson played, fans flocked to see him. Attendance at National League games jumped by more than a million during his first season with the Dodgers. He led the team to the league championship that season and was named Rookie of the Year.

Robinson's daring on the basepaths drove pitchers wild with worry. The moment he reached first base the crowd would begin screaming. He would take a very long lead, crouching on the balls of his feet, his arms outstretched, ready to take off for second base or dive back to first.

There are a number of players today who display Robinson's speed and boldness on the basepaths, but in 1947 he was unique. Managers played a cautious game in those days, looking for their big hitters to drive in the base runners.

Robinson helped to change that strategy. Sometimes he would walk or hit a single, steal second, go to third on an infield out and score on a fly ball. That kind of performance dimmed the need for the big hitter.

In 1947, Robinson's first year, the average National League team stole 45 bases over the season. Today, there are many *players* who are capable of stealing that many bases in a season. And some, such as Tim Raines of the Montreal Expos or Rickey Henderson of the New York Yankees, have stolen more than twice that number—more than 90 bases—in a season. Obviously, Robinson and the black players that followed him, by bringing speed to baseball, revolutionized the game.

After Jackie had been with the Dodgers a couple of years, he stopped being meek and humble. When he got spiked, he would spike back. When a pitcher threw at him, he would retaliate. He argued with umpires and rival players. He fought with his own managers and league officials.

Robinson's change in attitude earned him a great deal of criticism. He was called a "loudmouth," a "troublemaker," and a "hotheaded popoff." But, as Branch Rickey pointed out, Robinson was simply displaying qualities that many people admire in white players but cannot bear to see in blacks. He had simply become what he had always been, a fighter on the field, a player who absolutely hated to lose.

Robinson played for the Dodgers for ten years, helping to power the team to six pennants and, in 1955, to a World Series win. In six of those ten years, Robinson batted .300 or better. His career average was .311. Twice he led the league in stolen bases. He was named the league's Most Valuable Player in 1949.

A first baseman in 1947, he was chiefly a second baseman from 1948 to 1952. He ultimately played every position except pitcher and catcher.

In 1947, Robinson was the only black man in baseball. He was followed by Larry Doby, an outfielder for the Cleveland Indians, the first black player in the American League; by catcher Roy Campanella and pitcher Don Newcombe of the Dodgers; pitcher Satchel Paige of the Indians; and outfielder Monte Irvin of the New York Giants (now the San Francisco Giants).

All had played in the Negro leagues. Robinson, Campanella, Paige, and Irvin were elected to baseball's Hall of Fame.

In 1959, after the Boston Red Sox signed Elijah "Pumpsie" Green, every major league club had at least one black player.

Robinson, besides being noted for his aggressive base running, also earned a reputation as an exceptional clutch per-

Jackie Robinson stole home—in an era when stealing any base was a rare and exceptionally daring move. *Courtesy of the Los Angeles Dodgers.*

former. His last appearance in this role came in the 1956 World Series. The Dodgers faced the Yankees and were down, three games to two. Their situation was grim.

In the sixth game, neither team could score. It was still 0–0 when Brooklyn came to bat in the last of the ninth. With one out Junior Gilliam walked. Then Pee Wee Reese laid down a sacrifice bunt, allowing Gilliam to race to second. Now there were two outs.

The Yankees decided to walk slugger Duke Snider to get to Robinson. Bob Turley was pitching for the Yankees. Robinson hammered Turley's second pitch all the way to the wall in the deepest reaches of left field, sending Gilliam home with the game's only run.

Robinson retired from baseball when the Dodgers traded him to the New York Giants in January 1957. He was elected to baseball's Hall of Fame in 1962.

After retiring from baseball, Robinson became a business executive and was active in politics. He joined the administration of New York Governor Nelson Rockefeller in an effort to improve conditions for the poor.

Not long after his retirement, Robinson discovered that he had diabetes. In time, the disease severely weakened him and caused his eyesight to fail.

In October 1972, Robinson was honored at the World Series in Cincinnati. Ten days later he died of a heart attack.

In the years that followed his death, Robinson's widow avoided the spotlight. In one of her rare public appearances, she threw out the first ball of the fourth game of the 1985 World Series, the Kansas City Royals vs. the St. Louis Cardinals.

She spoke to Dave Anderson of the *New York Times*, saying, "I appreciate the number of minority players not only in baseball but in all sports. But there have been only a token number of black managers and a token number of opportunities for black front-office people."

Several of the players who participated in the series that year discussed Robinson. "I don't remember too much," said Cardinal third baseman Terry Pendleton. "I know he was an excellent outfielder. I know he was one of the best at stealing home."

Outfielders Willie Wilson and Darryl Motley of the Royals spoke of Robinson's social importance. "He's the reason," Motley, a black, said, "why I'm playing in the World Series."

Additional Reading

Robinson, Jackie. *I Never Had It Made.* New York: G. P. Putnam's, 1972.

Rowan, Carl T. *Wait Till Next Year: The Story of Jackie Robinson.* New York: Random House, 1960.

Tygiel, Jules. *Baseball's Great Experiment: Jackie Robinson and His Legacy.* New York: Oxford University Press, 1983.

Bill Russell

Basketball's Best
1934–

It used to be that the center in basketball was a scoring machine, stuffing points like crazy. Not anymore. The center is still expected to be a good scorer, but shot blocking and rebounding are the center's foremost jobs today. Holding down the opposition scoring is what coaches want their centers to do.

Bill Russell, center for the Boston Celtics of the National Basketball Association (NBA), was the man responsible for the transformation. No one was better than Russell at blocking shots from any angle or height. No one was harder to force out of position or get around. No one was tougher to go through or go over.

"He changed the game," said Pete Newell, director of player personnel for the Golden State Warriors. "He was the first to bring into focus what a shot blocker could do."

Before Russell came along, defense was never very much in fashion, at least not as far as the center was concerned. The sight of the 6-foot-9 Russell slamming the ball back into the faces of shooter and sweeping the ball off the backboards was so unusual that one college coach, who observed Russell during his sophomore season at the University of San Francisco, described his style as "fundamentally unsound."

It was after Russell joined the Celtics in 1956 that his defensive skills began to be fully appreciated. With Russell at center, the Celtics became champions overnight. That was in 1957. In the years that followed, the team built a tradition of winning that is unmatched in modern professional sports.

Another great pro center, Willis Reed of the New York Knicks, once said of Russell, "He was the greatest. He was my boyhood idol. He stands above all the rest. There are men with God-given ability, and there are men who make the most of the skills they've got. Few fit both categories. Russell did. His record is his monument."

The record to which Reed was referring is extraordinary. In his thirteen years with the Celtics, Russell led the team to the NBA championship eleven times. He was named to the East All-Star team eleven times and won the league's most valuable player award five times.

In 1966, in addition to playing center, he took over as the team's head coach. He thereby became the first black head coach in pro basketball.

The climb to the top was anything but easy for William Felton Russell. He was born on February 12, 1934, in Monroe, Louisiana. He had more than a few bitter memories of his early childhood.

One incident involved his mother, Katie, a "gentle woman," as Russell has described her. She liked to dress in stylish street clothes. One day she was shopping in a new suit when a cop came up to her and said, "Who do you think you are, nigger? Dressed like a white woman. Get out of town before sundown or I'll throw you in jail."

"My mother came home in a state of shock," Russell says in his autobiography, *Go Up for Glory*. Bill was five years old at the time. He watched her sitting in the kitchen of their home, trying to understand why the cop had been so vicious.

Such abuse led the Russells to leave the Deep South and move to Oakland, California. Not long after, Bill's mother and father separated, and then his mother died. Bill and his older brother, Charlie, were raised by their father.

At Hoover Junior High School in Oakland, the tall and gangly Russell tried out for basketball but failed to make the team. Later, at McClymond's High School, he tried again. This time he barely made the junior varsity, having to share the team's fifteenth uniform with another player.

He kept growing taller, but he was also putting on weight and gaining in balance and poise. Although he played two years on the varsity, he didn't make enough of an impression to get mentioned on any of the area's All Scholastic teams.

He did have good games now and then, however. An assistant coach at the University of San Francisco saw him play one of them and offered Bill a scholarship.

"I lived right across the Bay and didn't even know there was a University of San Francisco," Russell was to say later. "It was the only scholarship offer I got, so I took it."

The University of San Francisco (USF) was virtually unknown in college basketball at the time. But Russell, along with K. C. Jones, who was later to be a Celtic teammate of Russell's, turned USF into a national basketball power. At one time, the team blazed to 55 consecutive wins. In the seasons of 1954–55 and 1955–56, USF was the nation's top rated college team and the National Collegiate Athletic Association (NCAA) champion. As for Russell himself, he was hailed as the nation's number one college player.

Even before he graduated, Russell began to receive offers from professional clubs. One came from the Harlem Globetrotters, the team of touring basketball funny men. The Globetrotters offered Bill a salary of $32,000 for his first pro year. That was an enormous sum for the day.

But Bill turned down the offer. A very proud man, it irritated him that the representative of the Globetrotters met with his coach at San Francisco and made the offer through him. The man scarcely paid any attention to Bill at all.

The year Bill graduated from San Francisco, 1956, was an Olympic year. He held off signing a contract with a professional team so he could compete with the United States Olympic basketball team. Olympic competition was held in Melbourne, Australia, and Bill and his teammates easily captured the gold medal.

The St. Louis Hawks owned the draft rights to Russell, but they traded the rights to the Boston Celtics for Ed Macauley. "Easy Ed" had been a college star at the University of St. Louis, and the Hawks expected him to attract fans in big numbers.

Arnold (Red) Auerbach, coach of the Celtics, was happy to make the trade. He believed in fast-break basketball, in the run-run-run game. But in his first few years as Boston's coach, Auerbach's tactics didn't bring the team any championships. What good is the fast break if you can't get the ball? What the Celtics needed was a big man to pull down rebounds at the defensive end of the court and start the fast break.

"I don't need shooters," Auerbach said. "Never did. I've always been looking for that good big man to get me the ball." Bill Russell was to be that man.

After Russell returned from Australia, he married his college sweetheart, Rose Swisher. The Russells went to Boston on their honeymoon. While there, Bill signed his first pro contract. It called for a salary of $24,000 for the season. That sum may seem tiny when

Bill Russell (seventh from left, standing) postponed joining a professional basketball team in order to play with the American team in the 1956 Olympics. His prudence was rewarded by a gold medal. *Courtesy of the United States Olympic Committee.*

compared to current salaries, but at the time the amount represented a new high for an NBA rookie.

Some people have said that Bill Russell could have won pro championships had he been teamed with three fourth-graders and a cocker spaniel. Not true. For a team to be successful in the pro ranks, players must represent several different talents. Then these specialists have to learn to work together.

To team with Russell, the Celtics offered a splendid array of talent. It included the sharpshooting Bill Sharman and fancy-dribbling Bob Cousy, perhaps the finest playmaker the pro game has ever known. Tom Heinsohn, who broke in with the team the same year Russell did, became one of the league's best scorers and offensive rebounders.

From the beginning, Russell was a marvel. In one of his first games he held Philadelphia's Neil Johnston score-less for thirty-eight minutes. It was usual for Johnston to score between 20 and 25 points a game. The next night Russell limited Johnston to four field goals.

"Nobody ever blocked shots in the pros before Russell came along," said Red Auerbach. "He upsets everybody. The only defense they can think to dish out is a physical beating and hope he can't take it."

Russell demonstrated that he could not only take the punishment but dominate teams while doing it. He took down 943 rebounds that season, an average of 19.6 rebounds per game, highest in the league.

The Celtics won the Eastern Division title in a breeze. In the playoffs they beat the Syracuse team, two games to one, to win the semifinals. They then faced the St. Louis Hawks for the title in a best of seven series.

The Celtics had no secret weapon. They relied on their fast break (as they were to do for the next decade). Russell would clear the boards, flip the ball to Cousy, who would fly downcourt with the ball, Sharman trailing. Then Cousy would either drive for the basket himself or flip the ball back to Sharman, who would pop his deadly jump shot.

The Celtics won three of the first five games and led through most of the sixth. But the Hawks, playing on their home court, edged into the lead at the buzzer. The teams returned to Boston for the seventh and deciding game.

Boston led, 121–120, with 2 minutes and 16 seconds remaining. Then Tom Heinsohn, their rookie star, fouled out of the game. Exhausted and emotionally drained, he collapsed in tears on the bench and buried his face in a towel.

The teams traded free throws. Then Russell blocked a St. Louis shot. The ball went to Boston's "super sub," Frank Ramsey. Ramsey tossed in a 20-footer. Boston's lead was three points, 124–121.

After another St. Louis free throw, Med Park, a St. Louis substitute, was fouled. If he could make both shots, the score would be tied. His first shot was good. His second shot caromed off the rim. Russell's powerful hands grasped the rebound.

Boston added a free throw to lead, 125–123. There were two seconds left to play.

Alex Hannum, the St. Louis player-coach, would not give up. He knew the clock would not start until someone on the court touched his team's in-bounds pass. His plan was to fire the ball the length of the court, hit the back-board, and have Bob Pettit, the team's best player, tap-in the rebound.

Hannum's throw was perfect. The ball rebounded into Pettit's hands. Six feet from the basket, he arched the ball up. The crowd gasped as it rolled around the rim—and out.

Bedlam broke out. The Celtics had won. They were champions of the world. What was to become the greatest dynasty in the history of professional sports had claimed its first title.

The NBA championship was Russell's third title within a year. He had led San Francisco to the NBA crown twelve months before, and the Olympic championship had come only six months after that.

At the end of the 1957–58 season Boston and St. Louis met again in the finals, and St. Louis got revenge. In the third game, Russell suffered a chipped bone in his right ankle and some torn tendons. He tried to play in the sixth game but was useless. The Celtics went down to defeat, 4 games to 2.

The Celtics recaptured the championship the next year, beating Minneapolis in the finals. They knocked off the Hawks for the title both in 1960 and 1961.

Russell missed four games in 1962 because of a muscle strain—and the Celtics lost all four. It marked the first time in five years that the team had a losing streak that long. It prompted one Boston newspaper reporter to pen this rhyme:

The Celtics had hustle
But they didn't have Russell,

So naturally wound up
Losing the tussle.

When Bill returned to the lineup, the Celtics ripped off six straight victories. "I guess that proves what makes the Celtics click," said Jack Twyman of the Rochester Royals. "Without Russell, they can be had."

Countless others must have agreed, for Russell was the runaway winner in the balloting for the league's most valuable player that season. He was now being acclaimed as the finest defensive player in basketball history.

But in the minutes before a game, Russell was anything but a daunting figure. He had a nervous stomach. He often got so deathly sick that it seemed certain he would never recover in time to play.

"I'm dying, Red," he would say to Auerbach. "I can't make it."

The coach was always sympathetic. "Just take it easy, Bill," he would say. "And don't worry. We'll start somebody else if you don't feel better by game time."

It was the right strategy. Russell never actually allowed his fluttering stomach to keep him out of the lineup.

Sometimes the pressure would be so great that Russell would get just as sick after the game as before. The final game of the 1962 playoffs between the Celts and the Los Angeles Lakers was one of the most tension-filled of Russell's career. With 7 seconds left and the score tied, Frank Selvy of the Lakers dribbled up the left side of the court and lofted a soft jumper from fifteen feet. The ball hovered on the rim, then rolled off. Russell soared over Elgin Baylor, seized the ball with both hands, and hugged it to his body as the buzzer went off. The game was in overtime.

Russell, totally exhausted and still clutching the ball, sank to the floor. He remained there without moving for about thirty seconds. Then he got up slowly and walked to the Celtics' bench. As the team gathered about him, the trainer poured ice water on the back of Bill's neck. Bill took a deep breath and stood up. As he walked out on the court to begin the overtime period, the Boston Garden shook with cheers and applause.

Russell grabbed two key rebounds during the overtime to help the Celtics win, 110–107. It was more Russell's victory than anyone else's. He had tied his own playoff record with 40 rebounds. He had scored 30 points and played all 53 minutes.

But the ordeal had taken its toll. When the game was over, Russell blindly followed his teammates to the locker room. Then he got sick. Then he began to cry.

Once he felt himself again, he met with reporters. "This one meant more to me than any other," he said with a grin. "But those Lakers give me the feeling that things aren't going to be the same next year."

Russell may have been an exceptional basketball player, but he wasn't very good at forecasting the future. The Celtics had no trouble with the Lakers or anyone else over the next four years, winning the championship each year.

During his career, Russell was often pitted against Wilt Chamberlain of the Philadelphia Warriors, the league's scoring champion season in and season out. Huge crowds flocked to see the two men whenever they met.

Russell always praised Chamberlain and even hailed him as the "greatest player of all time." What Russell had to say about his rival sometimes seemed intended to keep Wilt from getting stirred up. "I have a three-part defense I use against him," Russell once said. "One, I try to keep him from the ball. Two, if that doesn't work, I try to stay between him and the basket. Three is when everything else fails. I panic." With that, Russell would let loose with a loud burst of cackling laughter.

But Russell knew that Chamberlain was no laughing matter. One night Chamberlain scored 45 points against him. Russell cried afterward. "Pride has always been very important to me," he said.

Professional basketball has never seen the likes of Wilt Chamberlain, a devastating scorer. In his rookie season of 1960–61, Chamberlain averaged 38.4 points per game. Russell's average that season was less than half that, 16.9 points per game.

The following season, 1961–62, Chamberlain raised his scoring average to a startling 50.4 points per game, establishing a record that still stands. Russell averaged 18.9 points a game that season.

But while Chamberlain was able to score as no other individual had done before, he was not a consistent winner. The championships always seemed to go to Russell and his Celtic teammates. To many, Wilt came to represent individual achievement. Russell, on the other hand, was the symbol of teamwork, the unselfish player—just as happy to feed a teammate as toss the ball up. And he was also a great defensive star.

Russell took over the job of coaching the Celtics for the season of 1966–67, while continuing to play. Perhaps that was a mistake, or maybe Chamberlain was concentrating on teamwork more. Whatever the reason, the Celtics were trampled by Chamberlain's 76ers in the playoffs that season.

Russell came back the next year as a player-coach again. The Chamberlain-led Philadelphia 76ers won the Eastern Division title by eight games, and it seemed as if a new dynasty was beginning. But in the Division playoffs, the Celtics cooled off the 76ers, 4 games to 3. It was Boston's tenth NBA championship in eleven years.

Before the 1969–70 season, Russell, with a year to go on his contract, decided to retire. He explained his decision in an article in *Sports Illustrated.* He noted that he had played some 3,000 games of basketball, "organized or other," adding, "I think that's enough."

He complained that his knees hurt. "They've been hurting for ten years," he said, "and my ankle has been hurting ever since I broke it in 1958."

But Russell declared he wasn't giving up the game because he played in pain. His interest in the sport was ebbing. ". . . I am not involved anymore," he said. If he continued to play, he'd be playing only for the money, he said, and he didn't want to do that.

Russell described himself as a "professional entertainer," and said that the field of entertainment would be a "natural path" for him to follow. For a time, he was a television sports commentator. Critics applauded him for his confident naturalness.

He was back in basketball in 1973

with the Seattle Supersonics, signing on as coach and general manager. In 1974–75, under Russell's leadership, the Supersonics made the playoffs for the first time. Russell was elected to the Basketball Hall of Fame in 1975.

Many great centers have followed in Russell's wake. They include Bob Lanier of the Milwaukee Bucks, an exceptional shotmaker; Artis Gilmore of the Chicago Bulls, perhaps the strongest center to play the game, aside from Chamberlain; Moses Malone of the Philadelphia 76ers, the best rebounding center of the 1980s; and, of course, Kareem Abdul-Jabbar, the great All-Pro center of the Los Angeles Lakers who, as a scorer, rewrote the NBA record book.

But none—Lanier, Gilmore, Malone, or Abdul-Jabbar—was the equal of Bill Russell. He was a dominating force in any game in which he played, the most devastating player in the history of the sport. And he was, as *Sports Illustrated* once called him, "a one-man revolution."

Additional Reading

Russell, Bill, as told to William McSweeny. *Go Up for Glory.* New York: Coward-McCann, 1968.

Russell, Bill, and Taylor Branch. *Second Wind: The Memoirs of an Opinionated Man.* New York: Random House, 1979.

Babe Ruth

Baseball's Greatest Player
1895–1948

Thanks to his ability as the sport's first great home-run hitter and his colorful personality, Babe Ruth was the biggest hero baseball ever produced. He had such an enormous influence on baseball that historians of the sport often refer to the 1920s as "The Babe Ruth Era."

Ruth, who joined the New York Yankees in 1920 after several seasons with the Boston Red Sox, hit more than 50 homers in four different seasons, including a record 60 in 1927. Before Ruth, no player had hit more than 24 homers in a season. Ruth's record of 714 career homers lasted for almost forty years.

Ruth's home run totals so impressed major league owners that they livened up the baseball in 1921. Their motive was to get more players hitting home runs and thus boost attendance in every park in both leagues. As a further aid to batters, such trick deliveries as the spitball and mudball were forbidden. Batters began trying to take advantage of these changes. More and more became full swingers, like Ruth, rather than poke and place hitters.

But neither free-swinging batters nor a ban on trick pitches nor the "rabbit" baseball could produce another Babe Ruth. He was one of a kind.

Mention the name Babe Ruth and many people call up the image of an overweight slugger who always swung for the fences. This is only partly true. Ruth was a complete ballplayer, one of the best of all time.

As a left-handed pitcher with the Boston Red Sox, he won 18 games in his rookie season of 1915. He won 23 games the next year and 24 games the year after that. The Red Sox then decided to assign Ruth to the outfield because they wanted his powerful bat available every day. Ruth's record of pitching 29⅔ consecutive scoreless innings in World Series play stood for 43 years before Whitey Ford of the Yankees broke it.

Ruth was a splendid outfielder, able to cover plenty of territory despite his bigness. He had an excellent arm and a keen baseball sense. He always seemed to be positioned in the right spot. He could be depended upon to throw to the right base.

Besides his many talents, Ruth had a theatrical flair; he was a showman. He married his second wife, Clair Hodgson, early in the morning on the opening day of the 1929 baseball season. The new Mrs. Ruth watched the game from a box seat. The bridegroom hit a home run. As he rounded second base, he stopped and swept off his cap in a deep bow to his bride.

There are countless other stories about Babe and his sense of the dramatic. More than once he visited some sick child in a hospital and promised to hit a home run—and did. He opened Yankee Stadium with a home run against the Boston Red Sox. At the age of forty he closed out his career as a player by smacking three mighty blasts out of Forbes Field in Pittsburgh.

The most talked-about and written-about incident of his career took place during the 1932 World Series, the last in which Ruth played. The Yankees faced the Cubs at Chicago's Wrigley Field. The score was 4–4 when Ruth went to bat in the fifth inning with the bases empty. Charley Root was pitching for the Cubs.

Ruth had lifted the Yankees into a three-run lead in the first inning by smashing a home run off Root with two men on base. Now, with Ruth at the plate again, the crowd booed loudly.

Root pitched and Ruth swung and missed. Ruth stepped out of the batter's box and lifted a finger. "One," he was saying.

Root poured a second strike past Ruth. Again the Babe stepped out. This time he raised two fingers. "Two." Then Ruth, according to witnesses, took his bat and pointed it dramatically forward toward the bleachers in right-center field. And that is where he hit the next pitch.

Ruth's home run made the score 5–4. Lou Gehrig followed with a homer, and the Yankees won, 7–5. The victory gave the Yanks a 3–0 victory lead in games. The next day they ended it.

"It was impossible," wrote Paul Gallico in *Farewell to Sport*, "to watch him at bat without experiencing an emotion." Said Gallico: ". . . when he connected, the result was the most perfect

Babe Ruth (with teammate Lou Gehrig) set a record for home runs that was to remain unbroken for almost forty years. *Courtesy of the National Baseball Library, Cooperstown, N.Y.*

thing of its kind, a ball whacked so high, wide and handsome that no stadium in the entire country could contain it. . . ."

The name of Babe Ruth appeared in the newspapers so often that reporters and columnists invented nicknames for him. They called him "The Sultan of Swat" and "The King of Clout." "Bambino" was another favorite, which headline writers sometimes shortened to "Bam."

His on-the-field exploits and his off-the-field antics provided the press with a never-ending stream of material. There was his salary for one thing. He was paid astronomical sums by standards of the time. In 1922, Ruth signed for $52,000. By comparison, Wally Schang, the team's catcher and one of the best in baseball, was earning $10,000. Pitcher Bob Shawkey, a 20-game winner three times, was receiving $6,500. Babe received $70,000 from 1927 through 1929 and $80,000 in 1930 and 1931.

Ruth had a gusto for living, but sometimes he went too far. In 1922, for instance, he left the field to pursue a fan in the stands who had been taunting him. He drank too much; he gambled too much. He quarreled with Yankee manager Miller Huggins and baseball commissioner Kenesaw Mountain Landis. He even played some bad baseball.

At the annual dinner of the Baseball Writers Association of America, Jimmy Walker, a New York state senator and later the mayor of New York, made a public plea for Ruth to reform, asking Ruth to be mindful that he was an example to the youth of America. Ruth, deeply moved, got to his feet and, with tears streaming down his face, promised to behave for the sake of the kids of the nation. And he kept the promise. He was never in serious trouble again.

George Herman Ruth was born on February 6, 1895, in Baltimore, Maryland to George and Kate Schamberger Ruth. The building in which he was born at 216 Emory Street is now the Babe Ruth Birthplace Museum. A life-size model of the hero stands at the door. The museum also houses the Baltimore Orioles' Hall of Fame.

Ruth was brought up on the south side of Baltimore, close to the waterfront, in a poor, rough neighborhood. Eventually seven other children were born to the Ruths. The father owned a saloon. Both of his parents worked hard.

Young George's father faced constant problems in running the saloon. His mother was often sick. They did not have much time to look after George. He seldom went to school, preferring to roam the streets with friends. "I learned to fear and hate the coppers and to throw apples and eggs at the truckdrivers," Ruth declared in later years. It has been written that young George chewed tobacco, drank whiskey, and stole. "I was a bum when I was a kid," Ruth once told Bob Considine.

The older he got, the more difficult George was to control. The Ruths eventually felt forced to place their unruly son in St. Mary's Industrial School for Boys on the outskirts of Baltimore. St. Mary's was a reform school. Boys who went there were labeled "bad."

The school was staffed by the Xaverian Brothers, a Catholic teaching order. Physical exercise was considered very important. The approximately 800 boys who were cared for at the school played soccer, handball, volleyball, and basketball. They also participated in track, boxing, and wrestling.

The favorite sport was baseball. Teams were organized on all levels. Ruth caught, played third base and pitched. By the time he was eighteen, George was the biggest boy in the school and the best baseball player. He hit some tremendous home runs. When he was twenty and in his last year at St. Mary's, he hit a home run in almost every game he played.

Word of Ruth's heroics reached the ears of Jack Dunn, owner and manager of the Baltimore Orioles, then members of the International League. Dunn went to St. Mary's to scout Ruth. In the game Dunn saw, Ruth hurled a 6–0 shutout, striking out twenty-two batters. Two weeks later, Dunn signed Ruth to his first professional contract.

Since Ruth was not yet twenty-one, the superintendent of St. Mary's was his legal guardian. It was arranged that George would be "paroled" in the custody of Jack Dunn. When the Orioles went south for spring training in 1914, George Ruth went with them. "He was free," writes Robert W. Creamer in his dramatic biography of Ruth. "After all those years, he was finally out of the cage, and no one was ever going to get him back in one again."

To the veteran players on the Oriole team, Ruth was an innocent young kid. They referred to him as "Dunn's newest babe." And soon they were calling Ruth by the nickname "Babe," which was common in those days. The newspapers picked it up and then the fans did.

It didn't take Ruth long to justify the faith that Dunn had in him. He won eight of his first nine games, often aiding his own cause with long-ball hits.

The powerful Orioles seemed headed for the International League pennant, but the fans never responded to the team's excellent play.

At some games there were no more

Sent to reform school in his youth, Babe Ruth conducted himself as a model of good behavior after he attained stardom. *Courtesy of the National Baseball Library, Cooperstown, N.Y.*

than 150 people in the stands. Dunn had to sell his star players to keep from going broke. Ruth was one of the players Dunn peddled. In July 1914 the Babe was sold to the Boston Red Sox.

When the season was over, Ruth, who was twenty, married Helen Woodford, a seventeen-year-old waitress from Boston. Helen Ruth died tragically in a fire in 1929.

By 1916 Ruth was being hailed as the best left-handed pitcher in baseball. He had a 23–12 record that year. He was impressive as a slugger, too. Since he was the only member of the Red Sox able to draw fans, the management decided he should concentrate on hitting and play every day. The changeover from mound to outfield began in 1918. By midseason the following year, Ruth was an outfielder, and except for a few brief appearances for publicity purposes he did not pitch again.

The modern American League record for home runs at the time was 16, held by Ralph (Socks) Seybold of the Philadelphia As. Seybold had retired in 1908. The all-time record holder was Edward (Ned) Williamson, who had collected 27 home runs for the Chicago White Stockings in 1884.

Ruth started pursuing both records. Fans jammed ballparks to watch him. Newspapers used special boxes on the sports pages to help keep track of the chase.

On August 14 Ruth hit his 17th home run, establishing a new American League record. His 20th homer was his fourth grand-slammer of the season. It stood as the major league record until Ernie Banks of the Cubs hit five in 1955.

On September 20, in the second game of a doubleheader against the White Sox at Fenway Park, Ruth tied Williamson's mark. He broke the record a few days later in New York, blasting a tremendous drive over the roof of the Polo Grounds.

Ruth ended the season with 29 home runs. His final homer of the year was struck in Washington, the first he ever hit there. It gave him the distinction of hitting at least one home run in every city in the league. No one had ever done that before.

Nowadays, to hit 29 home runs in a season is considered a rather modest achievement. Several players in each league are capable of doing it. But in Ruth's day, it was extraordinary. Imagine a player today hitting 65 or 70 homers. That would be a feat comparable to what Ruth did in 1919.

After the season Ruth was hailed as the greatest home-run hitter baseball had ever known, and he had only 49 homers in his entire career.

Despite the fact that Ruth was a national sensation, his team, the Red Sox, were in deep financial trouble. The club management decided to put Ruth's contract up for sale. The Yankees agreed to buy Ruth from the Sox for $100,000, the biggest amount ever paid for a player.

The Babe's popularity skyrocketed in New York. The Yankees played their home games at the Polo Grounds, located in Upper Manhattan, when Ruth first joined the team. In 1920, when the team was in the thick of the pennant race and Ruth was belting home runs at a record clip, the stadium was filled to capacity in one game after another. That year the Yankees became the first team in baseball history to draw over a million fans for a season.

Ruth almost doubled his record in 1920 when he hit 54 homers. The career record for home runs at the time was 136, held by Roger Connor. Ruth surpassed Connor's mark in 1921. Thus, in his third season as a full-time hitter, Ruth became the all-time home run champion.

Ruth hit 59 homers in 1921. But he did not surpass 59 until 1927, the year he hit 60. That deed, along with his .625 batting average in the 1928 World Series (10 hits in 16 at-bats), are considered the standout statistical achievements of his career.

Ruth hit his 700th homer in 1934. At the time, only two other players had struck as many as 300. When Ruth retired in 1935, his career total stood at 714. He had more than twice as many homers as the second man on the list.

At the time of his retirement Ruth also held the record for the highest slugging average for a season, .847, which he set in 1920. He also had the highest career slugging average, .690. (A slugging average is obtained by dividing the total bases reached on safe hits by the number of official times at bat.) Those two records still stand.

Ruth's record of 60 home runs fell in 1961, when Roger Maris of the Yankees hit 61 homers. Ruth's career record of 714 homers stood until Hank Aaron of the Atlanta Braves hit his 715th homer in 1974. Aaron ended his career with 755 home runs.

In 1935 Ruth joined the Boston Braves as a player, assistant manager, and vice-president. Despite the many titles, he was never happy with the club and left after three troubled months. He had one memorable game with the Braves, hitting three home runs against the Pittsburgh Pirates, the last homers of his career.

Babe was hired as a coach by the Brooklyn Dodgers in 1938 in an obvious attempt to boost attendance. The Dodger players loved him. They would cluster around him in hotel lobbies to listen to his tales. But Ruth's stay with the Dodgers was shorter than his sojourn with the Braves.

In retirement Babe played golf and bowled. He played himself in the movie, *Pride of the Yankees,* based on the life of Lou Gehrig. He had his own radio show for a time.

In 1946 Ruth learned he had cancer. A day was held in his honor at Yankee Stadium in April 1948. About 60,000 people turned out. When Ruth spoke, his voice was weak and raspy. "There have been so many lovely things said about me," he declared, "I'm glad I had the opportunity of thanking everybody." Then he smiled, waved to the crowd, and walked slowly to the Yankee dugout. Two months later he died.

Additional Reading

Creamer, Robert W. *Babe: The Legend Comes to Life.* New York: Simon & Schuster, 1974.

Smelser, Marshall. *The Life that Ruth Built: A Biography.* New York: Times Books, 1975.

Jim Thorpe

America's Great Athlete
1888–1953

Jim Thorpe was nineteen, a lean, strong six-footer, when he tried out for football at the Carlisle Indian School in the fall of 1908. To make the team, Thorpe had to pass a "test" that had been devised by the team's coach, Glenn (Pop) Warner.

Warner instructed Thorpe to stand at one of the goal lines. He then positioned the entire first string team around the field. The ball was to be punted to Jim, who would attempt to carry it through the players all the way to the far end zone. Few players had ever gotten as far as midfield, much less the goal line.

Warner signaled the punter. The ball soared into the air. Thorpe gathered it in, charged straight ahead, then wheeled and twisted his way through the entire squad.

The coach could hardly believe his eyes. He ordered the drill to be run again. Thorpe ran straight through everybody a second time.

When Warner said to him, "You know, this was supposed to be tackling practice," Thorpe replied, "Nobody tackles Jim."

Few people did in the seasons that followed. Not only was Thorpe devastating as a ball carrier, he passed, punted, blocked, and kicked. He played football as a teenager and was still playing it twenty-five years later as a professional.

He tried baseball, too. The 1913 World Series with the New York Giants highlighted his eight-year career.

At the Olympic Games at Stockholm, Sweden, in 1912, Thorpe performed the dazzling feat of winning both the five-event pentathlon and ten-event decathlon. No athlete had ever done that before.

King Gustav of Sweden presented the winners their gold medals. When it was Thorpe's turn, he draped the medal about his shoulders and said, "Sir, you are the greatest athlete in the world."

In the years since, King Gustav's words have been echoed and reechoed. In 1950, Thorpe was declared the "best athlete of the first half of the century" by an Associated Press poll of hundreds of sportswriters. Many experts agree that he will still be Number 1 in the year 2000.

But while Thorpe's life had its moments of high triumph, it was frequently marred by tragedy and despair. His is not always a pretty story.

The man whose athletic prowess led him to become a sports legend in America developed his speed, strength, and agility on the broad, flat prairieland of central Oklahoma. There, on May 28, 1888, near the town of Shawnee, he was born to Charlotte View and Hiram Thorpe. He was one of twin boys. The other was named Charles.

Jim's father was half Irish, half native American. His mother was the granddaughter of Chief Black Hawk, one of the great Sac and Fox warriors.

The Thorpe family had been granted 160 acres of farm and forest land by the federal government. As a boy, Jim farmed and helped out with the hogs and cattle. He tracked game, hunted and fished. He was ten when he bagged his first deer. He could ride a wild pony and was an excellent shot with a rifle.

He and Charles attended a grade school on the Sac and Fox reservation. They had been going to school for only a few years when Jim suffered the first of a number of personal tragedies. Charles was stricken with pneumonia. Doctors could not reduce the high fever that racked his body. The boy grew weaker and weaker and finally died. Jim had lost not only his twin brother but his closest friend.

When Jim was fifteen, his life changed abruptly. An official of the Carlisle Indian School, traveling across the Sac and Fox lands scouting for new students, stopped near the Thorpe home. Carlisle (no longer in existence) was a well-known institution operated by the federal government to teach Indian boys various trades. With a student body of more than one thousand, it was housed on an old army post near Harrisburg, Pennsylvania.

The official talked to Jim to find out whether he would like to attend Carlisle. Jim decided he would. He arrived at Carlisle in the fall of 1903. There and then the Thorpe legend began. He was, in his own words, "just a skinny little jigger" at the time. But he was growing fast.

Jim had been at Carlisle only a few weeks when he received the tragic news of his father's death. Jim's mother had died several years earlier. The people he loved the most were now gone. There was no one left.

Jim became an apprentice tailor at Carlisle and joined the tailors' football team in the school's shop league. In 1906 the tailors won the league championship.

One crisp fall day, Jim stopped to watch tryouts for the track team. One after another, the candidates muffed the high jump, nudging the bar to the ground. I can clear that bar, Jim thought. Although he was wearing heavy clothing and thick boots, he soared over the bar easily.

Pop Warner, the Carlisle football coach, happened to be passing by and saw Thorpe go over the bar. He knew he could make use of a boy with that kind of skill. He persuaded Jim to try out for the football team.

After Jim had passed Warner's "test" and made the team, he sat on the bench for the first few games. Then, in a game against Penn, the starting left halfback (a position now called running back) was injured, and Jim was sent in. He was new to the position and did not know the plays. The first time they gave him the ball, he was flattened behind the line of scrimmage. Carlisle lost five yards on the play.

"Give it to me again," Jim said in the huddle. Flashing his speed and flicking his hips, Jim ran 65 yards for a touchdown. Warner counted the Penn tacklers strewn about the field. There were seven of them.

From that beginning, Thorpe's football career took off like a rocket. The Carlisle team won ten of thirteen games that season, and Thorpe's name was in the headlines often. The following spring, Jim blossomed as a track star. He was seldom beaten as a sprinter, hurdler, or high-jumper. He also starred in lacrosse and was a hard-hitting first baseman on the baseball team.

Sports were his whole world. And Carlisle was becoming his home.

In the spring of 1909, Thorpe began making plans for summer vacation. Many of the Carlisle students were assigned to work on farms during the summer months. Jim had done farm work the summer before, and he didn't like it.

Warner suggested that Thorpe and two of his teammates, Joe Libby and Jesse Youngdeer, go to North Carolina and play baseball for the summer. Teams in the Eastern Carolina Association were looking for players, Warner said. They each could earn around $25 a week.

It was common practice in those days for college players to sign up with little-known professional teams for the summer. Many players used false names to deceive officials. Thorpe did not.

Jim pitched for Rocky Mount that summer, winning 23 games. The following summer he went back. He played for Rocky Mount for a while and then switched to a team in Fayetteville. Shortly after, the league folded and Jim returned to Oklahoma.

Late in the summer of 1911, Jim received a letter from Warner. "If you come back to Carlisle and start training," the coach said, "I think you can make the Olympic team that is going to Sweden next year."

Jim had missed Carlisle, his friends, and teammates, and he jumped at the chance to return. He was bigger now, with a thick neck and heavy thighs. He was faster, too.

Thorpe hadn't touched a football for almost two years. Warner used him only sparingly in the first game of the season against Dickinson College. Although Thorpe played only seventeen minutes, he scored seventeen points.

Thorpe was merely warming up. The next week he scored three touchdowns in Carlisle's defeat of Mount St. Mary's.

Pittsburgh, a powerhouse of a team, was next on Carlisle's schedule. Carlisle was very much the underdog. The Pittsburgh players were determined to "get" Thorpe. Every time he carried the ball, two or three or four Pittsburgh players piled upon him. He felt the sting of knees, elbows and fists. But the rougher they played, the rougher *he* played.

"This time left tackle," he would shout to the players across the line, and then he'd grab the ball, clutch it to his belly, and hurl his body at left tackle. "Center," he called out. Then he'd hit into the middle of the line.

Throughout the afternoon, Thorpe kept challenging the enemy tacklers to stop him. But they could not. He leveled them with straight arms or sent them reeling with his quick hip thrusts. Carlisle won, 17–0. Said one sportswriter: "The Red Man is all they say he is—and more."

Carlisle downed Harvard that season, 18–15, in what was one of football's most stunning upsets. Harvard had been ranked the No. 1 team in the country before the game. It was another brilliant day for Thorpe, as he scored every one of Carlisle's eighteen points. When the train carrying the team arrived in Harrisburg from Boston, the entire student body was on hand to greet the players.

The next spring, Thorpe had no trouble making the Olympic team. He was so confident of his skills, he never felt

At the 1912 Olympics, Jim Thorpe achieved an unprecedented victory when he won both the pentathlon and the decathlon. *Courtesy of the United States Olympic Committee.*

the urge to practice hard. In Sweden, waiting for the games to begin, Thorpe took long naps in a hammock while the other athletes practiced running, jumping and throwing.

One day he heard someone mention the distance that the leading competitors in the broad jump were expected to leap. Thorpe got out of his hammock, measured off the distance, and looked at it closely. Certain that he could jump that far, he climbed back into the hammock and continued his nap.

Thorpe's reluctance to practice did not seem to do him any harm. In winning the pentathlon gold medal, he was first in four of the five events—the broad jump, discus, and 100-meter and 200-meter dashes. He was third in the javelin throw. In winning the pentathlon, Thorpe ran up a point total that was twice that of his nearest rival, Ferdinand Bie of Norway.

The pentathlon was tough, but the decathlon was much tougher. Indeed, it is considered the most grueling Olympic test of all. Thorpe placed first in the shot put, high hurdles, high jump, and 1,500-meter run. He finished no worse than fourth in the six remaining events—the pole vault, javelin, broad jump, discus, 100-meter dash, and 400-meter run. Thorpe scored an incredible 8,412 points, a full 700 points ahead of Hugo Wieslander of Sweden, the runner-up.

When Thorpe returned home, there was a parade through the streets of New York in his honor. At the White House he received the personal congratulations of President William Howard Taft.

Once back at Carlisle, he plunged into the fall sports. Thorpe's greatest days in football that season came against Army, ranked as the Number 2 team in the nation. As usual, Carlisle was the underdog.

Carlisle scored first when Jim stormed into the middle of the Army line and wrenched into the end zone, carrying three Army tacklers with him. Not long after, Jim threw a pass for a second touchdown, and later in the game he fielded a punt on the Carlisle 10-yard line, headed for a sideline, cut back, and then ran straight down the field for a third touchdown. But the touchdown was called back because Carlisle had been offside.

Army punted again. This time Thorpe picked up the ball on the Carlisle 5-yard line and ran 95 yards into the Army end zone. The final score saw Carlisle on top, 27–6.

One Army player had injured his knee trying to tackle Thorpe. He had to be helped from the field, and he never was able to play football again. The player's name was Dwight D. Eisenhower, who was to become the thirty-fourth President of the United States.

"Thorpe gained ground; he *always* gained ground," Eisenhower was to say in later years. "He was the greatest man I ever saw."

Jim was at the peak of his career when, in January 1913, an event occurred that was to cast a shadow over the rest of his life. A newspaper reported that he had been paid for playing baseball in the Eastern Carolina Association several years before. This raised the question whether he had actually been an amateur in the Olympics. The news flashed around the country.

The Amateur Athletic Union (AAU), which decided upon the status of team members, asked Jim to explain. He instantly admitted receiving money. "I didn't know that I was doing wrong," he said, "because I was doing what many other college men had done, except that they did not use their own names."

The AAU could not be swayed. The organization ruled that Thorpe had been a pro at the time he had competed in the Olympics. The International Olympic Committee stripped Jim of his medals, ordered him to return them, and erased his name from the official Olympic records.

Thorpe's great pride did not permit him to speak out. He accepted the AAU's harsh verdict stoically.

Thorpe spent the next sixteen years of his life as a professional athlete. He tried baseball first. Several major league teams had sent scouts to Carlisle to try to get Jim's name on a contract. He finally signed with the New York Giants. (The team moved to San Francisco at the end of the 1957 season.)

The Giants had won the National League pennant for three consecutive years beginning in 1911. Jim, who arrived upon the scene in the spring of 1913, found the team brimming with stars. It was tough for him to break into the starting lineup.

The fiery John McGraw managed the Giants. McGraw believed in hard work and long practice sessions. Thorpe, who played the outfield, did not. Thorpe believed baseball should be fun. He and McGraw often feuded.

Before the season was very old, McGraw sent Thorpe to a Giant minor league team in Milwaukee. Jim played there for most of the season of 1913 and 1914. However, he was recalled for and played in the 1913 World Series, which the Giants lost to the Philadelphia As, four games to one.

During his first season at Milwaukee, Thorpe married Iva Miller, whom he had known at Carlisle. The couple had four children.

In 1917 Jim was hit with another tragedy. His three-year-old son, Jim, Jr., whom he adored, came down with infantile paralysis. The vaccines now available that help prevent polio had not yet been discovered. Jim's son died in a week.

Jim went on a rampage. He disappeared and no one could find him. Then one day he was back and playing baseball again. He wore the familiar grin and joked with his teammates, but he had been deeply scarred.

Besides the Giants, Thorpe played briefly for the Cincinnati Reds and Boston Bees. It was sometimes said that Jim's career was hindered because he had difficulty hitting curve balls. In his six-year major league career—269 games—Thorpe batted .252. This suggests that the curve, or something, was troublesome.

After the baseball season ended in 1915, Jim received an offer from the Canton (Ohio) Bulldogs to play professional football. The pro game was much different then. There was no league, no formal schedule. Often players were paid out of what could be collected by a passing of a hat among the spectators.

Jim Cusack, who owned the Canton team, offered Thorpe a salary of $500 a game. "You're paying him too much," Cusack was told. But the Canton owner believed there was magic in Thorpe's name, that big crowds would pay to see him play. Cusack was right. Canton had been averaging about a thousand fans a game, but with Thorpe in the lineup, attendance jumped to 6,000 a game and then to 8,000.

Playing pro football against Jim Thorpe was something like being in a street brawl. He wore special shoulder pads of hard leather. "They hit like iron," said George Halas, who had played against him. "He blocked with his shoulder, and it felt like he had hit you with a four-by-four. He was a great defensive player, too. If he hit you from behind, he'd throw that big body across your back and about break you in two."

Another player of that period, Pete Calac, once said, "Jim had one way of running I never saw before. Not everyone wore helmets in those days, and Jim would shift his hip toward the guy about to tackle him, then swing it away. And then when the player moved in to hit him, he'd swing the hip back hard against the tackler's head and leave him lying there.

"He talked a lot during a game, too. I mean, he'd say to a tackle on the other side of the line, 'I'm coming right over.' Then, like as not, he would."

Thorpe was still with the Bulldogs in 1920 when representatives of eight of the pro teams then active got together to form an organized league. They called it the American Professional Football Association, and they elected Jim as the league's first president.

Thorpe served as president for a year and also continued playing. In 1922 the league changed its name to what it is today, becoming the National Football League.

Thorpe was aging. His skills were eroding.

On November 30, 1929, the Associated Press carried this story: "Chicago—The Chicago Bears routed their ancient rivals the Chicago Cardinals, 34–0, in the annual Thanksgiving Day game at Wrigley Field today. Jim Thorpe played a few minutes for the Cardinals, but was unable to get anywhere. In his forties and muscle-bound, Thorpe was a mere shadow of his former self."

Difficult years followed. Thorpe had trouble getting work. He drank too much. Now when his name appeared in the newspapers, there was usually sadness connected to the story. One told how he was digging ditches for a living. Another reported he was broke and couldn't afford to buy a ticket for the 1932 Olympics, held in Los Angeles.

His first marriage had ended in divorce. His drinking led to the breakup of a second marriage in 1945. The same year, Thorpe married for a third time.

Thorpe lived in California during the last years of his life. He died of a heart attack in his house trailer in Lomita, a suburb of Los Angeles, on March 28, 1952. He was a couple of months shy of his sixty-fifth birthday.

The saga of one of the world's greatest athletes did not end with his death. Through the years his family and friends struggled to have Jim's medals and titles restored. Their efforts met with success in 1973 when the AAU reversed its position. Thorpe's titles should be restored, said the AAU. Two years later, the U.S. Olympic Committee followed the lead of the AAU and also changed its position.

One stumbling block remained—the International Olympic Committee. Not until 1982 did the IOC vote to restore Thorpe's titles. In January the following year, new medals were presented to his children in a ceremony in Los Angeles.

Jim's name, however, did not go into the record books as the sole winner of the pentathlon and decathlon. The IOC continued to recognize the second-place finishers, Ferdinand Bie of Norway in the pentathlon, and Hugo Wieslander of Sweden in the decathlon, as winners. Thorpe's name was merely added as a co-champion. This decision has been widely criticized. If Thorpe's status has been changed, if his offspring have been awarded his medals, then he should be declared the sole winner, the critics say.

The chapter concerning Jim Thorpe and the Olympics seems to be closed. But another remains open. When Thorpe died, his third wife dictated where he would be buried. She chose the town of Mauch (pronounced Mock) Chunk in northeastern Pennsylvania. Some civic leaders in Mauch Chunk believed that being known as the burial place of the great Jim Thorpe would give the town a boost. There was talk of a new hospital and a Jim Thorpe museum. Town officials agreed to change the name of the town to Jim Thorpe (the name by which it is known today) in exchange for Thorpe's body. Thorpe's widow agreed to these terms.

The odd burial arrangements upset Jim's seven sons and daughters. They felt that their father's body was sold as a tourist attraction. Moreover, they said that their father's soul was doomed to wander aimlessly until his body could be returned to his native Oklahoma and given a proper Indian burial. The family wants the town to give up the body so it can be buried with his Indian ancestors. "Dad's been dead almost thirty years, and his spirit is still roaming," forty-five-year-old Jack Thorpe, one of Jim's sons, told *Sports Illustrated* in 1982.

Up until 1985, the efforts of Jim Thorpe's family to have his body moved to ancestral ground had not been successful, but the family continued in its quest. The sadness and controversy that often characterized Jim Thorpe's life seem to pursue him in death as well.

Additional Reading

Newcombe, Jack. *The Best of the Athletic Boys.* New York: Doubleday & Co., 1975.

Wheeler, Robert W. *Jim Thorpe: World's Greatest Athlete.* Norman, Oklahoma: University of Oklahoma Press, 1979.

Johnny Unitas

Mr. Quarterback
1933–

A quarterback in the National Football League has to know how to handle the ball smoothly to execute fakes and hand off on running plays. He has to know how to read defenses and call plays. And it doesn't hurt if he knows how to run a little.

But most of all, a pro quarterback has to know how to throw the ball. Throwing the ball is what Johnny Unitas did best.

No one was better than Unitas when it came to quick and accurate short passes, and he was a great long passer, perhaps the best pro football has ever known. From his rookie season, 1956, until his retirement in 1973, Unitas completed the most passes in football history (2,830) for the most yards (40,239) and the most touchdowns (342). (Fran Tarkenton later topped

these records.) Unitas set another mark by throwing at least one touchdown pass in 47 consecutive games. Three times he was the NFL's Most Valuable Player, the first time at twenty-five.

Unitas guided the Baltimore Colts to classic triumphs over the New York Giants in NFL title games in 1958 and 1959. Twice he saw the Colts go for Super Bowl glory. In Super V in 1971, his passing helped the Colts achieve their only Super Bowl win.

In 1971, when *Sport* was celebrating its twenty-fifth anniversary, the magazine chose Unitas as pro football's top performer during those twenty-five years. He is, said *Sport*, "the one man against whom all other quarterbacks are measured."

The glowing praise, the trophies, and the titles—Unitas shrugged them off.

246

He rarely showed the slightest bit of emotion. A Colt official once said of him: "If Unitas completes a pass or if he has one intercepted, he comes off the field looking the same. If you hadn't seen the play, you couldn't tell from his expression whether he had thrown a touchdown pass or fumbled."

This trait gave evidence of another of Unitas's strengths—the ability to remain cool under pressure. "You can't shake him," Merlin Olsen, an All-Pro tackle for the Los Angeles Rams, once said. "Once in a while the defense gets there, knocks him down, stomps on him, hurts him. The test of a quarterback is what he does next. Unitas gets up, calls another pass, and drops back into the pocket. Out of the corner of his eye, he may see you coming again, and I swear that when he does, he holds the ball a split second longer than he really needs to—just to let you know he isn't afraid of any man. Then he throws it on the button."

Unitas did not look like a hero. A trifle stoop-shouldered, he stood 6 feet; he weighed about 190 pounds. Until the final stages of his career, he had a bristly crew cut and boyish face. He could have passed for a college senior. His feet toed in and he always wore high-topped black shoes, the kind that linemen of the day often wore.

He had an unusual way of throwing. Unlike most passers, he finished his delivery with his palm toward the ground. This, along with his straight overhand technique, produced a ball that delighted receivers. But it put an enormous strain on Unitas's elbow. As early as 1960 he was beginning to play in pain, and by the end of the decade his career was in jeopardy from a torn muscle on the inside of his forearm. Off-season therapy in 1968 helped to make the arm healthy again. But he could no longer toss those 60- or 70-yarders. Even to throw 40 yards made him wince.

A painful throwing arm wasn't Unitas's only physical problem. He badly jammed two fingers of his throwing hand in the early 1960s. He had to have knee surgery in 1965. He also had fractured ribs, a broken back, and a shattered collarbone.

Through it all, Unitas adjusted, making the experts realize how many talents he had besides a great arm. His toughness, his brilliant play calling, and his willingness to gamble—all of these combined to make Johnny Unitas the dominant force in any game in which he played.

"Nothing ever bothers him," a teammate once said of Unitas. "That's because he never worries about what happens on the field."

Unitas learned early in life about courage and confidence. "The things

Johnny Unitas, quarterback for the Baltimore Colts, overcame serious physical setbacks at the outset of his football career and went on to become one of the game's most legendary Baltimore players. *Courtesy of the Baltimore Colts.*

I've done," he once said, "well, they're nothing to be so proud of when you look at what Mother did."

He was very proud of his mother. Johnny Unitas was born on May 7, 1933, in Pittsburgh, Pennsylvania. His father died when he was five. His mother raised her four children by working as a scrubwoman in downtown office buildings. She also went to business school to study bookkeeping and later worked as a bookkeeper for the city of Pittsburgh.

Johnny grew up with an interest in sports. At St. Justin's High School he played basketball as well as football. He wanted to go to Notre Dame, but a coach there took one look at his 6-foot, 145-pound frame and told him he was too skinny to play college football.

Unitas then accepted a scholarship to the University of Louisville. As a freshman quarterback, he quickly demonstrated his ability to take charge. Louisville was playing the University of Houston. It was late in the fourth quarter, the score tied, 21–21. Louisville had the ball on Houston's 40-yard line. It was third down with two yards to go for a first down.

In the huddle, as Unitas got set to call the play, the team's veteran fullback declared, "Give me the ball; I'll get the two yards."

Unitas stared at him icily. "When I want you to take the ball, I'll tell you," he snapped. Then Unitas called a pass and threw for a touchdown.

The Pittsburgh Steelers drafted Unitas in 1955 and invited him to their training camp, then let him go. The club gave him $10 in bus fare to get him from their training camp in Olean, New York, to his home in Pittsburgh. Unitas, married now, and with a baby to support, decided he'd hitchhike home to save the money.

Despite this setback, Unitas didn't give up on himself. He sent a telegram to Paul Brown, coach of the Cleveland Browns, and asked for a tryout. Brown wired back, saying it was too late in the training season to invite him to camp but that he'd be glad to take a look at him the following summer. Now Johnny had something to look forward to.

He took a job as a construction worker that paid $3 an hour. He also began playing for a semipro football team in the Bloomfield section of Pittsburgh, the Bloomfield Rams. The team played on Thursday nights on a dimly lit dirt field. Sometimes only a hundred or so spectators turned out. Johnny was paid $6 a game.

But Unitas still had visions of becoming a quarterback in the National Football League. His teammates kidded him about his dream. "Sure, he was the best ballplayer in our league, and everyone knew it," one of his teammates once recalled, "but it still didn't make any sense for a guy playing sandlot ball to be talking about signing with the Cleveland Browns. Guys would needle him. 'Hey,' some guy would yell, 'did you hear about me, Unitas? The Los Angeles Rams want me.'

"But it didn't bother Johnny any. He kept his mouth shut and played the game. You had to admire him."

Unitas never did try out for the Cleveland Browns. In February the next year, 1956, Unitas received a call from the Baltimore Colts asking him whether he would like to come to Baltimore in May to demonstrate his skills for coach Weeb Ewbank. If Ewbank liked him, Unitas would be invited to the Baltimore training camp in July. Naturally, Johnny said he'd be there.

How had the Colts learned about Unitas? One story has it that a Baltimore fan wrote to the club to say there was a quarterback with the Bloomfield Rams they should take a look at. In later years Ewbank was to say with a grin, "I always accuse Johnny of writing that letter."

Unitas quickly impressed Ewbank with the power and accuracy of his passes. "And he was very eager to learn," Ewbank has said. "I liked that."

Unitas won the job as the Number 2 quarterback for the Colts. When the Number 1 quarterback, George Shaw, was hurt and lost for the season, Unitas took over. In his first game the Colts faced the Chicago Bears. The first pass Unitas threw was intercepted and returned for a touchdown. He fumbled three times, and all three times the Bears recovered. The final score: Chicago, 58; Baltimore, 27. But Johnny wasn't the least bit shaken. He told the club, "If you just give me a chance, I'll show you what I can do."

He showed them in 1957. He completed 57.1 percent of his passes for a league-leading 2,550 yards and 24 touchdowns. The Colts finished with a 7–5 record, their first winning season ever.

The next season, Unitas steered the Colts to victories in their first five games. But in the sixth game, Johnny was injured. Leveled by a Green Bay linebacker, he cracked three ribs and suffered a punctured lung. It looked for a time as though he would be on the sidelines for the rest of the year.

But after a week's rest, Unitas insisted he was ready to play. He was fitted with an aluminum corset to protect his ribs and sat out only two games.

Unitas led the Colts to a 9–3 record and the championship of the NFL's Western Division. The Colts met the New York Giants for the league championship on a gray winter afternoon at Yankee Stadium. It has been called the greatest football game ever played.

With two minutes to play, the Giants led the Colts, 17–14. The Colts had the ball on their own 14-yard line. In the huddle, a stony-faced Unitas told his teammates, "This is where we find out what we're made of."

They found out fast. Unitas quickly began to move the Colts. He calmly threw three passes to end Ray Berry that ate up 62 yards. Then, with seven seconds remaining, Steve Myhra kicked a field goal that tied the score.

Now it was sudden death, an overtime, the first in NFL history. The first team to score would be the winner, the champion of pro football. Anything—a touchdown, a field goal, or a safety—would do the trick.

The Colts kicked off. When the Giants couldn't move the ball, they punted.

Taking over on his own 20-yard line, Unitas sent L. G. Dupre around right end for 10 yards. After a pass went incomplete, he called on Dupre again, sending him up the middle. Dupre got three yards.

On the next down, Unitas dropped back to throw. He scanned the secondary for Ray Berry. Berry was covered. But Unitas caught sight of fullback Alan Ameche cutting into the open. Instantly Unitas whipped the ball to Ameche, and the Colts had another first down.

Another handoff to Dupre netted seven yards. But then a 12-yard loss made it third down and 15 to go for a first down. As Unitas pedaled back to throw, he saw defensive back Carl Karilivacz, the man assigned to cover Berry, fall down. Berry darted toward the sideline, unaware that his defender had fallen. More important, Berry hadn't gone deep enough. He was still several yards short of a first down. Coolly, Unitas kept the ball cocked and at the same time waved Berry to go deeper. At the last split second, Unitas threw to Berry for a first down on the Giant 42.

As he hunched over the center to take the snap, Unitas glanced at the Giant defense. He noticed that Giant linebacker Sam Huff had dropped back a few yards to help out on pass coverage. Unitas had called a pass play in the huddle, but now, at the line of scrimmage, he barked out signals for a new play. Instead of a pass, he called a run, handing the ball off to Ameche, who slanted into the opening that Huff had created when he dropped back. Ameche gained 23 yards.

A pass to Berry and another to Jim Mutscheller brought the ball to the one yard line. The Giant fans sat in stunned silence. Unitas handed to Ameche again and the big fullback blasted into the end zone.

The Colts were the champions. When the final gun sounded, thousands of spectators flooded out of the stands.

Joyous Baltimore fans tore down the goalposts and ripped up sod from the field.

That night, when the Colts' plane landed at Baltimore's Friendship Airport (now Baltimore-Washington International Airport), a mob of 30,000 was waiting. They cheered the players as they made their way to special buses, and then they surrounded the buses, shouting and chanting.

With that game, the Colts became one of the National Football League's premier teams. Five years before, the struggling franchise had been brought to Baltimore from Dallas. Only once before in the team's struggle for existence had the Colts managed to win more games than they had lost. Now they were numbered among the football elite.

The game also had lasting impact on pro football. It created a new level of interest in the sport and won for it an acceptance it had never enjoyed before.

In 1959, the Colts captured the Western Division title and again beat the Giants to capture the league championship. Unitas was in exceptional form. He ran for one touchdown and passed for two others in Baltimore's 31–16 victory. In total, he completed 18 of 29 passes, good for 274 yards. During the season, Unitas set an NFL record by throwing 32 touchdown passes.

Unitas remained the Colt quarterback until 1972. The team won the Conference championship in 1968, but it was a dismal year for Unitas. He missed most of the season with an injured elbow. In Super Bowl III, won by the New York Jets, 16–7, Unitas came off the bench late in the fourth quarter to lead Baltimore to its only touchdown.

Two years later, in Super Bowl V, Unitas again completed the Colts' only scoring passes as they whipped the Dallas Cowboys, 16–13. It was Unitas's first and only Super Bowl win.

Unitas was sold to the San Diego Chargers early in 1973 and played in five games in the season that followed. Then he called it quits.

After his retirement, Unitas was a television broadcaster for several years, providing the color commentary for NFL games. He was elected to Pro Football's Hall of Fame in 1979.

As the man who put Baltimore on the football map, Unitas did not remain cool in 1984 when the team moved abruptly to Indianapolis. He spoke out angrily against the franchise switch that left Baltimore without representation in the NFL.

During the 1980s, Unitas did promotion work for several companies and appeared at charity golf tournaments. Golf, he admitted, had become his favorite sport.

In Baltimore, Unitas could be seen frequently at his restaurant, chatting with customers and autographing souvenir menus. Considering its owner and his talents, the restaurant had an appropriate name. It was called the Golden Arm.

Additional Reading

Unitas, Johnny, and Ed Fitzgerald. *Pro Quarterback: My Own Story.* New York: Simon & Schuster, 1965.

Unitas, Johnny, with Harold Rosenthal. *Playing Pro Football to Win.* Garden City, New York: Doubleday & Co., 1968.

Ted Williams

The Slugging Professor
1918–

"Hitting a baseball—I've said it a thousand times—is the single most difficult thing to do in sport." Ted Williams said that.

But, judging from the record book, hitting baseballs did not appear to be terribly difficult for Williams himself. In the years before and after World War II, the tall and rangy Williams, left fielder for the Boston Red Sox, was baseball's home-run king and the greatest hitter in the game. Six times he led the league in batting. His career average was a sparkling .344.

Williams achieved a batting average of .406 in 1941. That is certainly not a statistic that can be associated with anyone having a "difficult" time of it. In the more than forty years since, no batter in baseball has been able to average two hits out of every five trips to the plate. (Two, however, have come fairly close—Rod Carew with a .388 average in 1977, and George Brett, who hit .390 in 1980.)

The final afternoon of Williams's 1941 season has become part of baseball folklore. Williams began the day hitting .399. The Red Sox were in Philadelphia for a doubleheader against the Athletics at Shibe Park. Williams went six for eight in those two games, boosting his average to the .406 level.

Sharp-featured and handsome, Williams was several inches over 6 feet; he weighed about 190. Those numbers gave birth to his nickname—"The Splendid Splinter."

Williams was a great student of hitting. His book, *The Science of Hitting,* written with John Underwood, first published in 1968 and still in print, is considered one of the clearest explanations ever written of the principles involved in putting the bat to the ball.

Williams said a good swing was based on three rules. First, the batter has to get a good ball to hit. Indeed, Ty Cobb once criticized Williams for waiting for the perfect pitch. "He takes too many bases on balls," said Cobb.

Second, Williams stressed "proper thinking." That meant knowing the pitcher and pitches. It meant getting the right pitch to hit. "If a pitcher is throwing only fastballs and curves," Williams once said, "and he's getting only his fastball over, then you're crazy to be looking for a curve."

Williams once said that some of the great classic hitters—such as Willie Mays and Mickey Mantle—could have been even better if they had thought more at the plate. "They struck out too much," Williams said.

"Look at DiMaggio. He struck out only a half or a third as many times as he walked. It meant he was looking for his pitch. He was in control, not the pitcher."

Being quick with the bat was the third rule that Williams cited as being important in achieving a good swing. He stressed that "the hips set the swing in motion and lead the way."

His uncanny ability to tell a bad ball when he saw one made Williams extremely difficult to pitch to. If the pitcher missed the plate by so much as the width of a Wheaties flake, Williams, after striding to meet the pitch and cocking his bat, would let it slip by. As a result, Williams drew many bases on balls. He was also often handed free walks when there were runners on base. It is thus easy to understand why Williams led the major leagues in bases on balls for six consecutive seasons beginning in 1941.

When Williams retired, he was second on the all-time list for getting the most walks. He was fifth in lifetime batting average. He was third in home runs. He was sixth in runs batted in. He was eighth in runs scored.

What Williams achieved is even more impressive when you consider that his career was twice interrupted by military service. He spent four years as a Marine Corps pilot in World War II and the Korean War.

Not wartime service, not Hall of Fame pitchers such as Bob Feller or Early Wynn, nor the unusual defensive alignments some managers tried against him could stop Ted Williams. He was a quality hitter up until the very end of his long career. In 1957, when he was 39, he led the league in batting with a spectacular .388 average. And in 1960, his final season as a player, the 42-year-old Williams hit .316. The very last hit of his career was a home run—number 521.

Theodore Samuel Williams was born in San Diego, California, on August 30, 1918. His father traveled a great deal, and Ted seldom saw him. As a result, he was especially close to his mother, a Salvation Army worker.

He talked often to his mother about his dream—to become a major league baseball player. He practiced constantly in the backyard. Often he imagined he was Bill Terry, first baseman for the New York Giants (the team moved to San Francisco in 1958) and, like Williams, a left-handed batter.

Terry was a student of hitting. His studying paid off. In twelve years with the Giants, his average fell below .300 only once. In 1930, when Ted was twelve, Terry hit .401.

At Garfield Grammar School in San Diego, Ted tried out for the baseball team. The coach decided he would make a good pitcher. But Ted could hit, too, and when he wasn't assigned to pitch, he played the infield or outfield.

Ted went on to pitch for Horace Mann Junior High School and later for Herbert Hoover High School. At his high school graduation, Ted was awarded a silver trophy on which were engraved his batting averages—.586 for his junior season, .403 as a senior.

After he graduated, Ted played for a team representing a local American Legion post. One day a scout for the New York Yankees, who had been watching Ted play, visited the Williams home. He told Ted and his mother that he might be interested in signing Ted to a contract to play for the Yankees. Ted was thrilled to death, but Mrs. Williams wouldn't hear of such a thing. New York was much too far from San Diego, she said. The scout left without getting Ted to sign.

When Ted was finally permitted to play professional baseball, it was with a local team, the San Diego Padres. He joined the Padres in 1935, signing a $150-a-month contract. (The Padres were a minor league team at the time, members of the Triple-A Pacific Coast League.)

The Padre manager soon discovered that Ted was a much better hitter than pitcher and switched him from the mound to the outfield. In 1936, as a part-timer, Ted batted .271. But the next year, as a regular in the outfield, "The Kid," as he was called, hit .291. Some of his homers were among the longest ever seen in the Pacific Coast League.

The Boston Red Sox had been interested in Williams for over a year, and after the season ended, the club exercised an option it had been granted to buy Williams's contract. The Red Sox gave up four minor league players, plus $25,000 in cash.

Mrs. Williams was not happy when she learned that Ted was going to Boston—that was as far from San Diego as New York—but she realized that Ted had to live his own life, and his life was baseball.

Ted was stunned by the news that his contract had been sold to the Red Sox. He had dreamed of playing in New York with either the Giants or the Yankees. He had never thought about going to Boston.

Williams reported to the Red Sox at spring training in Sarasota, Florida, early in 1938. The camp was a painful experience for him. In those days veteran players needled the rookie players. Ted was one of the targets. But he refused to accept the taunts, hurling back insults of his own. The veterans didn't like that. "Like children, rookies should be seen and not heard," said one.

Things got worse. Ted's temper often flared. The veteran players started calling him Ted the "San Diego Saparoo."

The needling and wisecracking began to affect Ted's performance. When he would take his turn at the plate, he was often thinking about what someone had said to him. Since he wasn't concentrating, pitches that he would ordinarily have hit went whizzing right by him for strikes.

One day Red Sox manager Joe Cronin took Ted aside and told him he was being sent to a Boston farm team in Minneapolis. "We've got a lot of good veteran outfielders," said Cronin. "If we kept you, you wouldn't get to play every day. Down at Minneapolis you will."

Ted was crushed. He hated going back to the minor leagues. He felt certain that he could hit major league pitching.

At Minneapolis in 1938, Williams was a sensation. He led the Triple-A American Association in hitting with a .366 average and in RBIs (runs batted in) with 142. He slammed a league-leading 42 home runs.

When Ted joined the Red Sox in Sarasota for spring training in 1939, he made up his mind to keep his mouth shut. He would concentrate on his hitting, not on insults. He hit fiercely all spring. When the Red Sox arrived at Yankee Stadium in mid-April for the opening of the season, Ted was the team's starting right fielder.

Williams was almost everything the Red Sox could have hoped for as a rookie. He batted .327. His RBI total of 145 was the highest in the league.

But there were some sour moments. One day about a month after he had joined the Red Sox, Williams let a base hit skip through his legs. Then he turned to run after the ball. Some fans thought he didn't run fast enough. The next inning, the fans began to hurl insults at Williams.

No player likes to be called names or insulted. Ted Williams hated it. He yelled insults back at the fans. After another bad incident, Williams vowed, "I'll never tip my hat to them again."

And he kept his promise. Whenever he hit a home run, Williams would circle the bases with his head down, then duck into the dugout. No matter how long or loudly the crowd cheered, Ted would not tip his hat.

In the years that followed, there were many other examples of Williams's lack of maturity. He would sometimes fling his bat high into the air when he failed to get a hit. In the outfield, he would kick the turf or turn his back on the play. He once spat at the Boston fans. He heard boos in every city in which he played.

But when he concentrated on the job, Williams did everything well. He could run the bases with the best. He ran fast; he slid hard. He had a strong and accurate throwing arm. And with his long strides, he could cover an entire zip code.

Of course, hitting was what Williams really liked to do. The year 1941 was a high point for him as a hitter. He was the hero of the All-Star Game, belting a tremendous home run with two outs in the ninth inning that won the game for the American League. He also hit .406 that year, becoming the first player to do so since his boyhood hero, Bill Terry, had accomplished the feat in 1930. And Williams was, at twenty-three, the youngest player ever to top .400.

Williams won triple-crown honors the next year, 1942, leading the American League not only in batting, with a .356 average, but in homers with 36 and runs batted in with 37.

During World War II, Williams served as a Marine Corps pilot. He was away three years. By the time he left the service, he had flown eleven hundred hours.

It was 1946 when Williams rejoined the Red Sox. Again he was the All-Star Game hero. During the contest, he faced National League pitcher Rip Sewell, who had made a career of frustrating batters with his "eephus" pitch. Sewell would lob the ball about 20 feet into the air and let it fall very slowly toward the batter. Most batters popped up the pitch. When Sewell lobbed the eephus ball at Williams, Ted took two quick steps forward and lashed the ball out of the park. No one had ever hit a home run off an eephus pitch before. "I'm sure glad Ted Williams doesn't play in the National League," Sewell said afterward.

Ted's home run off Sewell was one of the five hits he had in five trips to the plate that day. He also collected five RBIs. "I call him the best hitter the game has ever seen," said Steve O'Neill, manager of the American League team.

While the All-Star Game was a bright spot for Williams in 1946, the World Series was anything but. The Red Sox played the St. Louis Cardinals. The Cards adopted a method of defending against Williams that had been used by American League teams that season. Devised by manager Lou Boudreau of the Cleveland Indians, it was called the Boudreau shift. It took advantage of the fact that Williams almost always pulled the ball—that is, hit to right field.

In setting up the shift, the shortstop and third baseman joined the second baseman and first baseman on the right side of the second base. The center fielder was shifted into right-center field. The left fielder was drawn in almost to third base.

Teams that used such a defense were practically conceding Ted a single. All he had to do was poke the ball into left field. But when he pulled the ball,

as he normally did, six fielders were waiting for it.

Ted eventually learned to outwit the strategy. He changed his stance, setting up a little farther from the plate, and pushing the ball to the left side. But in the 1946 World Series, the strategy handcuffed him. He hit only .200 as the Red Sox went down to defeat, four games to three. "I was just terrible," said Williams afterward.

Ted was anything but terrible in 1947 when he won his third batting title, hitting .345 and winning his second triple-crown. The next year, with a .369 average, he won the batting crown a fourth time.

After the Korean War broke out in 1950, Ted went back into the Marine Corps. He spent much of 1952 and 1953 piloting jet fighter planes over Korea.

Williams was back in baseball in 1954 and still far from finished. In 1957, at thirty-nine, he won the batting championship a fifth time, with a .388 average. He took his sixth title in 1958, hitting .328.

Late in the season of 1960, Williams announced he was retiring. In his final appearance at Fenway Park, Ted came to bat in the eighth inning with the score tied, 3–3. The pitcher delivered a fastball. Williams unleashed that long, loose swing and sent the ball soaring out of the park. The fans stood and

Ted Williams of the Boston Red Sox hit his 500th home run with this swing on June 17, 1960. *Courtesy of AP/Wide World Photos.*

cheered as Williams circled the bases. He crossed home plate and hurried into the dugout—and did not tip his cap.

Williams retired to his comfortable home in Islamorada in the Florida Keys. He spent the bulk of his time fishing for bonefish and tarpon. He later acquired a fishing camp on the Miramichi River in New Brunswick, Canada. There he spent the summers in quest of Atlantic salmon.

In 1969 Williams was lured out of retirement to manage the Washington Senators. While he had some success with the team and, indeed, was named manager of the year in 1969, he was happy to quit in 1972. He later called managing a "pain."

On the other hand, he found it "fun" to help young Red Sox hitters. He went to the Boston training camp every year for spring training. "Hips ahead of hands," he would tell the young hitters. "Hips ahead of hands. Get your body into the ball before it reaches the plate."

"He's not quick to criticize or change you immediately," said one Red Sox prospect. "He watches, and then when he talks, people listen. He tries to be positive in his approach. He'll say, 'You've got a good swing, but there's not enough action into the ball. Cock your bat back farther.'"

It is universally agreed that no man knew more about hitting a baseball than Ted Williams. His legacy is six batting titles and a magnificent career that spanned two wars and more than two decades and sometimes seemed as if it might go on forever.

Additional Reading

Williams, Ted, with John Underwood. *My Turn at Bat: The Story of My Life.* New York: Simon & Schuster, 1969.

Williams, Ted, with John Underwood. *The Science of Hitting.* New York: Pocket Books, 1968.

SPORTS FIGURES
BY PERIOD OF GREATEST ACHIEVEMENT

1900–1920

Ty Cobb
Jim Thorpe

1920–1940

Red Grange
Walter Johnson
Jesse Owens
Babe Ruth

1940–1960

Roger Bannister
Jim Brown
Babe Didrickson
Bob Mathias
Willie Mays
Jackie Robinson
Ted Williams

1960–

Muhammad Ali
Larry Bird
Wilt Chamberlain
Nadia Comaneci
Julius Erving
Peggy Fleming
Wayne Gretzky
Gordie Howe
Jean-Claude Killy
Billie Jean King
Martina Navratilova
Jack Nicklaus
Bobby Orr
Pelé
Bill Russell
Johnny Unitas

Index